THE NERVE-FRAZZLING THRILLER
THAT ONLY THE AUTHOR OF
AUTOPSY
COULD HAVE WRITTEN!

With all the spellbinding force and nonstop sus-
pense that made AUTOPSY a runaway bestseller,
John R. Feegel creates the story of Bill Trumbull,
expert medical pathologist—a man who's performed
hundreds of autopsies, who knows what a murder
scene looks like . . . and who's tired of his cold,
distant wife.

Murder is the only answer, but there's only one life
he can take in good conscience—his own. With
chilling care, Trumbull stages his own fake murder
—an ingeniously contrived death scene that will
guarantee his wife a bundle in insurance cash, and
keep the cops and the most sophisticated forensic
analysts from unraveling the truth: that he is on a
yacht, with his beautiful mistress, heading for
Guatemala.

Only, death also sails the bay . . .

Other Avon Books by
John R. Feegel

Autopsy   36905 $1.95

DEATH SAILS THE BAY

JOHN R. FEEGEL

AVON
PUBLISHERS OF BARD, CAMELOT AND DISCUS BOOKS

DEATH SAILS THE BAY is an original publication of
Avon Books. This work has never before appeared in
book form.

AVON BOOKS
A division of
The Hearst Corporation
959 Eighth Avenue
New York, New York 10019

First Avon Printing, June, 1978

AVON TRADEMARK REG. U.S. PAT. OFF. AND IN
OTHER COUNTRIES, MARCA REGISTRADA,
HECHO EN U.S.A.

Printed in the U.S.A.

Chapter One

BILL TRUMBULL REACHED beyond his microscope and picked up the phone. Unconsciously he dialed 256. As it rang for the third time an impatient frown crossed his brow and then, at the end of the ring, it was answered.

"O.R.," said a lazy voice.

"Betsy?" Trumbull said knowingly. His memory flashed to her buttocks gyrating sensuously on a mahogany coffee table as she danced at the chief of staff's New Year's Eve party. "What's his honor doing in there now?" He picked up his cigarette and took an absent-minded puff.

"Still chopping on somebody's tit," the O.R. nursing supervisor supplied mechanically. She not only chewed gum, but snapped it into the phone as she spoke.

"Tell him the lump is benign."

"It'll break his heart."

"What heart?" Trumbull needled.

"He was set up to do a radical."

"Then tell him to cut off his leg if he has to whittle on something."

"Which one?" the O.R. asked playfully.

"The little one, sweetheart, the little one."

Trumbull put the phone back on its cradle and smiled

1

at the ceiling. This had been the third frozen section that morning and he was beginning to feel the strain of being the only pathologist in a two-hundred-bed hospital. Things were different when he had been one of eight pathologists at Tampa General Hospital downtown. They could share the load. But in a small hospital, keeping five surgeons happy in the operating room, six mornings a week was more than he had anticipated. When he had first taken the job it was a challenge to convert the old, poorly managed hospital lab into an automated machine that could spit out clinical tests with instantaneous and, as one of the local "pink ladies" had drawled, "utterly amazin' accuracy."

Trumbull turned abruptly back to his microscope and took another look at the tissue specimen from the breast lump. The stroma gave a slightly pink reflection as he passed the glass slide under his medium-power lens. The epithelium was slightly disorganized and one duct exhibited a single focus of apocrine metaplasia. "Still benign," he reassured himself. There was still time to change the diagnosis to cancer and condemn the woman to a radical mastectomy, but she had escaped.

He peered down the barrels of his binocular microscope until it was almost out of focus, and suddenly felt weary. The days had multiplied on themselves and the vacation that he had promised himself had by now faded into a dream. If he had been someone else— someone who had come to him for medical advice— he would have told him to take a few weeks off immediately. Such kindnesses were reserved for others. Never himself.

He looked at the cigarette in the ashtray. He guessed that it was number seven for the day. How many people had he scolded professionally for their smoking? How many PTA's and civic clubs had he lectured on the effects of cigarette smoke on the bronchial mucosa? He butted the cigarette longer than usual and renewed his pledge to quit—one of these days.

2

The stack of slide trays waited patiently on the desk in front of him. Each tray contained several carefully prepared slices of tissue, excised at surgery the day before and then stained with almost religious dedication by his lab tech. Each presented a new look at a surgical lesion that he had seen many times before. The names and hospital numbers changed, but the diseases remained the same. His four thousandth case of appendicitis looked pretty much the same as the fourth. Only occasionally did a weird tumor come along to break the monotony of his daily practice of pathology.

William J. Trumbull, M.D., fellow of the College of American Pathologists and also fellow of the American Society of Clinical Pathologists, was thirty-eight years old, although he looked a few years younger. When he had finished his internship, his dream of one day being the head of his own hospital laboratory and thus responsible for the microscopic diagnoses of rare diseases seemed almost unobtainable. While his medical school classmates went into general practices around the country and were making their down payments on the traditional Cadillac, he had packed his family off to a four-year residency in the leaky basement of Denver General Hospital. In the morgue at D.G.H., he cut tissue slides on an almost endless parade of nameless patients, and acquired the exposure to disease, tumors, and surgical mistakes required to change a physician into a pathologist. A senior instructor had remarked that one could learn enough pathology in a four-year residency to pass the pathology boards, but that it took ten years to become competent. In the meantime, he would be dangerous.

As Trumbull approached his tenth year of practice as a pathologist he knew that the instructor had been right.

He shoved the stack of slides to the far side of his desk and felt his heart skip when they almost fell to the floor. His chair creaked as he swiveled back in it and emitted a long sigh. Maybe that vacation should not be postponed much longer, he thought. Absently, he picked up the *Journal of the American Medical Association* and glanced at the table of contents. More disease, more tumors, more reports of obscure medical researchers who injected unknown things into anonymous rats to report meaningless reactions. His fingers flipped to the classified ads in the back section. Usually, he read these ads to enjoy a Walter Mitty-like reverie over the opportunities that beckoned from other cities, other hospitals, other associations, and other countries. All of which remained harmlessly unobtainable.

The classified jumble passed through his brain like the babble in an Arabian marketplace. In crying for some sort of doctor or another, every hospital promised "a lighter load," "good fishing nearby," "congenial associates," or some other dream. Most medical ad writers seemed to have been instructed to, "Promise them anything but get them."

He strained his eyes to focus on a short and therefore cheap ad that read:

PATHOLOGIST wanted. Board cert., any age. Small religious hosp. in Guatemala. Hard work. No questions asked. Write Bro. Timothy, S.J., St. A. Gonzaga Mission, Chichicastenango. A.M.D.G.

Bill Trumbull's eyes fixed on the last four letters. His undergraduate days had been spent in a Jesuit college in Massachusetts, and the motto of the society had appeared on his classroom papers almost daily. A.M.D.G.: To the Greater Glory of God. Here was a Jesuit brother who was asking for help in his struggle to operate a mission hospital in the jungles of Guatemala. His "no questions asked" clearly indicated his desperation.

Trumbull folded the *JAMA* back on its binding and reread the ad as he lit another cigarette. He found his attention almost magnetized to the page. The voice of

4

his secretary calling his name seemed distant and un-
real.

"Dr. Trumbull," the voice repeated. A feminine hand
reached out and shook him by the shoulder. "Dr. Trumbull," the voice said insistently.

"Huh?" he said, startled. "Mary Nell? What's up?"
Trumbull recovered his composure and turned the
JAMA face down on his desk.

"Mr. Harrison would like to see you this afternoon,"
the secretary said. She looked at her boss and tried to
gauge the fatigue she saw in his face.

"Tell him . . ." Trumbull paused inappropriately,
mentally framing an obscene reply. "Tell him that I'll
call him later." He thought of the hospital administrator
and was painfully aware that he did not want to talk
laboratory complaints that afternoon. Harrison was easy
enough to get along with, but most days there was
plenty to do in the lab without administrative problems
as well.

"Yes sir," the secretary said as she slipped quietly out
of the pathologist's office. "I'll call him."

"Yeah," Trumbull said absently as he turned over
the *JAMA* and reread the Guatemala ad. "Chichicastenango," he said almost inaudibly.

Trumbull had looked up Chichicastenango a few
years before when he was planning to go to Guatemala
on a vacation to investigate some Mayan ruins. The relatively isolated mountain town had caught his attention
when, in describing the bustle of the marketplace, his
Central American guidebook noted the strange mixture
of paganism and Catholicism that had developed
among the Indians. Travel to the little city was hard to
arrange, and treacherous once off the main road out of
Guatemala City. A man could easily drop out of sight
in any one of the small villages that surrounded Chichi.

Stimulating retinal cells by pressing his fingers
against his eyeballs, he saw a few orange-red and off-
green flashes. He wondered if he could get away with it.

He thought of his wife and the children. Lately, home had not been a happy place for him. His wife, Agnes, had undergone a hysterectomy after years of vague female complaints, and psychologically, the results had been less than ideal. On several occasions at surgical-pathological conferences, Bill Trumbull had argued with the gynecologists that the early removal of the uterus, even if the ovaries were left intact, resulted in severe damage to her identity as a woman. The patient turned into a spayed, resentful female for whom the world held little joy or expectation. Over the years, many gynecologists had ganged up on him for his heretical ideas, and since these men contributed a major portion of the surgical specimens from which he made his living, he did not insist on the point.

Despite the endocrinologists' facile and supposedly reassuring explanations of temporary hormonal imbalance, Agnes's hysterectomized personality had undergone such a striking change that eventually Bill Trumbull had come to avoid going home. She became suspicious. She searched his wallet, finding nothing unusual. She called his office and annoyed his staff. She accused him of preferring his work to his family. In general, she became unbearable. The bickering over nothing and the relentless hostility had spread malignantly into his relationship to the children. It was a time in their lives when the children needed a strong father figure to stabilize them. For a while, Bill had tried taking them on outings and entertaining them with the usual backyard activities. But pal relationships were not easy for this pathologist to foster, and impossible for him to fake. As a result, the games were abandoned as quickly as they had been started, with neither father nor children objecting. Agnes had increased her mother-protection over them and, at times, Bill worried that this might dilute the masculinity that every father hopes to see in his sons. So far it hadn't, but the closer relationship between Agnes and the children had pushed him even further out of the family picture, until at last he was left with only his work to occupy his energies and emotions. Her accusation had become true.

It was probably because of the unhappy relationship with Agnes that he had begun seeing Martha Holland. Of course, there were also Martha Holland's own unfulfilled needs and her almost instantaneously enthusiastic response to his early, awkward advances. She was a reasonably successful, divorced lady lawyer who, quite simply, had been too smart for her husband. Her husband had grown tired of, and then angry at her superior abilities, even though she had tried not to flaunt them. Despite her best efforts, she was never quite able to let her husband lead in their marriage dance, and so it broke apart. Amicably, of course, but with legal as well as emotional finality.

Dr. Trumbull looked up at the certificates on his office wall and frowned. He thought of all the sleepless nights spent in the acquisition of these scraps of gold-sealed wallpaper and wondered what he would have become if he had channeled the same energies toward some other area. He had often thought that if he had not become a doctor, he would have wanted to be a lawyer. But now, it was too late for such dreams. He had chosen his role and felt trapped by it.

Trumbull drummed softly on the desk top and then suddenly tore the classified ad page from the medical journal. He slipped it into his shirt pocket and took his jacket from the office closet. Stuffing one arm into the jacket, he shook his head as if to disagree with himself, and put the coat back on its hook. He left the closet door ajar slightly as he returned to his desk, then reached for the light switch on his microscope but decided against turning it off. He lit a cigarette and the smoke climbed upward and caused him to squint an offended eye. He scribbled a note to his secretary that said simply, "I'll be right back."

The pathologist left his office and hurried into the

7

hospital blood bank. The technician was on a break and the donor room was empty. It had taken a great deal of effort on his part to get this blood bank approved by the American Association of Blood Banks, but he had persevered through the corrections of each minor deficiency that the A.A.B.B. inspector had listed until at last validation had been granted. Now the hospital was qualified to take in its own donors, process the blood, and dispense it to patients. Previously, the blood had to be purchased from large commercial sources, hepatitis and all.

Trumbull reached into a neatly arranged drawer in the donor table and took out a disposable plastic syringe. He slipped the syringe and a few sterile-packed needles into his pants pocket and returned to his office. One of the chemistry techs scurried out of a lab and into the corridor as he passed, too preoccupied with her mental calculations of some new cardiac's SGOT to notice the 10-cc syringe bulging in his pocket. Conspicuous as Trumbull felt it made him, it was actually no larger than a fountain pen, and was not out of place in the pocket of a pathologist anyway.

Trumbull looked quickly around his office and paused briefly in the doorway. With a thin smile he walked back to the desk, carefully placing his still-burning cigarette in the ashtray. He positioned it so that as it burned it would not roll out onto the desk. Then he exited his office quickly and silently, leaving the door open. No one saw him as he walked down the laboratory corridor toward the back fire exit. Even if anyone had seen him, they would have thought nothing of it. He could have been taking one of his short trips to the post office, the bank, or the little nearby public library.

It was almost ten o'clock by Trumbull's wristwatch. Plenty of time, he reassured himself. He eased himself into his two-year-old Thunderbird and backed gracefully out of his assigned space in the doctors' parking lot. The transmission whined softly as he nosed the car down the main street of the small town and headed for the business section. He gave his habitual cautionary beep as he passed a blind alley in the center of the block where the deputy sheriff's car was concealed. The deputy liked to play traffic spy from that hiding place, but everyone knew he was there and braked slightly before passing the alley.

Trumbull pulled his car into the parking lot outside the bank. Trying to appear casual, he paused before the entrance to the building and delivered a short pep talk to himself. Make it good, Bill, he urged himself. This is hurdle number one, and if you can't get by Mavis Drawdy, you might as well forget the whole thing. He opened the door to the bank and went in.

"Mornin' Doc," Henry Kirk said in passing. Henry Kirk was one of the town's leading druggists and therefore an eager greeter of all physicians, even if he had to cross the street to do it. As usual, Trumbull deliberately and carefully ignored the pharmacist's salutation. He went straight to the savings-account teller and waited for an obese, molasses-slow black woman to withdraw sixteen dollars and forty cents and convert it into a cashier's check made payable to Sears. Trumbull chewed anxiously on his lower lip as he waited and looked over the black woman's shoulder at Mavis Drawdy. He telegraphed impatience, and she did not miss it.

"I'll be right with you, Dr. Trumbull," Miss Drawdy said pleasantly. She pronounced the title *"Doctor"* with such an official ring that only a stone deaf idiot could miss the implication, but the black lady was too preoccupied with putting her check into a battered handbag to catch the hint to hurry. Mavis Drawdy flashed her eyes impatiently toward the ceiling to show Dr. Trumbull that if she had had her way, segregation would still be a way of life in Orangeburrow, Florida.

When the woman finally turned the clasp on her bag

and moved away, Trumbull stepped quickly to the counter and leaned closer to Miss Drawdy than was customary. At first, the plump, middle-aged teller was pleased by the unexpected proximity, but her attitude turned to curiosity when she saw how nervous the pathologist was.

"Miss Drawdy," Trumbull almost whispered, "Please withdraw all of my savings and give it to me in small bills." He briefly looked her in the eye and then shot a quick, nervous glance toward the door.

"Is something wrong, Doctor?" she whispered in return, glancing toward the door.

"No, nothing," he said, almost stammering. "Please hurry, Miss Drawdy." He glanced obviously at his watch.

"Yes, Doctor. It will take me a few moments." She scurried off toward the files and came back with his account card. "You know, of course, that at the present time, you have seventeen thousand, three hundred and sixty-eight dollars and forty cents in the account." She looked at the doctor over the rims of her glasses.

"Yes, yes, I know that, Miss Drawdy. Small bills, please."

"How small?" she asked suspiciously.

"Twenties and under. And put it in one of those cloth bank bags." He squinted impatiently.

"Yes sir. Right away." She went to the end of the teller's section and unlocked a steel drawer. She took out several bulky bundles of currency and stacked them on the counter in front of her, counting aloud to herself. Trumbull shifted his weight from foot to foot in a manner that would later be described as "visibly upset" by one of the assistant bank managers who could see him from his office across the lobby.

Mavis Drawdy stole several glances at the pathologist as she assembled the stacks of bills. She thought of calling the bank manager on the phone and telling him of the doctor's unusual request, but then reconsidered. It was not bank policy to question its depositors on any transaction that was apparently legal. The manager periodically lectured all employees that they were never to express approval or disapproval of a depositor's legitimate request. She would now hold the manager to his own rules. Miss Drawdy brought the money to Dr. Trumbull in two bulky cloth bags bearing THE ORANGEBURROW BANK in fading blue stencil.

"Would you like to use one of the offices to count it, Doctor?" she offered. She searched his face for some clue to the cause of his anxiety.

"No, that'll be all right, Miss Drawdy, I'm sure it's all here." He signed the withdrawal slip that she had prepared for him and swept the two bags into his arms.

"But, Dr. Trumbull," she protested mildly, "the bank cannot assume responsibility for . . ." Her voice faded into the hum of the air conditioner in the window as he hurried to the door and out into the parking lot. Trumbull locked the bank bags in the trunk.

He wheeled the T-bird out of the lot and onto the street, turning at the corner to head for the interstate highway. It was about fifteen miles to Lakeland, the nearest city of any appreciable size. He had been an active member of the medical society in his own county and had never really taken part in professional activities in Lakeland and assumed correctly that he would not be recognized there.

Trumbull was careful not to exceed the speed limit along the interstate or on the downtown Lakeland off-ramp. The last thing he needed that morning was a speeding ticket. He wished himself no cops, no witnesses, no bad luck of any kind.

As he neared downtown Lakeland, he stopped at an isolated phone booth. Consulting its battered directory, he tore out the yellow pages containing the addresses of several stores. He wasn't very familiar with the layout of the streets in Lakeland, but the city was small, and he had no trouble locating the first address. He

11

parked the Thunderbird a few doors down from the store and walked calmly toward the entrance. The sign in the window announced: SALE!! ALL WIGS AND COSTUMES—ONE HALF OFF!! Today was really not Trumbull's day for bargain hunting. Just a simple, quick purchase of a few masquerade items without too many questions would do. The old-time bakery-shop bell over the door jingled as he entered.

"Good morning, sir," said a doe-eyed teenager in tight, faded dungarees and sandals. "Can I help you?" She smiled disarmingly and showed the braces on her upper teeth.

"Yes, thank you, miss," Trumbull said, turning toward the costumes filling the shelves. He was careful to expose as little of his face to the young lady as he could without appearing suspicious. "I'm planning to attend a costume party in Miami this weekend and I'd like to see a long-haired wig and matching mustache."

"Something like a pirate, maybe?" the girl asked.

"More like a hippie," Trumbull said somewhat absently. "Not too conspicuous, you understand, just long enough to help me look the part."

"I think I have just the one for you, sir," the girl said. She walked to a selection of wigs at the rear of the store and settled on a straight-combed shoulder-length brown number. Handing it to the pathologist, she said, "Try it on."

Trumbull held the wig in front of him upside down and then, stuffing his own hair into the elastic opening, threw it backward over his head. The long hair fell down over his neck in a jumbled mess. He arranged the strands with his fingers and looked at himself in the mirror.

"You can comb that one," the girl said proudly. "It's one-hundred-percent human hair."

Trumbull felt a slight twinge of disgust as he wondered about the previous owner of the hair, but managed to keep a placid facial expression.

"Expensive?" he asked absently. The color and the length was about perfect for his plans, and with five hundred dollars in his pocket, he wasn't really concerned about the price. It had simply occurred to him that no one would buy a wig without asking the price.

"Fifteen dollars," she supplied.

"And the mustache?" He was still adjusting the wig, keeping his arms and hands more or less in front of his face.

"Oh, yes! The mustache," she chimed. "Let's see. That's a pretty deep brown." She was picking her way through a deep wooden drawer beneath the counter. "Did you want to match the brown or go for a darker red? Some men have red mustaches, you know."

"I think the same brown would be about right." He began to sweat slightly despite the air conditioning.

"Maybe a little gray in it?" she asked as she presented him with several packaged, false mustaches. Trumbull quickly picked through the selection, finally opting for a full, somewhat bushy brown piece that made him look like a British aviator in a World War I movie. He held it up in front of his face and grinned slightly as he looked at himself in the mirror.

"You stick it on with this stuff," she said. She held out a small tube containing a substance that looked like airplane glue. "It comes off easy with soap and water," she reassured him. "Not the mustache, the glue."

"I'll take them both," Trumbull said.

"Great!" she said with teenage enthusiasm. "I'll put them in a bag for you." Her eyes twinkled as she asked, "You didn't want to wear them home, did you?"

"Not today," he said, jocose in return.

"Not that anybody would notice you, I guess. Half of the guys I know wear their hair about that long."

"I guess it's the style," Trumbull agreed.

"Right on," she mumbled. She was preoccupied with the monumental task of adding fifteen dollars for the wig and three dollars and fifty cents for the mustache and glue. "That'll be eighteen dollars and fifty cents, plus tax," she announced. "And the tax comes to . . ."

"Seventy-four cents," supplied Trumbull.

"It does?"

"It does." He gave the girl one of the twenties that he had just withdrawn from the bank and waited with suppressed impatience for her to make change.

"Nineteen-twenty four, twenty-five, fifty, twenty dollars," she counted, dropping the coins in his hand. "And thank you. I hope you have a nice time at the costume party."

"Thank you. You've been very helpful."

Trumbull took his purchases and left the store, taking care not to slam the door or otherwise attract attention. Easing the T-bird out of its parking space, he drove off to resume his scan of street signs. About twenty blocks along the street he came to a motorcycle agency and drove into the parking lot.

Signs in every window screamed that the agency carried every conceivable type of motorcycle with every conceivable type of engine, attachment, and capability. Trumbull parked his car near the rear garage door and took several hundred more dollars from one of the bank bags in the trunk. He then moved the bags to a safe place under the front seat. He entered the shop and was greeted simultaneously by an exuberant salesman and the distinctive smell of heavily oiled machinery.

"May I show you something in a bike?" asked the salesman, rubbing his hands together. Trumbull made a mental note to advise young men planning to become salesmen never to rub their hands together when approaching potential customers.

"Yes, I'd like to see one of those little trail motorcycles. You know, the ones the kids ride on vacant lots before they're old enough to get licenses?"

"I know just what you have in mind," the salesman gushed. "Is it for your own son?"

"Yes, and it's a surprise. His birthday, you know. I want to take it home with me."

The salesman nodded enthusiastically.

"We have just the model you need, sir," the salesman said, placing his hand gently on Trumbull's shoulder. His sales instructor had probably advised him to make flesh contact with every customer sometime during the pitch. Of course, the instructor did not know how much Trumbull would hate being touched that particular day.

"And it will have to fit in the trunk of my car," said Trumbull with nonchalance. "Otherwise the surprise will be spoiled."

"I understand perfectly, sir. I think this little Nagayami will just fill the bill." He had led the pathologist to a rear section of the showroom and was pointing to a miniature motorcycle with tiny, fat wheels and what seemed to be a disproportionately large seat and engine.

"Will it perform on the road as well? When he's old enough, I mean," asked Trumbull.

"Yes indeed it will, sir. It will do about forty-five miles an hour and deliver an economical seventy-six miles to the gallon. All you need are plates and a helmet."

"A helmet?" Trumbull asked absently. He did not want to appear too well informed about the state of Florida's motorcycle regulations.

"All riders and passengers are required by law to have a helmet on their heads when riding motorcycles in the state of Florida," the salesman lectured.

"Who sells them?"

"We carry a full line, sir. About how big a boy do you have?"

"Oh, he's a husky lad," Trumbull said. "I guess his head size is about the same as mine." He glanced at the price tag on the bike. It read three hundred and fifty dollars.

"Any special color for the helmet?"

"No, anything will do. Look, I'm in a bit of a hurry. I'll take this machine, but I wonder if you'd do me a little favor?" Trumbull smiled warmly at the salesman.

"I'd be happy to help you however I can, sir. The Chopper House is at your service to—"

"Yeah, swell," interrupted Trumbull. "What I want you to do is to roll this thing out into the parking lot and show me how it works. You know, give me a quick lesson so that I can instruct the boy when I get it home."

"No problem whatsoever," said the salesman. "Harry!" He called to a mechanic who was out in the garage. "Roll this Nagayami out to the lot and set it up to drive."

"And fill it with gas," suggested Trumbull quietly.

"And fill it with gas, Harry," the salesman repeated as if hypnotized. "How did you wish to arrange for the payments, sir?" he asked gently.

"Cash. And don't forget the helmet."

"Yes sir!" said the salesman, rubbing his hands again. Then he scurried off to make out the sales slip as Harry grunted the heavy little machine out of the display room and through the rear door. Trumbull pulled enough twenty-dollar bills from his pocket to pay for the bike.

The salesman rushed back with a fistful of papers and continued to write on them as the engine of the Nagayami roared in the parking lot.

"What name shall I enter, sir?"

"Name?" asked Trumbull. There was a sudden lump in his throat.

"The warranty. We stand behind all of the parts for a full year."

"Armstrong. Charles Armstrong," said Trumbull, recovering his composure. "Twenty-two South Ashland Drive, Lakeland." He watched the salesman enter the phony name and address on the sales slip.

"Is that out in that new development south of town?"

the salesman asked casually. "Getting so I don't know the street names anymore."

"Right." Trumbull smiled gently and handed the salesman the small bundle of twenties.

The mechanic had no difficulty showing the pathologist how to operate the little motorcycle. The machine was incredibly easy to handle and Trumbull felt an adolescent thrill as he gunned it around the parking lot. The mechanic instructed him how to shut off the gas lines for safe transportation and then helped him lift the machine into the trunk of the T-bird. The trunk lid would not shut tight with the motorcycle inside, but Harry quickly produced a short length of rope and tied it down.

"Happy riding," the salesman shouted as Trumbull drove out of the lot. Trumbull smiled and waved at the gushing little man who was still clutching his written record of the transaction in his hand.

His next stop, at a dry-goods store, produced a pair of ordinary denim dungarees and a matching denim jacket. With these items deposited on the rear seat, he headed the Thunderbird back onto the interstate and headed toward Tampa.

As he got to the Orangeburrow exits, he inched cautiously to the right and made his way onto a little-used off-ramp without a tire squeal. It bordered on the rear entrance to the regional high school and was heavily traveled only when the students were coming or going to class. Now it was a little after one o'clock in the afternoon and the students were all inside.

He eased the car toward the high school parking lot and looked over the cars. In a moment he spotted what he was searching for. In a secluded spot under a large live oak, there was a student's motorcycle that couldn't be seen from the school windows. Trumbull drove quietly over to the tree and stopped long enough to scan the yard carefully again. There was no one around.

Trumbull took a small adjustable wrench from the glove compartment. He left the T-bird's engine running as he walked casually to the motorcycle and unscrewed the soft steel bolts that held the registration plate to the rear bracket. Taking it back to his car, he put the plate on the seat beside him and drove quietly away.

The road signs announced that Tampa was still sixteen miles away when he turned off the highway and onto a deserted country road. The whole area had recently been dug up by massive earth-moving machines that gouged out tons of soil containing microscopic shells from which processing plants extracted phosphates, acids, and other chemicals for the fertilizer industry. Boatloads were shipped daily from the Tampa ports to destinations all over the world. The phosphate industry had been one of the economic mainstays in Hillsborough and Polk counties for many decades. Some experts said that the area boasted the richest deposit of phosphates in the world. But environmentalists said that it was a colossal rape of the Florida landscape, leaving massive holes to fill up with water.

The water flowed into the pits from the surface and sometimes from deep springs that were tapped when digging machines had scooped too far down. Every year the medical examiner's office was consulted on a drowning case or two in these pits. Unaware or unafraid of the incredible depths, kids used them as swimming holes. Some of the pits that connected to deep springs maintained a swift flow that made them, for all practical purposes, bottomless. Though the chemical industrialists had lately begun to "re-contour" the land and convert the mined areas into golf courses and citrus groves, in most places, the ravaged landscape with its dangerous holes remained.

Trumbull stopped his car alongside an isolated phone

booth. After popping a dime into the slot, he dialed a familiar number and waited for a pleasant but mechanical voice to announce, "Law offices of MacDonald, Chittly, Holland and Wallace."

"Miss Holland, please," he said simply. Although divorced, she preferred to use her maiden name.

"Thank you, sir. I'll connect you."

There was a brief delay and a series of clicks as the connection was made.

"Miss Holland's office. May I help you?" said another professional but friendly voice.

Trumbull bit slightly on the side of his tongue and stuffed it toward one side of his mouth. The secretary might have recognized his normal speaking voice.

"I want to speak with Miss Holland, the lady lawyer," he said with an obvious impediment.

"Certainly, sir. May I tell her who's calling?"

"Mike Castonella."

"Do we have a file on you that I might give Miss Holland, Mr. Casperella?"

"No. No file. Tell her I want to be a new client." Trumbull figured that any lawyer would bite quickly on the bait of new business.

"Yes sir. Just one moment."

There was a brief pause as the message was transmitted to the lawyer by her efficient secretary.

"This is Miss Holland," a voice said precisely, but not pompously.

Trumbull knew Martha Holland's secretary well enough to know that she would not listen in on their conversation. Even so, he did not intend to take any chances.

"Martha. Just listen," he said in his own voice. "Use your private line and call me right back at 555-7618. Got it?"

"Yeah, I have it. What's up, Bill?"

"Call me. And keep still about who called you just now."

"No problem there. My secretary thinks you are some Italian criminal defendant."

"Good. Tell her you sent me to one of the Spanish lawyers. But call me right back." He put the receiver back on its cradle and waited impatiently for the phone to ring. It rang in less than one minute.

"Now, what the hell is going on?" she demanded.

"I'm going to do it," he said with determination.

"Do what?"

"Cut and run, Martha. I told you I was fed up with the whole rat race. Today is the day."

"You mean it?" On past occasions, when they had both had enough to drink and they were too tired for more sex, she had heard him ramble on before about escaping to some romantic South Sea island.

"I really mean it. I'm going."

"But what about Agnes and the children?" she inquired almost instinctively. Sometimes she was a woman, but she was a lawyer all the time.

"I'm going to set them up beautifully," he said with a smile in his voice.

"What do you mean, 'set them up'?" Her professional antennae were buzzing. "You got some crazy scheme cooked up in that formaldehyde-soaked brain of yours?"

"I'll tell you all about it when I see you this afternoon."

"See *me*? Where?"

"At your beach house." His mind quickly flashed to the beach house that she kept on a deserted stretch of the gulf coast north of St. Petersburg. It was deserted because the area was so expensive. Anyone wealthy enough to buy property along that stretch did not want neighbors close by.

"What time? I've got clients this afternoon," she protested ineffectually.

"Whenever you can make it. I'll let myself in with my key. But look, try to be as early as you can. There is a lot that I have to go over with you." He paused to let his remarks excite her curiosity. "And Martha—"

"Yeah?" she asked with genuine interest.

"You've got to keep this whole thing quiet. If you even mention my name, or tell anyone that you're going to meet me, I'll end up in prison or something. I'm not kidding." His tone was insistent.

"Bill!" she snapped firmly. "What the hell are you up to?"

"Trust me. It will be all right," he said reassuringly.

"You're not going to . . . kill Agnes, are you?" Her voice was shot through with concern and disbelief. She had never considered Bill Trumbull to be homicidal. She knew that he was occasionally capable of irrational acts motivated by the strain of his practice and his homelife, but she did not seriously think he was the type for premeditated murder.

"No, sweetheart. Not even close. I'm going to kill myself." He laughed inappropriately into the telephone.

"Damn it, Bill. Will you cut the crap and tell me what is going on?" She considered Bill Trumbull's suicide even more unlikely than his being capable of homicide.

"This afternoon. But don't blow it, please."

"OK. But be careful, whatever you're up to."

"And no matter what you may hear, just don't believe it. I promise I will see you this afternoon."

"I'll be there," she said softly.

He put the phone gently onto the hook and got back into his car. Driving carefully down the country road, he remembered that he had taken his sons along a road just like it when they were experimenting with father-son games. He turned off the paved road and onto a sand trail that led to one of the larger water-filled phosphate pits. The soft sand grabbed at the tires of the heavy T-bird and he found it a little difficult to steer.

"Come on, baby, Don't get stuck now," he said to his car. The machine responded to his coaxing and drove easily to the edge of the pit. He stopped the car and turned off the engine. Carefully investigating the perimeter of the pit for sound or movement, he soon decided there was no one else there. No fisherman hoping for a fat catfish. No teenage lovers. No bums keeping out of sight from the sheriff. He was perfectly alone.

He got out of the car and took the little motorcycle out of the trunk. He attached the stolen license plate to the rear bracket and replaced the tools in the trunk of the T-bird, removing the tire iron as he did. He placed the tire iron on the front seat and changed his clothes. The denim pants had to be rolled up an inch or so, and the jacket fitted loosely.

Trumbull took the syringe out of his trouser pocket and attached the sterile needle. He pulled his sleeve up to his elbow and gave it a slight twist to constrict the veins. With an awkward backhand movement, he slipped the needle into a prominent vein and withdrew the full 10 cc's of blood. He ignored the puncture in his arm and rolled down his sleeve.

He carefully applied a few cc's of the blood to the steering wheel, the driver's window, and the tire iron. The rest of the blood was scattered, drop by drop, along a short trail from the car to the water's edge. Returning to the car, he pulled a few hairs from his head and pressed them firmly into the partially dried blood on the tire iron. Squinting, he examined the tool to be sure that he had not left any fingerprints in the blood smear. He replaced the plastic cap on the needle and put the syringe in his pocket.

Trumbull stepped back to survey the scene. It was remote enough to be appropriate and yet popular enough with local fishermen to be discovered in a day or so at the most.

He started the engine of the Thunderbird and turned on the radio. The disc jockey gushed about some newly released clash of noisy guitars that bore little resemblance to what Trumbull considered music; he went for the big band sound of the forties and was visibly unimpressed by the rock groups.

He rolled his office clothes into a ball and secured them with the belt. The denim jacket was loose enough to allow him to stuff the clothes under it. He carefully dropped the tire iron near the opened front door of the T-bird and faked two drag marks toward the water.

Trumbull then walked backward toward the motorcycle and started it without difficulty. He stuffed the money bags into the opposite side of his jacket and drove the motorcycle along the sandy trail to the paved road. At the edge of the road, he parked the bike in some weeds, tall enough to hide the machine from view, and walked back to the T-bird. It was still running. He took a last look at the car and satisfied himself that the whole scene looked just good enough.

Wearing the long-haired wig and the mustache and the helmet, he looked quite different from the neat, well-dressed pathologist who had been seated at his microscope that morning. He was confident that even if he were seen on the road, no one would recognize him. He took a medium-sized rock, put it in the unmarked bag from the costume store, and threw it into the pit. It sank immediately. He watched the circle from the splash progress toward the shore in a slowly expanding gentle wave, and smiled to himself.

Trumbull left one shoe near the car. He slipped on a pair of sneakers he always carried in the trunk and tied the other shoe to his belt.

Then the pathologist selected a branch from a large bush that grew wild around the phosphate pits. Starting at the car where he had left the shoe, he brushed his way backward along the trail toward the motorcycle. He was careful to use crude but effective brush marks in erasing his footsteps and tire marks. Trumbull was sure that the officers from the crime lab would spot the erasure and that it would add to the suspicion of his violent death.

He stuffed his denim jacket into his pants and fastened the stiff, new snaps securely. He gave one last glance toward the car now hidden in the weeds and raised his hand in a mock salute.

"Rest in peace, Doc," he said aloud. He started the

little Japanese machine and putted his way carefully, quietly, and totally unnoticed to Martha Holland's beach house. Even there his luck held out, for no one saw him arrive or bury the motorcycle in a shallow grave on a stretch of beach completely hidden by the dunes. He chuckled to himself as he thought of some twenty-first-century archeologists unearthing a new motorcycle, a stolen license plate, a helmet, and a business suit without a label and one shoe.

Trumbull was unable to repress a wide grin as he stood alone at Martha Holland's bamboo bar and made himself a very large martini.

Chapter Two

MARTHA HOLLAND STARTED as she rushed into the "Florida room" of her beach house and saw Bill Trumbull in shoulder-length hair and bushy mustache, sitting on the low sofa. His feet were propped on a glass coffee table.

"What the hell is all this?" she asked in impatient and carefully measured tones.

"The great exodus!" he exclaimed. He threw his arms in the air and sprinkled Beefeater's all over her genuine south Georgia hooked rug.

"OK, Moses, but why the Halloween costume?" She put her handbag and the two law books she'd been carrying on the edge of the bar. She always took a file folder or a book or two home from the office. It made her look industrious, she had said.

She moved toward him quickly and gave him a generous kiss on the mouth.

"Worried?" he mumbled, still kissing her.

"Of course I was worried, you crazy son of a bitch. First, you gave me that insane phone call at the office, and then I didn't see your car when I got here. You're damned right I was worried." Her tone scolded him, but ever so carefully. "Where the hell is your car, anyway?"

"Catching flies, I hope," he teased.

"Flies? What flies? What are you talking about, anyway?" She reached for the half-empty bottle of Beefeater's and splashed some into a short glass. She called these iceless, vermouthless, straight-gin drinks "martinis."

"It is gracefully parked next to a phosphate pit, playing rock and roll to the mosquitoes," he chuckled.

"Are you drunk?" she asked in a suddenly serious tone.

"Not nearly enough," he said, squinting through his glass at the sunset rays over the Gulf of Mexico.

Martha Holland pried the heels of her shoes off with her toes and padded over to the sofa. Her end-of-the-day feet left brief, moist footprints on the black slate tiles of the Florida room.

"OK," she said with theatrical weariness. "You've had your jokes. Now clue me in on the whole deal." She collapsed with a loud sigh onto the low sofa. Bill Trumbull walked to the westward windows and continued to grin. The red glow of the sunset created a halo around his head.

"And take off that ridiculous hair. You look like some Jesus freak."

"I didn't strive for a biblical image," he snorted, pulling the wig from his head. "Can I leave the mustache glued on? I'm beginning to like it." He stroked the bristles sticking out from his upper lip with loving care.

"It all began . . ." she prompted, waving her glass.

"It all began this morning at the hospital when I read this ad in a medical journal." He threw the torn-out classified-ad page into her lap. She quickly scanned several dozen "help-wanted" ads. The lady lawyer only partly understood their medical jargon.

"So you're taking another job?" she asked, still searching the page.

"Not exactly. Check the ad halfway down the middle column."

"Let's see," she mumbled, "psychiatrist needed for multi-specialty clinic in St. Louis? You? A shrink?"

"No, ninny. The one a little farther down the page. Think exotic," he prompted.

"Exotic. Exotic . . ." Her eyes continued to scan the entries. "Holy shit!" "S.J." and "St. A. Gonzaga Mission" in the small ad were enough to put her mental gears in fast forward. "You're not going to run off and join the Jesuits!"

Trumbull laughed out loud. "Not *join* them, sweetheart, just hide with them for a while."

"In Guatemala?" she shrieked.

"What better place than Chichicastenango?" Trumbull held his hands above his head like a flamenco dancer and began snapping his fingers rhythmically.

"But, why Chichi—whatever it is?"

"Why not?" he asked, holding his palms upward and shrugging largely. "Who'd ever think of looking for me there?"

"But, what was all that bullshit this morning about the secrecy and prison? Hell, Bill, anybody can get on an airplane and . . ." She waved her hand around the room in a manner suggestive of a genie, "and disappear."

"But *they* get caught!"

"And you won't, I suppose," she mocked.

"And *I* won't. That's why all the Mickey Mouse this morning."

"And the long hair and mustache."

"Exactly."

Trumbull proceeded to tell Martha Holland about the note he left at the hospital, promising his return; the bloody car, still running, at the edge of the phosphate pit; and the little Japanese motorcycle.

"They'll get you for that license-plate theft," she warned professionally. "That's no joke, you know."

"But, they won't ever see me again, Martha."

She stared blankly at him for a moment and then

looked suddenly into the yard. "What little motorcycle?"

Trumbull winked and pointed out toward the beach dunes. "I planted it." He gave her a broad, silly smile that was somehow disarming.

"On my property?" she yelled. "And with a stolen plate? You'll get me disbarred!"

"How could they tie you to the motorcycle or the stolen plate?" he asked. "They really haven't got any connections between you and that bike. OK, so some kid came over here when you were gone and buried the motorcycle he stole."

"Yeah, but they'll connect the motorcycle with you somehow, and then you with me. That's all I need." Martha was visibly worried.

"No, Martha," he said, calming her, "I bought the little motorcycle under a phony name and address. There's no link. Honest!" He stuffed his hands into the pockets of his denim pants and hunched his shoulders slyly.

"OK, Houdini. Where do you go from here with this crazy scheme? Out to a waiting Nazi U-boat by rubber raft?" She was trying to convince herself that the whole thing was some kind of a joke.

"Better than that," he grinned. "How 'bout a thirty-two-foot sailboat?"

"Oh no!" she protested. "I'm not getting involved with this mess. If you want to foul up your whole career and run off to some jungle clinic, that's your business. But not in my sailboat." She was shaking her head decisively and marching toward the bar for more of her version of a martini.

"Just lend it to me," he persisted. "I'll see to it that it gets sent back."

"From where? Chichi-whatchamacallit?"

"From Mexico."

"Mexico?"

"Look, Martha, it's easy." He came closer to her and

put his hands on her shoulders. "You've been in those sailing races from St. Pete to Cozumel. They never have any big problems, do they?"

"Sure, Doc. But those guys are expert sailors. A Charlie Morgan or a Ted Turner, you're not. The guys who run in the ocean-racing conference know how to handle a sailboat in rough seas. Guys like that can—"

"You've seen me handle your boat before, Martha," he argued gently. "I know I can make it across the gulf. What the hell. The sailing problems are the same whether you're out for a day on the bay or gone for a week. It still comes one day at a time."

"You'll get yourself killed." She was shaking her head slowly and soberly. "Why don't you go by Pan Am?"

"I'd get caught for sure. Some old lady would remember a mole on my wrist, or something. It's too risky, Martha. I really need your boat. I'm too far into this to back out now. I'd look like an idiot if I did."

"Good-bye, sailboat," she said sadly. A small smile altered the set of her lips but did not much diminish the severe frown on the rest of her face.

"It's insured," he said quickly. He half-kissed her on the mouth. "Besides, you've got more money in your own name than any woman has a right to."

"Big deal. You're only interested in my money and my brains." She returned the second half of his kiss and stood closer. "Why can't you be a chauvinist pig and want me for my voluptuous body?"

In fact, Martha had no reason to apologize for her body. While not exactly "voluptuous," she was certainly well proportioned. Her problem was not in attracting a male. She had a harder time convincing one that she was serious and that her being a lawyer would not be a threat to his tender male ego.

"I am, I am," he said playfully. He reached back and slapped her behind with both hands then squeezed it sensuously. Softening immediately from defensive sarcasm to genuine affection, she leaned her head toward him and pressed her lips to his cheek. She felt his warm breath on her hand as she reached up to caress his face.

"Why Mexico, Bill?" Her voice was tiny and filled with concern.

"Because I'm too poor a navigator to sail Ole Duckie to Guatemala." He sometimes wondered if she had christened the sailboat Ole Duckie just to keep nautical friends from referring to it too seriously in conversation. So, she made it sound like the S.S. Bar of Soap floating in the bathtub. In fact, it was a well-equipped fiberglass sailboat with an inboard diesel engine, outfitted as a sloop. It was forgiving and handled easily. Martha had received more than her fair share of expert, personal instruction between advances made by the more amorous members of the yacht club. With these few years of experience behind her, including a couple of S.O.R.C. races to the Dry Tortugas and to the east coast of Mexico, she ranked among the more capable sailors in the state. By now she could single-handle the craft although she preferred not to. She insisted that for her, sailing was a social experience, not a navigational challenge.

"What makes you think that you can even hit Mexico?" she purred, trying not to dissipate the warm feeling that was rapidly enveloping both of them as they continued to stand tightly together.

"Because, once I fumble my way out past the number one whistle and into the gulf, all I'll have to do is set the compass on due west and let her go," he whispered in an equally inappropriate, intimate voice.

"You don't care where you hit Mexico?" she sighed.

"In fact, I won't hit it," he said, biting her ear. "I'll stop the damn thing a few hundred yards just before that."

"Or sooner, if you don't know where the reefs are," she mumbled, squirming as she responded to his nibbling as a woman rather than a lawyer.

"How can you tell . . ." he paused to kiss her several times quickly, ". . . where the reefs are?"

"You follow . . ." she returned the kisses, ". . . the charts." She was holding him tightly now. His hands touched her in places that silently called out to both of them. They moved to the sofa and collapsed gently into its cushions.

The sun had set and the beach house seemed unusually dark when, a few hours later, they disentangled themselves from each other. In the distance, the surf sent its deep roar to remind the unmindful ear that it was still out there, and would always be.

Martha Holland reached up and switched on the lowest power of the three-way table lamp. She unconsciously adjusted her hair. Bill Trumbull was still sprawled, semiconscious and satisfied, across the sofa.

"Not bad for an old, exhausted doctor," she teased. "When do you plan to shove off?"

At the mention of shoving off, he became alive again. He opened one eye and managed a small grin. "As soon as the boat is stocked and ready." He fussed with the stiff brass buttons on his new denims and moved to the window facing the black Gulf of Mexico. Somewhere offshore a navigational light winked a tiny eye at him in a four-second code.

"The sails are all on board," she said dully. "All you'll need is a week's supply of water and food and a few cans of fuel for insurance."

"Fuel? I'm not going to *drive* to Mexico, you know."

"You might," she said knowingly, "if there's a storm. The engine will help to keep your bow into the wind. She's also got a storm jib, just in case."

"You make it sound like the *Kon Tiki*," he chuckled. Inwardly, he was quite aware of the dangers involved in a solo voyage across the gulf. It would be a major challenge for an expert; for a novice it might well be suicide.

"I've been out there, Bill. I know how rough it can get." She extracted two cigarettes from her handbag and threw him one without looking his way. She waited silently for the snap of his aged Zippo. "There . . . are . . . easier . . . ways to get killed," she puffed.

"But I died in a phosphate pit," he announced triumphantly.

"Why don't you just call the whole thing off?" she said calmly. "We could drive over and reclaim your car right now. The sheriff probably hasn't found it yet. And even if he has, you could explain the blood as a fishing accident, and that your car got stuck."

"Too late, Martha," he said, shaking his head wearily. "I've wanted to break out for quite some time now. You know that. We've talked about it a million times. There's nothing left for me at home anymore. Or even at the hospital, for that matter." He puffed anxiously on his cigarette. "Going back is just not the answer. Don't you see? This way, the insurance company will take care of the family and I'll be out free."

"That's called fraud, you know," she said in a professional tone. "So far, you're only involved in a crazy situation that might be embarrassing to explain. Assuming, of course that no one saw you steal the kid's license plate at the school. But once you let them file that claim with the insurance company, you'll have a bitch of a time explaining why you're not really dead when they catch up with you."

"Catch up with me?" He laughed out loud. "How are they going to catch up with me? Do you think that Brother Timothy is going to turn me in to the local police in Guatemala?"

"Do you know this Brother Timothy?"

"No, but what's the difference? He won't ever hear of the disappearance or the evidence of any violent death in a phosphate pit in Florida. All he will ever know is that I'm an American doctor that God dropped right in his lap, 'no questions asked.'"

She moved closer and stood beside him silently. She knew there was no reason for further argument about his scheme. She had become an expert in reading the moods of witnesses from their voices. Bill Trumbull's was serious, determined, and anxious.

"OK," she sighed. "I'll drive."

"You'll what?"

"You'd get killed surer than hell, Bill. If you've got to go through with this, I'll sail you over to Mexico."

He put his arms tightly around her waist and, looking into her eyes, pulled her body against his own. Suddenly he smiled and appeared more relaxed.

"And stay?" he asked.

She shook her head. "I don't think that jungle life is my bag, Bill. I'll wait around back here until you're sick of whatever you find over there, and then I'll bail you out of the whole mess. Or at least find you a more comfortable place to hide. Like Paris, or somewhere."

"Maybe someday," he offered softly. They looked at each other for a moment longer than Martha Holland could stand. She tore herself from his arms and began to bustle around the room defensively. She hated to cry in front of any man. Even Bill Trumbull.

"Well!" she exclaimed abruptly rather than sob. "I'd better see about the arrangements." She put in a guarded call to her office answering service and announced that she'd decided to take a few days off to attend the Chicago law seminar she'd been planning to skip. Since her partners had originally urged her to attend the seminar, her last-minute change of heart would probably be more pleasing than annoying to them. Her secretary would shift her clients to other members of the firm and the world would go on, even though Martha Holland usually behaved as though it would stop without her.

She frowned slightly. "We can't very well outfit the boat tonight, but I suppose we can go check it out, at least."

"But if I'm seen around your marina, I'm dead."

"The night man is at least a hundred and fifty years old and he hasn't actually checked on the boats in fifteen years. We just keep him on because he's a retired Navy chief, and because the insurance company gives us better fire and theft rates if the marina is attended."

"What would the old fart do in case of fire?" Trumbull asked absently.

"Sleep through it, I guess," she shrugged. She reached for the keys to her car and nodded toward the door. Trumbull held up the blue-stenciled bags.

"Did you rob the bank too?"

"Only my own money. But the girl at the bank will tell them that I looked nervous when I withdrew it."

"How much?" she asked as a frown of legal worry invaded her face.

"A little over seventeen grand. That should pay the fare to Mexico and set me up in Chichi for a week or so." Trumbull was grinning like a small boy.

"Sounds like you're planning to buy this Chichi place."

"Well, I figured that if I ran out of money, you could send me a few bucks from time to time." He pushed her playfully toward the door of the beach house. Her MG was parked in the driveway just outside.

"Let me make sure that no one is around," she offered. Trumbull got the bank bags with the money and stood quietly in the darkened doorway and listened unconsciously to the rumble of the surf as Martha Holland walked to her car. She appeared to be unlocking the door, but was actually casing the grounds like a cautious burglar. After a moment she gave him a little wave and he got into the car quickly.

"I don't know how you manage to get in and out of this damned thing," he grumbled as he stuffed his legs into the small passenger compartment.

"You'd be surprised just what you can get done in an MG if you are willing to be very careful about it."

"And cooperative, too, I'll bet," he added.

She flicked on the lights and backed the sports car onto the empty roadway. The smallness of the car and the stiff British springs gave Bill Trumbull the feeling that they were flying down the narrow beach highway, though Martha, mindful of nosy traffic cops, was careful not to break fifty. In his Thunderbird, a hundred was still comfortable, but in the MG not only did everything go by faster, but it was all knee high.

After several miles of beach road and little hoop-de-doo bridges that bounced Bill Trumbull to the canvas top, Martha squealed the MG into her assigned space at the Boca Palma Yacht Club. The night man was visible in the little house at the entrance to the dock area. On the opposite side of the parking lot there were cars belonging to some late diners at the main clubhouse. There were no other cars in the area reserved for boaters.

"Let me go down and get rid of old Salty Sam," she said quietly. "You can come when you see him leave the cabin on the dock."

"What are you going to tell him?"

"I'll tell him that I want to check something on the boat and then I'll send him over to the clubhouse for a chicken sandwich. He'll go. He's a sweet old guy. You can sneak on board while he's gone."

"Send for two sandwiches. I'm starved."

"Too risky," she cautioned, shaking her head. "There's plenty of snack stuff on the boat. Open a couple of cans of something." She got out of the car and walked briskly to the guard's station. Trumbull slipped down on the MG's seat as low as he could and watched Martha's charm envelop the old man. He could not hear what she was saying, but in a few minutes, the old man got up, put on his battered Navy cap, and walked toward the main clubhouse. Martha made a careful wave toward the MG and Trumbull picked his way along the sand fence to the opened dock gate. Wordlessly, he took the boat key from Martha as he passed, and hurried along the deserted dock, carrying the money bags.

Next to the dock a long row of sailboats bobbed silently on their forward lines. An occasional halyard clanged rhythmically against an aluminum mast as the wind tapped out an undecipherable code to no one. Trumbull walked nervously and quickly past the smaller boats, ranging from twenty-four to twenty-eight feet, and approached Martha's thirty-two-foot fiberglass sloop. Trumbull stepped onto the blue-trimmed foredeck and felt the beamy sloop dip slightly under his weight. He remembered that Martha had refused the teak cockpit decking that the manufacturer wanted to install on the basis that too much work would be involved in the upkeep of the wood. Originally, the hull had been done in white anti-fouling paint, but the stains from oil spills in the water had forced Martha to repaint it a deep barn-red the previous spring.

The designer of the craft had installed a centerboard that dropped below the fixed keel, giving the six-ton boat greater stability in heavier winds, and shallow draft capabilities for running close to shore in Tampa Bay. Running aground in Tampa Bay or around Sarasota was no reflection on anyone's sailing abilities since the water was notoriously shallow and also subject to shifting sandbars. However, the bottom was soft and generally free of rocks, and getting off a sandbar became more of a social event than a maritime drill. Occasionally, someone on a sandbar would have to walk his anchor out and kedge off, but more frequently, an inboard engine would provide just enough power to grind the boat through the mud and back into deeper water.

Trumbull opened the padlock and silently slipped the hatch boards out. He was careful not to show a light as he eased his way into the cabin. The cabin smelled of unventilated fiberglass. The lights from the yacht club danced across the water in the marina and flashed around the inside of the boat. Alongside, he could hear the gentle lap of the waves as they relentlessly tested the integrity of the hull.

He reached inside the small cupboard beneath the galley sink and found a canned cocktail. He could not quite read the label in the dim light but prayed for a daiquiri. A warm manhattan greeted his tongue. He grimaced in distaste and resumed sipping the drink.

The boat tipped gently, and then he heard Martha's low heels click across the deck toward the cockpit. She was one of those comfortable sailors who did not bother their guests by requesting they take off their shoes before boarding. In fact, the fiberglass deck was tough enough to take most anything except Spanish dancing in spiked heels.

"Bill," she whispered hoarsely into the darkness of the cabin below. A paper bag containing the sandwich crackled in her hand.

"Welcome aboard," a voice said from the darkness.

"Turn on a cabin light or the watchman will think I fell into the marina and drowned."

"You turn them on. I'm too comfortable on this bunk."

Martha grumbled a few mild obscenities and felt her way toward a forward cabin light. The cabin was suddenly filled with the white light of the twelve-volt battery-powered system that operated whenever the boat was not connected to a power source on shore. Some of the larger boats stayed plugged into shore when they were at dock to keep their freezers and ice machines working. But Martha's sailboat was not big enough to be in that class.

"The guard brought a ham sandwich from the club. They were out of chicken," she said, fixing her hair and dropping the paper bag on a counter top. She slipped off her shoes and padded to a small radio that served as both entertainment and weather-report receiver. She turned the knob and the soft, romantic strains of a St. Petersburg FM station favored by retirees filled the cabin.

"Keep playing that Jackie Gleason and I'll never leave," Trumbull said in a sultry voice. He had stretched out on the starboard bunk, the warm canned manhattan was balanced on his chest. It rose and fell with each breath.

"I think it's just as well if you didn't anyway. It's safer."

"Didn't what?"

"Leave the boat. After all, you made it on board and no one saw you. Why risk running up and down the dock now?"

"You want me to just lay here and wash down my only sandwich with this warm booze?"

"You can switch to warm beer if you get sick of manhattans," she chuckled. "Those manhattans have been on board since Judge Flanagan crewed the last race to Clearwater with me. Hate 'em myself."

He lifted the nearly empty can and toasted the skipper smartly. "Here's to the judge."

"All I'll have to do," she offered enthusiastically, "is to go buy us some supplies tomorrow and bring them on board a little at a time, so that I don't look like I'm outfitting this boat for the Galapagos Islands. No one will even know where you are."

He sipped the last of his manhattan thoughtfully. Even Martha winced to see him drink it warm.

"You might be right," he conceded. He sat upright on the bunk. "But do you really think you'd be able to bring all that stuff we'd need out here without attracting any attention?"

"Sure—I put stuff on this boat all the time. Nobody counts the number of trips I make along the dock. 'Specially in the daytime when there's no watchman. Most of the other boat owners don't show up until the weekend anyway."

"Unless they're down here fooling around with their secretaries," Trumbull suggested.

"Well, hell. They certainly wouldn't bother you then," Martha said with finality.

"How come you're so cooperative in this crazy affair anyway? You want to get rid of me or something?" he asked casually.

"Look" she said firmly, sitting on the bunk beside the pathologist. "You've already stolen a license plate and left plenty of indication that you intend to defraud the insurance company. If the sheriff isn't hot after your murderer at this very moment, I'd be greatly surprised. That's why I'm so suddenly cooperative. You really don't have any easy way back at this point." She brushed a lock of hair from his forehead and fingered his frown.

"Careful, or I'll begin to think you're really interested in my welfare," he said defensively. He put his hand on the back of her arm and squeezed gently. She let him pull her slowly toward him.

"I think you're perfectly insane," she whispered, accepting his kiss.

"Nobody's perfect," he sighed.

Shifting to a more comfortable position, he reached up behind his head to move a flashlight that protruded slightly from a shelf and threatened to whack him on the back of the head if he became careless. He kept his eyes fixed seductively on Martha as he moved the light a few inches along the shelf. His groping fingers were surprised by the unmistakable, cool smooth metallic feel of a gun.

"What's this for?" he asked, palming the .38 Smith and Wesson.

"Careful. It's loaded," she said quickly. "I used to keep it at the house, but I figured it would be safer here." She exhibited an expression that said she did not like guns.

"What do you shoot with it?"

"So far, one shark—I think."

"What did he do to you?" the pathologist asked, examining the weapon.

"He just kept swimming around the boat one day, making some of my friends on board a bit nervous. One of them took a shot at it."

"And missed?"

"Nope. The water got all bloody. Just like the movies. Oh, he never surfaced and surrendered, but we were pretty sure that he had been hit."

Trumbull nodded understandingly and put the gun on the bunk beside him. He tried to resume the romantic mood with Martha, but the gun had made her nervous. She stood up and adjusted her clothing.

"When it's quiet, I'll clump down the dock and make sure that the dockmaster sees me go," she said, looking out at the still marina.

"Why not stay here with me," Bill Trumbull teased. He held out his hand.

"We've got plenty of time for all that when we've made it safely out of this damned harbor," she said. "If you want to call it off, now's the time."

He shook his head firmly. "No going back," he said.

Martha was framed in the hatchway and never looked better to him. He put out the cabin light and moved up against her in the darkness. He could feel her heart beating nervously.

"You can bring me the stuff and get the hell out before it's too late," he offered in a whisper. "Tell 'em I stole the boat."

She shook her head gently and then rested it on his shoulder. "I know you're crazy, Bill, but I can't let you go out there alone." She raised her head and looked at him. The dim reflected light of the marina bounced off a small tear that ran down her cheek.

"Maybe you're the crazy one," he said softly.

Chapter Three

By jogging around his duplex house twenty-four times at 4:30 in the morning, the police sergeant in the traffic helicopter had psyched himself up for the boring job of watching the endless stream of daily commuters on the thruway. Without his daybreak run and a thermos of hot *café con leche,* he would be inclined to let the drivers below find their own accidents along the approaches to Tampa, and to find himself a light touch in the I.D. section.

It was already 7:30 and the heaviest flow was beginning to back up along the interstate with some exit ramps badly congested.

"You're doing a real fine job looking out for each other down there," the eye-in-the-sky said with phony cheerfulness. "Keep a safe distance and everybody will get to work safely. The inbound lanes are getting pretty full around Fortieth Street and some of you folks should think about taking an alternate route to downtown. We can't all use the same exit and jam up those older streets. Keep up the good work now." He nudged his pilot in the ribs and the chopper responded like a neck-reined quarter horse. The police sergeant snapped off his radio transmitter and squinted eastward into the sun.

"Let's take a look at the eastern part of the highway," he shouted at the pilot. "That Disney World traffic has made the east part of county into a real trouble spot. Time was when it was nothing but a couple of farm trucks on that stretch. Now it's solid commuters from the suburbs and rental cars going to the airport from the Magic Kingdom." He shielded his eyes from the glare that flashed from the lakes below and lit another cigarette. "You been there, Harry?"

"Where?" the pilot asked, banking slightly to get a view of wherever he thought the sergeant was looking.

"Disney World."

"Nope." He leveled the copter again, muttering under his breath.

"Some joint," the sergeant shouted over the noise of the engine.

"Rather fish, myself," the pilot shouted back.

"Well, you've got to go at least once. For the kids, I mean." The sergeant adjusted the radio dial to tune in the morning disc jockey show that carried his periodic traffic announcements. He had become so used to the job that he heard only his own cues from the D.J. and hardly ever followed the music or the rest of the show.

"*My* kids would rather fish," Harry announced loudly.

"Than Disney?"

"Than anything."

"Ever ask them?"

"Wouldn't dare. They might want to go to Disney World."

The police sergeant looked over at his pilot to make sure that he was grinning. Suddenly, a flash of light leaped at the sergeant from the general area of the phosphate pits below. His subconscious computer immediately registered the incongruity of a flash in that desolate area. He nudged the pilot and pointed toward the pits.

"Let's take a look over there, Harry," he shouted, pointing vigorously.

The pilot put the helicopter into a left turn that made the sergeant's experienced stomach squirm.

"What are we looking for? Catfish or raccoons?"

"Not sure," said the sergeant. "It just seemed like a . . ." He squinted toward the phosphate pits and was rewarded with another smaller, brighter flash. "There!" he shouted triumphantly. "Bet you my ass that's a windshield."

"Some bet," Harry muttered to himself.

"Probably a stolen car. Let's check it out."

"As if we didn't have plenty to do watching those idiots drive into town." Harry dropped the chopper several hundred feet and aimed at the small black dot that was rapidly becoming a parked car. He brought the chopper across the car at an altitude of a few hundred feet but did not stop. Both of the police officers glanced quickly at the car as they flew by and went into a high left banking turn for another sweep.

"Don't raise any dust," the sergeant remarked out of habit and training. "Drives the fingerprint boys crazy."

"Crazier."

"Looks hot to me," the sergeant observed expertly. "Doors open. Nobody around. Sure ain't no fisherman."

"How can you tell?"

"Don't see any beer cans around." The sergeant flipped his radio dial to the police circuit and pressed the transmitter button. "Sky bird one to base," he said mechanically.

"Roger, sky bird. This is baseland. Go ahead," a female voice said flatly.

"We have an apparent signal ten at one of the phosphate pits off of Merckle Road. Better have it checked out. Over."

"Roger, sky bird. Acknowledge. A signal ten. Say again the location. Over."

"I make it Merckle Road about three miles south of the interstate. It's a Thunderbird, parked next to one of the old pits. Can't see anyone working phosphate out of this pit at this time, but it looks like there's an old dirt road into the place. Over."

The pilot made another pass over the car and both men strained to give the scene a more careful look.

"Roger, sky bird. I copy. Will do. Over."

"Keep it up and I'll get you a job on the real radio, honey," the sergeant teased.

"Out, sky bird."

The police receiver crackled to silence. The sergeant unconsciously heard the D.J. say, ". . . and now, here's our eye in the sky, Sergeant Joe Flag."

Sergeant Flag switched his radio to the AM band and pressed his transmitter lever. "OK, all you folks. You're doing real fine now. Keep that safe distance. Let's not be in a big hurry and we'll all get downtown to work on time." He looked out of the helicopter toward the phosphate pit area and saw only one farm tractor inching its way along a secondary road. "There's a lot of cars on the interstate westbound this morning, but let's all drive carefully and avoid that accident. Remember that driving is like baseball: It's not how many hits you get, but how many times you get home safe." He glanced at his pilot and shrugged helplessly. "This is Sergeant Joe Flag, your early-morning eye in the sky."

The D.J. picked up the cue and flipped on an up-tempo country-and-western selection without announcing the title or the artist.

The chopper pilot looked at Sergeant Flag and shook his head sadly. "That traffic report came pretty close to outright fraud," he shouted.

"Hell, nobody believes us anyway," Joe Flag said a little too softly to be heard over the roar of the engine.

* * *

It was almost an hour later when a green-and-white sheriff's patrol car found the dirt roadway into the phosphate pit and wallowed through the soft sand toward the Thunderbird. Deputy Fletcher had not yet noticed that there were no tire tracks leading into the pit. He had received what he considered to be a routine call from the dispatcher notifying him that there was a possible stolen car at that location. He was not exactly pleased about the uncertain address he had been given and the prospects of dulling his newly shined service boots with soft phosphate dirt, but it was better than the jimmied windows and broken fences that had to be checked out in following up the morning burglary complaints.

As the patrol car churned through the weed-grown trail, the abandoned Thunderbird suddenly came into full view. Fletcher eased the cruiser up to the back of the T-bird and automatically took down the Florida tag number on his clipboard. The printed sheet of hot cars on his clipboard contained thefts only eight hours old, but the Thunderbird's plate number was not on the list.

"Goddamn fishermen," Fletcher mumbled as he opened the door of the patrol car and stepped out into the soft sand. His shiny black boots took on a fine powdery coating with the first few steps.

"Anybody home?" he called loudly. Hand still cupped to his mouth, he waited like a slightly irate statue for a reply that he somehow knew would not come. "Hello?" he repeated more forcefully. "Anybody here?" Absorbed by the open phosphate pit, the tall weeds, and the hum of disinterested insects in the brush, his voice was echoless. He picked his way toward the driver's side of the sports car and looked in through the open door. Deputy Fletcher was careful not to touch any part of the door as he began his preliminary inspection.

47

"She's still on," he mumbled as he noticed the key in the ignition. He took a ball-point from his shirt pocket and carefully depressed the horn. There was no sound. "Dead," he said aloud.

He stood a few feet back from the side of the car and slowly scanned the vehicle from front to back. His eyes focused on the tire iron lying in the soft dirt near the left front wheel. Half crouching, he squinted at the tool and tried to convince himself that he really saw dried blood and hair on it. A single drop of sweat wandered lazily down the middle of his back as he bent over the tire iron in the hot Florida sun.

"Signal ten be damned," he whispered. "Looks more like a homicide to me." He carefully retraced his footsteps to his green-and-white, slid in behind the wheel, and turned the ignition to beef up the radio-transmitting power.

"Car nine," he said quickly.

The base dispatcher acknowledged his call.

"Ah, this is car nine," he repeated needlessly. "I'm out here in the east county checking out that signal ten that the chopper spotted?" His statement was inflected like a question not because he needed or wanted an answer, but because his Tampa Bay upbringing gave him no other choice. "Be advised that on checking out this here vee-hicle, I am of the distinct impression that this may be a signal five also. Over."

"Roger, car nine. Repeating, I read you as, 'possible signal five over the possible signal ten' at your location in progress. Over."

"And, Dolly? Let me have a quick listing on Florida 3WW-2525, current year. And you'd better send me out an area supervisor. Over and out." He closed his cruiser door to contain the cool air that belched from his air conditioner and threatened to condense on his uniformed knee.

"Roger, car nine. Will do. Stand by." The radio gave a metallic click as the headquarters dispatcher ended her transmission. Deputy Fletcher shook a cigarette from the half-empty pack on the seat beside him and tapped it firmly on his thumb nail to repack the tobacco. He looked at the Thunderbird pensively as he lit up and took two long silent puffs.

"Surer than hell he's in that phosphate pit somewheres," he mumbled into his slowly rising cloud of blue-gray smoke. He glanced at his watch and sighed deeply. He wondered why he couldn't have been assigned some other case. He wondered why this signal ten couldn't have turned out to be an abandoned vehicle needing only a tow back to town or a couple of teenaged kids playing zipper games in the back seat. "Just my luck," he announced to the world. "A goddamned homicide to spoil a beautiful day."

The deputy's brain filtered the irrelevant radio dispatches aimed at other cars on other assignments without calling his attention to them. He absently considered the fate of a fat, imaginary catfish feeding on the rotting flesh of the dead body at the bottom of the phosphate pit, and wondered if it would change the flavor of the fish. "Hell," he said aloud. "Crabs eat dead stuff all the time and nobody minds their taste. The biggest ones come from around the sewer pipes from the hospital. Least that's what the nigger kids that catch 'em say."

"Car nine," the radio said without warning.

"Nine," he responded.

"Car nine, be advised that your request for a make on Florida 3WW-2525, reads as follows: registrant, William E. Trumbull. Address of record, 1306 Bramble Drive, Orangeburrow, Florida. No record of being missing or stolen to date. Over." Except for an undeniable Southern accent, the dispatcher's pronounced words were as crisply distinct as a robot in a science fiction TV series. Fletcher jotted the message on his clipboard form and reached for the transmitter.

"Roger, Dolly. How 'bout my area supervisor?"

"Acknowledge, car nine. Be further advised that area supervisor is en route."

"Roger. Car nine out." Deputy Fletcher put the transmitter back on its cradle and slipped into a more comfortable slouch to avoid the direct rays of the sun that burned through his car windows and made pancake griddles of his vinyl car seats.

A small breeze, ineffectual against the humidity, stirred a small stand of tall weeds at one end of the phosphate pit. Fletcher remembered that when he was a boy, he would imagine big gators coming through the tall weeds whenever the wind made them sway. His eyelids became heavy and he recalled the tall weeds around Old Port Tampa just before he dozed off, oblivious to the dispatcher's announcements.

Deputy Fletcher was not sure whether his own sudden snorting awakened him or whether the small, playful whine of the siren from the sheriff's cruiser behind him had shocked him back to consciousness. He sat up quickly and straightened his wide-brimmed hat as he opened his car door and stepped out to greet his supervisor.

"Mornin', Sergeant," he said, offering a poorly executed hand salute.

"Mornin', Fletcher," the sergeant said casually. "I been fixin' to get myself lost in these damnable phosphate pit roads. If you hadn't made them tire marks in to here, I'da like to never found you." He leaned slightly out of the open window of his patrol car and squinted at Deputy Fletcher.

"Yes sir. This here's some kind of a hideaway, all right." Fletcher grinned and assumed a softer, more "country" accent to match the homespun attitude of Sergeant Orville Grubbs. Sergeant Grubbs had been "with the sheriff," as he put it, for twenty-four years and was approaching retirement, not that he had anywhere to go or anything else to do when retired. Check-

ing unlocked gas stations, mediating domestic argu-
ments, and looking into reports of stolen barbed wire
were about all he knew and all he cared to know.

His assignment as an area supervisor had taken him
out of the office where his antiquated methods had
almost driven the younger men crazy. He had been
assigned to the east county, of course. It was sparsely
populated and hardly needed patrol, to say nothing of
"area supervision." Sergeant Grubbs was aware that
this job was a kind of putting him out to pasture, but
did not complain. He hated the office work even more.

"What kind of trouble you causin' today, Fletcher?"
He puffed noisily with mild emphysema and obvious
overweight as he struggled out of his green-and-white
cruiser and walked toward the Thunderbird. Fletcher
was again aware of the soft sand and dust collecting
on his carefully polished boots. Sergeant Grubbs wob-
bled toward him, oblivious to the dirt and probably his
shoes as well.

"You got Doc Trumbull's car here, Fletcher," the
sergeant announced flatly. "He around?"

"Doc who?"

"Dr. Trumbull. The pathologist. From Orangeburrow. Works over at the hospital." Grubbs was casually
but expertly scanning the back and driver's side of the
T-bird as he spoke.

"How did you know all that, Sergeant?"

"'Cause I know just 'bout everybody in the east part
of this county." Grubbs was not bragging. He was simply stating a fact.

"Those there are my footprints," Fletcher offered.
Grubbs ignored both the announcement and the footprints as he chugged his way toward the open door of
the car. He pushed his hat back on his head and looked
inside the Thunderbird, satisfying himself that there
was nothing in the front seat. Then he turned to face
Fletcher.

"What makes you think this is a signal five?"

"Well, there's a lot of things," Fletcher said cautiously. "There's that tire iron over there." He pointed to the tool near the left front wheel. "Looks to me like there's blood and some hair on it."

Grubbs looked at him skeptically. "Blood and hair, huh? You workin' for the crime lab now, Fletcher?" The sergeant leaned over the tire tool and looked at the dried material on one end. He was silent for a long time and then stood up, scratching the back of his neck.

"What do you think, Sergeant?"

"Boy, they pay me to report things, not to think. Thinkin' is for some of those new fellas who don't have to wear uniforms. These days, they do about all of it."

"I mean do you think that's blood and hair on that tire iron?"

"Mebbe. Can't rightly say. They got tests they do to tell that." The sergeant was looking farther on toward the lake, and noticed the shoe.

"Whose shoe is that?" he asked Fletcher.

"The doc's, I guess. Ain't mine."

"Lucky it ain't. Lord knows where the foot is."

"In the pit, I reckon," Fletcher volunteered.

Grubbs nodded his head slowly. "Could be. Poor ole Doc," he added. "Wasn't no bother to no one. Did a pretty good job over at the hospital too, they tell me. Used to do all them lab tests, you know. The ones they do on the blood they take out of your arm at six in the morning? They took all kinds of blood out of me once. And just to fix a hernia!" He poked at the shoe with a stubby forefinger but made sure not to mar any fingerprints left on it. The label said Florsheim and the shoe had not been polished recently.

"How'd they come out?" Fletcher asked casually.

"How'd what come out?"

"The tests they done on you."

"Oh, OK, I guess. Leastwise, I ain't heard no more

from nobody about them. Figgered they'd have called me if they found something bad. It's been a couple of years." He walked to the front of the car and looked at it carefully. The headlights were not broken and there were no dents in the fenders. Grubbs recalled a hit-and-run case where the dents in the fender and hood had been matched by the medical examiner to the height of the victim's leg fractures and scalp lacerations. The car was positively identified several days later, even though the driver had replaced the broken headlight. Since that case, Grubbs had made it a point to personally inspect each car that he came into professional contact with. He hadn't turned up another suspect car in the intervening years, but the one solved hit-and-run case had psyched him up enough to keep him looking tirelessly.

"Been over this car pretty good, Fletcher?" He walked along the right side of the Thunderbird and looked it over carefully.

"No, sir. I thought I'd leave that for the crime lab. You find something?"

Grubbs shook his head and spit into the dust. "Good thinkin', Fletcher. Best thing is to stay out of their way. If you check everything out all by yourself, the lab fellas will say that you loused up their precious evidence. But if you don't look the case over at all, the lieutenant will jump on you."

"Can't win for tryin', Sergeant."

Grubbs had made it all the way around the car and looked into the front seat again. "Key's still on," he remarked. "Bet she's out of gas."

Fletcher took an involuntary step toward the gas flap.

"Don't touch that gas cap!" Grubbs shouted without looking at Fletcher. "Whoever drove this heap here might have stopped for gas on the way. Fingerprints, you know."

"But, the prints will be from the gas station attendant. Not the driver's," Fletcher protested, defensively.

"Mebbe. Mebbe not. If the prints are the gas station boy's, we might be able to find him and trace the car back at least that far. But, remember, some guys like to put their own gas caps on. Lose one and you'll see why."

Grubbs poked at the radio knob with his pencil. It turned easily. "Radio's still on, too," he mumbled to himself as he squinted to see what station it had been playing.

"You want me to call homicide and tell them that you agree it looks like a signal five?" Fletcher was already walking back to his cruiser, if only to get out of the sun.

"You might as well," Grubbs shouted from inside the doctor's car. He was trying to look under the seat but his belly limited his search. "Tell them we think the body is in the phosphate pit, so they'll need to bring out some frogmen. Better tell Captain Rizzolo too. He don't like to be left out of a good murder scene."

Captain Rizzolo had come up through the ranks to head the homicide section of the sheriff's department. His early years as a policeman had been spent on the city force, but when the old sheriff quit and a man whom every cop in the county respected took over, Rizzolo had been among the first to submit an application for transfer. The new sheriff had to be careful not to encourage a personnel raid on the city police force, but he had an obligation to put together a stronger department than his predecessor had left him with. Rizzolo's application had been accepted almost immediately.

The sheriff had made him second in command in the homicide-and-robbery section, and then had promoted him to captain and section head in just two years. Though the men admired Rizzolo's careful work and his ability to get along with just about all of them, they knew as well that, if necessary, he was a tiger. Tough on any deputy who fell down on the job, and merciless with any of them who were even suspected of dishonesty.

Rizzolo was forty-two, thick-chested and shorter than most of his men. Though he allowed his deputies to wear their hair long and to grow mustaches, he continued his own lifelong practice of wearing a crew cut, a clean-shaven face, and white socks. Remarks about his being an Italian redneck did not bother him in the least.

"Do you think Captain Rizzolo will come way out here?" Fletcher asked.

"Bet your ass he'll come. And he'll check out every damned thing that the I.D. guys turn up. That's how he is."

"Think he'll show up in a frogman suit?"

"Funny. Very funny. Why don't you ask him when you put in the call for the lab truck?"

"Right, Sergeant. I'll do that," Fletcher chuckled.

"And, Fletcher . . .?" Grubbs called, prying himself from beneath the driver's seat of the car. "You'd better get yourself down by the paved road and show him where to turn in here. Rizzolo won't put up with poor directions from us, and I couldn't even start to tell him how to find this place on the radio."

Fletcher was opening his car door to make his call when he noticed the dirt roadway.

"That's funny, Sergeant," he said loudly.

"What is?"

"The dirt road into here. There's your tire tracks and those there are mine," he said, pointing to the tread marks in the sand. "But there ain't none at all for that T-bird."

Grubbs made his way to the back of the Thunderbird and looked at the smooth sand extending from the rear tires and down the sandy roadway. He frowned, as if that would help him to think more clearly.

"Been wiped clean," he said softly. "Probably with a piece of brush. See the scratch marks running sideways? Somebody has swept the whole road."

Grubbs' sweat had made dark areas on the front and back of his uniform shirt.

Chapter Four

AT HOME, Agnes Trumbull felt alone again. The alarm buzzed impatiently and she renewed her vow to replace it with something more pleasant-sounding. For no reason, each morning when the buzzer intruded on her sleep, she remembered how that little electric clock had been dropped by the movers and at that moment acquired its grating tone. At that time, Agnes and Bill Trumbull were in the process of moving from the hospital where they had just completed a rotating internship, to Denver, where Bill was to begin his residency in pathology. Like other women whose husbands were involved in post-graduate medical training, Agnes had adopted the "we" in her descriptions of Bill's educational experiences. Medical wives did not feel the least bit self-conscious about this choice of pronoun. They felt intimately involved in the daily aspects of the training that their husbands suffered through. The details of difficult cases and the daily rebukes by senior instructors were as familiar to the wives as to the house staff doctors themselves, and made them an important part of their laundry-room conversation.

This morning, Agnes had nothing planned, but plenty to do, as usual. After the breakfast hassle with the kids, and the struggle to the school, she hoped that she could scare up a tennis game with Mary LaFontaine, the wife of the local radiologist. This "sporting engagement," as Mary's British husband would label it, would be contingent on the number of martinis that Mary and Bruce LaFontaine had consumed the evening before. Bill Trumbull liked to chide Bruce on the fact that he was British-born and Scottish-trained, but carried around a French name. LaFontaine was happy to remark that the English Channel was quite narrow and that crossing it had been no more difficult for his father than for his sperm to swim upstream. In fact, LaFontaine's father had had the assistance of a French single-seat fighter that had chased a Messerschmitt around the skies over Calais until—badly off course, a little shot up, and very low on fuel—he had pancaked near Brighton, England. After a while, his passionate urge to return to France had been replaced by another passion, and he had married a barmaid in London. The result became Dr. Bruce LaFontaine.

Agnes swept her hand across Bill's side of the bed and sighed deeply. In the early days, beginning with the clinical assignments at the hospital during medical school, she had been willing to accept his not coming home as part of the sacrifice required to transform a college boy into a doctor. Later, it was part of the similar sacrifice required to transform a doctor into a specialist. Now, she reluctantly accepted the fact that his nights out were related to his frustration and boredom at home rather than to his medical practice at the hospital.

At the downtown hospital, there had been more frequent emergencies, and more middle-of-the-night frozen sections on unscheduled cases. But at the little country hospital where he now practiced alone, there were few real emergencies and almost none of these required the pathologist himself to respond.

For a while, she wondered about his absences and the gap that had grown between the two of them and would cry easily, though she made sure that he was unaware of her grief. Later, she contrived to make him fully aware of her unhappiness, and wept whenever he gave her the slightest cause. Still later, when she saw that he was unconcerned with her red eyes, depression, and general irritability, she cried alone once again. After several months of that, and after a psychiatrist friend of the family had seemed to suggest that her solitary weeping was "unhealthy," she had ceased it altogether.

His side of the bed was as smooth that morning as it had been when the maid had made it. Agnes slept in a single, unmoving curl that became animate only when gently prodded by Bill Trumbull's infrequent sexual urges at home. Until a few months ago, Agnes used to carefully disturb her husband's side of the bed when he stayed out all night, to indicate to the maid that he had really been there. The maid was never fooled, and the psychiatrist had asked Agnes about that defense mechanism too.

She clicked the radio on and walked quietly out of the master bedroom. The radio promised a nice day in a cheerful voice that suggested that the announcer was either a full-blown psychotic or that he was scheduled to get off in an hour or so. People who were happy, cheerful, and bubbly in the morning should be held highly suspect, she had once remarked.

Agnes Trumbull glided silently along the carpeted hallway and looked in on the sleeping children. Tom, the littlest, slept in a ball, while his sister was spread-eagled across her bed like some pioneer captured and sacrificed on an anthill by marauding Indians. These two were six and seven, respectively, born late in residency, and unused to being anything but a doctor's children. The oldest boy, John, was fifteen, and had dim recollections of his father going off to the hospital in a white, starched uniform, with books under his arm and stacks of homework to do at night instead of playing ball in the backyard like the other boys' fathers did.

Agnes was reluctant to disturb the peacefulness of the morning by awakening the children, but the clock said that the car pool to the parochial school was due at the front door in thirty minutes. She reached for Tom's exposed foot and stroked it gently. He had a pretty face, with blue eyes that only closed three quarters when he slept. His behavior, however, was less than angelic, a fact that pleased both his father and his grandfather.

"Morning, Mr. Tom-Tom," Agnes purred as she stroked his tiny foot. The little man emitted a long-suffering groan that suggested that his clandestine TV watching had gone on longer than his mother had been aware. "Time for my first-grader to go off to school." She stroked the blond hair from his eyes and kissed him gently on the cheek. He stretched, yawned, and put his arms toward his mother. He would have preferred to remain asleep, but was affectionate enough to accept his mother's caresses without hesitation.

"Can I have two nickels for lunch today, Mom?" he asked quickly.

"Two nickels for what?" she said sympathetically.

"He wants bubble gum," his sister said from the doorway. She had awakened with the first words from Tom's room and was by nature too nosy to let anything escape her immediate and personal attention.

"Na-uh!" Tom denied vigorously. "It's for a pencil." His tone implied that had his mother not been present, he would have stuck his tongue out for emphasis.

"Bubble gum," his sister Cathy repeated in a sing-song.

"Pencils," he insisted.

"Bubble gum."

Tom charged out of the bed toward Cathy. His mother prevented the mayhem by lifting him, still running and fighting mad, into her arms.

"Come on, mama's boy," she said tenderly. "I'll give you some Cocoa Puffs."

"And bananas," he said, snuggling closer to her and working her for every last thing he could get.

"Cathy, you wake up John and tell him fifteen minutes to school," Agnes ordered crisply as she carried Tom down the stairs to the kitchen.

"But he'll beat me up," Cathy pleaded.

"Wake him and run," Agnes retorted over her shoulder. "He's just like his father."

She had promised Bill—and herself—on several occasions that she would stop making derogatory comparative statements about his personality in front of the children. Her own personality and the childhood influence of her own father made her characterize the man she had married as unloving. Her biting comments had contributed to their growing further apart until, at last, her criticisms of Bill Trumbull had become justified. He had become hard and unloving toward her, and yet he knew that he was not destined to be content with anyone else.

Perhaps he was not destined to be content with anyone.

An hour later, kids off to school, Agnes settled into a blissful mental state that she reserved for the "second cup of coffee." The tennis match had been called off by Mary LaFontaine on the pretext of a headache, which Agnes correctly interpreted as a hangover.

She lit her first menthol cigarette of the morning, and congratulated herself on not lighting up earlier. The woman's page in the Tampa *Tribune* was open in front of her and she tried to imagine the actual execution of the steps in a foreign-sounding recipe that was printed alongside a photograph of a chicken in an unpleasantly red sauce.

The front doorbell rang with one chime missing in its Westminster bongs, making a sound like a musical smile with an absent front tooth. She had asked to have it repaired or replaced, but Bill had said that it had a humbling effect on the otherwise pretentious $75,000 house that he had had built in a fashionable area of Orangeburrow. All of the houses there were a little too big for their intended purposes, but never quite big enough to completely satisfy either the suburban wives or the building contractors.

Agnes's mind flashed to an image of her next-door neighbor who would, no doubt, be calling to share a cup of coffee and to bring the latest gossip about the rest of the town in her own, "down home" Mississippi accent. Agnes really didn't mind the drawl as much as her rural expressions. Such expressions as "useless as the left hind tit on a bore hog" left Agnes groping for images, and totally distracted her from the conversational topic at hand.

Agnes adjusted her hair and opened the door suddenly. Her planned greeting of "How y'all," made it only to the "H" which continued as an inappropriate hiss. She was greeted by a plump, middle-aged, dark-complected man in a plain brown suit. He was accompanied by a neat, tall, uniformed sheriff's deputy.

Their green-and-white stood in the street patiently, its blue "bubble-gum machine" on the roof resting.

"Mrs. Trumbull?" the man in the brown suit inquired politely. "I am Captain Rizzolo with the county sheriff's office." He put his big blunt hand out gently. "This is Deputy Keaton."

"How do you do, Captain," Agnes said, shaking his hand and nodding to the well-pressed deputy. "Won't you come in, what can I do for you—I think there's some coffee left," she gushed all at once as her surprise and anxiety joined together to rattle both her brain and her tongue. "I hope the children haven't done something terribly dreadful," she said, showing them the way to the living room.

She wished she hadn't mentioned the children; suddenly she saw herself on a witness stand being reminded of this spontaneous admission of guilt.

"No, ma'am, nothing like that," the captain offered quickly. "Nothing like that at all." He was quite aware of the fact that everyone feels a little nervous when the sheriff calls, and that nothing is gained by putting off the reasons for the call. "It's about Dr. Trumbull," he said.

They had entered the living room but were not yet seated. Agnes turned abruptly and faced the captain. She almost covered her mouth with a limp hand, and her eyes were suddenly blurry.

"An accident?" she asked, unbelieving. He always drove too fast, she said to herself.

"No, ma'am, not an accident. At least not as we see it at this time," Rizzolo said. "I'd like for you to sit down, Mrs. Trumbull."

Agnes sat down obediently and silently. She could feel her heart beginning to pound in her chest and the back of her throat suddenly ached with dryness. She found herself focusing on the neat row of bullets in the deputy's beautifully shined black belt and avoiding the captain's face.

"We found the doctor's car, Mrs. Trumbull, and we need to ask you a few questions," Captain Rizzolo said gently, but without apology. It was always referred to as "a few questions," he thought to himself. In fact, it was never a few questions.

"First of all," he continued in response to her faint nod, "did the doctor come home last night?"

Agnes shook her head and glanced quickly into his face before turning away again to study the deputy's belt. "Sometimes he has to be at the hospital all night," she said. "You know, emergency surgery cases?" She looked up at Rizzolo's expressionless face. "They might need him to ..."

She realized that this simple explanation of his absence from home all night might satisfy the ladies, but would not be sufficient for the captain. If it were, the captain would not be sitting in her living room.

"Mrs. Trumbull," Captain Rizzolo said softly and

with surprising sympathy. "We have reason to believe that Dr. Trumbull may have met with serious trouble yesterday or last night, and we need your help in trying to find out just what might have happened to him."

"What do you mean, 'serious trouble'? Is he hurt or something? Where is he?" She looked at him and then to the implacable deputy before turning back to the captain in search of visible signs. Their faces were still professionally expressionless. She felt herself collapsing inside.

"First of all, Mrs. Trumbull, I want you to know that we are doing everything to determine exactly what may have happened out there, and—"

"Out where?" she demanded.

"At a phosphate pit south of the interstate. We found his car." Captain Rizzolo paused to give Mrs. Trumbull time to grasp each fact as he carefully presented it. On previous occasions he had had to begin a homicide investigation by interviewing the surviving wife or husband, and was well aware that the fear of what might have happened could almost close the mind to what, in fact, did happen. The simple questions that need to be answered in the beginning could go unheard and misunderstood. Horrified parents might identify an article of burned clothing from the victim of a car crash and, experiencing overwhelming grief, not remember talking to the investigating officer at all. Some even denied their signature on the bottom of a statement recorded by a certified court reporter. This temporary amnesia was due to the shock and the deep need to block totally unacceptable facts from the conscious mind. At a later time, when the brain had had time to convince itself that the horror was indeed true, the shocked next-of-kin were often able to function in a rational way, remembering not only what was said, but details of dress, manner, and climate.

Captain Rizzolo did not think that Agnes Trumbull looked totally irrational. Her shock reaction seemed genuine, he thought. Rizzolo was trained to notice the initial reaction of the wife, husband, or lover of every homicide victim, and insisted on being present when the nearest survivor was told about the death. He was convinced that his gut reaction gave him a sure indication of the truth or untruth of the statement the person gave at that moment. If they looked well prepared, Rizzolo was ready to pursue the questioning along a different line than if the survivor looked obviously and genuinely shocked at the news.

"But what would he be doing at a phosphate pit?" Agnes asked.

"We don't know, ma'am," Rizzolo said. "Did he call you or anything yesterday at any time?"

The deputy had silently and unobtrusively slipped a small spiral notebook from one of his shirt pockets and was making cryptic notes as the conversation went on.

"Nothing since after he left . . . yesterday morning," she said. She tried to swallow but her mouth was too dry. Her voice cracked slightly as she spoke. "Is he . . ." she paused, not really wanting to ask the question, and yet compelled from deep within herself to go on. "Is he dead?"

Captain Rizzolo put his hand on hers and looked into her eyes. "There's no need to think that, Mrs. Trumbull," he said. "At least, not yet. We only have the preliminary reports from the scene." He paused to let her savor his reassurance, and for her anxiety to abate somewhat. "It's just that I couldn't allow anyone to ask you these questions on the phone. I had to come here myself. Just to be sure."

"Sure of what?" she asked, cautiously.

"That the information we obtained from you was, first of all, consistent with what we found, and that any questions we might have to ask would not upset you unnecessarily." He continued to hold her hand. The uniformed deputy noticed, but did not smirk. He thought his captain was being smooth.

"But what *did* you find?" she insisted, taking her hand back.

"Ma'am, I'm not at liberty at this time to disclose all of our findings. First of all, a lot of these things that we are just guessing at might not be true, and knowing everything that we found out there would probably upset you for no reason. But I still would like to ask you about a few things."

Agnes Trumbull shrugged helplessly. She considered calling Barry Ackerman, a family friend and a local criminal lawyer, but decided that there was no need for that. Not yet, at least.

"You say that Dr. Trumbull left for work at his usual time yesterday?"

"Yes."

"And went right to the hospital?"

"Yes."

"And drove the Thunderbird?"

"Yes."

"And didn't call you at all during the day?"

"He never does."

"And didn't come home at all during the night?"

"No." Her negation was less emphatic than her yesses.

"Nor did he call last night?" The captain's tone was softer and almost sympathetic.

"No."

"And did he have any real enemies?"

"Enemies?"

"People who, you know, might have made threats against him. Someone he may have made mad at him?"

"Captain," she said formally, "Dr. Trumbull was a pathologist. Who would get mad at a pathologist?"

The captain accepted the minor challenge and thought for a moment. "A family who did not want an autopsy? . . . A surgeon that he called wrong on some big diagnosis? . . . A girl friend's husband? . . . A—"

"Really! Captain! There is no need for you to be insulting." Agnes Trumbull rose from her chair and walked to the window. She stood looking out, her arms folded tightly across her chest.

"I'm sorry, Mrs. Trumbull. It's just my job. I have to think about bad things because I have to investigate bad things. Nobody ever gives me a pleasant case to work on." He walked toward the door, motioning for the deputy to follow. "That will probably be enough for now, Mrs. Trumbull." He opened the front door and allowed Deputy Keaton to precede him.

"Oh, one more thing, ma'am." He stooped slightly and picked up a paper bag that he had left behind a low bush near the doorstep. He reached into the bag and took out its contents.

"Is this your husband's shoe?"

Agnes Trumbull looked blankly at the single shoe and recognized it immediately as one of Bill Trumbull's scuffed wing tips.

"I'm not sure," she said dully. Her confusion was beginning to get to her. "I'm just not sure," she said again, slowly closing the door in the captain's round, tanned face.

Chapter Five

SEVERAL TIMES THAT DAY, Martha Holland was sure she had completely lost her sanity. Her mental conversation with herself had been incessant and, on several occasions, she had almost convinced an imagined Bill Trumbull, hiding somewhere inside her brain, that the whole scheme was a mistake. Each time, she had been shocked into the reality of what she was doing by a question from a salesperson. First in a marine supply store, then in a grocery store, and now, the liquor store.

"Are you sure that you want all that whiskey and stuff in pints, ma'am?" the clerk asked.

"Huh? Oh, yeah. Thanks. How much is it?" Martha said, resuming full consciousness.

"It comes to fifty-two dollars and eighty cents," he said, reading the cash register tape like a stockbroker.

"The pints will store easier," she said self-consciously. "I live in a trailer." She gathered up the re-packed liquor case and attempted to lift it from the counter. The change from the purchase that she held in one hand weakened her grip on the box, and it threatened to fall.

"Let me help you, ma'am," the clerk said as he came from around the counter. "You might drop all that, and wouldn't that be a shame?"

"Yes. A terrible shame," she chuckled. She quickly thought of the car out front. In addition to containing many bags of groceries, it was loaded with rope, fishing tackle, marine shackles, sea charts, and other items of nautical hardware that would arouse the curiosity of any young man.

"No, wait," she said as he reached for the box, "I think I can make it alone."

"Nonsense," he said, laughing her off. He assumed it was a women's lib statement and wondered why the females of the country chose to give up their protected positions as inferior but coddled creatures.

He was already elbowing his way through the glass door with the carton of whiskey when Martha Holland caught up with him. She had taken time to stuff her feminine junk back into her handbag, and during the repacking, he had grabbed the box and was gone.

It was one of a chain of cut-rate liquor stores throughout the state, located in a part of town that she hardly ever frequented. She was trying to follow Bill Trumbull's admonitions to the last detail, and not arouse even the slightest curiosity. The liquor store boy had really been the first person to show any interest in what she had bought or how she had managed to get it to the car.

To avoid any suspicions, she had divided her grocery purchases among several stores. She had purchased bagsful of canned meats, stews, beer, fruits and vegetables, as well as candies, cookies, and crackers. All of these items were in small-sized cans that two people could easily finish at one meal. Martha had wondered, absurdly, if any of the stores took this as an open defiance of their large-economy-size efforts to ease up on the consumer's pocketbook.

Near the door of the liquor store, the cardboard Carlsberg beer girl stood like a silent sentinel. She held out her cardboard tray and smiled sweetly as the boy held the door open for Martha Holland with the corner of the box.

Martha glanced up and down the parking lot as she emerged from the liquor store. She tried to be casual about it and, in fact, the store boy didn't notice her nervousness. He balanced the corner of the liquor carton against the side of the car and waited for her to fumble the car keys out of her cluttered handbag.

"They're in here somewhere," she mumbled into the mess in her purse.

"It's OK," the boy said with an obvious air of masculine superiority. He was about twenty-three and needlessly handsome. Martha would have enjoyed giving him a swift kick in the ass, but then he would have dropped all those pints, and since they were outside the store, she recognized that "title," if not possession had passed to her. A "sale," as her commercial law professor used to remark nasally, had been consummated.

She found the keys and attempted to insert the one for the trunk into the driver's side door. The store boy's grin widened considerably as he noticed the error. Martha Holland thought about the price of the liquor in his arms and again repressed a swift kick.

She opened the car door and motioned him toward the inside of the MG with a curt thrust of her head.

"I really dig this car, ma'am," he said, stuffing the liquor case into the tight space behind the front seats. "Corner well?"

"Yeah, yeah. Corners like a goddamn dream," she said, sticking a quarter into his hand. That was not where she would like to have stuck the quarter.

The boy headed back toward the liquor store, tossing the tip into the air and catching it backhanded, like a Harlem Globetrotter. Martha felt a sudden urge to gun the car forward and run him down for his insolence.

She had focused all of her attention on the boy and

failed to notice the man gently tapping his finger on the driver's side window of her car.

"Hitting the sauce, Martha?" the voice asked playfully.

She turned to her left and saw the hand at the window. Like the voice, it was terribly familiar.

"Jesus Christ," she said softly but audibly as she looked up to recognize the smiling face of Bruce LaFontaine, M.D.

"Not quite," LaFontaine laughed. His eyes said that he had been hitting the sauce himself.

"Hi, Bruce," Martha said, recovering about 40 percent of her composure. "What are you doing in this part of town?"

"I might ask you the same thing, Martha. Got somebody stashed over here?" He weaved slightly as he managed to stand and talk at the same time, apparently straining the residual sober part of his brain.

"This is near to the apartment of a friend of mine, Bruce," she supplied as casually as she could under the circumstances.

"Really? Over here? What's his name?" Bruce LaFontaine laughed aloud at his own remark.

"Girl friend, Bruce, girl friend!"

"Of course! Just kidding, Martha." He quickly reached for another subject. "Say! Why don't you pop over to the house tonight and have a couple with Mary and me? She'd love to see you again." Dr. LaFontaine had reassumed his British composure when he ceased his sexual innuendoes. He was confident that she would not accept his invitation.

Martha remembered Mary at the last cocktail party thrown by the Crewe of Venus at one of the downtown hotels. Mary had been both drunk and a bit put out about not being named to some damn fool committee that had charge of some obscure aspect of the annual Gasparilla celebration. Mary was not skillful in hiding her displeasure, and, to the obvious delight of Bill

Trumbull and Bruce LaFontaine, had literally socked a dowager widow.

Bill Trumbull and Martha Holland had decided mutually to arrive "stag" for that particular Crewe of Venus party. Their coincidental meeting there was held in high suspicion by several ladies present, including Mary LaFontaine. Agnes Trumbull had been convinced that the party would be worse than dull and didn't come at all.

The social events attended by local high society had somehow reminded Martha of her grandfather's definition of a horse show as, "a bunch of horses' asses showing their horses' asses." His appraisal was not appreciated or shared by those ladies of Tampa society who really had nowhere else to go after they were all dressed up in evening wear.

"Some other time, Bruce," Martha said as she started the MG. "I'm kinda late." She smiled a small smile that said she was willing to be minimally pleasant, but really wanted to get away. Even Bruce LaFontaine could read the smile. His blood-alcohol level helped him ignore the body language to bug off, and he leaned heavily on the car.

"Looks like you're packed for a trip around the world," he said, glancing around the inside of the car. He grinned widely and breathed gin fumes in Martha's face. "You sailors are strange people."

"Actually, it's a trip to the moon, Bruce. I've been promising myself a trip to outer space for quite some time." She tried to be casual about her reply, and half regretted being so sharp-tongued. She didn't want to encourage any further conversation about her car or its contents. She would not let herself underestimate the observatory powers of this well-trained radiologist even when drunk. She instantly recalled an evening lecture at the University of South Florida when a psychologist had remarked that during the war, the German government had used pathologists and radiologists to make daily readings of aerial photographs of enemy territory. The theory was that pathologists and radiologists had been trained to observe the overall patterns of things in their microscope slides and X rays, and to form subconscious memory impressions about the smallest details. If the idea was correct, these medical specialists should have been able to spot the slightest change in the photographs—say, the addition of some camouflaged unit. Martha was not able to remember whether the psychologist had said that the use of these physicians had been a success or a total flop. Either way, it made her nervous to see the sharp, but now half-bloodshot eyes of this radiologist scanning the inside of her car. She took small comfort in the fact that Bruce LaFontaine knew she was a sailor, and therefore might not concern himself about the sailing hardware that stuck out from between bags of groceries and from behind the case of liquor.

"You really do need a lorry, my dear," he suggested.

"It does get a bit cramped in here some days, Bruce." She put the small car in reverse and allowed it to bump backward slightly. Dr. LaFontaine took the hint quickly and stepped back from the car.

"I'm actually planning a little weekend trip up to the Homosassa River, and I've just got to run. I'll give Mary a call real soon. Good to see you, Bruce."

"Bye, bye, Martha. It's good to see you too. Be careful out there in that boat of yours. I'll tell Mary that I happened to run into you." LaFontaine was smiling and waving as Martha backed the MG out of the parking lot and gunned it onto the street.

I'll just bet you'll tell her, Martha said to herself as she watched the radiologist get smaller and smaller in the rearview mirror. "Well," she sighed, "maybe that blows the whole deal. And maybe just in time." She frowned and continued to talk to herself as she drove back to the marina.

On the boat, Bill Trumbull had spent an awful day. The cabin had become very hot and the sun had tried to melt the fiberglass decking. Bill Trumbull was too nervous to do more than crack the forward hatch about half an inch, and to take the top board out of the aft companionway to give himself at least a chance for a breath of fresh air. Very little air seemed to enter or leave the cabin but he was afraid to run the bilge blowers, even though the little battery-powered motors made only the slightest whine.

During the morning, he had started at the jump of every mullet in the almost still water, and at every human sound that wafted across the marina. He had stripped down to his undershorts and looked like a pot-bellied customer of some Turkish bath as the trickles of sweat ran down his chest and back, and produced wet footprints on the thin carpet of the main cabin area. From time to time, he allowed himself a cautious peek through the windows of the main cabin. Once before, when sailing on a bright sparkling day with Martha, he had called them "portholes" in an attempt to sound nautical. But Martha had pointed out that they weren't round and didn't open, so she considered "porthole" to be an overstatement for what clearly appeared to her to be oval, water-tight, little windows that let in light and occasional drops of water along their seams in heavy seas.

For part of the morning, Dr. Trumbull had kept himself busy by reading Chapman's bible on small-boat handling and piloting. The chapters on recognizing the changes in the appearance of the waves in a gale-force storm gave him a slight constriction in the throat. He had not seriously considered the unpredictability of the weather in the Gulf of Mexico. The sailboat was not equipped with weather radar, the way that many of the larger boats were, and the shore radio stations were not able to broadcast their forecasts to the middle of the gulf, he thought nervously.

In fact, Martha's radio equipment was quite capable of picking up the offshore marine broadcasts, but Bill Trumbull had never seen it in action. Luckily, Martha had never actually needed this weather-watching equipment, though over the last several months, she had attended small classes where she had stuffed all kinds of sailing and meteorological knowledge into her legal brain. As a result, she actually felt capable of running up a storm jib or even dragging a mainsail behind the boat as a makeshift sea anchor if faced with a hurricane. Martha had been skeptic enough to conclude that her instructors themselves hadn't had the opportunity to fight and then survive a raging hurricane at sea. However, it was something to do on rainy nights at the yacht club instead of drinking at the bar with landlocked businessmen or reading Joseph Conrad stories in the stuffy cabin.

Earlier that morning, two kids in a pram had sailed right into the stern of Ole Duckie in their frantic attempts to make a last-minute turn in the marina. The daytime dockmaster had blown his whistle and chased them out of the marina, but had not come on board Martha's sailboat to look for any damage. The little pram was light enough to bump the bigger sailboat without damage to either of them and the dockmaster knew it. But from the inside, Bill Trumbull thought that he had been rammed by an enemy submarine. The fiberglass hull had echoed the noise of the collision like a drumhead and had startled him out of a sweaty midmorning nap. He could hear the voices of the young sailors as they argued and blamed the poorly executed coming about on each other, and their shouts of joy at finally bringing the bow around to a new course out of the marina and back into Tampa Bay.

The children's voices and the sound of the dockmaster's whistle had made Bill Trumbull think about his own kids at play in the playground at the parish school. He wondered if the sheriff had found his car and if they had told Agnes yet.

He experienced intermittent waves of panic and confidence as he wondered if the sheriff's men had overlooked the tire iron with the blood and hair on it, followed by sober thoughts that convinced him that the efficient investigators from the sheriff's office would find everything.

But what if the girl in the costume shop had remembered selling him the wig? But how could she? She had never seen him before. And besides, she didn't look like the type of girl who noticed or remembered very much.

But what about the guy who sold him the little motorcycle? Wouldn't he be suspicious that he had paid for the bike in cash? But why should he? After all, he had explained about it being a surprise birthday gift for a kid. That should take care of the salesman. Hell, lots of people pay cash for things. Especially guys who had a chance to luck into a bundle of cash without records, like doctors or vegetable sellers, and guys like that.

But what about Miss Drawdy in the bank? Maybe he had made her a little too suspicious with his nervous act. Maybe she called the police right away and they found the car last night after a big search with planes and searchlights. That would have given them several hours' jump on the case.

He paced the narrow walkway of the cabin nervously, his hands clasped behind his back professorially.

Maybe they would call Martha's office to ask about him. But why would they call Martha Holland? Hell, there wasn't enough to put them that close together. Maybe a couple of close friends suspected something between them, but it certainly wasn't public knowledge.

Nobody would put out an A.P.B. on a pathologist

missing just one night, he reassured himself mentally. He allowed himself the luxury of one small grin of confidence that froze and died on his face as new worries came to haunt him.

Jesus! He thought. Maybe I did too good a job! Maybe I clobbered them so hard with the evidence of foul play that they're combing the whole damned bay for me.

A chopper from MacDill Air Force Base flew over the marina at about 1,500 feet. Bill Trumbull was sure that it was some part of an organized police search that had enlisted the Air Force and the whole Coast Guard to comb the bay for clues. He pushed his face awkwardly against a window and watched the chopper disappear toward MacDill in an unswerving line. He regained some of his waning confidence. Nobody searches in a straight line, he lectured himself. And besides, they couldn't possibly get the Air Force mobilized that fast to look for some unknown civilian. The President, maybe. But a small-town pathologist? Not a chance.

He opened another slightly rusty can of chili with beans and ate it cold. Not really cold in the hot, airless cabin, but at least unheated. He was afraid to use the alcohol stove. The grease at the top of the can had congealed and it coated his tongue like an anesthetic. The chili made his mouth burn slightly and a sip of warm 7-Up was of little help. He had found a case of canned 7-Up in the bottom of the ice chest, but half of the cans were empty, proving that Martha was some kind of an aluminum-recycling nut.

The air in the warm ice chest had smelled unusually stale. It was mixed with a peculiar odor of unventilated fiberglass and spilled sweet gherkin pickle juice. The sailboat did not have electrical refrigeration, but depended on its ice compartment being pre-chilled with ice, and filled with fresh ice cubes for the actual sailing. Many of the day-sailors didn't bother to chill the box at all. They carried ice cubes in a Styrofoam ice chest that could be hand-carried. Enough to get them through the day, but little more. The real day-sailors drank their beer warm like the British. That way, they didn't notice as much when they ran out of ice in the middle of the bay.

A fly buzzed near, then sat casually on the edge of his chili can. As it ate some of the sauce, Bill Trumbull wondered if the pepper burned the fly's mouth as much as it had burned his own. He watched the fly for a moment without moving. The fly ate confidently and stayed long enough to wash his face with his two busy front legs. Bill wondered if the fly knew it was on a boat in the company of a screwball pathologist. He wondered if the fly would even care if it knew all that. The fly could come and go, as long as it avoided his enemies and stayed out of the path of insecticide sprays. The pathologist watched the little animal for longer than he had ever studied an insect before. He felt envy for it and then pity. He was jealous at first of the fly's freedom but was sorry for its brief and apparently meaningless existence. Yet in some way it was a triumph for the life process that began as a maggot in some piece of rotting dead meat. It was a sign that the brief capture of molecules from the physical world and their temporary rearrangement into a living, independent creature would somehow go on, regardless of man's own destiny or thoughtless efforts to disrupt the balance of what he called nature.

The doctor wondered if some of the carbon and nitrogen that the fly had captured for his own body cells had ever been a part of a human body. Maybe they were distant cousins by virtue of their having shared the same carbon, the same oxygen and the same trace metals they both needed to sustain their lives. Neither of them could keep the atoms for very long and each of them relied on the same common pool of them for constant supply. The fly might get his from rotten meat in the bottom of some garbage can, while the pathologist might prefer the Capuchina filet at the Spanish Park Restaurant, but both of them released the same atoms back into the environment when they were, at last, unable to hold on to them, and forced to give them up.

Bill Trumbull brushed his biological cousin away with a gentle wave of his 7-Up can. The fly buzzed the cabin noisily and contemptuously, and flew out into the blue sky through the space at the top of the companionway hatch. He, at least, was still free.

A firm footstep on the forward deck caused Bill Trumbull to slip into the head and pull the door shut quietly. He took the .38 Smith and Wesson with him. The main cabin had been hot, but the small airless head seemed unbearable with the door closed. The seawater in the head smelled of dead microscopic marine animals mixed with his own urine. He had been afraid to work the hand-pumped flushing mechanism. The through-the-hull outlet was well below the water line, so that splashing would not have been a problem, but the head pump would have made a considerable amount of noise.

Rivulets of sweat joined each other in several places on his back and hairy chest, and ran down into his shorts, causing him to itch intensely. His grip on the revolver was wet and unsure. He was far from an expert with handguns, but somehow the revolver made him feel more secure.

The curtain on the little window in the head was drawn shut except for a small crack at one end where the fabric had shrunk away from the metal rod that was supposed to hold it. He strained to look out of this crack without success.

As he leaned up against the window to look out, his leg bumped the upraised toilet seat and it fell with a sudden crash. Trumbull's heart skipped several beats.

He closed his eyes and held his breath as if to recapture the fugitive noise.

The footstep on the deck was followed by several others as someone made his way toward the aft end of the boat. Trumbull was sure he heard the unmistakable clump of a sheriff's boot. He realized that he was trapped and would have nowhere to go when the big, uniformed deputy came to throw open the door to the head. He tried to listen over the pounding of his heart.

He pictured the embarrassment of Agnes and the children. He knew he would be thrown out of the medical society when the Tampa *Tribune* got hold of the story and printed it on the front page. He saw himself being dragged before the scowling Norman Rockwell-like board of trustees of the hospital. He then saw himself before a judge in a black robe that accented his shiny, bald head as he glared down from a terribly high bench. His wife and children were there, crying as he was sentenced to several years in the state prison at Raiford for attempting to defraud the insurance company. An old, long-since-dead doctor that had signed his Florida medical license was suddenly there in the courtroom, laughing out loud and tearing his license into tiny pieces.

The footsteps had made it to the cockpit and hands were lifting the remaining hatchway boards out of the slide. He could hear the boards piled in a clattering stack on one of the cockpit seats. The hatchway was now completely opened to the outside.

The footsteps came down the short ladder into the main cabin and became silent again as they hit the carpet. The boat swayed almost imperceptibly as the intruder moved through the cabin. Trumbull strained his ears to pick up the slightest sound, but no more noises came. He tried not to breathe at all.

Suddenly, the door to the head was jerked open. Trumbull had shut his eyes rather than face the uniformed deputy and the muzzle of the police special revolver that would be pointing at him.

He raised his hand in front of him in a frightened gesture of defense and there was a sudden roar. In his panic, the pathologist had fired his .38 by mistake. His ears rang and his nose registered the distinctive odor of burned powder.

"Bill—" a familiar voice said in the darkness.

"Christ!" Trumbull said suddenly. In front of him, half on the bunk and half on the carpeted floor, lay the dying body of Martha Holland. There was a large entrance wound in the left side of her chest. The doctor fell toward her and lifted her almost-lifeless face with his hands. Her eyes stared blankly ahead, and only a shallow gurgle come from her throat. His experienced fingers told him immediately that she was dead. Her blood covered his hands as he pulled her body into the middle of the cabin.

"Martha," he said, helplessly. He knelt beside her and wept openly. He was no longer concerned about noise or lights, or escape plans. He knew that the whole insane scheme was over, and that he had ruined everything. Martha Holland had become a tragic monument to his idiocy. He wanted to run up the dock to the yacht club and tell them all what he had done, but his legs would not respond. He was forced by his own paralysis to sit awkwardly in the middle of the cabin, holding Martha Holland's head, and rocking back and forth, like a mournful child cradling some life-sized, broken doll.

Bill Trumbull was not sure how long he sat there holding Martha and staring into her face. The air had become cold and the marina was dark. The blood on his hands had dried where it had been smeared thin. The thicker pool of blood beneath her body was still wet and sticky. The dim light of the marina showed him the reality of his nightmare, but spared him the grim details.

Incredibly, the shot had not been heard—or, at least, no one had come to Martha's boat to ask what had happened. He remembered Martha's remark that noises inside the boat that were in direct contact with the hull, were partly insulated from the outside, while hull noises were transmitted through the water, like a giant drum.

He pushed the button on his digital wristwatch with a bloody finger. It was 10:17 P.M. He sat quietly for a few minutes and tried to imagine that he was a patient that had come to Dr. Bill Trumbull seeking advice for this problem. Even this psychological ruse was almost useless. He was barely able to see anything but the immediate problem and objective thought ran away from him, down mental alleyways, chased by panic.

Bill Trumbull's legs sent previously ignored internal signals that Martha's dead weight was deprived of circulation. Responding heavily to these sensory impulses, he wriggled himself out from under her cold, stiffening body, and sat on the port bunk. His pants were soaked with blood. As the circulation returned to his numbed legs, he felt the chilling wetness, mixed with the millions of tiny needles that told him that his feet were still alive.

There was a small blanket folded at the head of the starboard bunk. Trumbull moved Martha's body to the bunk, placed a cushion beneath her head, and covered her with the blanket. These purposeful acts seemed to slip his brain back into gear. He began to anticipate the difficulties that would begin for him with his announcement of Martha Holland's accidental death. The medical examiner in that county was a onetime friend of his, and a fellow pathologist, but no amount of explanation was going to account for the shooting of a prominent female lawyer, by a doctor who had just attempted to fake his own murder. Somewhere in all of that, he reasoned, the state attorney would find sufficient grounds for a long series of hearings, charges, announcements to the press, and an inevitable trial. Oh, there would be private statements of apology and regret, of course, but what state attorney could afford to pass up that kind of publicity?

Trumbull began to see his only way out. So far, he had not been identified with Martha Holland as she went about her errands, picking up the supplies for the boat. She had smuggled him on board without anyone's knowledge, and except for her car in the yacht club parking lot, no one knew that she was there. It would be a while before anyone would question her absence. On many previous occasions, she had sailed out of that very marina to enjoy the bay under the stars. Her sailboat, chugging out of the basin at that time of night would probably be noticed, but Trumbull could not think of any reason why anyone would care.

Bill Trumbull crouched in the aft hatchway and cautiously looked around the marina. There was no one in sight. The other boats were quiet, and even the dockmaster's shack had cut down to a small, obvious night light. There were a few people in the main building of the yacht club, but their party noises ensured that any ordinary sound from the marina would certainly go unnoticed.

He kept low, and made his way forward to the bowlines. The deck cleat gave the lines up easily, and he eased them over the side. He was not a good enough sailor to know that Martha would have thrown them onto the dock, staying dry and awaiting her return. He also did not know that she would have taken these lines with her if she had expected to be gone more than a day.

Still crouched, and moving as quietly as he could, Trumbull slipped back into the cockpit, released the starboard stern line, and pulled Ole Duckie out of her slip by means of the other stern line. So far, the sailboat had made no sound to announce its nocturnal departure. There was no wind to push the boat into any of her neighbors. She was content to stand silently in the middle of the marina, half pointing toward the outlet into the bay.

Trumbull returned to the darkened cabin and felt around for the ignition key. It was hanging near the master electrical switch, and the small panel of toggle switches that opened the various circuits on the boat. He was not sure which switch was which, so he threw them all. The small blower motor began to whine somewhere behind the inboard engine, and the bilge fumes, if any, were pumped out through the ventilators. The bilge blowers were not being used as a safety feature, in this instance, but went on working as a mechanical testimonial to his good luck and the fact that he did not know which switch turned off the noise.

Trumbull slipped the key into the ignition slot in the cockpit and gave it a turn. The engine responded with unexpected promptness, and the sailboat began to chug its way out of the marina. In his fumbling with the toggle switches, Trumbull had also turned on the red and green running lights on the bow, the white stern light, and a single, white light, three-fourths of the way up the mast. Though he was certainly not aware of it, he was, at that moment, properly lighted as a sailboat under power.

Trumbull squinted into the darkness ahead. A single, white blinker, guarding the entrance to the yacht club basin, lay at the end of a string of unlit, one-armed poles that showed where the channel was, more or less. New ecology regulations had virtually forbidden the removal of the sandy shoaling that threatened to obliterate the channel entirely, one day. Inexperienced sailors followed the chart and risked running aground on the sandbars that lay hidden beneath the surface. Experienced sailors followed the visible markers, keeping well to the middle of the channel, and, whenever possible, sought out "local knowledge" to keep them off the bottom. Bill Trumbull's local knowledge was limited to a couple of sail-outs with Martha Holland at the wheel, himself at the beer cooler, and no one really paying too much attention to the course.

This time, with Martha's lifeless body on board, Trumbull's luck outweighed his skill. He missed every unlit marker and all of the uncharted sandbars.

He had made no attempt to raise a sail or even to remove the boot from the main. Aimed straight ahead, he guided the sailboat out of the marina at a steady three-and-a-half knots, and in a few minutes, glided past the white, four-second entrance light. A large, black cormorant awoke with a start, and flapped away into the night. Ahead lay the black, threatening expanse of Tampa Bay.

The U.S. Coast Guard maintained a zigzag of red, green, and white blinker lights on nuns, cans, and towers that made sense to the professional harbor pilots that brought the big tankers and bulk phosphate carriers into Tampa from Egmont Key, some forty miles away. To a lesser navigator, the water-level view of this irregular string of Christmas lights was little more than a hopeless, mazelike confusion of colors and twinkles. Each of the lights had a code number and letter which enabled any boater armed with a standard sea chart of the bay to look it up and identify his position. Tampa Bay was more than nine miles long by thirty-five miles wide and the commercial traffic, typified by the *Yokohama Maru*, a multi-ton Japanese phosphate bulk carrier, traveling at twenty-five to thirty-five miles per hour, and requiring more than a mile to come to a stop, frequently made night sailing a dangerous and therefore exciting experience. Night sailing was only dangerous and exciting if the skipper was competent and could identify the type and direction of the big ships by their running lights. For Bill Trumbull, night sailing was something closer to suicide.

Dr. Trumbull sat quietly at the helm and listened to the rhythmic chug of his little, four-cylinder, Atomic-4 gasoline inboard engine. It could deliver about forty horsepower, but the pitch of the propeller and the internal mechanics of the drive system gave it incredible power, inch by inch, when it was asked to plow through a soft sand bar. The whole sailboat would labor and shudder if the engine was asked to make more than eight knots. At a cruising speed of three-and-a-half knots, the boat knifed through the water with romantic ease.

There was almost no wind on the bay that night. The water was like glass and offered no resistance to the smooth, fiberglass hull. Across the bay, to the east and a little to the south, Trumbull calculated by fuzzy memory and poor dead-reckoning that there was a relatively uninhabited stretch of mangrove that had been declared an ecology preserve for birds and shallow-feeding fishes. He had no idea what navigational light configuration he should have to sail safely to that area —and avoid the sandbars at the same time. Squinting, he was just able to make out a blinking red light on the horizon, more or less in the direction that he thought he wanted to go. He took it to be a red blinker along one of the cuts to the international channel, about half-way to the Sunshine Skyway Bridge. In fact, he was looking at a red blinking light on the top of a radio tower, several miles inland. But the general direction was, by blind luck, essentially correct.

The pathologist stepped up the engine speed to about four knots and mentally calculated that it would take him about three hours to reach the mangrove area. Stars twinkled above him as a tantalizing but, for him, useless aid to navigation. There was no moon to brighten the water as he slipped along through the darkness.

Down below, Martha grew colder as her body heat oozed through the blanket and into the chilly, moist air. Above her head, a ship's compass rested comfortably in its wooden case, waiting to be carried into the cockpit and snapped into its deckside holder. Bill Trumbull could have read it easily enough, if he had known where it was, and how to attach it in the bracket. But at that moment, with his brain still numbed by the shock of Martha's death, Trumbull was afraid to adjust any part of the boat, leave the cockpit, or take his eyes off of the distant, red blinking light.

He was constantly aware that his progress across the bay had nothing to do with his skill as a sailor. His mind raced, with patchwork images of investigations by police, Martha's internal injuries, and unrelated scenes of the children and Agnes. He fought with himself to keep his mind focused on the progress of the boat and his own escape. As a doctor, he was well aware of the unreliable workings of the human mind under severe stress. To whip his brain back into obedient service, he forced himself to review the various types of ovarian tumors, but found himself wandering instead, into scenes from medical school, when he had invented these personal, mental tricks to learn and then recall these complex classifications.

He could still hear old Dr. Magner, whinily cataloguing tumors in his strong Toronto accent. He could still visualize him at the front of the classroom, his hands thrust into the pockets of his Harris tweed jacket, and his teeth tightly clenched around the badly chewed pipe that went with him everywhere.

"The ovarian tumors are benign and malignant, cystic and solid, functioning and non-functioning," Magner used to say. "The benign, cystic masses may be neoplastic or non-neoplastic. The commonest cysts are follicular. Nothing more than blighted eggs. The pseudomucinous cystadenocarcinomas are the ones you'll remember, because some of these buggers will run to ten or twenty pounds and you'll wonder how in the bloody hell the woman hid all that material in her belly. . . ."

Trumbull snapped back to reality. Several miles down the bay, a small, green blinking light came into view and took over his attention for a few moments. He had no idea where it really was and what it signified. For a few moments, he tried to gauge how far away it was, but then realized that without landmarks for comparison, the task was hopeless for him. Panic began to swell within him and he returned to the red blinker and his mental gymnastics.

"The tumors of the ovary that will fascinate you for a lifetime are the hormone-producing ones," Magner said to the medical school class. "Some of them, like the arrhenoblastoma can produce male hormones that will make a woman grow hair on her face and deepen her voice like a man. On the other hand, a granulosa cell tumor can occur in the ovary of a child and produce enough female hormones to change her into a well-developed little woman, with pubic hair and good-sized breasts, even at the tender age of six or eight. . . ."

Trumbull wondered absently about the stacks of notes that he had taken at these endless lectures in medical school. He visualized them in a Canadian Club carton on a shelf in the garage. The sudden thought of home constricted his throat and blurred his eyes. He fought back harder. The mental games worked well for him. They kept him from submitting to the panic that lurked within him and prevented him from thinking about Martha's dead body. He forced himself to move from ovarian tumors to brain tumors, and experienced even more difficulty in recalling the details of the classifications accurately. In his small hospital practice, he had not seen very many brain tumors, since these specialized cases were usually shipped off to the university center almost as fast as they were diagnosed.

Trumbull had piloted the sailboat for more than three hours now, and the stars seemed to change, conforming to his course. The night air, heavy now with moisture that clung to the fiberglass decks and gave them a just-washed look, bit through Trumbull's shirt and reminded him that he was cold.

The dark shadow of the shoreline lay before him, devoid of detail and blending into the equal blackness of the water. He could not tell where the land and the water met. All the lights now lay off to his starboard and seemed much farther away. He hoped that he had found the mangrove area in the southeastern part of the bay. There was nothing visible or audible to reassure him that he had arrived, or to challenge this conclusion. As far as he could tell, guiding the sailboat without compass or chart, he had sailed in a generally straight, south-easterly course and had, fortunately, met no other vessels in the crossing. It appeared that, wherever he was, he had arrived.

Trumbull knew that the sailboat would not be able to sail into the mangrove area without running aground. He also knew that if she ran aground, it would attract the attention of every passing pleasure boater the following day. They would all streak over, shout halloos and ahoys, before finally boarding her to discover Martha's body. He considered wrapping the body in the sail and weighting it down with tools and canned goods, but then he remembered that as the tissue decayed and produced gas, her body would become buoyant, and surface within a day or so. He knew that it would take about one and a half times her living body weight to keep her down after she started to rot and bloat with gas. He did not think that he had sufficient weight in tools and other sinkable objects to insure that she would stay on the bottom, and he worried that she might be carried along by the tide, half-submerged, to surface in some threateningly unpredictable location.

Trumbull shut the small engine down and put out the running lights by throwing all the toggle switches. He allowed the sailboat to drift gently in the darkness, and groped his way down into the stuffy cabin. In a small locker under the alcohol stove, he located a short length of plastic tubing that Martha used to empty her drinking-water tank when the contents became too foul for consumption. He was suddenly struck by an idea.

He measured an arm's length of the plastic tube and cut it off with the sail knife that was always kept in the emergency toolbox. Then, working in the dark, he slipped the tube down Martha's nose, into her esophagus, and threaded it into her stomach. He found the alcohol stove's funnel and attached it to the tube. With some difficulty, and considerable spillage, he slowly poured the stove alcohol into the funnel and felt for its disappearance with an index finger. He poured about a pint into her stomach before he removed the tube and replaced it and the funnel in the locker beneath the stove and stowed the alcohol jug. He knew the alcohol would not enter her bloodstream effectively, but he was confident that the peculiar smell of the denatured stove alcohol would not be overlooked by the medical examiner if her body was found before it rotted away.

He arranged her body on the bunk to simulate sleep and returned to the emergency toolbox. He found a small, disposable flashlight that Martha liked to hand out to passengers on night cruises, and used it to find the latches that closed the small hatchway to the engine compartment beneath the cockpit floor. Reaching the engine compartment, he shined the light around carefully so as not to direct it into the cockpit where it might be seen by someone on shore. He identified a one-and-a-half-inch plastic pipe that carried water from a hull fitting to the engine for cooling, and tried to pry it loose. The plastic pipe was designed to stay attached to the fitting, and it did. He took the sail knife out of the emergency tool box and, with clumsy effort, sawed his way through the plastic. As he entered the middle of the pipe, the water from the bay began to squirt in all directions. At last, the pipe was sawed through and the water rushed in and swirled around the base of the engine, filling the bilges faster than he thought it would. Luckily for Trumbull, Martha had never installed automatic bilge pumps with direct connections to the batteries.

He dropped the knife on the cabin floor and began to stuff his shirt with the money from the bank. It was bulkier than he wanted it to be, but with a little effort, it all fit inside the shirt. Trumbull took lead weights from Martha's fishing box and put one in each bank bag before dropping them overboard. He picked up the gun and stuffed it into his pants pocket. The discovery of the gun, he reasoned, would precipitate a search for a bullet wound that might otherwise go undetected in a rotten, apparently drowned body. Trumbull had had several opportunities to examine rotten corpses during his pathology residency, and knew that the greasiness and odor would discourage all but the most ambitious of police investigators. He also knew that the Tampa medical examiner would look at the body regardless of the state of decay. His expert examination was a risk that Trumbull was going to have to accept. He knew that he would never be able to get Martha's body off the boat and swim to shore with it without drowning or being forced to abandon it halfway there. She would have to remain on the boat.

Trumbull knew that his only chance was to sink the boat, and hope that she would not be discovered for weeks. And then, he hoped that the death would be attributed to an accidental drowning, when the boat sank as she slept.

He emptied the rest of the canned cocktails to help convince any curious investigator that she must have been drunk when the accident occurred.

The water had risen in the bilges to spill onto the carpeted floor of the cabin. He knew that it was time to begin his swim to shore. If he remained on board to ensure the sinking of the boat, he would be caught by the sunrise and possibly discovered. The dark swim was his only hope.

He glanced around the cabin in the darkness and searched his brain for items that might be traced to him rather than to Martha. None came to mind. He repressed an urge to kiss Martha's cold cheek once more, and went up the steps to the cockpit without looking back.

The water had risen rapidly within the cabin. Trumbull climbed over the safety railing and lowered himself into the black, cool water of Tampa Bay.

He was not an expert swimmer and the clothes that he wore did not make it easier. The money in the shirt began to weigh heavily as it soaked up water and stuck to his skin. The gun in his pocket felt like an anchor. His burden allowed him only a painfully slow breast stroke that seemed to defy his progress toward the black shoreline. In the darkness, he could not tell how far away the shore was, and he felt his heart quicken with fear as he felt for sand with his feet and found nothing but bottomless water.

Behind him, immediately hidden by the night, the sailboat sat lower and lower in the water as it gracefully settled toward the bottom of the bay. Its heavy keel kept it upright and controlled the sinking so that it did not capsize. Trumbull had left both the forward and aft hatches open to allow the air to escape as the boat sank.

The rising water in the cabin had reached Martha Holland's lifeless face when Bill Trumbull felt the thump of the first sandbar against his waterlogged sneaker. Soon, he was able to wade to shore and to disappear among the mangrove and sea grape that grew thickly in this protected area.

He threw himself on the mud-and-sand shore between the mangroves and was glad to have the mosquitoes biting him. When he finally caught his breath, he strained unsuccessfully to see the night-shrouded sailboat, some three-quarters of a mile offshore, as it settled into the bay. But, if he had seen it, he would have been horrified to find that while the boat had sunk just as he had planned, the mast stood proudly out of the water like a flagpole over a flooded schoolyard.

He turned and continued to stumble his way inland, deeper into the thick mangrove, while the darkness was with him.

Chapter Six

THE PANEL TRUCK from the diving club had little trouble grinding its way up the abandoned road to the phosphate pit. Sometime back, an enterprising member, transplanted from up North, had donated his useless snow tires for excursions into soft sand. The idea had been met with back-slapping laughter by the native Floridian members, but these grins dried up when the truck proved to be as mobile as Rommel's tanks.

The sheriff's department didn't have a frogman staff of its own, and a decade or so earlier, skin diving and scuba were considered rather frivolous tourist sport. The department became involved with it only when some civilian diver became trapped under a ledge in a cave dive or had an accident at the bottom of the bay. For years, bodies had been recovered by the tried and true methods of grappling hooks and systematic dragging by patient deputies and volunteers in rowboats. But as the sport of scuba diving became more popular all around the country and its very name began to sound less strange, the law enforcement agencies could no longer afford to ignore its possibilities in crime detection.

At first, there had been a few civilian divers who would volunteer whenever the newspaper published a report of a drowned fisherman, or when some frantic mother living near a deep irrigation ditch missed a pre-school-age child. After a couple of spectacular recoveries, these strange guys in frog suits with tanks and flippers were not only tolerated by the police agencies, but were actively sought after.

Some of the more advanced departments around the state, like Miami, had established full-time sections with trained divers on staff. Other parts of the state still relied on the volunteers from the diving clubs.

That afternoon, when the phone rang in his suburban barbershop in Brandon, Bob Wrigley had a sudden premonition that he was going to be called out. It was not that he was psychic, but that he enjoyed that kind of exciting fantasy when the phone interrupted his boring afternoon of haircutting and empty conversations with his regular customers.

At first, his partners in the barbershop had shared his excitement in a sheriff's call for Bob's frogman services. Later, they became hostile and objected to his being away from the shop as often as he was, looking for stolen cars in canals and fishermen that sent their rowboats back empty. Finally, they worked out a fair schedule that would allow each of them about equal time to do his own thing, and the four of them had settled down to peaceful coexistence. The nondivers again became interested in Wrigley's gruesome stories about submerged bodies and how it felt to grab a half-decayed arm in the dark at the bottom of a stagnant canal.

Bob Wrigley no longer shared those kinds of stories with customers in the chair since the time, about a year ago, when one of them threw up on the floor and walked out with half a layer-cut. But after a few beers at the Stagecoach Lounge, he could be coaxed to let go some inside experiences that would keep his drinking buddies glued to their barstools—not that it took much glue.

It had only taken him a few minutes to finish off the customer in his chair before going home for his diving gear. Since he kept his diving club's panel truck at his house, he didn't need to drive all the way downtown to the clubhouse to get it. The club was located in a neighborhood that was hard to protect from burglary and vandalism, and Bob Wrigley, one-time organizer and former two-term president, usually took the truck home to safeguard their collection of tanks, regulators, suits, and the piles of assorted other junk that the sport seemed to require.

For a while, they had tried to make the club a paying venture and bought a cheap compressor to use in a tank-filling concession. But they were only able to attract a few customers other than their own membership, and after using up their individual hundred-dollar investments, the members accepted the fact that it was meant to be a club and not a business. They still managed to sell a tank or two of air or some odd piece of equipment to an outsider, but more often than not, the sale generated a conversation between the customer and an enthusiastic member, and the outsider became an insider. A quickly calculated discount on the price of the equipment took care of the dues, and the new members would quickly fit in with the disorganized group that called itself the Tampa Bay Diving Club.

At home, Wrigley put in a call to Tinker Herndon, a local fireman and slightly crazy diving club member and his favorite diving partner. Tinker's firehouse schedule permitted him great flexibility. Wrigley was not averse to diving alone, but the rest of the club membership had voted against that kind of recklessness, especially when the water was unknown, or when the dive was of an official nature. The sheriff had concurred after one diver had become snagged for a while on a piece of automobile junk at the bottom of the bay near the Sunshine Skyway while looking for a drowning victim and fighting an underwater current of more than eight knots. From that day on, divers involved in body recovery were put on a strict buddy system, and the sheriff provided additional men in boats or on shore to assist them.

Like Bob Wrigley, Tinker Herndon was twenty-eight years old. Together they could put more diving experience and expertise at the sheriff's disposal than any other two men in the bay area. Wrigley was fully certified by the National SCUBA Association as a qualified diving instructor, and Herndon had passed all the tests except the written. He was unquestionably qualified in the practical areas but was simply unable to grasp such technical concepts as partial pressures of oxygen, nitrogen narcosis, and carbon dioxide tensions in the human bloodstream. Herndon felt far more comfortable with a mask and a pair of flippers than he did with pen and ink, but the accrediting board required more than practical competence. They had found that the understanding of the physics and chemistry of dissolved gases could be as important to a diver in trouble as his knowledge of how to unhook his tank and drop it.

At the phosphate pit, Wrigley obeyed the sheriff's deputy and drove the panel truck into the tall weeds away from the Thunderbird. He noticed that the area around the car had been roped off and several men were picking up objects almost too small to be seen, like a flock of hungry birds.

"Those guys lose their collar pin?" Herndon grinned from the passenger seat.

"Hell, they might even sift the whole acre," Wrigley replied. "I seen 'em do that once out near the bridge where a guy was shot clean through, and they come up with a .22 bullet. Trouble was, it weren't the bullet that killed the guy they found. It was from some kids target shootin'."

"No shit?" Herndon was craning his neck to get a better look at the deputies as they inched the truck into the assigned parking area.

98

"That's the trouble with a lot of these scenes. They send in a bunch of I.D. techs and these guys have to pick up a whole bunch of stuff, tag it, and cart it all downtown before they know whether any of it is evidence or not." Wrigley shook his head sadly, as if to say that he knew a better way to do it, but no one had ever asked him for advice. In fact, he didn't know a better way of clearing a scene for trace evidence, and it was quite unlikely that anyone of authority would ever ask him about the collection and preservation of evidence.

Wrigley got out of the truck and pulled his pants up over the small potbelly that he was growing. He slapped it luxuriously and reminded himself that one of these days he was going to drop five or ten on some low-carbohydrate plan. With him, it was not just vanity or the local Heart Association's TV scares. His skintight rubber suit became uncomfortable when there were a few more pounds to squeeze into it than there were when he had been measured for it.

Herndon moved around to the rear of the panel truck and opened the double doors. A cartoonlike frogman had been painted across them. It showed a skinny man-form in flippers, mask, and wet suit lying underwater on his back reading a book. The figure had his legs crossed casually and his head was propped up on a large, friendly looking starfish. Some of the diving club members said that the guy was reading a book on how to surface without precipitating a blood nitrogen problem. One member suggested that he had taken a waterproof porno book down to the bottom of the bay to be alone with it. In any case, half of him swung in each direction when the rear doors were thrown open.

"Let's leave the stuff in the truck till I get a chance to talk with the sheriff," Wrigley said calmly but with authority. Herndon had little initiative, so Wrigley automatically took charge of the situations in which they dove together. The arrangement was ideal. Herndon stretched sensuously in the sun and squinted at the crime scene area. The gleaners were still gleaning.

Wrigley recognized the stocky, muscular form of Captain Rizzolo coming toward him even before he was able to make out the policeman's face. Rizzolo walked as if he were twenty pounds overweight, had corns on one of his little toes, and was carrying a gun under his coat. He was sweating profusely as he approached the divers and the truck.

"Glad you all could come out," he said loudly. He shook Wrigley's hand enthusiastically.

"Captain, good to see you. You remember Tinker Herndon. A buddy of mine." Wrigley grinned at both of them.

"Good to have you with us, Tinker." The homicide captain returned Herndon's extra-firm handshake. "Another barber?" he asked Wrigley.

"Nope. A fireman," Wrigley supplied before Herndon could.

"City?"

"Eight years," Herndon said in a tone that announced that he was comfortable in the job.

"Well, you won't find any fires down there." Rizzolo threw his head sharply toward the water. Except for the bustle of the sheriff's men, the whole scene was incongruously peaceful. The water reflected the cloudless blue of the Florida sky and an occasional breeze moved quietly across the surface, rippling it in small waves that chased each other aimlessly, as if they were full of fun. The tall weeds took up each breeze like a respondent section of a symphony and danced with each theme before releasing it to move on across the countryside. Nature gave no sign that a dead body might be hidden in the depths of this tranquil pond.

The three men stared silently at the water. Rizzolo thought that it was a colossal pain in the ass; an impediment to his recovery of a dead body and to the forward progress of his investigation. Herndon thought that it was a little frightening. He was uncomfortable with uncharted and unknown waterways, especially those that had been created by mining or by damming a river. Full of hidden caves, these were often catchalls for abandoned stoves, stolen cars, and dead trees. All of these things gave Herndon a mushy feeling somewhere deep in his abdomen. Wrigley welcomed the whole scene as an opportunity to escape from the world on top in favor of the cooler, darker, wet environment of the dive. Peace began just beneath the surface. He knew that the first sounds of his exhaled bubbles rushing by his mask and the effortless glide through the water would be all that he would need to find himself. His only regret would be his biological demand to return to the surface to replenish his air supply. Wrigley truly envied the fish that were able to explore the ocean floor without returning to the surface for air. His fearless curiosity about the darkest recesses of the bottom had frequently caused a diving partner to abandon him rather than share the risks.

By some stroke of luck or some kind of an occult agreement between his inner soul and the whole aquatic environment, Wrigley had never been bitten by a fish, stung by a vicious creature from the dark ocean floor, or even threatened by a giant clam like Jon Hall in some old South Sea island movie. More than once, he had overstayed his air tanks and had surfaced a little too quickly, or at least faster than more cautious divers would allow themselves. Once or twice he had snagged himself on sharp metal sticking out from dumped junk, but generally, he had led a charmed underwater existence.

His friends had warned him that he was long overdue for an unlucky experience, and that when he ran into trouble it would likely be big trouble. Such warnings evoked only a small laugh from Wrigley. Once, after he had heard an international diving expert tell how he had been knocked unconscious by a love-struck sea turtle, Wrigley had had serious thoughts about his own diving safety for almost four minutes. But that was all the time he had been willing to squander on the so-called dangers of the deep. This was his favorite place, and he would not think of it as less than perfect. Though he often recalled that the nun who had been his third-grade teacher once said that nothing in the world was perfect, he was sure that she had never experienced scuba diving or sex.

"Is your doctor down there due to his own stupidity or through the courtesy of somebody else?" Wrigley asked blankly.

"He was helped," Rizzolo said, flatly.

"What happened?" asked Herndon.

"We think he was abducted by someone, forced to withdraw all the money in his bank account, and then driven here. They apparently hit him over the head with a tire iron from his own car."

"They?" Wrigley interrupted.

"Well, maybe there was only one, but it seems more likely to me that there was more than one of them. Dr. Trumbull was a fairly capable guy, they tell me, and I just bet that one guy alone would have had his hands full." Rizzolo warmed up to his own theory. He didn't mind sharing it with the two divers who had volunteered to help him. The more they knew, the more enthusiastic they were likely to be in their search for the body. Besides, no matter how confidential he tried to keep the early investigation, the newspapers would print it all anyway. The reporters claimed that the public had a right to know. Rizzolo thought that they were just answering an unacknowledged inner drive to be professional gossips.

"You found the money?" Herndon asked.

"Hell, no, we didn't find no money." Rizzolo was visibly astonished at Herndon's question.

"Then how'd you know that the doctor took out all his life savings from the bank?"

"Because the bank teller called up the office about ten minutes after he was in there yesterday morning," the captain said patronizingly. "She said the doc was as nervous as a cat."

"Pretty sharp of her," Wrigley said. "I'll move my holdings over there tomorrow." He laughed gently.

"All forty-seven cents of it?" Rizzolo offered, chuckling good-naturedly.

"Hell, he's got a fortune in illegal treasure that he dug up from down around the reef in the Bahamas and the Keys. Didn't he ever tell you about all that stuff, Captain? He's just afraid that the state boys will swoop down on him and cart it all off to Tallahassee for taxes. He keeps it hid under the floor of his barbershop." Herndon was enjoying his lies a lot more than Wrigley, who wasn't convinced that Rizzolo knew it was meant to be a joke. Besides, he did have a few illegal pieces from old Spanish wrecks that he took out and looked at whenever he felt sure that the state wasn't looking over his shoulder.

To the state of Florida, recovered treasure that went unreported and untaxed was no joke. And who would they suspect other than free-lance divers? Who else would be willing to go down into some badly charted wreck and bring up old coins, old guns, and other junk covered with barnacles, just for the fun of it. Occasionally a diver would claim that he had made a fortune in recovered treasure, but Wrigley figured that if a guy really recovered something valuable from an old wreck, he'd damn sure keep his mouth shut about it. The ones that bragged about their finds had probably never seen a wreck.

"Of course, we didn't give the bank teller's story any thought until this thing with the car today," Rizzolo explained, returning to his theory. He did not allow himself the luxury of concentrating on what seemed extraneous details. His single-mindedness sharpened his investigational skills and made him difficult to work for at times. One of Rizzolo's guiding axioms was that a homicide not cracked in the first forty-eight hours was likely to remain unsolved. That axiom was not always true, but Rizzolo used it to push his men along more urgently than they were willing to push themselves.

"Got any idea what kind of water that is?" Wrigley asked conversationally. He was busy unpacking the panel truck.

"We contacted the phosphate company that dug the pit a couple of years back, but they ain't too much on keeping those kind of records," Rizzolo said. "You know, they keep a lot of records about what they get out of these places, but not much on the hole itself. We even tried to locate the dredge operator, but he don't work around here anymore."

"He got smart and found an honest job?" Herndon quipped.

"Guess so. But they make damned good money on these rigs. He used to operate a great big shovel almost day and night, like some of them do. They would dig up this crap in the big scoop and dump it in front of a nozzle that would wash it all into a twelve-inch pipe that ran clear down to the phosphate plant. Made their bundle and moved on, I guess. Can't find any of those guys now." Rizzolo squinted into the sun as if to gauge the time.

"They probably wouldn't remember one of these holes from the other anyway," Wrigley observed. He stacked the air tanks side by side in the soft sand and concentrated on a tiny screw on his own regulator.

"Expect to use all them tanks?" Rizzolo asked.

"Hard to say. Don't know how long it will take to dive this pond for you."

"We did get hold of the regional director for the Mid-Florida Water Management Council, though," Rizzolo continued. "He said that a lot of pits in this general area were connected to underground streams that might just go on for miles and miles." The captain reported this fact without emotion, unaware of the effect it had on the two divers. Wrigley and Herndon exchanged long, silent glances like two pilots who were about to board their planes for a particularly dangerous bombing run over enemy territory.

"Did you drop a lead line for depth?" Wrigley asked cautiously. He continued to stare at Herndon.

"Eighty feet," the captain said.

"All over? No real deep spots?" Wrigley tried to look unconcerned, but his unflinching gaze told another story that both divers understood quite well.

"Over toward one end there was a deep area, but that's not anywheres near where we think they dropped the body." Rizzolo pointed toward the far right side of the phosphate pit. It was a hundred yards or so from where the Thunderbird was parked.

"Did the guy from the water management council say anything about stream movements or currents?" Herndon asked. He continued to be busy with his equipment and did not look up as he casually questioned Rizzolo.

"Nope. I didn't ask him. Why should I? You guys figure that this here pit connects with some underground river or something?" Rizzolo was becoming visibly concerned.

"Maybe," Wrigley said flatly. He pulled his rubber shirt from a wooden box inside the panel truck and winked at Herndon. The wink was enough to keep Herndon from carrying that line of questioning any further.

"Figure it will be cold down there, Bob?" Herndon asked.

"Shit, you guys, it's eighty-five out here," Rizzolo said, ridiculing the suggestion that it might be cold anywhere.

"You're right. The surface water is probably about seventy-four degrees, Captain," Wrigley said quickly.

"But if we find a connection to some uncharted underground stream, it's liable to be down to forty or fifty."

"In Florida?" The captain was sure that his leg was being pulled.

"In that part of Florida, anyway," Herndon pointed out. "When you get down eighty feet and better, there isn't much sunshine that gets through to warm the water up."

"Add that to a spring-fed underground stream and you can get temperatures that will turn a man blue in just about no minutes flat," Wrigley added. He slipped out of his pants and took off his shirt unself-consciously. Herndon stepped behind the truck to strip to his shorts and start to wriggle into the pants of his wet suit. Wrigley pulled his wet suit pants on a little quicker than his partner and sat down on the rear end of the truck zipping up the insides of the ankles.

He was reminded of the few pounds that he had put on when he felt the tug of the rubberized band around his waist. His jacket slipped on easier than the pants, but the front zipper balked slightly at his growing pot-belly.

"Better do something about that," Rizzolo offered with a chuckle.

"A hundred women think it's cute," Wrigley shot back.

"A hundred women that would admit to knowing you?" Herndon joined in playfully. "What would that be, the zoo parade?"

Wrigley slid his finger along the side of his nose in a poorly disguised Italian salute.

Several yards from the car, a sweating sheriff's deputy paddled an eighteen-foot aluminum boat toward the shore. The underside of the bow made a grating sound as the metal rubbed against the reeds and then the sand of the shoreline. The sound reminded the deputy of his early school days at Our Lady of Perpetual Help, and of a skinny kid in the fifth grade who used to scratch his fingernails across the blackboard just to be annoying. Even now, as an adult, the deputy had only to remember the school to feel a shiver up his spine.

Wrigley stopped to pull a sand spur out of his foot as Herndon put the air tanks and regulators in the boat. For comfort's sake, both of them preferred to keep their wet suits zipped only halfway up the chest prior to submersion and to leave their hoods off.

Herndon spat in his mask and massaged the saliva across the inner surface of the plastic faceplate. The deputy watched, horrified. He thought it was a particularly disgusting trick and wondered why the frogman didn't wash his mask before he came out to the scene.

"How far out there you gonna want to go?" the deputy asked. He had been working in the hot aluminum boat for about two hours and longed for a few minutes in the shade. He dreamed of a cold Busch rolling down his throat, but knew that with Rizzolo on the scene, he would not even get a rest. The deputy would have been happy to spend all day in another small boat provided that he was dressed in his old fishing clothes, had a cooler full of cold beer, and got at least an occasional nibble from some cooperative fish. But sitting in a police boat, fully uniformed, dropping a lead line over and over again to measure the depth of this pond was not his favorite sport. The monotony had dissipated the initial enthusiam he had felt when he volunteered to plumb the pond instead of searching the weeds for little pieces of other people's trash.

His boredom had made some of his depth measurements less precise than they should have been. This was particularly true in an area over to the right where, for several moments, he wasn't sure whether there was no bottom at all or that the sun had begun to play tricks with his brain. Since it had been sixty-five to eighty feet everywhere else in that pit, he found it more than hard to believe that one area could just drop out of sight when he lowered his lead weight on the light-gauge nylon line.

Rather than fight with his own common sense, the deputy had recorded the right end of the pit as "apparently deeper than 80'" and let it go at that. He was convinced that no one in the department would believe it if he had reported that he had let out a little over two hundred feet without hitting hard bottom. And besides, he reasoned, the captain would have only made him go out there in the sun and do it all over again. Finally, he concluded that the reason for that absurd depth reading was that the line had probably become snagged on some root down there.

The deputy hadn't noticed the pull on the line from the current that swept by at 125 feet and carried his six-ounce lead weight along with it like a lost toy.

Wrigley struggled with his flippers. "Far as I'm concerned, you can just anchor about ten yards or so offshore. I'm going to go in from here." He sat in the shallow water at the edge of the pit and was careful not to grind the small sharp rocks into his rubberized butt.

"Falls off right smart," the deputy volunteered.

"Most of these dug ponds do," Herndon said confidently. He began a short swim to acclimate himself to the water. He rolled and dived without tanks or regulator like a porpoise on a honeymoon. The deputy watched him and remembered the Sunday in July, six or seven years before, when he had taken his family to the county park near Lithia to swim and cook hot dogs. His brother-in-law had come down from Lima, Ohio, and that had served as an adequate excuse to actually go into the water. Otherwise, he took the position that that sort of stuff was for the tourists.

"We'll use the boat as a floating base and keep our gear in it. Less sand that way," Wrigley said, struggling with his hood and then with his mask. He slipped his arms into his backpack and adjusted to the weight of the single tank. He preferred a single tank because it gave him greater mobility, although it provided a smaller supply of air.

The deputy found himself being shoved off by Wrigley and quickly sat down to regain his balance as the boat floated free. He paddled out about thirty-five feet and stopped.

"That's a good spot to start with," Wrigley shouted from the water. The hood over his ears made him unsure how loud he was really shouting.

"Be careful, you guys," Rizzolo called out. He stood helplessly on the shore and watched as the deputy handed Herndon his tanks and regulator. Wrigley treaded water easily with his flippers and strong legs and helped Herndon into the backpack. They had often gone through the whole process in the water just to stay in practice. Ordinarily they both would prefer to suit up in the boat and then slip over the side. But the small boat the sheriff had provided looked much too tippy for that kind of athletics, and both divers had chosen to stay in the water and struggle with the tanks and packs.

Both divers tried their regulators and carefully monitored each other as they made final adjustments. It was to be a buddy dive all the way and the other man's equipment was as important to each man as his own. They carefully inspected the gauges, air lines, regulators, every strap and buckle and snap. When they were satisfied that they were fully prepared, they exchanged knowing nods.

The deputy handed Wrigley a battery-powered light that was small enough to hand-carry, and tried not to look upset about the water that the divers splashed on his well-pressed green uniform.

Wrigley felt the excitement at the water rushing along his suit and the initial roar of his own exhaled bubbles as he flipped downward and started his dive. Shortly, as he became accustomed to his underwater environment and began investigating its details, he would no longer hear the bubbles or feel the light movements of the water. He was almost home. The bright sunlight faded into diffused pale-blue columns of fog as the billions of tiny phosphate particles still suspended in the water gleamed and danced in the disturbance he had created.

The two men descended slowly, adjusting to the pressure and the darkness. The anchor line was visible for a while off to the left of Wrigley's bubble line, and it remained there in his memory even after he was no longer able to see it. He snapped on his light and watched the beam fight its way through the water for a few feet before it was consumed by the phosphate particles and the blue haze. Wrigley decided that the light would be useless for a wide search, but if they found anything it might be handy for a closer inspection.

Wrigley slowed his rate of dive when his trained ears and experienced skin told him that they were approaching the bottom. Both divers had cleared at about fifteen feet and neither had felt particularly uncomfortable since that depth. They had felt increasing pressure in the ears and the masks pushed back against their faces more firmly, but the dive had so far progressed without irregularities. Wrigley pulled up into a rest stand and was surprised to feel his right flipper brush against a hard object. He curled over to look at what he had touched and slid his hand gingerly along the edge of an old abandoned car. It was at least twenty years old and had obviously been dumped into the pit. There was no engine or windshield. Wrigley moved his light along its rusting side to show it to Herndon.

They had reached the bottom of the pit.

Herndon made a pointing gesture toward something he had bumped in the dark and Wrigley gave him the light. He watched the dim beam become an almost undiscernible glow as Herndon swam away only a few feet. Even without the light, Wrigley continued to explore in small circles around the bottom of the pit. He carefully felt his way, hoping to encounter the soft-ness of a submerged body, and yet not truly welcom-ing a dead invader in his underwater wonderland. Div-ing accidents and dead bodies gave the whole sport a bad name. People were scared enough of the water without adding to their fears by publicizing cave-diving accidents, air-embolism cases, and Loch Ness monsters that lurked in every dark shadow.

Wrigley's groping on the bottom yielded several de-caying tin cans, random pieces of automobile junk, and an abandoned kitchen gas stove. Herndon had found a fisherman's anchor jammed beneath a rock and a piece of farm machinery that he was unable to identify.

Wrigley caught up to Herndon and tapped him on the arm. He pointed to his watch and peered at it my-opically in the beam of the light. They had decided in advance that these dives would be limited to fifteen minutes; ten minutes had passed. He made a gesture to indicate that they start up, but that first they try a quick exploration of the area to the right end of the pit. Herndon nodded in agreement and they glided off ef-fortlessly, leaving two trails of bubbles behind them like the snow-mist that follows a downhill skier.

Wrigley swam slightly in the lead, and as he skimmed along the soft bottom he recognized that the floor of the phosphate pit began to slope sharply downward. He was about to call Herndon's attention to the in-creasing depth when a sudden chill passed across his back and left arm. A light tap on his leg signaled that Herndon was already aware of the sudden change in the temperature. In the near-darkness, Wrigley turned to face his partner as they brought their masks close enough to communicate by facial expressions. His raised eyebrow and widened eyes was answered by Herndon's anxious nodding in the direction of the deeper, darker water ahead. Wrigley returned a hand signal that asked his partner to allay his fears and venture on a little farther with him into the black water ahead. Herndon shrugged and swam along.

Bob Wrigley abandoned his effort to follow the bottom that was falling off so abruptly. Suddenly, he was experiencing pressure problems again. The water had become very cold and Wrigley felt the unmistakable pull of a swiftly moving stream. He had come across strong currents on other dives and could instantly judge the lighter movements that could be felt at the outer edges of an underwater river where the warmer water merged with the stream and was rapidly sucked into it.

Wrigley took a few cautious strokes farther and immediately felt the pull of a current stronger than any he had ever experienced before. He turned to face Herndon to wave him back, but the warning was not needed. Herndon had already recognized the rapid movements of the water and had no desire to test its strength against his own. He pointed frantically at his watch and then toward the surface.

Wrigley knew that Herndon was right. This was no time to explore a cold, fast-running, uncharted river at the bottom of a phosphate pit. He gave a signal to his partner and they both started back. They had to swim harder than Wrigley expected when they turned away from the edge of the turbulence. His efforts made him use more oxygen than he had anticipated, and Herndon's increasing anxiety caused him to breathe faster. Both divers pulled their safety valves and went on reserve air for the ascent.

It was Wrigley who took charge of staging the way up, accurately estimating the depth by the pressure on his skin and within his ears. At his signal, both divers paused for the required time at selected levels and gave the gases dissolved in their bloodstreams a chance to diffuse out without forming crippling or even fatal bubbles in their brains.

Herndon burst from the surface of the pit with a relieved gasp and spat out his mouthpiece. He yanked his mask off and gulped in the hot Florida air. Wrigley surfaced beside him with much less drama and no sign of panic.

"That's a goddamned river down there, Captain," Wrigley reported as he crawled onto the shore and stood up. He flapped his flippers in front of him for stability and unzipped his wet suit jacket. Herndon rested at the edge of the aluminum boat as the deputy took his air tank and backpack aboard.

"No body?" The captain was disappointed.

"Not sure yet. But my bet is that it went down the drain." Wrigley pointed toward the right end of the pit.

"You mean right out of the whole pit?" Rizzolo was puzzled. The water looked calm enough to him.

"If not totally out, then at least farther down in that hole than anybody is going to be able to dive to get it back."

"Rotten goddamned luck, Wrigley," Rizzolo said, mopping his brow with a dirty, wrinkled handkerchief. "Rotten goddamned luck."

Wrigley waved to Herndon and slipped off his flippers. "I'll dive it a few more times to convince the widow that we really looked, Captain, but that's a real son of a bitch down there."

Rizzolo turned away from the diver and walked back toward the Thunderbird. The I.D. boys were dusting every surface and examining every piece of lint on the carpet. For all practical purposes Wrigley and Herndon had done their jobs. True to form, Rizzolo had discarded them as quickly as he did the butt of his cigarette.

"Send me a bill," Rizzolo said over his shoulder.

"Sure," said Wrigley. He knew that no one would pay it, and he really didn't care. Diving was diving. And if you're a diver, that's all there is.

Chapter Seven

"AND REMEMBER," Rizzolo said to his class of rookie deputies and Tampa-area patrolmen, "when a witness gets served with a subpoena duces tecum, that means that he is supposed to show up in court with his old records. —Not a couple of dusty Glenn Millers or Jack Teagardens, you understand, but old business records." There was a polite chuckle from the small collection of policemen in the class. This was mixed with and almost lost in the shuffle of chairs, feet, and books slapping closed as the crime-scene class came to an end. Rizzolo did not really have time for that kind of academic nonsense anymore, but he recognized that there was no one else to teach the class if he quit. The department was already strapped for applicants and teaching personnel were at a premium everywhere across the country.

A small cluster of more-than-eager police rookies gathered around Rizzolo's desk as he collected his papers and stuffed them into his aged leather briefcase. He used to boast that there was not another briefcase like it in the world. Those who saw it prayed that he was right.

"But how come there were no tire tracks leading out

from the phosphate pit?" one of the rookies asked quietly.

"Covered 'em up," Rizzolo grunted. "Looked like they used some kind of a piece of brush or tree limb with leaves. Left a lot of little scratch marks, the way you would if you worked a big piece of brush back and forth across a sandy trail."

"Does that mean that there were some kind of identifiable tire markings and the killers wanted to hide them?"

"So far, that's as good a theory as any other, Ames," Rizzolo said, complimenting his student. "At this point, we have to assume that somebody wanted to make it hard to I.D. those tires . . . unless he just needed a quarter of a mile of sweeping exercises."

It was Rizzolo's habit to use current cases in his lectures whenever possible. His idea was that a fresh case would catch the interest of the new men quicker and hold it longer than some canned narration of a 1926 shooting in Chicago. Using a hot case gave the rookies a sense of belonging to a team that was still faced with an unsolved problem. They might contribute very little, but at least it kept them awake during classes and made the instructor get his facts straight. Rizzolo and the other instructors ran the risk that the new men might challenge them on some detail gleaned from newspapers or TV. Rizzolo did not want parrots in uniform. He wanted to train police officers. To do that, he had to start with ordinary men and build a sense of pride within them that would keep them straight while they continued to acquire the technical skills that would forever set them apart from the ordinary citizen. Once they had been trained as cops, they would always remain cops, Rizzolo reasoned. On or off the force, active or retired, in this county or in some other jurisdiction, straight or renegade, they would think like cops and act like cops.

"You think that the guy had some kind of crazy

racing tires or a foreign tread . . . you know, like on a sports car?" another of the rookies asked hopefully.

"But, even some American sports cars use foreign tires and most imported cars end up with American tires, so what can you make out of that?" Rizzolo teased.

"Somebody used up a lot of time and sweat to hide some kind of tracks, that's all I can make out of it, Captain." The rookie was backing off.

"Right," Rizzolo agreed. "And left us plenty of damned crude brush marks, too. The guy didn't seem to mind at all that we noticed that he swept the tire marks away. That's the hell of it all." He continued to stuff his lecture papers into his battered briefcase. "You're Hanson, right?" Rizzolo squinted at the rookie over his glasses, now well down on his nose.

"Right, sir. Hanson, John J. Number eight seven three."

"Well, Hanson, take that sweeping episode as a homework problem. Share it with your friends in the class. Bring me back eight hundred and seventy-three reasonable explanations for why some dude would sweep a dirt road leading out from an abandoned phosphate pit after he dumped a doctor's body in the water."

"Excuse me, sir, but how come you're sure that the body is in the pit?" Hanson persisted.

"You're right. I'm not sure at all that the body is really in the pit. The frog guys said that the pit connects with a fast underground river. They want to bet their flippers that the body got carried out of the pit by that river after somebody dumped it." Rizzolo arched his eyebrows pending Hanson's reply.

Hanson's eyebrows were also elevated, but combined with pursed lips his expression was more confused than quizzical.

"Guess the frogmen know their trade," Hanson conceded slowly, "but I'd feel a lot better about it if they had brought up the body."

"So would we both. So would we both." Rizzolo

squinted at Hanson as if to admit that the younger man had as much right to come up with a new idea as anyone else. He continued to squint silently at the rookie as he considered the alternatives to the body being carried away by the current. It was a run-it-up-the-flagpole frame of mind that he often allowed himself when analyzing his own hypotheses about crime scenes. If he didn't question his own theories, who would? His rank and departmental stature scared away most criticism and other reasonable opinions that he knew he often needed desperately.

"Work on it," he said abruptly to Hanson. He walked briskly from the classroom and down the hall to his office. He grunted but did not speak to the other detectives who acknowledged him as he entered the cluttered and busy homicide area. A new detective waved a piece of paper at him as he crossed the room and headed toward his private office. He brushed the young detective aside like a pesky gnat and instantly regretted it. The detective turned away from him without malice and left him with the solitude that his expression and purposeful, deliberate gait clearly demanded.

Rizzolo opened and closed his door quickly and noisily, and slumped in his chair. Then he cupped his face in his hands and sighed deeply. He did not like to feel unsure about anything. It bothered him and it bothered everyone who worked for him.

He picked up the desk phone and quickly dialed an inside number. He balanced the phone between his ear and his shoulder as he slid open his desk drawer and took out a large paper clip, which he unbent to use as a toothpick. He promised himself again that he would at least let that cute dental hygienist clean and scrape his teeth, even if he refused to let the dentist poke around in his mouth. This promise would be broken just as all his other dental promises had been over the previous five years.

"Lieutenant Turner, please," he said briskly as soon as a female voice answered the ring at the other end.

A man's voice responded with almost no delay. Rizzolo wondered just how close he had been sitting to his secretary–file clerk, grade IV.

"Lieutenant Turner," the busy-sounding voice acknowledged. The tone was firm enough to belong to the head of the crime lab section, without suggesting impatience.

"Turner. Did you finish processing that car?" Rizzolo asked without introduction or warning.

"Which car, Captain?" Turner asked, seeming annoyed at Rizzolo's lack of precision.

"The T-bird, Turner, the T-bird."

"Yep. Got almost nothing."

"Nothing?" Rizzolo sounded gypped.

"Nothing much, anyway. The doc's prints are all over the thing and the Texaco station manager from Goat Hill Road handled the front of the hood, but the rest of it has been wiped clean."

"What about this Goat Hill guy?"

"Nothing there, Captain. We called him as soon as I made him from the prints. Figured it was a gas station man 'cause it was greasy and was right where a guy would close that hood from up in front. You know, with two hands? He'd kind of push down on the hood and—"

"Yeah, yeah, Turner. I know how to close the hood of a car. Even a T-bird. What else did you get?"

"We had the garage man's prints on file 'cause he was an auxiliary a couple of years back. Name of Peacock."

"And . . . ?"

"And he's clean. One of you boys called him and he remembers servicing the T-bird the day before the doc went to the bank. Clean all the way around."

"He knows the doc?"

"Serviced his car for a couple of years."

"Anything else about the car, Turner?"

"Not much. Radio was left on. So was the engine. But it ran out of gas."

"How long you figure that T-bird would idle if it had been driven a couple of times back and forth from the doc's home to the hospital and had a full tank to start with?" Rizzolo was just thinking out loud and Turner knew it.

"Dunno. Maybe ten, twelve hours. Hard to say. Want us to fill it and run it to see?"

"Not yet. By the way—what station?"

"Texaco."

"No, dummy. What *radio* station? You said the radio was left on. I'll bet you don't even know." Rizzolo needed small, sadistic thrusts at his officers to keep him on an even emotional keel.

"Don't bet your badge, Captain. It was 'WMDN, your country-and-western home on the air.'" His mimicry of the down-home twang that the announcer used to identify the station was almost perfect.

"You mean Bobby Gentry and all that? That was the doc's music bag? Shit, I'd have taken him for a University of South Florida, FM-classical freak long before I'd have handed him over to the shit-kicking set."

"I guess a lot of people like it, Captain," Lt. Turner offered blandly. He rolled his eyes toward heaven for patience.

"And the tire iron?"

"Type A, positive. Human blood. Human hair, caucasian type. No prints." Turner was a machine.

"His type?"

"Right. We checked it out with his own blood-bank records at the hospital where he had his lab."

"He gave blood at his own blood bank?" Rizzolo was mildly astonished.

"Every time they ran out and needed a pint for some emergency surgery, the doctors and nurses would roll up their sleeves. Dr. Trumbull included."

"No crap? Now, that's real gung-ho of them, ain't it? Never figured the doctors to give blood like that. What kind was he again?"

"Group A, type Rh positive," Turner said slowly and carefully. His precision was almost insulting, but Rizzolo missed it.

"And it's a match with the blood on the tire iron?"

"A match, Captain."

"But no prints."

"You know how hard it is to lift a print off of smooth metal, Captain." Turner sounded a little defensive, but not afraid of his senior officer. He would bow to Rizzolo in homicide, but nobody could put Turner down in identification and criminalistics.

"The Canadians claim they have a way of spraying the victim and dusting a print right off of his skin," Rizzolo said, playfully.

"Champion for the Canadians," Turner said, doing his best to sound like Toronto.

"You vacuumed the car, of course."

"Every speck of dust, every flake of tobacco, every piece of lint. All negative. Nothing turned up except eighteen cents in assorted U.S. coins, a Juicy Fruit gum wrapper, and an old Texaco credit card receipt dated three weeks ago." Turner was becoming a little annoyed. His report on all that would be out promptly, with copies to Rizzolo and every senior officer concerned, if they would only stop calling him on the phone.

"Did it look like somebody cleaned up the car?"

"Not really. It had a normal messy flavor." Turner sighed heavily, hoping that Rizzolo would take the hint and hang up.

"How about the rest of the T-bird? Hub caps, under the seat, trunk—" Rizzolo paused suddenly as if he had just thought of something new. "This guy involved in any narc traffic? How 'bout a big baggie of horse in the left rear? Come on, Turner, make us a real case out of all this bullshit."

"No help, Captain. We took that car apart. Nothing

anywhere." Turner made it a point to sound more and more weary. He was working on Rizzolo.

The captain sighed deeply. He pitched the disfigured paper clip toward the metal wastebasket in the corner and winced as he heard a wooden thud that signified yet another miss.

"What about his doctor's bag. Did it get ripped off?" Rizzolo threw a new paper clip and was gratified to hear a metallic clang when it hit the wastebasket.

"Pathologists don't carry doctors' bags, Captain," Turner said heavily.

"They don't?"

"No."

"Not even with autopsy tools and rubber gloves?" Rizzolo was grinning at his end of the phone. "Some of them forensic pathologists show up with a bagful of weird tools every time we find a rotten body somewhere."

Turner was silent for a while.

At last he offered, "Maybe medical examiners are different kinds of pathologists than the guys who work in the hospital labs." He knew that Rizzolo would have just sat there silently until he came up with some kind of an answer.

Rizzolo contributed a small, almost obviously cynical chuckle. "Ever try to get one of those hospital pathologists to look at a body that's been in the bay for a week or so? They all run like it was the plague. The medical examiner don't run."

"Maybe his nose doesn't work," Turner suggested.

"Who?"

"The M.E. How else can he stand those bloated bodies with the maggots crawling out of them?"

"Job security, Turner. Job security. He probably figures that the county will keep on paying him if he goes on doing autopsies on those stinkers." Rizzolo was laughing, really laughing, for the first time that day.

"Oh yeah—there was one funny thing, Captain,"

Turner said, getting a sudden flash that he felt forced to share.

"That-a-boy, Turner. I knew you'd hit on something. Lay it on me." Rizzolo was mentally rubbing his hands together.

"The trunk. There was an oil spot on the floor of the trunk and somebody had spilled a little gasoline in there."

"OK." Rizzolo waited patiently. "OK. And...?"

"That's all. End of message. I just collect the facts. You're the one who tells us all what they mean."

"Oil and gas on the floor of the trunk? So what, Turner? What does that make him?"

"Beats the hell out of me, Captain. Oil and gas in the trunk. That's all. Spare was OK. The rest of the trunk was clean."

"Except for the tire iron."

"Yeah, except for that. But even there, the tire and tools and the jack were not thrown around all over the trunk the way you might expect they'd be if some guy was messing around looking for something to zap the doc with."

"Now make us something out of that oil and gas in the trunk, Turner. Look into your crystal ball."

Another paper clip clanged in the corner. Rizzolo wondered how much he had cost the county in paper clips since he had been with the sheriff's department. He figured that in the long run it was cheaper than sick leave if throwing them kept a man from getting an ulcer.

"How 'bout a lawn mower?" Turner offered.

"Make it an outboard."

"Don't see why, but we'll work on it, Captain." Turner chuckled and carefully replaced the phone on its cradle. He was free of Rizzolo.

"Because I don't think that doctors carry lawn mowers in their Thunderbirds or even know whether their lawns ever get cut, that's why," Rizzolo said out loud to himself. He put the phone down and swiveled his chair around to face the window. The city looked unperturbed, implacable, and unwilling to rush into Rizzolo's office with a quick solution to his latest murder case. The citizens would be briefly concerned while they drank coffee over the morning *Tribune,* while the radio gave out highlights of the case between records, and for three minutes at six o'clock when the TV showed a few film clips of the sheriff's office, a patrol car with a flashing light, or a pan shot of Dr. Trumbull's house. But for the rest of the day and all through the night, the case would be Rizzolo's and nobody else's.

At home, Agnes Trumbull had spent the day in a numb state of shock. She knew that it was all true, but somehow was also sure that it couldn't be. As soon as the sheriff had brought the news of Bill's disappearance and with it the presumption of a brutal homicide, the children had been picked up at the local Catholic school. This was to spare them the embarrassment of unthinkingly cruel comments from their schoolmates and to prevent any threats to their safety. Rizzolo had learned long ago to assume that one death was sometimes the first of a series. A vendetta against a whole family by some psycho was not impossible, although Rizzolo had never been personally involved in one. It was his practice and a departmental rule to offer immediate protection to the surviving next of kin until a motive for the murder could be established.

So far, there was nothing in this case to suggest that Agnes Trumbull or her children were in any real danger.

The children had thoroughly enjoyed the ride home in the sheriff's patrol car. Tom wanted to hear the siren and was gratified by a low whine as the deputy gently pressed the floor button. Cathy was interested in the radio that spoke "mostly numbers," as she reported it later, and through which the deputy could have talked "with any policeman in the world right from his car."

John, the oldest, had not been entertained at all. He knew that a deputy would not have been dispatched to bring him and his siblings home from school in the middle of the day unless something terrible had happened. The deputy had not volunteered any details, thereby adding to John's anxiety. John maintained enough composure to avoid upsetting the others during the ride, and silently rejected the official put-off that he would be told what was wrong by his mother when they reached home. He swallowed the growing lump in his throat and fought back tears as he attempted to distract Tom and Cathy. He assured Tom that the deputy's gun was real and that the bullets in the belt were all capable of shooting a robber. John quickly wondered if there had been a robber at his house after he had left for school. Maybe someone had come and hurt his mom. His mind flashed to one of those school lectures that the crime prevention deputies delivered annually and their unspecific warnings about the horrible things that happened to kids who accepted rides from strangers. He remembered vowing silently that he would always feel responsible if something terrible ever happened to his mother when he could have stayed home and protected her. But then, he wondered, somewhat perplexed by his old resolution and the realities of the present situation, how would he know which days to stay home and which days to go to school?

The squealing and the gibberish of his little brother and sister intruded on these serious thoughts as the patrol car turned into the driveway of their house. There were several other cars around, but only two of them were painted the familiar green and white. He correctly guessed that the other two were unmarked units. Who else but a police department official would drive around in an almost chromeless, blackwalled, two-door, cheap-model car with a conspicuous, although inverted, spotlight at the driver's side door post?

There was a uniformed deputy standing at the door as John and his sister and Tom bounded across the lawn to enter the house.

"Momma! We rode home in a police car!" Tom exclaimed with excitement as he rushed through the entrance hallway and into the family room. His wide eyes were matched by those of his sister who shared his excitement, but with caution. John followed more deliberately, and was perfectly serious.

"Mother, what has happened?" John asked Agnes Trumbull in a matter-of-fact tone that would do justice to the anchorman on the six o'clock news. He was fifteen, but at that moment Agnes saw a man emerging in him. He was almost man enough to relieve her of part of her own anxiety. Almost man enough to embrace and surrender the whole problem to. And yet, still a little boy who would fold quickly when told about his father's death. A little boy who would need his mother's love and comforting.

But the little man stood there unflinching, offering her a comforting hand, helping her gather in the two littler ones, and not yet retreating from her eyes, now reddened by crying.

"John," she said as flatly as she could, "it's your father." Her lower lip trembled and gave the whole thing away.

"Was he killed?" John asked quickly. The tears came fast now and burst through his facade of maturity before he could stop them.

He experienced an immediate and consuming anger. He was mad at something or someone, or everything and everyone who had conspired to injure his father. He wished suddenly for someone—anyone—against whom he could direct his reprisal. He knew that her answer to his question would be yes, but he did not want to hear it, and, screaming, burrowed his head into his mother's lap and jammed his hands tightly over his ears to block out the world and all of its horrible realities. He felt only the firm petting of his mother's hand on the back of his head and neck, squeezing him with alternating gentleness and pleasurable pain to tell him without words that she was still there.

He didn't hear himself screaming, "No, no, no," into the folds of his mother's skirt or realize how much time had elapsed before the firmer hands of a deputy sheriff interrupted his hysteria by pulling him away.

Agnes Trumbull did not try to talk to him, or offer explanations until he had had enough time to work through part of his sudden and overwhelming grief.

"John, there is no proof yet that Daddy's dead—or even hurt," she offered soothingly. It was this comment that attracted his little sister's attention and cued her to join in the crying. She had missed the point up to that moment, but when she responded, Tom chain-reacted to her tears and cried openly. He was still not quite sure what it was all about.

"Then why is the sheriff here, and all those police cars?" John screamed at her defiantly. It was as if he were blaming her and the sheriff for the creation of a problem bigger than he could possibly cope with.

"They're here to help us, John," Agnes said with strength.

"I wish they'd all go away," he sobbed, running from the room and dashing up the stairs to retreat into his own bedroom. His brother and sister were coaxed away to another part of the house by a sympathetic neighbor woman who, until then, had stood around helplessly.

Agnes had tried to cooperate with the sheriff's detectives who had arrived shortly after Rizzolo to ask her detailed questions and make pages of notes on long yellow pads. Deputies had secured the doors to screen out curiosity-seekers or those whose offers of help were little more than obvious dodges to gain entry into a house that presented the prospect of a grotesque but welcome break in the average suburban housewife's dull routine.

She had supplied the detectives with a list of friends and acquaintances who knew or probably knew Dr. Trumbull's daily routine, and a list of others she could think of who might have had a grudge against him. They had solemnly promised her that the latter roster would never be disclosed, and that those she put on it would never find out about their inclusion. That promise had helped her to be more liberal in supplying names. Making a list of anyone—literally anyone, as the sheriff's detectives had said—who might possibly hold the slightest grudge against a man as active as the opinionated pathologist she had married had been easier than she had imagined it would be. At first, she had protested that there simply were no enemies. But the detectives had given her an expert explanation of how little it might take to generate hard feelings in some closet screwball. The task then became easier and easier until, at the end, she had found herself in danger of putting just about everyone they had ever known on the damned list.

She felt that she was now a victim too. The investigation, the questions, the strangers who came into her house to inquire into her private life with Bill Trumbull —all this had conspired to rob her of the luxury of grief and, somehow, of a portion of her identity as well. She began to feel resentment and withdrew from the detective's questions long before Rizzolo was satisfied. His years of experience allowed this withdrawal as a temporary and strategic concession to Agnes Trumbull, the widow. He knew that he would have many other opportunities to talk to Mrs. Trumbull before the disappearance of her husband was solved.

Chapter Eight

THE NEXT MORNING, the Tampa *Tribune* was trying to say it all, imply still more, and yet honor the promise that the editor had once made to Captain Rizzolo. The *Tribune*'s editor and Rizzolo had become friends over another notorious case, and each had learned to respect the other's job. Rizzolo was willing to part with the facts that he knew the newspaper needed, but he had to protect his investigation by extracting a halfhearted promise to soft-pedal the gory details so that a jury could be found later. A motion for a change of venue could easily be based on indiscriminate reporting that managed to prejudice those who might be chosen as jurors. A change of venue only moved the same trial out of town, and caused the witnesses, police officials, technicians, and other personnel costly and inconvenient travel.

The headline said: LOCAL PATHOLOGIST FEARED MURDERED IN PIT. The newsphoto was an aerial view of the phosphate pit area with a lopsided "X" that looked more like an Iron Cross medal marking the spot where the Thunderbird had been found. Rizzolo noticed that he had been quoted or given as the source for statements nine times in the story, but the newspaper treatment of the story was otherwise fair. It was sensational enough to sell copies, probing enough to excite the reader, and factual enough to keep the reporter off the police shit list for future items.

The *Tribune* told its readers how the car had been found near the pit and that a tire iron with blood and hair on it had been recovered. These items had been sent to the crime lab for further study and tests. The new local crime lab had taken over trace-evidence, serological identification, ballistics, and other criminal-istic testing procedures, but frequently the FBI still got the credit because for years they had done all of these complicated procedures by mail.

Rizzolo folded the *Tribune* badly and finished his coffee in one continuous and quite audible slurp as he got up from the breakfast table. The coffee was not very good, but since he made it himself every morning, he had no one else to blame.

His unmarked unit waited in his driveway. He had no sooner turned the key in the ignition when his radio began to crackle with an official dispatch. His brain was able to monitor a dispatch while, consciously, Riz-zolo devoted his mental energies to something else en-tirely. Yet, if he wished, the Captain could reach back into his memory bank and pull out the essential facts of some radio bulletin that had been made hours and sometimes days before, even though the case had not been his. This talent amazed the younger deputies, but Rizzolo shrugged it off as a curse coming with years of experience on the job. He told them that if Leonard Bernstein could hum snatches from a thousand sym-phonies, why shouldn't the chief of homicide be able to remember a few routine police dispatches?

Rizzolo eased the car off the thruway and onto a cobblestoned city street. His office was downtown and, incongruously, in another police jurisdiction. The city police investigated crimes inside the city limits while the sheriff watched over the rest of the county. But since the sheriff's office and headquarters were located inside the city limits, the city police had to patrol the sheriff's front door.

Two prisoners from the jail trotted out to take possession of Rizzolo's car almost before he got out of it. A newspaper exposé had put an end to a previous practice that all ranking officers, councilmen, and the mayor's staff could have their private cars washed and waxed by prisoners. The inmates had literally fought over the opportunity to get out into the fresh air and sunshine and to make a few coins by taking care of these cars. But after the newspaper story, the whole process was scrapped by a single, direct telephone order from the governor's office.

Wash jobs were now limited to county-owned, "official" cars, and even then, the prisoners had to be bona fide volunteers.

"Check the oil, too, will ya?" Rizzolo barked at the first prisoner.

"Yassah," said the black prisoner, grinning and Uncle Tom-ing Rizzolo insolently.

Rizzolo looked at him with contempt. Not for his offense—petty larceny and fighting in a public place—but for the theatrical nigger that he played whenever an officer was around. Whenever he saw Rizzolo, he bowed and scraped right out of a 1930's movie, knowing all the while that neither he nor Rizzolo was buying any part of the performance.

Rizzolo let the glass door to the sheriff's headquarters hiss quickly shut and then turned abruptly to catch the prisoner spitting on the fender of his car. The prisoner knew that Rizzolo would turn around to watch him after entering the building although he could not see the captain through the morning glare off the glass door. So he legitimized his private act of contempt by rubbing the spit into the dust on the fender with the sleeve of his gray jail uniform and then faking a careful inspection of the small circle of shined paint he had produced.

There was a litany of "Mornin', Captain" as Rizzolo

made his way down two corridors to his office on the
second floor. The waxed tiles reflected a wavily sur-
realistic image of the ceiling lights fifteen feet above.
As Rizzolo entered his office, he made his first two
points of the day with the toothpick that he had chewed
on all the way from his home.

He looked at the stack of files on his desk. Some of
the cases were under investigation and others, flagged
by folded subpoenas on their jackets, waited patiently
for their day in court.

On the top of the stack was a new folder marked
TRUMBULL, WILLIAM E., M.D., HOMICIDE. Rizzolo took the
homework out of his briefcase and slipped it under the
new Trumbull folder. Inside the folder were written
reports from detectives, the crime lab, and random
scraps of information, including that morning's *Tribune*
story. One of the reports read:

TO: Captain Rizzolo
FROM: Lt. Isaac
RE: Trumbull, Wm. E., M.D.
CODE—HOMICIDE—FILE OPEN
Undersigned visited Southern MidFlorida Hospital, Orangeburrow. Confirmed that Trumbull, William E., M.D., subject of file, was employed at said
institution for past seven years. Interviewed Laboratory staff personnel (see list attached). U/
signed not able to establish any history of trouble
between subject—well trained, usually considerate
—and others at work site. Undersigned interviewed
Courtney Haskall, administrator of said hospital.
No evidence of stolen property, scandal involving
narcotics or malpractice, etc. U/signed not able to
establish any complaint from any former patients
at hospital via interview with Haskall.

Routine check of hospital employees reveals a
Roosevelt Hawkins, black, male, age 24, previously

known this office, file S.O. 187462-68, B&E, stolen property, convicted, served 2 years of 8 year sentence. Hawkins interviewed states his conviction not known to hospital. Confirmed by Haskall. Hawkins denies all contact with subject doctor. Hawkins' whereabouts turned over to Robbery. No current file on Hawkins per Robbery.

Impression: Hospital scene and personnel, clean. U/signed not able to establish suspect in homicide or motive.
2100 HRS. R. Isaac, Lt. HCSO
cc: Routine per S.O. directive 3/70. File.

Rizzolo shuffled the paper to the bottom of the folder and quickly reviewed another nonproductive report on an interview conducted by a uniformed deputy. The bank teller, Mrs. Drawdy, confirmed her previous report without significant addition. The report noted that Mrs. Drawdy herself checked out reasonably clean. She had been seeing a bartender at a Lakeland lounge, but since she had been divorced and living quietly for the past three years, the deputy and his reviewing sergeant did not feel that this was worth a follow-up. Rizzolo agreed.

Several sheets of legal-sized paper in the Trumbull file were stapled together at one corner and began to blossom like an exotic plant as Rizzolo picked them up with one hand. The front sheet was titled PROFESSIONAL ASSOCIATES and the corner opposite the staple bore a faded red-rubber-stamped announcement that the packet was "incomplete." It had been compiled by several members of Rizzolo's staff, and had used several sources, beginning with the most obvious, the roster of the doctors with whom Trumbull practiced daily.

Rizzolo didn't recognize the names of many of the doctors on the list. He seldom went to doctors, and when he did, it invariably turned out to be one of the

Spanish-speaking physicians associated with a Cuban Health Club that his mother had enrolled him in as a child for twenty-five cents a week. Over the years, the medical care offered at the Cuban club had gradually changed from annual physicals for cigar workers to a reasonably modern clinic with up-to-date equipment, several non-Spanish doctors, and an incongruous fifty-year head start on the concept of prepaid health care in the United States. The weekly rate was no longer twenty-five cents, but many of the patrons who had been lifelong members of the club were carried for embarrassingly low fees.

Rizzolo scanned the brief biographical sketches on each of the doctors at Trumbull's hospital and repressed a yawn. He saw nothing of interest in the two surgeons who for ten years had practiced together in an office near the hospital. One detective had supplied the fact that Trumbull had put the younger of the two surgeons on the tissue committee report for several consecutive months for consistently removing totally normal appendixes and for performing hysterectomies on ladies that Trumbull had judged to be too young or too healthy. Neither Rizzolo nor the detective felt that that was sufficient to elevate the surgeon to "suspect" status in the case. Besides, Rizzolo added mentally, a disgruntled surgeon who wants to get rid of a troublesome pathologist doesn't do it by hitting him over the head with a tire iron and throwing his body into a phosphate pit. A surgeon, by his very nature and training, would choose some more exotic method, like the injection of a weird drug.

The next to the last staff sketch was of Bruce LaFontaine. Rizzolo began to read it with one eye, and that half closed. The report supplied the usual material about the doctor's training and the fact that he was apparently very successful in his radiology practice at the hospital. LaFontaine was listed higher than all the other staff doctors as to the probability that he had frequent social contact with Bill Trumbull. It had not been hard for the detectives to uncover the fact that the Trumbulls and the LaFontaines were often seen together at Tampa social events, and that they had even taken a vacation trip together.

Rizzolo made a mental note to see if they had become even cozier: might there not be some romantic link between Bill Trumbull and Mary LaFontaine or between the radiologist and Agnes Trumbull? Rizzolo's interview with Agnes Trumbull had not given him the impression that she was the type to develop extramarital romantic ties. Her personality seemed to suggest that she would offer precious little romance to anyone, including, probably, the man she had married. Rizzolo's cynicism was only partly congenital. The rest of it had come from years of police work, mountains of lies, cover story after cover story, and the conviction that everyone except his own mother was a lying bastard. Even there, Rizzolo was willing to admit with a wink that he had never had the opportunity to cross-examine his mother on her relationship with his father.

Rizzolo wrote Bruce LaFontaine's name and office address on the back of a cheaply printed card that announced that the bearer was in the faithful employ of the sheriff, slipped it into his shirt pocket, and walked quickly out of his office. He seemed preoccupied.

Rizzolo eased his car into an angled space that was marked FOR DOCTORS ONLY, and told the radio dispatcher as much. He wondered if the dispatcher would start a rumor that he had some kind of a malignant tumor since he had signed out to a radiologist's office. Rizzolo resigned himself to the fact that like trying to correct a newspaper story, the more one offered evidence of the truth, the more people believed the false report.

The radiologist's private office was located in a small two-story professional building across the street from the hospital. The more urgent or complex cases were handled in the hospital radiology department. LaFontaine had opened the small office only to accommodate general practitioners who had offices around the hospital, and who wanted simple cases looked at without incurring the expense of the hospital.

Rizzolo walked slowly down the corridor of the building toward LaFontaine's office. Many of the names on the other doors were the same as those on the list that his detective division had prepared for him. Rizzolo was prepared to interview as many of them as needed to uncover any connection between one of them and the pathologist's death. But, deep within his policeman's heart, he knew this list of doctors would yield little. However, a policeman's intuition is often as keen as that of a woman, and hunches had to be checked out and laid to rest, one by one, just as thoroughly as real facts were.

The door to the office belonging to Bruce LaFontaine, M.D., claimed that only diagnostic radiology was practiced inside. LaFontaine had never attempted to set up a therapeutic radiology section. The volume of cancer cases to fry with a big cobalt machine was small enough to make private radiotherapy a financial disaster, and besides, most small-town people preferred to go to the big city to have highly specialized treatment, even if it could been done easier, quicker, and cheaper at home. The trip to the nearby big city or to the university medical center helped convince the patient that he was receiving high-powered, expert medical care, and maybe getting better.

As Rizzolo entered LaFontaine's office a large palmetto bug struggled out from partial entrapment in the fibers of the carpet and lurched outside onto the high gloss of the waxed corridor tiles. Rizzolo remembered reading somewhere that when man had finally managed to contaminate his whole world with radioactivity, the cockroaches would survive and take over. The palmetto bug that came out of LaFontaine's office may have been an advance scout for the civilization to come.

The recent high school graduate at the reception desk in Bruce LaFontaine's office glanced up quickly at Rizzolo as he entered the room, and then instantly resumed her typing rather than offer a greeting. The typing was obviously a difficult task for her judging by the frown she wore while closely inspecting each of the two characters that she had managed to type after Rizzolo shut the door. The captain stood silently in front of her desk and felt like his suit didn't quite fit.

It didn't.

Rizzolo unfolded his pocket I.D. wallet and waited for the receptionist to look up, recognize the badge, and stop ignoring him. He had a sudden urge to pull the paper out of the typewriter, crumple it, and throw it on her desk, but he repressed it. No sense starting off an interview with a suspect by mistreating his office girl.

Nearly half of the goldfish in the office aquarium came to the outer wall of their glass home to look at Rizzolo, but none of them seemed impressed with the fact that he was a captain in charge of homicide.

The girl at the desk squinted at the badge and the I.D. card inside the unfolded wallet.

"Oh, wow," she said softly.

"I'd like to see Dr. LaFontaine," Rizzolo said gently.

"Huh? Oh . . . yeah . . . sure," she said. She changed gum-chewing rhythm and dialed a single digit on the phone to use it as an intercom. She offered a half-smile at Rizzolo as the phone grunted metallically in her ear.

"Doctor LaFontaine?" she asked needlessly when her call was answered. "There's a policeman here to see you."

"Sheriff," Rizzolo corrected quickly.

"Sheriff, I mean, Doctor." She replaced the phone quickly. "He'll be right out," she explained.

Rizzolo nodded at the girl and flipped his I.D. closed. He kept it in his hand, ready to show to Dr. LaFontaine as soon as the opportunity presented itself. He didn't have long to wait. A dark brown door to the left of the receptionist's desk opened rather quickly and a tall, youngish-looking man dressed in a long white coat stepped out. He extended a hand in Rizzolo's general direction. He wore a film badge radiation detector on his lapel and his last name was printed across the front of it.

"I'm Bruce LaFontaine," he said spiritedly, emphasizing the "I" more than was necessary. "How can I help you?" His voice was just crisp enough to identify him as British-born.

"Captain Rizzolo, sheriff's department."

During the firm handshake that followed, each man tested the other's character in the ageless fashion. Without loosening his grip, Dr. LaFontaine slipped his other hand around Rizzolo's shoulder and moved him gently toward the still opened door to his office.

"I believe I spoke with a detective from your department yesterday," LaFontaine said as he closed the door. With a gracious sweep of his hand, he offered Rizzolo a leather chair in front of his neat desk.

"Right. I read his report. I just wanted to meet you and run a few additional questions by you, Dr. LaFontaine. Just routine. Just routine."

The radiologist had moved to his chair behind the desk, and just prior to sitting down he arranged his starched white coat to minimize wrinkles. Rizzolo slumped into his chair as if he had been boiled in his suit and then dumped suddenly out of a bucket.

"That was a terrible thing about poor Bill Trumbull," LaFontaine said softly. "I don't believe it even yet."

"Oh? Why's that, Doctor?" Rizzolo arched his eyebrows to encourage an answer.

"Oh, I don't know, Lieutenant—"

"Captain."

"Captain. Excuse me. I don't know. It just doesn't seem to fit a chap like Bill Trumbull, that's all. I mean, getting kidnapped and thrown into some sand pit, or whatever." Doctor LaFontaine was shaking his head slowly as he spoke and from the look on his face, one would think that he had just tasted something very unappetizing.

"Why do you say 'kidnapped'?" Rizzolo probed. He slid the nail of his left pinky sideways into the small space between his two lower middle teeth.

"Well, that's what I gathered from the newspaper account of the whole affair this morning. Sounded rather like he was forced to draw out his money from the bank and then was robbed out there in the pits. Horrible." He shuddered eloquently with his shoulders.

"But you don't buy that?"

"The *Tribune*?" LaFontaine looked quizzical.

"No, the story. I mean, you doubt that that's what really happened?"

"Well, I really don't *know* what happened at all, Inspector, you see."

"Captain, Doctor."

"Captain. Yes. Excuse me. I mean I really can't say just what may have in fact transpired out there between those two."

"What two?" Rizzolo's attention suddenly increased.

"Trumbull and the murderer, of course. That two," LaFontaine sounded as if the answer were insultingly obvious.

"Not three? Or four?" Rizzolo nudged.

LaFontaine rotated his eyes toward the ceiling. "Well, you know what I mean, Captain." He flopped his hand in the air to dismiss the distinctions that Rizzolo had called his attention to. "I mean, Bill Trumbull was not a troublesome man, you understand, but no one would be able to just walk into his office at the hospital, drag him out, make him go to the bank, withdraw all his money, and then do him in at some rock pit without one hell of a struggle somewhere along the line. That's just the way he was." LaFontaine finished his sentence with a shrug and his shoulders remained in the air, almost touching his ear lobes. That, and his equally Gallic facial expression contrasted markedly with his fading British accent and manner.

"Then how do you think the whole thing happened, Dr. LaFontaine?" Rizzolo's expression promised that he'd be receptive to just about anything.

"Oh, Lord, I don't know," LaFontaine began, looking at the ceiling and pursing his lips. "Maybe he just bugged out."

"Bugged out?"

"Yes. You know. Packed the whole thing up. Went over the hill, don't you see."

"And why do you think he would do something like that?"

"Well, we all get fed up with our lot, sooner or later, don't we, Captain?" LaFontaine made it sound as normal as apple pie. Rizzolo caught himself nodding in agreement.

"And one day we just say 'the hell with it all,' and hop the next plane to Kenya, or someplace," the doctor continued.

"Why Kenya? Did Dr. Trumbull know somebody in Kenya?" Rizzolo's brain was scanning stored information at an incredible rate, trying to find any mention of Kenya in the Trumbull case. No Kenya data was retrieved from his memory bank.

"I don't mean, Kenya like *Kenya*, Captain, I mean Kenya like in someplace else! Someplace to get away to. Could be Miami Beach, I suppose, but I would doubt it."

"Why do you doubt it?"

"Because Bill Trumbull used to tell everyone how much he hated Miami Beach. Too hot. Too expensive. Too many Jews. Too many Cubans. I doubt he went to Miami Beach." LaFontaine shook his head.

"But you're convinced that he wasn't killed?" Rizzolo was secretly overjoyed to hear another person express an idea that had been bothering him ever since the frogmen failed to produce Trumbull's body.

"Not exactly 'convinced.' More like a haunting suspicion," the doctor said.

"That's interesting," Rizzolo said. "How well did you know his wife, Agnes Trumbull?" Rizzolo was convinced that responses to that kind of question were more genuine when no preparation was allowed. He had hoped that the doctor might be caught off guard.

"Agnes? Agnes and I have been friends for quite some time." LaFontaine did not appear upended by the question. "We all were. Bill and Agnes and my wife Mary and myself."

"There was never anything—excuse me, Doctor, I do not mean to be offensive, but you understand my position in this case."

"Of course."

"There was never anything more between you and Mrs. Trumbull?" Rizzolo's emphasis on "Mrs." made the suggestion sound quite indecent.

"No, never. Agnes and I were merely good friends, that's all."

Rizzolo watched LaFontaine's hands for any small involuntary movement that would suggest that he was not comfortable with his own answers. He detected no nervousness.

"And how about Dr. Trumbull and your wife? Was there ever anything there that made you suspicious of anything at all?" Rizzolo had raised the issue of infidelity and there was no sense in backing away from it at that point. He continued to study LaFontaine closely as he screened the reply.

"Nothing at all, Captain. Bill Trumbull was never particularly fond of my wife anyway. He always thought she was a little stupid, I think. And, frankly, I suppose he was right. In any event, I consider the possibility of an affair between my wife and Bill Trumbull to be quite remote. Quite remote indeed."

"Did you ever suspect Dr. Trumbull of fooling around with anyone else?" Rizzolo tried to make his questions sound as casual as possible, but he was sure that they were hitting like bombshells, despite LaFontaine's calm demeanor.

"I don't think he really did, no."

"Not at all?" Rizzolo frowned slightly.

"Oh, maybe a flirtation or two with a nurse. You know. But nothing serious about it."

"Nurses like who?"

Dr. LaFontaine felt a sudden urge to say "like whom" but repressed it. "Oh, nobody in particular. I mean, I can't supply you with a list of names. There just wasn't anyone in particular with whom I would link up Bill Trumbull. Except—" He paused to evaluate his idea.

"Except who?"

"Oh, it's really nothing," LaFontaine chuckled pleasantly.

"No, go on. You were going to suggest someone?" Rizzolo felt the hair on the back of his neck tingle slightly. He enjoyed the excitement of a new lead in a homicide case.

"Well, Bill Trumbull had a passing interest in a lady that we all knew. But I don't think it ever amounted to anything. A drink or two. Saw each other at parties. That sort of thing. Nothing serious about it at all."

"One of the nurses?" Rizzolo slipped his small notebook out of his inside pocket and prepared to enter a name.

"Oh, no, no. Not one of the nurses," the doctor chuckled. "As a matter of fact, she is a lawyer."

"A lady lawyer?" Rizzolo registered immediate astonishment and disappointment. A female lawyer was too far from the barefoot-in-summer, pregnant-in-winter type of woman he felt comfortable with.

"And a pretty good one, too, from what I hear."

"They'll be into everything before too long," Rizzolo said wearily.

"They haven't done too badly in medicine," LaFontaine taunted. He pronounced "medicine" in two syllables, like a good Britisher.

Rizzolo nodded his head. "We've had a couple of female deputies that weren't too bad either. Guess it will just take some getting used to. But, tell me about your lady lawyer friend."

"Name's Martha Holland. Practices downtown in one of the bank buildings. Member of a substantial general law firm, I understand, but tends to specialize in domestic relations—family problems, that sort of thing."

"Like what, exactly?"

"Like your divorces, your adoptions, your general custody problems. You know, domestic tranquillity, and all that rot?"

"But she knows Bill Trumbull? Excuse me. I mean Dr. Trumbull."

"Quite all right, Inspector. We all have first names." Though in fact, LaFontaine never permitted anyone other than close friends and fellow physicians to call him by his.

"Thank you," the captain said without offering his own first name. His father had selected one so Italian that he preferred to use only his initials, E. J.

"I guess she saw Bill Trumbull from time to time, but I really doubt that they had anything serious going on between them." He lowered his eyes at the sheriff's department captain. "If you know what I mean."

Rizzolo nodded his head somberly. "I think I do, Doctor," he said. "Where did you say her office was located?"

"Well, she should be in her office, but I'm not sure, actually."

"Oh?"

"You see, I found her buying a fairly large quantity of staples and sailing tack, and I rather suspect that she might have taken off on a short voyage. She's something of a sailor, you might say."

"No, I didn't know that." Rizzolo caught himself picking up the doctor's British speech rhythms.

"Quite. Tampa Yacht Club, the Southern Offshore Racing Conference, or whatever they call it. That kind of thing." He paused to see that Rizzolo was following. "She sometimes sails off for days and days."

"Where does she park her boat?" Rizzolo had flipped to a new page in his spiral notebook.

"I believe the verb is 'moor,' Inspector."

"Who?"

"Sailors. One doesn't *park* a boat, but *moor* it. In a mooring, as it were. Martha Holland *moors* her boat somewhere over near Clearwater. I'm sure her office would fill you in if you properly identify yourself."

"Right, Doctor," Rizzolo said, rising from his chair and obviously ending the conversation. "I'll show her secretary my badge over the phone."

"Splendid. I'm sure that would do the trick." He assisted the homicide captain to the door. "If there is anything else that I can do for you—anything at all—please don't hesitate to call."

Rizzolo was sure that the doctor would instruct his secretary to be anything *but* accommodating to the sheriff's representatives in the future. Rizzolo shook the radiologist's hand and walked out of the office with a determined pace.

"Odd," LaFontaine mused softly, after the captain had left.

"Pardon me, Doctor?" his receptionist asked, snapping her gum.

"Oh, nothing," he said quickly. "But, you really cannot show someone a badge over a phone."

Chapter Nine

By FIRST GRAY LIGHT, Bill Trumbull had stumbled and crawled his way through the thick mangrove swamp and found a tiny island with an even smaller beach. The night swim from the boat had washed the blood from his pants, but the salt water had given him an unpleasant sticky feeling that urged him to take off his clothes as soon as possible. At sunrise, he stood naked, hanging his wet clothes on the sea-grape bushes that grew freely along the inland edge of the sandy shore.

The $17,000 was equally wet. Trumbull calculated that it would have taken two bushels of clothespins or a ton and a half of small rocks to hold the money down on the sand. As neither was available, he divided the bills into soggy stacks and laid a large piece of driftwood across them to keep them from blowing away if a breeze came up. Due to the hour, there was little danger of any wind, for a while.

He took the .38 out of his pants pocket and inspected it carefully. His knowledge of firearms was so limited that he was not sure if the unused cartridges would fire after the swim ashore.

The sight of the gun reminded him of Martha's dead body lying submerged in the cabin of the sailboat. He looked out toward the bay, but his view of the sailboat was blocked by the mangroves.

He punched the display button on his digital wristwatch, but got no response. With a sudden surge of frustration and disgust, he pulled the watch from his arm and threw it into the bay. A brown pelican, previously uninterested in the doctor's activity, flapped his wings frantically, and leaped into the air to escape the airborne timepiece. She glided away in a long, curving dive that allowed her to skim over the surface of the water at a consistent height of three inches. Bill Trumbull watched the bird and wondered why she never ground-looped or simply crashed into the water. Even pelicans, he reasoned, had to miscalculate sometimes.

Somewhere, not far away, he heard the purr of a small outboard motor and correctly imagined a fisherman, feeling his way around the shallow mangroves in search of an unsuspecting fish. It was impossible to calculate the distance to the outboard because the sound came and went among the small mangroves. Trumbull was nervous about the fisherman discovering him, and the thought of someone suddenly coming around the bend and finding him naked on the tiny uninhabited beach almost made him panic. He was without fishing gear, boat, snorkle, or other sporting equipment to legitimize his presence, and the money spread out on the beach made him ridiculous as well as suspicious.

He waited nervously until the sound of the motor disappeared. Trumbull shook his still-damp clothes and put them on. The pants felt cold against his legs and the wet shirt clung to his back, aggravating the mosquito bites that had come just before sunrise. The water in the bay was no longer at dead calm; the light breeze was a mute greeting to a new day. The morning littorals were beginning to flow across the surface of the land and out onto the bay, as the sun made its way west.

He stuffed the money back into his damp shirt and felt it stick to his skin like something dead. He put the .38 in his belt, but felt insecure about it. He remembered that as an intern he had seen a hunter who had developed gangrene of the right leg when he had shot himself accidentally while hopping a fence in pursuit of a deer. Trumbull put the gun in his pants pocket and felt safer about it, although he was not sure why.

The struggle inland cost him a tear in his pants and a painful scratch on his left leg. The brackish water stung the scratch when he was forced to wade from the island side of his mangrove to the mainland. The mud stuck to his feet, and tiny marine insects scurried away to avoid the footsteps of this unknown giant intruding upon their tranquil backwash home.

Trumbull was not sure what he would do when he finally came across another living human being. He hoped that it would be a peaceful encounter and that the whole countryside was not already crawling with deputies in search of him if they had not bought the murder; or in search of his killer if they had. Guilt gnawed at him and made him feel like the object of a manhunt. He made a conscious effort to convince his anxious brain that a search would be unlikely, even though he had certainly been missed at the hospital by this time. He was confident that even if the teller at the bank had reported his unusual behavior during the withdrawal, the sheriff would be reluctant to launch a full-scale search until his car was discovered at the phosphate pits. He knew that there was still a good chance that the T-bird remained hidden. Trumbull tried to convince himself that many cars remained abandoned for months before the law did anything about them. He mumblingly reminded himself about the elderly couple from Michigan who had accidentally driven their car into a deep roadside canal somewhere south of Lake Okeechobee and who had remained undiscovered until a grumbling fisherman hooked the tender several years later. The sound of his own voice helped him believe that the scene of his own faked death might still remain hidden.

The ground became firmer beneath the pathologist's feet and mangrove gave way to palmetto. Occasional palm trees offered shade and saw grass grabbed at his pants as he stumbled inland. Sand spurs stuck to his sneakers and pricked his skin, increasing the aggravating itch on his legs and ankles.

He came upon an ancient Indian shell mound and paused to rest at the top of it. As he lay there, looking up into the bright sky as he panted for breath, he visualized the hundreds of happy Indians who had gathered to consume these thousands of oysters, and to throw their empty shells on this huge calcified monument to their dietary habits. Some of these mounds had been carted away by the white settlers to build roads before they were recognized as natural historical monuments to the existence of the Caloosas and the other tribes, long since driven away and forgotten by the invaders.

In a flash of fatigue and fantasy, he saw a fat Indian sitting beside a campfire, being served a dozen oysters on the half shell by a beautiful naked girl. In his dream, the oysters were arranged on a Budweiser tray filled with cracked ice.

He must have dozed a few minutes, because suddenly there was a noisy blue-fly above his head, whining to his brothers about his discovery of a sweating, stinking man on an oyster-shell mound. Trumbull was not able to see the fly in the morning glare, but he monitored the noise with precision, hoping to be able to deliver a fatal slap the moment the insect landed on his skin.

Then there was a familiar but unexpected sound that made his eyes widen and his ears reorient themselves. Somewhere farther inland—a mile or less, he calculated—a large truck shifted gears and rumbled onto a highway. Trumbull was not familiar with the farm roads in that part of the county, known generally as the East Bay.

He resumed his inland trek. Around a small clump of palmetto, the ground became still firmer, and the little noises of man began to intrude on the insect and bird calls with greater regularity: a hammer knocking on a wooden wall; a metal tool falling on a concrete floor; human voices, indistinct but nonetheless real. Bill Trumbull approached the noises cautiously, almost afraid to confront people again.

After another hundred yards of picking through the low palmetto, a single building came into view. It seemed to be next to a narrow, unused road, and it advertised itself as a combination gas station and bait store. The two ancient gas pumps offered a mongrel brand that only the local farmers in pickup trucks and absolutely desperate travelers would put in their tanks. There were small stacks of empty oil cans between the pumps, and the roof of the station protruded a few feet from the front of the building, providing a small patch of shade for the almost motionless proprietor and his sleeping dog.

There were no sheriff's cars in sight anywhere. The road in front of the small station was not the main highway to Tampa, as Trumbull had incorrectly assumed from the first noises that he had heard, but only a narrow county road, now virtually abandoned since the construction of a larger bypass a few miles away.

As Bill Trumbull approached, the man slowly lifted his head to look up at him, but the dog slept on. The man was old, and the dog seemed older still. Inside the garage, a young man dropped his wrench on the concrete floor again and paused to take a look at the stranger.

"Mornin'," Bill Trumbull said to the old man. The dog opened one eye. The old man nodded silently and widened both eyes.

Trumbull wiped his brow with the back of his hand and emitted a loud breath. "Gettin' hot," he said.

The old man nodded again and the dog closed the eye. "Been fishin'?" the old man asked.

"Yep, and I got lost in the mangrove." Trumbull threw his head toward the bay.

"Ain't hard to do." The old man looked at the pathologist and surveyed his wrinkled clothes suspiciously. "Where's your boat at?"

"Somewheres out there in the mangrove. Ran out of gas. I'll pick it up later when I come back with the car." Trumbull wondered if he was talking too fast. He was not able to tell from the old man's implacable expression whether or not he was buying any of the story. "Got a phone?"

"Inside." The old man motioned toward the station door. "Takes two nickels. The dime slot is gummed up."

Trumbull felt for the coins in his pocket and knew instantly that there were none. He would have to change a wet dollar bill from inside his shirt, and he wasn't sure what the old man's reaction would be to the soggy money, or the unusual hiding place.

He hesitated further as he thought of the phone call to Agnes. He knew that his escape plan had been blown and that he needed a way back. There was no other way to start but with Agnes. He was sure of that now.

The old man watched him as he deliberated about the call, and wondered if the stranger was the crab-trap robber that he had been looking for. Strangers had a way of becoming the crab-trap robber for the old man, the longer he looked at them. The old man was wrinkled and bleached from a lifetime of overexposure to the Florida sun. The skin around his lips was perpetually cracked, and there were depigmented areas on the backs of both arms. Farmers who knew him and his crazy ways thought that his brain had been baked by the sun too.

That was probably why every stranger became the crab-trap robber for the old man. Over the years, the number of crabs that the traps had produced had declined as the shellfish were depleted and the pollution of the water increased. But the old man saw the drop in the crab catch as the work of the elusive crab-trap robber who came in silently and stole the crabs before the old man or his son could get there in the johnboat. Sometimes he found his floats damaged and the lines cut. He saw this too as the work of the crab-trap robber rather than the result of the steadily growing number of powerboats that churned up the bay every weekend.

He squinted at Bill Trumbull and tried to size him up. He certainly looked like the crab-trap robber, the old man concluded, although no suspect had ever been seen at any of his traps.

Trumbull sensed the careful appraisal and feared that a sheriff's bulletin had alerted the old man and his son to be on the lookout for him. He didn't know that the sheriff hardly ever came by to talk to the old man, or that the son had been arrested many times for drunkenness and disorderly conduct in Ruskin area bars, and therefore avoided all cops. His physician's brain had not yet registered that the old man was a psychotic and that his son was a mental defective.

"Where'd you put in?" the old man asked suddenly. That part of the backwash was nothing more than a tangle of mangrove, sandbars, swamp, and shell mounds that made boat launching almost impossible. The old man's bait house was on the only canal to the bay navigable by a small boat. He knew that the pathologist had not put in at his place that day.

"Down the bay, a ways," Trumbull said casually.
"Nearer to Bradenton." He did not feel comfortable in
that lie. He was not sure how far away Bradenton was.

The old man continued his curious examination of
the stranger. "Drive in there?" he asked suspiciously.

"Left the car and trailer," Trumbull added as con-
vincingly as he could. He felt increasingly anxious as he
watched the old man shoot a glance at his son in the
garage. The son returned the look in an obvious way.

"What's the name of this place, anyway?" Trumbull
asked, hoping to break in on the silent exchange between these two men.

"McCraw's. Bait, gas, and beer," the old man supplied. He turned his gaze away from his son and back
to Trumbull. "Been here for forty-two years. Sellin' bait
and crabbin'."

"How far south of route sixty are we?" Trumbull
asked.

"Depends how you go. Twenty-four and three-tenths,
one way. Little longer the other," the old man said
stiffly. He disliked giving information, as a matter of
principle.

Trumbull glanced down at his damp, wrinkled pants
and counted nine sand spurs around the cuff of the left
leg. The money in his shirt made him look pregnant.
He knew the old man's curiosity was growing with
every minute. He had to invent a way to get away from
this place.

"Anybody come by here that a fella could hitch a
ride with?" he asked pleasantly.

"Trucks, mostly," the son said dully. He had come
from the garage and stood just behind the pathologist.
His reply startled Bill Trumbull and he jumped.

"Kinda nervous, ain't ya?" the old man asked.

"He startled me, that's all."

"How come you walked up here out of the mangrove?" the old man asked again.

"I told you. I got lost. I was fishing. I ran out of gas." Trumbull swept his open palm toward the mangrove and the bay beyond it, as if to tell the old crabman where it was.

"You want to buy some gas?" the son asked.

"Well, not exactly," Trumbull said. "I need a ride to Tampa and I'll come back later for my boat. I want to go get my car and trailer first." He was not sure that he was making sense, but he felt more secure when he kept talking.

"How you going to get your trailer down through the mangrove?" the old man asked.

"Maybe I could paddle it up the canal you got over there by your dock." He motioned toward the bait dock on the narrow canal that had been dug over the years by a branch of the Alafia River as it wandered toward the bay. Tipped to one side as it lay against the muddy bank, the old man's johnboat was tied to the dock.

"You'd have to wait for the tide," the old man said knowingly. "They's not enough water to get by the sandbars now." He glanced at the sun and made an unannounced but expert calculation of the next tide.

"Maybe there'll be enough water when I get back with the trailer," Trumbull offered hopefully. The old man seemed unconvinced, and Trumbull was not sure why. There was some barrier to communication between him and this old man, and while he could sense it clearly now, he was unable to understand it. Trumbull did not know that he had become the crab-trap robber.

"You see any crab traps out there where your boat ran out of gas?" the old man asked.

"Hush up, Pa," the son said.

"I only asked him if he *saw* any crab traps out there where he says he ran out of gas."

"No sir, I didn't," Trumbull said blandly. He didn't know that there were hundreds of crab traps in the shallow waters of the bay, near the place where he scuttled Martha Holland's sailboat. He also didn't know that his denial was ridiculous.

"Didn't see a one?" the old man persisted.

"No." Trumbull felt uneasy with his answer.

The old man grinned at his son. "How do you figure that, son? A man comes up through the mangrove and palmetto and says his boat run out of gas, and then says he don't see even one crab trap. Make sense to you?" He urged a reply from his son by shaking his head.

"Sure don't, Pa," the son said. He moved toward the garage bench and picked up a tire wrench. The son slapped the tool into his palm in a threatening way as he returned.

"Why should I care about crab traps?" Trumbull asked. "I'm only interested in fishing. Redfish, mostly." He was not confident that his lies were convincing. He was not an experienced fisherman, and he was afraid that it was beginning to show. He had, in fact, never fished for redfish, but he had heard another of the doctors talking about going out for them somewhere around this part of the bay.

"Redfish, eh?" the old man said. "What do you use for bait?"

"Oh, the usual stuff." Trumbull smiled weakly.

"Like what?"

"Worms?"

"Mister, you're lyin' to me," the old man said. "And I know who you really are. Crab-trap robber!" He motioned toward Bill Trumbull with his arthritic hand and his son quickly responded by grabbing the pathologist's arm with one hand and raising the tire wrench over his head with the other.

The old man reached out and grabbed the front of Trumbull's shirt, as if to wring the truth from him. He gave the shirt a strong twist and two buttons popped off, exposing the soggy money underneath.

"What the hell?" the old man asked. Some of the

money fell to the ground. "This guy's got a shirtful of money!"

"From sellin' our crabs!" the son exclaimed.

"Yes sir. That's what it is," the old man agreed. He grabbed a handful of the money from inside the doctor's shirt and waved it around in his fist. "We done caught ourself the crab-trap robber this time, for sure. And this here is the money he got from sellin' our crabs to them Italians down the road." To the old man, this conclusion was perfectly logical. Justice, at last, was to prevail. The old man was sure of that.

"No, wait, I—" Trumbull protested. His head filled with tiny falling stars and a fragment of an old memory raced across a corner of his mind before all went black.

The old man's son had brought the tire tool across the pathologist's head, opening the scalp and rendering him unconscious.

The old man took the money from Trumbull's shirt and piled it clumsily in an empty oil-can box, then helped his son drag the doctor into a small shed behind the garage. They tied the pathologist's feet with a small length of rope and gagged him with his own damp shirt. The son rolled Trumbull over to tie his hands and felt the irregular, hard lump of the .38 in the pants pocket. He reached into the pocket with his greasy hand.

"He's got a gun, Pa!"

"I knowed it. I just knowed it." The old man was triumphant because they had captured such a dangerous man. "We got us the crab-trap robber at last, son." He danced a few steps in spite of his arthritic knees.

The son gave the gun to his father and the old man fumbled the unfamiliar object open. He squinted at the cartridges in the cylinder.

"He's done shot it once," he announced.

"At what, Pa?"

"You can't tell at what, you damned idiot. You can only tell *if* he shot it. Don't you know nothin'?" The old man picked at the spent cartridge with his stubby fingers, but it would not come out of the cylinder. Slightly frustrated, he snapped the cylinder shut and stuck the gun in his belt. "Tie him good, boy. I got plans for him."

The old man returned to the gas station and began to count the money. The tire tool lay on the floor of the garage. Blood and hair were smeared on one end of it. It looked about the same as the tire iron that Trumbull had left near the phosphate pit.

Chapter Ten

LIEUTENANT NELSON BRAX was not very happy in the
Coast Guard. He had originally joined because his college deferment was about to expire and no Navy ap-
pointments were available that year. His college fantasies had been filled with great sea battles, but he had
persuaded himself that a two-year hitch on board a
swift cutter out of a busy, northeastern seaport wouldn't
be too bad as a substitute. It would certainly beat
marching around in the Georgia dust with other
draftees of the U.S.

Brax had been assigned to Tampa and then to the
Federal Building downtown. There was a picture of a
fast cutter on his office wall, trading small-arms fire on
the Mekong River with some unseen enemy on the
shore. That was all that remained of Brax's maritime
fantasies; not even Tampa Bay was visible from the
window of his office.

His desk phone blinked and was answered with the
least possible interest as he continued to check off
routine items on an inventory form from the G.S.A. in
Washington.

"Lieutenant Brax," he said flatly.

"Lieutenant, there is a guy on the phone who wants
to report a sunken sailboat," the civilian secretary said.

"Is it in the waterway, or—oh, hell. I'll talk to him." He clicked on to the outside line. "This is Lieutenant Nelson Brax, United States Coast Guard. May I help you, sir?" He adjusted his tie in deference to the unknown caller.

"Yes, sir. This is Harvey Kernway? And I want to report a sailboat that is sunk out there in the bay."

"Yes, sir. How do you spell your name?" Lieutenant Brax had already begun to fill in Coast Guard form, CN-1081-5, preparing the first, or title page in triplicate, by using two badly worn one-third-size sheets of blue government issue carbon paper.

Harvey Kernway spelled his name twice and then supplied his home address, zip code, phone number, and area code. It was the area code for Tampa and all of west Florida, but CN-1081-5 had a box marked "area code" and Lieutenant Brax was a thorough Coast Guard officer.

"And I want to find out about salvage rights," Kernway said quickly.

"About what, sir?" Lieutenant Brax asked sleepily.

"About salvage rights. I mean, I found it, and I want to find out how I can go about claiming it. I mean, nobody else has called in first, have they?"

"Called in?"

"Y'know. To report this sunken sailboat. I mean, it's finder's keepers, isn't it?"

"Well, Mr. Kernway, there may be some salvage rights *if* this sailboat is actually abandoned by its rightful owner or owners, and *if* there has not been a prior claim made on the discovery of the wreck." Silently, Lieutenant Brax wondered where, in the Tampa Federal Building, he would be able to find a Coast Guard law book that would explain all of this to him before it got out of hand. So far, he was flying by the seat of his pants and wasn't sure of what the law on salvage was. He had hopes that the rescue station in St. Petersburg might know more about this area of maritime law.

"But you said that nobody else had called in," Kernway argued.

"In fact, Mr. Kernway, no one else *has* called in to report this wreck, but, in fact, Mr. Kernway, I don't believe that it would be necessary for anyone to actually notify the United States Coast Guard to actually claim an abandoned vessel. In fact, Mr. Kernway, I *believe* that all that a finder would have to do, would be to physically and actually claim the vessel before someone else, in fact, actually claimed it." Lieutenant Brax wondered if any of the things he was telling Kernway were true. They sounded good to Brax, at least.

"Oh, Lord. You mean, I should have stayed out there and tied my Boston Whaler to the mast, or something?"

"Possibly. In fact, Mr. Kernway, I'm not actually familiar with the precise mechanism by which a finder of an abandoned vessel actually makes his claim and—"

"But how would I get to shore, if I was still tied to the mast? I mean, would I have to stay out there, tied to the sailboat, to make my claim on her good?"

"I don't believe, Mr. Kernway, that I can, in fact, advise you on that precise point. But, I would like to know just where this wreck actually lies. Would you be good enough to tell me the exact location, sir?" Lieutenant Brax kept the phone at his ear as he swiveled around to face the wall charts of Tampa Bay. The charts had been printed in two parts that someone in the Coast Guard Office had clumsily taped together, making the middle part of the bay a no-man's-land of federal wall, instead of water and spoil islands.

"Well, are you guys going to go out there and get it, or what? I mean, if I tell you where it is sunk, how will I get to keep it? I mean, if it turns out that it is really abandoned, and if it turns out that I'm the first one to find it and lay claim to it, then how do I get to keep it?" Kernway was obviously worried.

"The United States Coast Guard is primarily interested in maritime safety and the saving of lives, in cases

like these. In fact, Mr. Kernway, we may not be actually interested in the ownership of the sailboat at all, if
it is not a threat to navigation or if there is no evidence
of any lives on board being in imminent danger."

"Well, there ain't nobody on board, if that's what you
mean."

"Oh? How do you know, Mr. Kernway?"

"Because all that's stickin' up out of the water is the
upper part of the mast, y'know what I mean?"

"The mast?"

"Yeah. Where the sails go up. You can see the rest of
the boat and all like that, if you pull up close to the
mast and look down in the water. Y'know what I
mean?"

"In fact, Mr. Kernway, you can see the boat actually
under the water?"

"Yeah. You can see the whole thing, clear as day.
Decks, cockpit, the whole works. And, there ain't nobody down there walkin' around on her."

"But where, in fact, is this sunken vessel located, Mr.
Kernway?"

"Well, OK. You know where the outlet is from the
Bahia Beach Marina? By the motel?" Kernway hoped
for a sign that Lieutenant Brax was following him.

Lieutenant Brax squinted at his wall charts. "OK, I've
got the area. Bahia Beach." He pointed at the spot with
his finger.

"OK, you run south of there about a couple of miles,
and then head over toward some mangrove near the
shore. Got it?"

"I see some mangrove areas here on the chart south
of Bahia Beach, Mr. Kernway. Is that where you
mean?"

"Yeah. Right south of there."

"But, there are no navigational routes through there,
Mr. Kernway. In fact, the area that you have desig-
nated is well away from the navigational channels."

"Yeah. I guess that's right. The channel markers are

way out from there. That's where I was fishing. Out by the channel markers. That's how I come to see this sailboat mast stickin' up out of the water. Right out of the water! I mean, I didn't know it was a sailboat mast at first, y'know, but I couldn't figure what it was. So, I pulled up my line and ran over there to give it a look-see, y'know what I mean? I mean, nothin' was biting out there, anyway, and—"

"Mr. Kernway—I'll be glad to notify the United States Coast Guard station at St. Petersburg, Florida, and ask them to dispatch a rescue vessel if you are suggesting that there may be survivors in the area, but—"

"Naw, naw. It don't look like nothin' like that. Nothin' like that at all. I mean, this is just a sunk sailboat. And all I want to do is claim it, if I can. Y'know what I mean?"

"The United States Coast Guard will offer aid to *any* vessel in distress, Mr. Kernway. Any vessel at all. In fact—"

"Well, yeah. OK, Lieutenant. Thanks a lot. I'll work on this some other way. Y'know what I mean?"

"Yes, sir, Mr. Kernway. Thank you for calling this to the attention of the Coast Guard. I've made a note of your name and your reported sighting. In fact, you can be sure that the matter will be fully investigated."

"Yeah. Well, OK, Lieutenant." Harvey Kernway had the impression that he was back in the Army and that he was trying to explain the obvious to one of the clerk-sergeants in the post commander's office. He hadn't been successful then, either. "Give me a call or somethin' if you find out what I should do about claimin' that sail-boat, OK?"

"We have your name and phone number right here. In fact, Mr. Kernway, the United States Coast Guard will be—"

"Yeah. OK, Lieutenant, I'll get back to you. Thanks for your time." Harvey Kernway put the phone down and felt relieved that he was no longer talking with Lieutenant Brax.

He threw his eyes toward the ceiling of his bedroom and sighed deeply.

"One more time," he said aloud, to no one. Kernway flipped open the front of the phone book and dialed the sheriff's office.

Chapter Eleven

E. J. RIZZOLO PARKED his car behind the county medical examiner's office. The space was marked INVESTIGATORS ONLY, but the captain of detectives was confident that no one would challenge him. Most of the M.E. investigators were retread detectives anyway. It was a good slot for a plainclothes cop who had put in his twenty. The job was more or less the same except that, instead of looking for suspects, he only had to search for the next of kin. At least, nobody ever shot at an investigator from the medical examiner's office. That might have been why the job was so popular. The M.E.'s office usually ran a waiting list of applicants.

The medical examiner's office was located in a new, one-story building that housed a morgue, dissection room, laboratories, and offices. In the old days, the medical examiner had been any one of the pathologists who might be on call at Tampa General. This gave the local police no system to work with. The result was hit-or-miss and generally unsatisfactory to everyone but the pathologists. They saw it as an economic shot in the arm for routine examinations that no one was particularly interested in performing, except for extra pay.

But with the arrival of Martin Flood, M.D., the community suddenly gained a well-trained, board-certified, forensic pathologist. Some of the older police officials resisted the changes that he brought with him from his training at the Medical-Legal Institute in Dallas, and all of the pathologists at Tampa General, whom he replaced, considered him a meddling intruder. He weathered all of these detractors and kept his professional sights set on the development of a new medical examiner's office for the area. After five years of dogged persistence, his efforts paid off, and the new office was opened.

Rizzolo had never been at odds with Dr. Flood over any of the cases they had collaborated on. Each had considered the other as a pro from the very beginning, and neither of them was willing to compromise his respective high standards of law enforcement and forensic science to pay lip service to an outdated departmental rule or to acquiesce to some inadequate pathological procedure. As a result, the two men became friends as well as professional colleagues.

Martin Flood, M.D., came to Tampa by way of a B.A. in liberal arts from Georgetown, an M.D. from Creighton, and a four-year pathology residency at Jackson Memorial Hospital in Miami. He took a fifth year at the M.L.I. in Dallas and was quickly certified in anatomic, clinical, and forensic pathology by the American Board. After certification, he had spent two years at the Armed Forces Institute of Pathology in Washington, D.C., getting rid of his service obligation, and feasting on the wealth of cases that were submitted from every branch of the military. But, as Martin Flood had observed when his two-year hitch was up, the A.F.I.P. was a great place to visit, but no one would want to live there.

Captain Rizzolo opened the front door of the medical examiner's office and walked in like he was part owner of the place. If he wasn't really part owner, he could rightfully claim the title of co-founder. His politicking among high police officials had been of great value in establishing a separate medical examiner's office, a fact which did nothing to weaken his close relationship with Martin Flood.

"Is your boss in, Amy?" he aked the blonde receptionist.

"Un-huh. You can go right in, Captain." She glanced at the drug salesman who had been waiting in the reception area for almost an hour, hoping to be able to demonstrate a new and somewhat self-serving method by which his product could be detected in blood. Doctor Flood had written a paper reporting the frequency of overdoses among users of this particular tranquilizer, and the company treated him with kid gloves. After that, whenever they developed a new test for this suburban poison, someone from the home office lab would be dispatched to Tampa to show it to Flood, hoping that he would approve. He seldom did, because it seldom worked.

Rizzolo went out of the reception room and walked quickly down the long corridor to the dissection room. At this time of day, there was little use looking for Dr. Flood in his office. He would be in the dissection room, doing an autopsy on some unexplained death, or supervising one of the forensic pathology residents from the medical school. He took up to three of them a year, for eleven months of what he called "real pathology." At the end of the year, all of them agreed with his characterization of the course.

The door to the dissection room had a spring lock mechanism which opened from the inside. Rizzolo rang the bell and waited like the Avon lady for the door to be opened.

A Latin inscription on the door said, "We do not mock the dead, but seek only to understand." Whenever he was asked the meaning of the motto, Martin Flood would invent a new and invariably absurd translation, trusting that the questioner was not a Latin

scholar. The Latin scholars, he reasoned, could trans-
late it for themselves.

The door opened and a large, slightly stooped black
man smiled immediately at Captain Rizzolo.

"Hello, Jerry," Rizzolo said, offering his hand, but not
before he was sure that the chief morgue deiner was
not wearing a bloody rubber glove.

"Captain Rizzolo!" Jerry Washington announced,
loudly. "Our favorite sheriff."

"Let's not let the real sheriff hear you say that," Rizzolo said. "Where's your boss?"

"He's here. He's here." The assistant grinned and
shook the captain's hand wildly as they entered the
room together.

"Looks like one of you is running for office," Martin
Flood said across his autopsy. He was working on a
young white female.

"That's the best part about being a subordinate,
Marty. You don't have to run for the job."

"Why don't you get yourself appointed to something
by the governor, like me?" Dr. Flood bantered lightly.
He was dressed in a green surgical scrub shirt, and
wore a white, plastic apron over it. His hairy arms were
bare, but his hands were covered with thin surgeon's
gloves.

"The governor would not appoint me to a dog-catch-
ing committee," Rizzolo snorted. "I'm local-born and
Italian, remember? To be on one of his teams, you have
to be a WASP."

"But, his grandmother was Jewish," Flood said with
mock seriousness.

"He only remembers that in Miami Beach," Rizzolo
added, approaching the autopsy table. He quickly
scanned the young woman's broken body, then emitted
a low whistle.

"Motorcycle," Dr. Flood said.

"Christ! What'd she hit, a truck?"

"Nuh-uh. She and her boyfriend hit an Olds, making
a left in front of them. She got booted out in the lot."

"Dead on the spot?"

"Good as. The boyfriend's a vegetable in I.C.U. She got the red-light ride to St. Joe's, but there was nothing left to work on when they got there. Ruptured her aorta." The pathologist held up the fragmented end of the girl's torn aorta and wiggled it at Rizzolo.

"That's all?" Rizzolo asked testily.

"As a matter of fact, she also broke her neck, both legs, and a bunch of ribs. Her helmet apparently kept her from fracturing her skull."

"Big deal," Rizzolo said, shaking his head. "We make 'em wear helmets so that they can smash up everything else they've got."

"We either get the damned motorcycles off the road or we dress them all in suits of armor," Dr. Flood mused. He was not a great fan of motorcycles. He had once told a gathering of their manufacturers in Washington that the machine was inherently unsafe. The motorcycle manufacturers had been upset by his remarks, but as a two-year officer at the A.F.I.P., Flood had not felt particularly vulnerable when they complained to his boss.

Dr. Flood was about forty-five now. He was not as tall as he wanted to be as a boy, but the years had given him a chance to adjust. His hair was getting grayer, and lately he was wearing it longer than he ever thought he would. This was not a response to the current style as much as a testimonial to his personal neglect. He liked to wear blue suits, black, wing-tipped shoes, and button-down shirts with striped ties. Some of his friends told him that his clothes made him look like an F.B.I. agent, but he had observed that modern federal agents wore beards, sandals, jeans, and body bugs to record their interviews with the junkies, the two-bit marijuana dealers, and street people.

He had married a nurse during medical school, but she had been killed in a car crash before his graduation. The accident had hit him pretty hard, and to keep him from going to pieces altogether, the pathologist

who had examined her body never told him that she
was newly pregnant. No one was sure whether he
had ever found out about the double loss that one car
and one bus had dealt him when they collided on an
icy Omaha street. In any event, he had buried himself
in his work, and had launched out to find the cure for
everything that plagued mankind before he finally accepted the loss of his spouse.

On recovery, he found himself unwilling to surrender
totally to another female. As a result, he became known
as a good date for nurses—interesting, easy with his
money, and relatively safe.

"You seen the one from the sailboat yet, Marty?" Rizzolo watched the pathologist weigh the dead girl's liver
on a large scale that hung over the table.

"Eighteen hundred grams," Dr. Flood said over his
shoulder to Jerry Washington, and then cut the organ.
"Not yet. I thought I'd wait till you got over here.
What's the story on her, anyway?"

"Some guy calls in, and tells us that he found a sailboat sunk in the bay."

"Tampa Bay?" Jerry Washington asked, eager to be
a part of the conversation between the two men that he
admired most in the world.

"Yeah. Down by Bahia Beach. Anyway, this guy says
that he spotted the sailboat's mast sticking up out of
the water, when he was fishing."

"Can you connect him to the body?" the pathologist
asked. "I mean, was he returning to the scene of the
crime, or something corny like that?"

"No, no. Nothing like that, Marty. This guy is stupid
and clean. We checked him out. But, he calls in to the
office and tells our operator about the sailboat that he
found, and the girl on the switchboard gives him to
lost and found." Rizzolo laughed gently.

"Lost and found?" Flood said.

"Yeah. Who knows? Maybe she was right. We never
had a sunk sailboat reported before, so how can I fault

her for picking on the lost and found?" The captain
shrugged in answer to his own question and watched
the pathologist bisect the girl's left kidney.

"Is that normal?" Rizzolo asked.

"Yeah. Normal. See here?" Flood pointed to one side
of the sliced kidney in his hand. "This is where the
urine is made, and this is where it comes down, along
here, and this is where it goes out to get to the bladder.
Isn't that marvelous?"

"No shit," the detective said quietly.

"No, Captain, shit is made somewhere else." He
flipped the kidney into the plastic garbage bag that
lined his collecting bucket. Later, he would put all of
these organs, garbage bag and all, back into the body
and have Jerry Washington sew it up with a continuous
baseball stitch.

"Why didn't you tell him to call the Coast Guard?"
Jerry Washington asked.

"We did. But he said that he had already tried that
route. He said that he got some guy who gave him the
run-around because there weren't any survivors. Who
knows? Maybe the Coast Guard sicced him on us?"
Rizzolo seemed to wrestle with his own question.

"So what happened?" Dr. Flood asked, squinting at
an ovary.

"So, we sent the patrol boat out and took the guy
along to show us right where he meant."

"Lucky for you guys," Flood taunted. "Otherwise,
they'd still be driving around the bay in your under-
sized speedboat, looking for the mast sticking out of
the water."

Rizzolo looked pained. "Well, I'll admit that my
patrol crews do better on land, but you don't have to
nurse a grudge just because they gave you a rough ride
when we found that Chinese sailor that fell off of the
freighter."

"Rough ride? It felt like we were shooting the rapids
on the Colorado River."

"Yeah. Well, anyway, this guy leads us to the spot, and sure enough, there's a sailboat down there in about twenty to twenty-five feet of water. We could see it plain as day."

"And?"

"And, we got a diver out there and sent him down to look it over. He's the one that discovered the body inside. And, that sure as hell cured the guy who was trying to lay claim to the boat."

"Didn't want any part of it if it had a dead body on board, eh?" Flood asked.

"Dropped it like a hot potato," Rizzolo said.

"Hot potato, on the bottom of the bay?" Flood teased.

Rizzolo shrugged away the remark. "So we're getting the salvage guys to come out with one of their big cranes and raise the boat. The crime lab will go over it as soon as they get it raised."

"Whose boat is it?" the pathologist asked.

"Hers."

"Hers? What did she do? Get caught in a storm?"

"Nope. There weren't any storms around. We checked it with the weather bureau. I think we've got worse problems."

"Like what?"

"Well, you know this buddy of yours that is missing from the hospital over in Orangeburrow?"

"Trumbull?" Dr. Flood's interest began to skyrocket. "What's this got to do with Bill Trumbull?"

"Well, I've been working that case too, and I'm not happy with the whole thing. Y'know. Some of the pieces just aren't fitting together the way I'd like to see 'em. Too many loose ends in that mess to suit me."

"You think he isn't dead?" Flood asked.

"Do you?"

The pathologist answered with a half-shrug.

"I'm not ready to stick my neck out yet, Marty, but the body in the sailboat is a mighty strange coincidence, if she isn't related to the Trumbull case in some way."

Rizzolo made an unpleasant face and turned away from the autopsy table as Dr. Flood opened the girl's stomach and carefully inspected its contents.

"McDonald's," Flood observed.

"Huh?" Rizzolo asked, without looking back.

"Two all-beef patties, special sauce, lettuce, cheese, pickles, onions, on a sesame-seed bun," Flood sang softly. He stripped off his gloves and abandoned the motorcycle case to Jerry Washington and his oversized turkey needle.

"God," Rizzolo said softly. "I'll never eat again."

"It will do you good," the doctor advised, patting the detective on his stomach. "Come on. Let's take a look at your sailboat lady." He turned and led Rizzolo toward the walk-in cooler that he had designed for the new medical examiner's office. His theory had been that a walk-in, or roll-in, cooler would eliminate a lot of body-lifting that the old, slab-type morgues required. So far, he had been right, but some of the assistants had complained that they were catching Boston-style colds in Tampa from going in and out of the big coolers.

"I haven't seen her yet, myself," Rizzolo said. "She was messy when they got her out of the sailboat, and it was all they could do to get her into one of your crash bags to bring her in here. You seen her yet?"

"No. They only brought her in last night. I figured I'd wait for you. You wouldn't want to miss anything, would you?" Dr. Flood slapped the captain on the back and reached for the cooler door latch.

"Just the smell," Rizzolo conceded. "I could do without that. Did they tell you who we think it is?"

"No. They haven't brought the file in to me. Why? Who is she?"

"The sailboat belonged to Martha Holland," Rizzolo announced flatly. "We checked the numbers on the bow with the tax and registration office."

"The lawyer? Hell, she handled a divorce for one of our surgeons over at the hospital. She was pretty good."

Flood paused to search Rizzolo's face. "But what would she have to do with Bill Trumbull's disappearance?"

"I've heard that she and Dr. Trumbull had something going on. Y'know." Rizzolo cocked one eyebrow.

"Bill Trumbull and Martha Holland?"

"That's the way I get it so far."

"Says who?"

"You know a radiologist named LaFontaine?"

"Bruce LaFontaine?"

"With the English accent."

"Yeah, I know him. Why?"

"He's the one that clued me about Trumbull and the lady lawyer."

"But, hell, E.J., Bruce LaFontaine is a first-class bull-shitter from way back. And he drinks like a fish." Flood had already begun to shake his head in disbelief.

"Look, I told you that I might be sniffing up the wrong tree, but you know me. I'll follow up any lead that anybody hands me."

"Y'know, E.J., I didn't know Bill Trumbull too well. I saw more of him when he was in the pathology group over at Tampa General. But when he moved out to that little hospital, we didn't get to see each other as often. He kind of got out of touch. So, I don't know who he's been seeing, or what he's been up to. But I wouldn't have picked Martha Holland as my first choice for him." The doctor gave a tug on the morgue door latch and it opened with a belch of frigid air that began to make wisps of fog as it mixed with the warmer atmosphere of the adjacent room. He switched on the light and moved toward the morgue cart on which his only current black-bag case rested. The long, rubber-ized zipper bags were reserved for bodies that were badly decomposed or mutilated.

"We didn't match her prints, by the way," Rizzolo admitted.

"Too far gone?"

"I.D. says she was beyond the washerwoman stage

that you see in your simple immersion cases. Maybe it was because the water was so warm. I think they want to give it another try after you get through with your examination."

"They want me to pull the finger skin off, or do they want me to inject the tips with glycerine?"

"Hell, I don't know, Marty. That sort of shit is definitely not my thing. I don't give a damn how they get their prints. All I care about is that we make the I.D."

Dr. Flood grabbed the cart with the black bag and pulled it toward the door.

"Let's take her out in the dissection room where it's warm," Flood suggested.

Rizzolo flapped his arms in an over-demonstration of how cold he thought it was in the walk-in cooler. "This is no place for detectives or brass monkeys," he said.

"It's only thirty-six degrees," the pathologist announced. "That's what one of our famous state laws calls for. Thirty-six degrees, if you're going to keep an unembalmed body around for more than twenty-four hours. I guess somebody's grandmother got left out overnight in some hospital pathology department, years ago. They turn black pretty damned quick, if you don't cool 'em." He pushed the cart into the dissection room and slammed the morgue door shut. The sound of the door closing reminded Rizzolo of a meat market cold locker; the latching mechanisms were exactly the same.

"Jerry, flip on the exhaust blower, will you?" Flood called to his faithful assistant.

"You seen her?" Rizzolo asked.

"Nope," Washington replied. "But, them bags don't keep in the smell when they are really rotten. Y'know, like one that has been left in a warm, closed trailer for a week? And I been in and out of the cooler enough times today to notice it right away, if she stunk really bad. She won't be too bad at all." He walked slowly to the big exhaust fan built into the back wall and flipped the switch. The fan was designed to rapidly draw out the air in the dissection room and with it, all of the unpleasant odors that a decomposed body could generate. It also evacuated most of the effective air conditioning from the room, but the men using the dissection room were willing to be warm rather than subject themselves to the unmistakable odor of a rotten human body.

"We'll soon see," Flood announced as he began to pull the zipper down along the full length of the bag. "Didn't she have any identification on her?"

"She didn't have anything in her pockets, Marty, but, like most women, she probably had a handbag with her. We're hoping that it's still in the boat. The I.D. boys are going to call me if they find it. Being sunk and all, the inside of that sailboat is bound to be a real mess."

"I'll bet," Flood agreed. "These zippers are strong enough, but the way they sew them into the rubberized plastic gives me a laugh. If you force them at all, the seam splits and it's good-bye closing up later."

Rizzolo was no longer listening. He stared at the black bag, waiting for its occupant to emerge. As the chief of detectives, the captain had seen more than a few dead bodies, but those that were found when the odor began to attract the neighbors and those that came floating in from the bay were the worst. For Rizzolo, it was almost a promise of things to come—when he would no longer laugh and hear music or smell popcorn or be thirsty or feel a cold beer on the back of his tongue. These bodies with accelerated decay gave him a chance to advance the film of his own life and see where he was going, inevitably, unalterably, and perhaps, inexplicably. The smell was the price he had to pay for the show, and many times, it was expensive enough.

"Will you recognize her?" Dr. Flood asked.

"I've got a picture of her in my pocket. It came from

her law office." He reached into his shirt pocket and produced a photograph of Martha Holland's face, split by a wide smile that showed as many teeth as a toothpaste ad. He was looking at it when the pathologist threw back the flap of the black bag and exposed the body.

Rizzolo looked up with an audible gasp that made Jerry Washington smile with satisfaction. Martha's hair was matted down over her bloated face. Her eyes protruded from their sockets and her tongue stuck halfway out as if to mock the professional efforts of both men. She was badly discolored where the blood had collected beneath the skin, and large blisters filled with foul-smelling fluid had erupted in many areas. Her skin was wrinkled in the places where she was not bloated, and she seemed two sizes too large for her clothes. The skin of her hands and feet hung in loose, precariously attached sheets. The bloodstain on the front of her blouse had been soaked away, and the bullet hole was obscured by a fold.

"I guess the marine animals didn't get to her yet," Flood remarked, as he adjusted the side flap of the bag so that it would not drip on their shoes.

"You mean, like sharks?" Rizzolo asked. He continued to stare at Martha's bloated and blackened face. The swollen lips protruded in a grotesque half-kiss.

"No. Crabs, small fish, turtles, things like that," Flood said. "Maybe they were scared off by the sailboat and wanted to give her a few more days before they got brave enough to come inside and start in on her." He looked closely at the eyelids. They half covered the dull, protruding eyeballs. "Still got lids. They tend to go first."

"You think it's her?" Rizzolo asked, clutching his photograph a little too tightly.

"Dunno. Let's get a look at your photograph." He took the snapshot from the detective and began a systematic review, looking first at an isolated feature in the picture, and then comparing it to the same area on the face of the dead woman. He compared eye ridges, nose angle, prominence of cheekbones, angle of jaw, set of chin, hairline, size of ears, and other constant features with professional detachment.

Flood began to nod to himself. "Yeah. That's her, E.J." He held the photograph up so that they could both look at it, and pointed out each of the facial characteristics that he had compared. He was careful not to touch the picture with his rubber-gloved finger, which by now had acquired a slight scum from Martha Holland's corpse.

"I'll run her dental chart before we're done with her," the pathologist said.

"I'll have one of my men track down her dentist and send him over," Rizzolo promised.

"Just her dental chart would be enough for now. Usually, what I get when the whole, living dentist shows up for his first look at a case like this, is vomit on the floor and a piss-poor consult from him. I'd rather start with the chart, do my own comparison, and then call in a dentist when I'm stuck." Flood shifted his attention to Martha's neck. There were no bruises on the outside of the throat. He began to unbutton her blouse, mentally noting that none of the buttons had been torn free, as might happen had there been a struggle. The blouse strained against the buttons due to the gas distension of the chest and abdomen.

"Oh, ho!" he said triumphantly, as the blouse fell open in his hands. "You're going to love this one, E.J."

"What have you got?" The captain of detectives stood on tiptoe to get the better look that could have been obtained by coming one step closer to the body.

"How about a nice gunshot wound of the chest?" The pathologist pointed to the round hole in Martha Holland's left chest, just above the upper edge of her brassiere.

"Gunshot wound?" Rizzolo ignored the odor and the foul water that dripped from the sides of the bag, and stepped forward. "I really didn't expect a gunshot wound."

"So, what does that do to your Trumbull theory? You think old Bill Trumbull decided to give up pathology and take up shooting lawyers for sport?"

"I'll bet we could find a few doctors who would be willing to volunteer for that kind of duty."

"Surgeons, mostly," Flood offered. "They're the ones that get hit the hardest by the lawyers, not pathologists."

"Well, you knew Trumbull better than I did, Marty. He was one of your friends, not mine."

"As I said, not mine, either, actually," Flood replied.

"How 'bout making me an educated guess about the caliber of that bullet hole," Rizzolo asked.

"C'mon, Captain," Flood pleaded. He called Rizzolo 'captain' only when he had caught him sounding stupid, and that was not very often. "You know we can't tell what caliber it is from looking at the wound alone."

"Well, it's not a .22, at least, right?"

"I'll concede that much to you, E.J.—Jerry! Give me a hand. I want to look at the back."

Jerry Washington moved instantly to stand across the body from the pathologist. He reached over, took the opposite arm and pulled the body halfway up. Some of the loose skin around Martha's wrist pulled free and bunched up under his gloves. Rizzolo winced at the sight of it.

Dr. Flood pulled the wet blouse up and inspected the back. The swelling made it very difficult for him to unhook the bra.

"I used to be able to do that with one hand, in a drive-in movie, when I was in high school," Rizzolo said.

"That's getting to be a long, long time ago." The pathologist finally undid the undergarment and looked closely at the skin beneath it. "There's a break," he said.

"What is?" asked the captain and Jerry Washington in unison. They paused to exchange amused glances at the coincidence.

"No exit. You want to help me find the bullet?"

"Look," Rizzolo said carefully. "I'll stand around here, taking pictures for you, jotting down your notes, and even running for your coffee. But one thing is for damned sure. I don't want to be in this room when you put your knife to this belly." He made a face that anticipated the foul odor that would escape from Martha Holland's bloated abdomen when it was opened.

"Chicken shit," the pathologist said.

"Chicken shit, I can stand. But, gas from rotten humans? No, thank you. Give me a call when you get the bullet out of her and I'll come hopping back and receipt it from you myself, if you want." He started for the door and paused when he had opened it. "But, I'll tell you what. To show you that I'm a good guy, I'll bring you something back with me."

"A big Italian sandwich?" Jerry asked, smiling.

"No," Rizzolo said sweetly. "Her dental chart."

Chapter Twelve

TINKER HERNDON STRUGGLED with his left flipper and squinted at Bob Wrigley. The sun was bright behind Wrigley's head, and Herndon couldn't be sure that Bob wasn't laughing at him.

"How do you find these messes to get us into?" Herndon asked. "Yesterday, the sheriff brings you out here to check out this sunk sailboat, and you go and find a dead woman on it."

"You could have come along and found her for yourself," Wrigley said, adjusting the regulator on his tank.

"I got to be a fireman some days. We can't all be hair butchers."

"You sat on your ass all day at the fire house, suckin' on the city's tit," Wrigley teased.

"Wait till your shop goes up. I'll call the Orangeburrow engine company and tell them to let the son of a bitch burn down."

"Along with ten solid years of *Playboy*? What are you, crazy?" Wrigley stood up and flapped his way over the rough decking of the barge, stopping at the edge to look down at the sailboat, lying on the bottom below. The water was fairly clear and the sun was bright. The sailboat could be seen easily.

The sailboat's mast stood in front of him like a flag-

pole. The stays were still attached to it, but Wrigley
knew that one of his first tasks would be to cut them.
The barge owner had already given him a large pair of
cable cutters for the job. An impatient man, the owner
was not interested in Wrigley's suggestion to undo the
four turnbuckles that held the stays tight to the deck.
Cutting them would mean another hundred dollars or
so to repair the damage, but the hourly rate for the
barge, the barge owner, the crane man, the tugboat and
crew, and the sweating deputies far exceeded it.

Rizzolo had engaged the Diver-Down Salvage Company to raise the sunken sailboat. The Tampa-based
firm was not the biggest or the fastest salvage outfit in
the bay area, but there was no one else available. The
other floating cranes were tied up for a week or ten
days, and that kind of a delay did not please Rizzolo.
The hundred dollars an hour that Diver-Down was
charging the county didn't please Rizzolo either, but he
wanted the job done. After Martha Holland's body was
found on board, Rizzolo would not rest until he had the
sailboat combed by his crime lab. Her known association with Trumbull had been incentive enough for Rizzolo to drain the whole bay, if necessary. Fortunately
for everyone that worked for him, the captain couldn't
think of a way to drain Tampa Bay.

A tug had brought the big barge and its crane down
the bay during the night. By first light, they had moved
the barge closer to the sailboat and had lined the
barge's bow up with the length of the sloop. The tug
captain had maneuvered the barge as skillfully as a toy
boat in a bathtub, and had held it in that position while
the crane man had dropped the huge steel-pipe spuds
through the round holes in the deck and into the muddy
bottom below.

The sailboat was in twenty-four feet of water at low
tide. The big spuds had hit the bottom with a thud and
had buried themselves five and a half feet into the mud
and sand. The salvage man had quickly turned the fast-

ening bolts and the barge had suddenly become steady as a rock.

Wrigley looked down her wide deck. The barge was 45 by 105 feet, and was made of steel. The decking was thick, wide planks that threw splinters into the air and groaned under the weight of the crane, each time the big machine moved along the deck. The big crane was powered by a loud, smoke-belching diesel, and moved along the middle of the deck, forward and backward, like a Sherman tank trapped on a drifting ferryboat.

The barge owner finished his conversation with the man in the cab of the crane and tossed his beer can into the water. He walked over to stand next to Wrigley.

"You look 'bout ready," he said.

"Yeah," Wrigley agreed. "We'll get down there in a few minutes, Mr.—er?"

"Connor," the big man said, holding his massive hand out. "But, everybody calls me Murphy."

"Murphy Connor?" Wrigley asked. "Sounds like they couldn't decide what your last name was going to turn out to be." He was careful not to suggest that they might have had trouble figuring out who Connor's father had been. Connor was far too big for that kind of a remark from a diver.

"Kind of. I used to fight under the name of Murphy. Back in the old days. I guess it stuck."

"Fight? Prizefight?" Herndon asked, joining the conversation.

"Oh, nothing big, you understand," Connor said. "Started in the Navy. Put away a couple of guys and made the mistake of thinking I was pretty good. But, after the service, I went a few bouts in New York and Boston before I found out that that ain't no way to make a living."

"You ought to be glad you quit," Wrigley said. "All those guys end up the same."

"You can say that again," Murphy-Connor said. "I got

me a job on a salvage rig and I've done this kind of stuff ever since."

"You own this one?" Wrigley asked, gesturing widely to take in the entire unit.

"Yep. Me and the bank, downtown. 'Course we don't own all of that big American walkin' crane. Got a piece of it though. It's easier that way. Ownin' a piece of the crane, I mean. Makes it easier to get 'em to come out in the middle of the bay to do a job."

"Some of those guys get chicken?" Wrigley asked.

"Shit," Connor said, spitting tobacco juice into the water. "All some of them crane men want to do is sit in some loading yard, lifting containerized freight into some Jap ship. Get 'em out here on one of these barges in a squall, and they like to shit their pants." He laughed and showed his yellowing teeth.

Wrigley estimated Murphy-Connor to be about fifty years old. He had sandy hair that was sparse in front, and his nose flaked continuously from repeated sunburning. He was at least six feet tall, and with his massive beer belly, his weight must have been 275. Everything about him was big and rough, and that's the way he liked it. It was appropriate for his chosen profession. A smaller, dainty man would never have survived in this brawny world of cables, block and tackles, cranes, and the salvaging of sunken ships.

Murphy-Connor wore gray work pants, steel-toed shoes, and the type of shoulder-strap undershirt that Wrigley had always associated with his grandfather. It was so mottled with holes at the sides that it looked almost like lace.

Murphy-Connor's arms were thicker than most men's thighs and even with their covering of fat, there was no mistake that the man was incredibly strong.

"I guess some of our summer storms can make a believer out of anybody," Herndon said.

"I seen waves hit as high as the middle of the cab on the crane," Murphy-Connor said. "And that's right here in the middle of the goddamned bay!"

182

"Not exactly diving weather," Wrigley conceded. "But, we sure as hell got us a good day for it today." He swept his hand along the cloudless sky like an orchestra conductor.

"It'll toughen up by late afternoon," Murphy-Connor said. "Always does, this time of year."

"We'll be done by then," Wrigley promised.

"You guys ever hooked up the straps before?" Murphy-Connor asked.

"No, not really," Wrigley admitted. "I was hoping you'd kind of brief me on just how you want this done."

"Well, it ain't much," Murphy-Connor said. "I'd just as soon have my own divers out here, but with the dead body you found yesterday, I'll go along with you, if that's what the sheriff wants."

"We've worked with the sheriff before," Herndon said, quickly.

"Oh, hell, don't get me wrong now," Murphy-Connor said. "I don't give a rat's ass who the divers is. We don't keep no divers on the payroll steady, or nothin' like that. It's just that the divers we gen'ly use is used to goin' down on wrecks and hookin' up the lines for the crane."

"I think Captain Rizzolo is thinking about how many guys he might have to call into court on this case," Herndon said. "He probably don't want too many divers testifying. It gets too confusing for the jury."

"What case?" Murphy-Connor said, shielding his eyes from the sun to get a better look at Herndon's face. "Was that woman you pulled out of there yesterday ... murdered?"

"Beats the shit out of me," Wrigley said. "All I did was to get her out of the boat and guide her up to the sheriff's boat. She was half rotten and full of gas. Damn near floated up by herself. They put her in one of them black bags right away, before I got a good look at her."

"How'd they know she was murdered, then?" Murphy-Connor asked.

"I don't know if they did," Wrigley said. "But they would have taken the body in to the medical examiner to make an autopsy. Anyway, they must have found something, 'cause the captain sure wanted this sailboat raised in a hurry."

"Amen to that," Murphy-Connor said. "He must be hell on wheels to work for. We damn near didn't get the job, 'cause we didn't want to bring this rig down the bay at night. But that Captain Rizzolo said it was pull her up this mornin' or forget about it."

"You made it down here all right, didn't you?" Wrigley asked. He glanced at the tug, standing silently beside the barge. There was no sign of life on the tug.

"Oh, hell, yes. Old Coony Daggit will bring that tug of his through anything short of a hurricane, day or night," Murphy-Connor said with a laugh. "He can drive that son of a bitch anywhere on the west coast, drunk or sober, without nobody wonderin' if he's goin' to make it. Old Coony's one of the old-timers."

"Where's he now?" Herndon asked. "I haven't seen anybody on that tug since the sheriff's boat brought us out here this morning."

"Sleepin', I expect. Stayed up all night, runnin' us down here at close to five knots," Murphy-Connor said. "This barge of mine ain't no speedboat, y'know. And, you put that big walkin' crane on her back, and you know you've got a load."

"Will he sleep all day?" Wrigley asked.

"More or less. He knows we ain't going' to move this here barge once we sunk them spuds in the mud. So, he's goin' to stay asleep, or drunk, or both, in that air-conditioned cabin of his until it's time for him to haul our ass back to port. What's he care? He's gettin' paid for just sittin' right where he's at. And that ain't all bad."

"Better'n getting yourself all wet, right, Tinker?"

"Depends on what you like, I guess," Herndon said. "You 'bout ready?"

"Yeah. I guess so. What's first here, Murphy?"

"First thing is to take them big wire cutters down on

the deck and snip them cables that come up to hold that mast. You know what I mean?" Murphy-Connor pointed into the water toward the sailboat. "One of you can handle that."

"Guess you get to stay dry for a while," Wrigley said to his partner.

"He's gettin' his ass wet, too," Murphy-Connor said quickly. "I want him to take this here line over to the mast and tie it fast. I'll hook it to the cable from the crane, and when you get them cables cut free, we'll lift that mast right off of the sailboat like a lollipop stick."

"Will it come right off of there?" Herndon asked. "I mean, don't you have to unbolt it or something?"

"This kind of a mast only has a pressure step," Wrigley explained. "It gets pulled snug onto the deck by its own weight and the tension of the stays that I'm going to cut. What kind of a sailor are you, anyway?"

"No kind of a sailor, that's what kind. I'd rather have a good engine pushing any boat that I'm on," Herndon said.

"You and me both," Murphy-Connor agreed. "And the bigger the better."

"OK," Wrigley said, explaining with his hands. "After we get the mast pulled off. Then what?"

"Then we pick the sailboat up," Murphy-Connor said simply.

"On what?" Herndon asked.

"On those big nylon straps." Murphy-Connor pointed to the straps lying in a heap near the crane. "All you got to do is make me a big sling under the sailboat, and we'll lift the bastard right out of the water." He simultaneously clenched his jaw and his fist as he spoke of the strength of the big crane.

"But that boat's going to be heavier than hell, filled with water like it is," Herndon argued.

"But we ain't goin' to lift the water," Murphy-Connor said. "All we're goin' to do is lift it up *in* the water, and let the displacement do most of the work."

"So, where will the water go?" Herndon persisted.

"The water will be sucked out by this four-inch, flexible pipe and that gas-operated pump over there." He pointed with his big hand. "After we get the sailboat raised up high enough so the water inside is at the same general level as the water outside. Get it?" He waited for Herndon to catch up. It only took the diver a few seconds.

"Ahhh," Herndon purred. "The sailboat will only be a shell around some inside water that will stay right in the outside water all the time."

"I think I understand it better when Murphy explained it," Wrigley said.

"But one of your problems is to find out where she's leakin'," Murphy-Connor added. "The water will continue to pour in the hole, wherever it's at. And that'll only make the pump's job that much harder."

"What if the whole side is stove in?" Herndon asked.

"Oh, we got ways to get around that kind of thing, too," Murphy-Connor explained, confidently. "For instance, we could drop a big piece of heavy canvas along the hole on the outside of the hull, see?"

"Yeah?"

"And then we could go inside the boat and pour some quick-settin' cement in a mold we'd build up against the hole." He paused to see if the divers were following him. They were. "And then, when the cement hardens —a couple of minutes, that's all it'd take—we can pump the water out, and she's on her way home."

"God damn!" Herndon said. "That's OK!"

"Do you really think she's got the whole side stove in?" Wrigley asked.

"Nah. There ain't no coral reefs around here," Murphy-Connor explained. "What you're goin' to find is a busted intake valve, or a pipe that's come off from some through-the-hull fittin'. Y'know. Like, the head busted loose, or the engine-coolin' line popped free. Somethin' like that."

"How come?" Herndon asked.

"'Cause, that's the way these sport sailboats and powerboats go down, usually," Murphy-Connor said. "It ain't never the builder's fault. It's always the asshole that owns it and then goes away and leaves his valves wide open."

"But the lady on this one was dead, Murphy. Gotta be something more here," Wrigley said.

"Dead drunk, you mean," Murphy-Connor offered. "Probably went to sleep out here and didn't wake up until she was drownded." He drew his stubby index finger across his throat to indicate her demise, if not the actual mode of her death.

"Can happen, I guess," Herndon conceded.

"Bet your ass," Murphy-Connor said. He indicated the big tugboat with a blunt wave of his hand. "Go over to Big Willie, over there, and open *her* petcocks. Old Coony would go down with her just as sure as shootin' and probably not even know what hit him. It ain't hard to drowned a drunk, once he's asleep and passed out from his booze. All he knows is the place is full of water, and he can't find his way out. 'Specially, if it's night."

"What do you want me to do if I find one of the pipes off of some fitting?" Wrigley asked.

"Stuff your Kotex in it, you asshole," Murphy-Connor announced. "Now, let's get on the job, or that sheriff's captain will chew my ass for runnin' up the bill." He waved at the crane operator, and the big machine roared into action. The forty-foot boom was swung over the mast. A hook and cable dangled lifelessly near the upper end, waiting to be attached. The divers pulled their masks over their faces, and fell off the barge backwards, landing on their air tanks with awkward splashes. Wrigley disappeared with the giant pair of wire cutters, and Herndon splashed around, near the mast, pulling the rope into place so that he could tie it on, and then attach the hook from the crane.

"You can put a bowline in the end of that line,"

Murphy-Connor shouted at Herndon. The diver's wet suit, holding tight around his ears, spared him the directions. In fact, he didn't know how to tie a bowline, but, instead he made an acceptable loop that slipped easily over the hook. He had already tied the other end to the mast in a series of boy scout half-hitches. He would never have been awarded a merit badge for his efforts, but Murphy-Connor knew that the aluminum mast did not weigh much, and it would not require much of a lift to get it off the step on the deck of the sailboat, once the stays were cut. He motioned to the crane operator and the line to the mast became taut. Almost simultaneously, the aft stay flopped loose, indicating that Wrigley had cut the first of the four.

Herndon swam a short distance away and treaded water effortlessly as he followed Wrigley's progress around the sailboat, when the other stays were cut, one by one. Murphy-Connor's arm had stayed in the air as a signal to the crane man to maintain the pressure on the line, but not to lift the mast as yet. Murphy-Connor waited for Wrigley to splash through the surface a few yards away from the barge before he ordered the lifting of the mast with a small but unmistakable hand motion.

The crane rumbled deeply, and the mast lifted skyward a few feet before the operator swung it gently and slowly toward the barge, where Murphy could get a hold of it with his banana-bunch hands. He nodded to the crane man to continue the lift, as he hand-over-handed the aluminum mast out of the water. Together, they manipulated the big mast onto the deck of the barge and released the lifting line.

"OK, you guys," he called to the divers in the water. "This ain't no Olympic game. Let's get these nylon straps down there to the sailboat, and get 'em ready to slip under." He dragged the big straps over to the end of the barge, and kicked them off unceremoniously. "They'll straighten out on the way down."

Wrigley had pulled the wet suit from one of his ears

to listen. He nodded theatrically at the barge man's instructions.

"When you get them down there, work one end of each of 'em under the hull of the sailboat, fore and aft. Kinda split the weight of the boat between 'em. Y'know what I mean? Here, you may have to dig in the mud to get 'em under the hull." He picked up a short shovel from the deck planking and threw it playfully close to Herndon.

"Hey! What the hell?" Herndon protested.

"Look out, Tinker," Wrigley warned. "Murphy's the kind of guy that calls a spade a spade."

"No, he ain't. He calls it a fuckin' shovel," Herndon shouted, imitating Murphy's clipped way of speaking.

"Whatever it is, get it down there and use it to get them straps under the sailboat," Murphy-Connor said. "I promised them deputies that when they got back the sailboat would be up and ready for them to ride it home."

"Ride it home?" Wrigley asked.

"Yeah. Somethin' about the captain wantin' one of 'em on the sailboat to 'secure the evidence' on the way back to my salvage yard."

"OK. So, we get the nylon straps under the sailboat. What then?" Herndon asked.

"Then, we take this center bar, here, and hook the straps up to each end." Murphy lifted the steel bar like a weight lifter trying for a world record. "Then we can hook the crane on to this welded ring in the middle of the bar. See?"

The divers nodded and treaded water.

"And if you guys have got them nylon straps on anywheres near the balance points on that sailboat, she'll come up like the flowers in spring." Murphy spread his arms to show how easy it was all going to be.

"What are you going to do while we're down there, diggin' these straps under the hull?" Herndon asked, spitting out water playfully.

"I just might slip over to that air-conditioned tug

galley and see if Old Coony left a beer or two for me and Oscar, up there in that hot crane cab." He laughed loudly, and slapped his belly with both hands.

Herndon pulled his mask down over his face and middle-fingered Murphy in the same motion. Murphy didn't see it, and if he had, he would have laughed amiably.

Wrigley swam over to the barge and handed the big wire cutters to Murphy.

"And, look—" Murphy-Connor said, seriously, "You guys be careful down there. I don't want nobody gettin' hurt over some shitty sailboat. This job is a cinch. Understand?"

"Yes, Mother," Wrigley said. He flipped his mask down and upended quickly, hoping to wet Murphy with the larger-than-necessary splash he made.

Murphy-Connor looked down into the water at the disappearing frogman. If his ears hadn't gone bad on him, he would have been down there with them, he thought to himself. He watched Wrigley descend into the depths "Shit!" he said aloud. He threw the cable cutters onto the deck of the barge. "Let's steal us a couple of beers from Old Coony!"

Chapter Thirteen

LIEUTENANT TURNER entered Rizzolo's office without knocking. This privilege came from their long association rather than equality of rank.

"The bullet's a .38, E.J.," Turner announced. He glanced around the room to make sure that they were alone. Turner always called Rizzolo "Captain" when anyone else was present.

"You're sure?"

"Uh-huh. Weight checks out." He tossed the small plastic vial that contained the bullet into the air and caught it skillfully. "Wanna see?"

Rizzolo reached for the vial and inspected it cursorily. "The doc marked it like he's s'posed to?"

"Flood? He's a pro. You know that."

"Yeah. What about the gun, Turner. What did you figure out on that?" Rizzolo picked at the masking tape around the top of the vial and glanced at the small label that was visible through the clear plastic.

"I'm betting on a Smith and Wesson."

"Why an S. and W.?"

"Oh, the twists, the spacing of the lands and grooves. Just a general gut feeling," Turner shrugged.

"Will the F.B.I. agree?"

"Oh, well, now, you know how they are. If we're lucky, they might agree that it's a bullet, and then they might tell us some umpteen kinds of handguns from all over the world that these markings are consistent with."

"Uh-huh." Rizzolo had managed to untape the vial and remove the surgical gauze-wadding from inside. The medical examiner had wrapped it in gauze to prevent any further scratches that might confuse or obscure the ballistics identification. Rizzolo could feel the bullet inside the gauze, and quickly exposed it on the blotter of his desk. He picked it up, and held it between his thumb and forefinger. He squinted at it as if he had microscopic eyes.

"Pretty good shape, eh?"

"Yeah, yeah. It's fine," Rizzolo mused, preoccupied. "Where did the doc say he dug this baby out?"

"In the back muscles, just below one of the shoulder blades."

"*Back* muscles?" Rizzolo was alarmed.

"Yeah. Well, he said it got there by going in from the front and running through to the back. He didn't mean that she was shot in the back."

"Oh, you scared the shit out of me. I thought he'd gone and found another bullet." Rizzolo smiled and relaxed a little. "What about the dental charts?"

"I sent a unit over to her dentist and picked them up right after you called. Dr. Flood has already made a preliminary check, and he says there's no doubt in his mind. It's her, all right."

"Martha Holland."

"Yeah. Martha Holland."

"So, what else are you running on her for me?"

"We typed her blood as group B, Rh negative," Turner offered.

"What's that make her?"

"Makes her a little rare, not much. Something like fifteen percent of the general white population. But, we've got nothing to compare it to. I mean, no blood-stains on anybody else's clothes, or nothin' like that."

"Patience, Turner, patience. You can't expect all the clues to fall on your desk in one day, can you? What else have you got?"

"I salted away some head hairs and pubic hairs. Just in case."

"Uh-huh."

"And, the doc says there was some funny stuff in her stomach."

"How funny?"

"Smelled funny, he said."

"Like what?"

"I dunno. He seemed to think it was a strange alcohol, or some solvent. I didn't smell it, myself. I'm going to send some of it off to the chemical lab and ask them to identify it, if they can."

"What's he mean by a strange alcohol or solvent?"

"He didn't say. I only talked to him for a few minutes when he finished the autopsy and wanted to get rid of the bullet."

"How 'bout her fingernails?"

"Too far gone to get anything out from under them, if anything was ever there, but Dr. Flood says that none of them was broken or torn."

"Was she screwed?"

"Not so's you could tell," Turner said with a little smile. "At least, there weren't any injuries down there that the doc could see. And neither of us have any hope of recovering sperm from her vagina or running an acid phosphatase that will mean anything."

"Too rotten?" Rizzolo made an unpleasant face.

"You'd better believe it."

"Pregnant?"

"Nope."

"Food in the stomach?"

"Nothing recognizable."

Rizzolo tapped his pencil on his desk for a few mental bars of "The Monkey Wrapped His Tail Around the Flagpole," and then abandoned it in favor of a bent paper clip. He twisted the clip for a moment and then threw it at the wastebasket.

"Missed," Turner announced.

"Bob Cousy, I'm not," Rizzolo admitted. He got up from the desk and reached for his jacket. It was sprawled on the nearest chair. "You seen the sailboat yet, Turner?"

"No, I haven't. I sent the truck over to the salvage yard when it arrived, but I haven't had a chance to get over there myself."

"You got somebody holding it down until the crime lab takes over?"

"There's the deputy that you assigned to ride back on it. As far as I know, he's still sitting on the deck, waiting to be relieved by somebody from homicide."

"Come on, then. Ride over there with me." Rizzolo walked so quickly to the door that it looked as if he wasn't going to stop to open it. Halting quickly, he turned the knob, stepped through, and turned to the secretary in the anteroom. "Call Lieutenant Turner's office and tell them he'll be ten-twelve with me. We're going over to the Diver-Down yard."

"Yes, sir," she replied, without shifting the phone receiver from her shoulder. "But, there's a call for you from Pinellas sheriff's office."

"Pinellas?" Rizzolo asked, a little annoyed. "We don't need any problems from St. Pete. What do they want?"

"It's a Lieutenant Norman, and he wants to talk directly to you, Captain." The secretary put on a sympathetic face.

Rizzolo sighed deeply and threw a look of deep frustration at Lieutenant Turner. "OK. I'll talk to him." He held out his hand for the secretary's phone rather than returning to his own desk.

"Captain Rizzolo," he barked.

"Captain, this is Lieutenant Jack Norman. With the Pinellas S.O.?"

"Yeah, Lieutenant. What do you need?" Rizzolo glanced at the ceiling, impatiently.

"We found a car here that I understand you might be interested in."

"A car? Whose?"

"Registered to a Martha Holland. That's M-A-R-T-H-A, first name, H-O-L-L-A-N-D, last name. We got a Tampa address from D.M.V. We found it locked and apparently abandoned in the lot of the yacht club near Clearwater."

"She's a signal five, Lieutenant," Rizzolo said flatly.

"So I understand. I called the car in to your stolen vehicle desk and they told me you were carrying her as a signal five. That's why I called you direct."

"Anything unusual about the car, Lieutenant?"

"Yes, sir, there was. The reason we checked it out in the first place was because somebody over at the yacht club called in a complaint about the smell coming from the car."

"Smell? What smell, Lieutenant? You found a body in the car?" Rizzolo glanced at Turner and raised his eyebrows.

"No such luck, Captain," Lieutenant Norman said. "All we found was some rotten meat and cheese and milk."

"Groceries, huh?"

"And a lot more stuff, too, Captain. Funny stuff. Like a lot of liquor in small bottles, and some canned goods. And some ropes and stuff. Y'know, the kind of stuff you would use on a boat if you was going out for a long time."

"She had a sailboat, you know," Rizzolo said.

"Yes, sir. We ascertained that fact from the dockmaster at the yacht club. We also learned that her sailboat has been missing for a while. Nobody here seems to know exactly how long. Would you like to have the boat's registration number and a description of the—"

"We found the boat, Lieutenant," Rizzolo said smugly. These interdepartmental competitions were always fun for him when he was on the winning side.

"You found the boat?" Lieutenant Norman sounded disappointed.

"Yeah, Lieutenant. And, she was on it."

"I see. OK then, Captain. Do you want me to ship the stuff from her car over to you, or what? I mean, do you think it's part of your signal five?" The Pinellas lieutenant seemed eager to be a part of the homicide case.

"Why don't you hold it at your place, and I'll send our expert, Lieutenant Turner, over to check out the car and the contents." He looked over the phone and made an impolite face at Lieutenant Turner.

"We'd be happy to have him, Captain. Of course, we have our own crew that would be quite capable of going over the car for you. But you tell him to come on over and to look me up when he gets here. Lieutenant Jack Norman. That's N-O-R—"

"Yeah, O.K., Lieutenant. I'll tell him. And, thanks for the call."

"I'd appreciate it if you'd keep me posted, Captain. I mean, maybe she was murdered in our county."

"If I find out that this is your signal five and not ours, Lieutenant, I'll ship her back to you on the next Greyhound bus."

"Bus, Captain? I don't—"

"Figure of speech, Lieutenant. Figure of speech," Rizzolo rolled his eyes for Turner. "I'll call you if we uncover anything pertinent."

"Same here, Captain."

Rizzolo hung up quickly. "Pinellas S.O. picked up her car with all the supplies in it," he explained to Lieutenant Turner. "I guess she didn't have time to get 'em on board her sailboat."

"What the hell does that mean?" Turner asked.

"Beats me," Rizzolo said. "Come on. I'll ride you over to the salvage yard."

The ride to the Diver-Down salvage yard, with Rizzolo at the wheel, was about as fast as Turner could tolerate. There was no red light; just a heavy, Italian foot.

"You been down this way before?" Turner asked Rizzolo, as they entered the shipyard neighborhood.

"A couple of times as a patrolman for the city. I chased a couple of kids out of here one night. But it's changed a lot. It used to be filled with big, rusty pieces of machinery, and barge parts, and boat sections, cranes. . . . All the stuff that would fascinate a kid."

Lieutenant Turner scanned the salvage yard and found himself looking at exactly the same items that Rizzolo had catalogued. He was about to ask Rizzolo what changes he was talking about when he saw the captain's big grin.

"You had me going," Turner admitted.

"While you're looking, see if you can spot a guy named Connor. A great big guy. But, they call him Murphy."

"A big, big guy with sandy hair, kind of balding in front, wearing an undershirt?"

"Yeah, Turner. That's him. Where is he?"

"Over there. By that deck housing." Turner pointed to the housing of a freighter, salvaged from a wreck a few years before.

"Yeah. That's him, all right. He cut that housing off of some Liberian freighter that sank in the channel behind the hospital. The company didn't pay his bill, so he kept the whole superstructure as his office. It's the only part of the freighter that didn't actually sink. He scrapped the rest, and made a bundle." Rizzolo eased the unmarked unit toward the office and parked it. Connor was halfway to the car before they could sign off with the dispatcher and get out.

"Captain Rizzolo?"

"Right," the captain said. "Talked with you on the phone. This is Lieutenant Turner from our crime lab and I.D. section."

"Lieutenant, glad to meet you. Your crime lab truck is already here." He wiped his hands on the front of his undershirt and shook hands with both men. "They're all over there by the sailboat."

"Have any trouble getting it up?" Rizzolo asked, looking over toward the boat, now standing proudly at the end of the salvage dock.

"When you get to be my age, Captain, you always have trouble getting it up." Murphy-Connor slapped the captain on the back and emitted a loud laugh. Rizzolo chose not to laugh and Turner failed to get the joke in the first place.

"Looks like it's floating high and dry, now," Turner said.

"It's a goddamned mess inside," Murphy-Connor said. "But your guys said don't clean it up or nothin'. So, we left it just like it was."

The deputy on the foredeck stood up and straightened his tie when Rizzolo approached. Rizzolo waved him off the boat with a flick of his hand, and the deputy responded without a comment.

"Where are the men from the crime lab?" Turner asked as the deputy passed.

"They're inside the boat, sir," the deputy replied. His green uniform pants were rolled up and he carried his shoes and socks in his hand.

"But nobody else went on board, right?" Turner asked.

"No, sir. No one."

"Good. You can go get yourself a Coke, if you want," Turner said.

"Thank you, sir."

Murphy-Connor watched the deputy hustle across

the dirty salvage yard toward the office. His feet quickly became black from the coal and cinders that had been used as fill when the county had built the area. "Looks to me like he's damned glad to get the hell off of that sailboat."

"I think he's afraid that the captain will give him another assignment if he sticks around," Turner said.

"He could be right," Rizzolo admitted. "You want to go on board, Turner?"

"Yeah, Captain, but let's not screw up my lab boys."

"Why'd she go down, Murphy?" Rizzolo asked. "Hole in the bottom?"

"Yeah, but not the kind you're thinkin' of," Murphy-Connor said. "She didn't hit nothin'. Somebody cut one of the intake pipes."

"Cut the pipe?" Turner asked.

"Well, plastic pipe. You know the stuff." Murphy-Connor made a circle with his thumb and index finger to demonstrate the approximate size of the plastic pipe.

"How'd you know it was cut?" Turner inquired.

"Looks like it was cut. That's all. You know how a plastic pipe looks when you take a knife to it?"

"Yes, Mr. Murphy, I know how it looks," Turner said impatiently.

"Kinda ragged?" Murphy-Connor persisted. "And with little cut marks around where the main cut goes? Like, somebody was tryin' to get a better bite on the pipe, but it slipped a couple of times?"

Rizzolo gave a chuckle. "Sounds like you ought to hire old Murphy here, as one of your crime scene analysts."

Lieutenant Turner softened and joined in the laugh. "Maybe you're right, Captain. Some of my men don't know that much about cutting a plastic pipe with a knife, I'm afraid."

"Shit, send 'em over. We cut plastic pipes all the time around here," Murphy-Connor said enthusiastically.

"How'd you plug the leak?" Rizzolo asked.

"We stuffed it with rags from the outside," Murphy-Connor said. "The inside's just like we found it."

"You think we could get the pipe off the fitting and save it as evidence?" Turner asked.

"Shit," Murphy-Connor said. "You can have the whole fitting, pipe and all, if that's what you want." Then he added, " 'Course, that might take some doin', and it would leave you with a hole in the hull to fix. But I could turn that plastic pipe off'n there without too much trouble, and leave the fitting. That'd be better, don't you think?"

"But, no additional marks," Turner added.

"Huh? Oh, yeah. I mean, no. I won't make no more marks on it. I'll put a soft rag between the pipe and the wrench."

"You want to print it first?" Rizzolo asked Turner.

"Why not?" Turner replied. "But don't get your hopes up. That whole boat's been sunk in seawater. We won't have a snowball's chance of lifting a print off of her anywhere."

They stood on the end of the dock, looking at the sailboat, wishing for clues. Suddenly, a man's head popped up out of the hatch.

"Oh, hi Lieutenant, hi Captain," the young man said. He had on the long gray smock that identified him as a crime-scene technician.

"Hello, Gibson," Lieutenant Turner said stiffly. "You get anything worth saving?"

The crime-scene tech held up a single baggie. "Just some of these empty canned cocktails, Lieutenant."

"What *about* the cocktail can, Gibson?" Rizzolo added.

"Nothing, Captain. Just an empty cocktail can. I thought I'd keep it and try to process it for prints, downtown. But I really don't have too much hope for it. This boat, here, Captain, has been—"

"Sunk," Rizzolo said curtly. "We all know that, Gibson." He glanced at Turner for sympathy, but received none.

"Huh? Oh yeah, Captain. That's right, excuse me." He disappeared into the boat again as quickly as he had appeared.

Rizzolo and Turner stepped onto the deck of the sailboat with the uneasiness of landlubbers unaccustomed even to the slight sway of a heavy boat on calm water. The outside of the boat looked normal except for the absence of the mast and stays. The sun had dried the fiberglass deck on the way to the salvage yard. It looked washed and ready. Their street shoes clicked along the deck and Turner almost slipped as his leather heels came in contact with the smoother fiberglass of the cockpit and found nothing to grip.

"Next, we'll have to fish you out of the water," Rizzolo said playfully. He offered Lieutenant Turner his arm for support. Turner accepted without embarrassment. He did not feel secure on boats and he didn't care who knew it.

Rizzolo stuck his head through the aft hatch and watched Turner's two men photographing the interior from every angle and dusting every conceivable surface for fingerprints that did not exist. He watched and admired their work silently. They were pros. They moved around the interior of the cabin like cats, touching nothing, forgetting nothing, and, unfortunately for the case, finding nothing.

"How can you guys find anything in this unholy mess?" Rizzolo asked, then emitted a long low whistle. The main cabin looked like a disaster area. Things that had been neatly stowed away had floated free when the boat went down, and were now lying in a big, wet heap in the middle of the cabin floor. The soggy and swollen pages of nautical books curled in on themselves, as if they were now ashamed to be read.

The foam mattresses on the two bunks in the main cabin dripped water continuously because no one had been authorized to squeeze them. The empty cocktail cans that Trumbull had enjoyed were scattered around without a recognizable pattern.

In the forward cabin, much smaller due to the bow structure of the sailboat, the sails rested neatly in their sailbags, undamaged and totally oblivious to their recent bath. The Dacron sails were designed for repeated exposure to moisture.

"I want you men to go over every inch of this boat," Turner said. "Look for bullet holes. Things that look broken. Signs of a fight. Scrapes on the wall. Anything out of the ordinary. Understand?" His orders were both routine and explicit. Both crime-scene technicians nodded in agreement.

"Either of you men know anything about how a sailboat works?" Rizzolo asked. The crime-scene techs shook their heads simultaneously. "Well, if you come across anything that looks strange, leave it alone and give me a call. If we can't figure it out, I'll find somebody over at the state attorney's office that knows sailing and ask them to help."

"Who have you got in mind?" Turner asked.

"I don't know, exactly, but some of those junior state attorneys are always showing up in the Sunday paper after one of them society races. I'll find somebody, if we need him. In the meantime, why don't you have these guys work this scene like a homicide in a car. The principles will be about the same, won't they?"

"That's a good idea, Captain," Turner agreed. "Check the ignition. Is there gas in the tank? Are the lights on? You know the routine."

"I'll tell you what, Turner," Rizzolo said after studying the mess on the floor and realizing how big the problem was going to be. "I'm going to leave this area for you and your team of experts. I think I can better serve the public back at the office."

"You're all heart, Captain," Turner said. "Leave me here and I'll hitch a ride back on the crime-scene truck when we finish."

"Ten-four, Turner," Rizzolo replied quickly. "C'mon, Murphy, tell me about how easy it was to raise this sailboat and why you're not going to feel guilty when you send the county a bill for a couple of grand."

"Hey, lifting it was easy, Captain," Murphy-Connor said. "The couple of grand is for having this rig to lift it with and knowing how."

"You're a seagoing junk dealer, Murphy, old boy. That's all you are." Rizzolo threw a light punch at the big man's shoulder, and he did not flinch. Rizzolo turned and stepped onto the dock awkwardly. Murphy-Connor stood unseen behind him, holding his arms out ready to catch the captain if he fell.

"There may be one more thing you can do for me, Captain," Murphy-Connor said as he jumped onto the dock with practiced ease.

"Yeah? What? Fix a ticket?"

"Not exactly. But you may get a call from somebody down around Bahia Beach, bitchin' about this little salvage operation of ours."

"Yeah? Why?"

"Well, Captain, while we was tryin' to get the barge with the crane on it in close enough to the sailboat to do you some good, old Cap'n Daggit had to run his tug through a whole string of crab-trap floats that was laid out down there."

"Coony Daggit?" Rizzolo asked, surprised.

"Yeah, Old Coony. Know him?"

"Is that old drunk still alive? I haven't heard from him since he ran a tug into one end of the Sunshine Skyway Bridge while he was hauling garbage for the city, a couple of years back. He damned near went to jail *that* time for destroying state property and operating a tugboat while drunk."

"I 'spect that some crab fisherman is goin' to be bent out of shape when he finds out that Coony chewed up a couple a dozen of his crab floats and lines."

"OK, Murphy," Rizzolo said reassuringly. "I'll alert the complaint desk and advise the irate citizen to submit a written claim for damages. The county attorney will just love to pay for a bunch of crab traps on a claim marked 'damaged during the investigation of a homicide.' That'll really blow his mind."

Rizzolo was still chuckling to himself when he reached his car. A belch of superheated Florida air met him as he opened the door and reached in for his radio transmitter.

"This is seven-fifty, and I'm ten-eight," he said. He returned Murphy-Connor's wave and spun the back wheels just a little as he turned around and headed for the main road.

Chapter Fourteen

THE DAY'S HEAT had already seeped through the walls of the shed and baked Bill Trumbull to a point, his medical knowledge told him, where his water balance and electrolytes were threatened. His hands and feet had ceased aching after the swelling around the ropes tying him tight had compromised the last of his circulation. The gag in his mouth had become wet with his own saliva while it lasted, and then dry when he ran out of it.

The day before, the crabman's son had brought him some water and some cold leftover fish, but so far, no one had opened the door today. From time to time, he had heard voices or boat motors coming and going. Trumbull realized that he had not remained conscious every minute of the day, and that even the moments he had been awake were blurred and confused in his mind.

It was only the heat, rising in the morning and then falling at night, that gave him any sense of time in the dark, hot shed. He wondered if there was a way out of this tiny prison, and then, after lying on the hard floor, gagged and fighting the repeated urges to vomit or scream, he began to hope for an even more pleasant escape; one that would eliminate his ordeal entirely and save him from the scandal that would smother him if he were rescued. His despair had shown him that death, even in a dark, lonely shed, could be a blessing.

Dried blood made his hair a thick, tangled mat. His head throbbed where he had been hit with the tire tool, and for a while he wondered if his skull had been fractured. But his neurological self-examination, limited as it was by his being tied, was finally abandoned when he realized that he had been able to sleep and regain consciousness without any significant loss of brain function. In a lower key of his numbed fear, he wondered if the blow on the head had started a slow-collecting subdural hematoma that might take days or weeks to kill him.

It seemed to Trumbull that it was late in the afternoon. Somehow, the heat was a little less intense, and the tiny points of light that came in through the cracks and nail holes in the wall seemed redder and less dazzling.

Outside, there was a muffled argument that suddenly grew louder, but no more distinct as two men made their way to the door of the shed. They paused there and continued speaking with considerable emotion. At last, he decided that it was not a true argument, but simply a heated discussion between two men. He wondered if one of them was a deputy.

Without warning, the door of the shed was thrown open, and he was suddenly blinded by the bright rays of the late-afternoon sun. Old man McCraw and his son stood in the doorway, looking in at him and no longer speaking. Trumbull blinked his eyes at them and did not move. He was suddenly afraid again, and his heart quickened its pace.

"Look at him, lyin' there," the son said, with obvious contempt. "Your men have been doin' a good job out there for ya!" The son rushed over to the corner where the pathologist lay curled and tied like a captured animal, and delivered a hard kick in the ribs. Trumbull yelled against the gag, then emitted a groan that registered only part of the pain that he felt in his side.

"Ain't enough, you got to come in here and rob our traps," McCraw said, joining his son at Trumbull's side. "You got to send your men over to destroy everythin' we ever worked for." He spat at Bill Trumbull, splattering him on the shoulder. Trumbull shook his head violently to deny whatever he was being charged with by these two angry men.

"That money you brung with you ain't enough for all the damage your people is doin' to us," the son said.

"People like you ain't fit to live 'round decent folk," the old crab fisherman said. He grabbed the gag and pulled it from the doctor's face. Trumbull began to work his lower jaw in a frantic effort to regenerate saliva. For a few moments, he was unable to speak at all.

The son started in again. "And there warn't no sign of that boat of your'n, neither." He raised his foot to kick the pathologist again, but hesitated contemptuously when Trumbull cringed to protect himself.

"I . . . didn't—" Trumbull tried to speak. His mouth was still painfully dry and his jaw ached badly.

"We seen 'em down there," the old man shouted, waving his arms. "No use for you to tell us otherwise. Didn't we, son? Didn't we see 'em down there?"

"Biggest damned barge I ever did see outside of Port Tampa," the son agreed. "And it had one of them big cranes on it, too." He brought his face close to the pathologist's to make his words more emphatic.

"Pickin' up every last crab trap, they was," McCraw said, shaking his head sadly. "Time was when they would come by and take a crab or two out of a full trap, and nobody'd pay no never-mind to it. But next, they come and steal the catch and the trap and the buoy, all together. And now this! They bring in a whole goddamned barge and crane!"

"But I didn't steal any crabs," Trumbull protested, despite his dry mouth.

"Lyin' son of a bitch," the younger McCraw said. He gave Bill Trumbull a knee in the side of the head and made him fall over on his side again. Trumbull strained against the ropes that held his hands and feet.

"You've got to believe me," Trumbull pleaded. "I don't know anything about crab traps or crabs, either, for that matter."

"Well, mister, you're sure as hell goin' to find out about 'em before it's all over," the old man said. An evil-looking smile covered his face.

"Look," Trumbull pleaded. "I'm a doctor from over in Orangeburrow. Give me a chance to use your phone, and I'll prove it to you." Trumbull knew that he would be abandoning all hope for escape from involvement in the death of Martha Holland and his own faked homicide, but he was convinced that this old man and his son were going to cause him great harm.

"You ain't callin' nobody," McCraw said. "Your kind just causes more and more trouble, the more chances they get."

"All right," Trumbull said. "If you saw a big barge out in the bay and it had a crane on it, it must have been sent down here to raise the sailboat."

"What sailboat?" the son asked.

"I came here on a sailboat and sank it off shore. Not too far out, either."

"You what?" McCraw asked.

"I sank the sailboat. It's a long story."

"You bet it's a long story, mister," the old crabman said. "And I had a belly full of it. Every year, I lose crabs and crab traps to fellers like you. But this is the first time they ever brought a whole barge down here to clean me out entirely. I wisht we could have got a shot at 'em. They was too far out." He glared at Trumbull and saw in the pathologist the personification of every difficulty he had ever encountered in life.

"He's a Communist, Pa," the son said dully.

"Or a Catholic, one or the other," the father added. "One's no better than the other."

"I told you," Trumbull said. "I'm a doctor from Orangeburrow. Let me call, and prove that much for you."

"You? A doctor? Don't make me laugh, mister," the crabman said. "You ain't got one piece of identification on you, nowheres. And you walked in here carryin' a gun, and lyin' about fishin' for redfish down in the mangrove."

"And he had all that money, Pa."

"Yeah, and that too," the old man agreed.

"That money came out of my own bank account." Trumbull said. "I can prove that too."

"You just took all that money swimmin', huh?" the old man sneered. "This here crook thinks we must be foolish, or somethin'."

"Did they find the sailboat out there?" Trumbull asked.

"We didn't see no sailboat," the old man said. "We got down around them mangroves in the johnboat when we commenced to hear all that racket offshore, and we seen 'em walkin' around on that barge, big and brassy as life, workin' with that big crane. We could tell right off what they was up to."

" 'They must be dredgin' the crab grounds,' I told Pa," the son put in, excitedly.

"They're fixin' to cut out our crab fishin' around here for good," the old man said. He turned and faced Trumbull again. "And you brung 'em. So, you know what they's up to. It ain't no sailboat they's lookin' for." He twisted the front of the doctor's shirt and made it difficult for him to breathe.

"No . . . really . . ." Trumbull gasped. "I don't know anything about that. They must be after the sailboat."

"If there was a sailboat out there, we would have seen it," the son said, simply.

"It's sunk," Trumbull said.

"He's crazy, Pa. Plumb crazy."

"That's the way them Communists want you to think they is, son," the father explained. "They act crazy so's you'll let 'em go. Then they come back and steal the rest of your stuff."

"You ain't gonna let him do that to us, is you Pa?"

"We didn't let any of them other guys cheat us and get away with it, did we, son?"

Trumbull suddenly imagined the father and son attacking the barge. He hoped that it hadn't been true, but he knew that if it were, the state attorney would find some way of blaming that on him, too.

"You remember that feller from the state road department?" the old man asked his son. "The one that said he was a hitchhiker? Now we really knowed that he was from the state road department, 'cause we could just tell. He was one of them that made the highway bypass this place. Used to sell a lot of gas before that."

"That guy had a pack on his back, and a beard, and all like that," the son recalled, happily. "But he didn't fool us none, did he Pa? He wasn't no hitchhiker. Leastwise, he ain't no more." The son gave out an explosive laugh that chilled Trumbull to the bone in spite of the awful heat that filled the little shed.

"Now, since this here robber is so interested in crabs . . ." the old man suggested.

"You gonna show him the crabs, Pa?" the son asked. "I mean, really show him the crabs? Real close up? Eyeball to eyeball?" The son laughed nervously again.

"The hitchhiker liked 'em, didn't he?"

The son jumped up and danced gleefully, rubbing his hands together. The memory of the hitchhiker and his fate had given him a half-erection. "Show him, Pa. Show him!"

"You check outside, son. Make sure there ain't none of them fishermen comin' back in for more bait."

"They's all went out, Pa. The last of 'em cleared out 'bout a hour ago." The son scurried toward the shed door and disappeared into the sunshine outside.

"What are you going to do?" Trumbull asked the old crab fisherman.

"We're goin' take care of another crab-trap robber. That's what we is goin' do," the old man said.

"They will be looking for me, you know. As a matter of fact, they've probably been looking for me for a couple of days. They think I've been killed." Trumbull was scrambling to appeal to some vestige of rationality in the old man's brain. It was obvious that he was not succeeding.

"If they think you've been killed, why would they waste their time lookin' for you?" the old man said with surprising logic. "They wasn't no one lookin' for you when you come walkin' up out of the mangrove."

"They just didn't know where I was. I'll bet the whole sheriff's department is out looking for me right now."

"Ain't been no sheriffs around by here today," the old man said.

"There will be. I'm sure of that," Trumbull promised. "And if they don't find me, you'll be in a lot of trouble over this."

"Mister, I been livin' on the edge of these mangroves for a good many years now. I comes and goes like I pleases. I fish when I want and where I want. I catch crabs when they is some. I don't catch none when they ain't none. And there ain't nobody what's goin' to come around here and give me no trouble. Leastwise, not over you."

"Yes, they are," Trumbull argued. "Look. Let me level with you. I got myself into some real trouble, and the sheriff is going to have to come looking for me. And if you say there was a big barge out there today, then that proves it. The sheriff's just got to come looking for me. Now, you let me go, and I'll get the hell off of your property, and the sheriff won't have any reason to bother you any further."

"What kind of trouble you into?" the old man asked, slyly. "You one of them guys runnin' dope off of them banana boats from South America? We seen some of them long-haired freaks around here last year. They cut out from the channel and somebody on the ship throws the dope off to 'em in a floatin' bag." He paused to remember and laughed to himself. "But they ain't goin' to bother nobody no more, either."

"No, damn it. I'm not running any dope or narcotics. My trouble's my own doing. There isn't time to explain it all to you now. Just untie my hands and feet and let me go."

"Ha! Now that's a laugh! I'm just likely to do that. Hey, son! This here crab-trap robber thinks we is goin' to cut him loose!" He shouted loud enough that the son reappeared in the doorway and joined in the old man's laughter.

"You tell him *how* we is goin' to cut him, Pa?"

"Not yet," the old man said. "I'm savin' that for later. When he meets the crabs."

The son stepped into the semidarkness of the shed. The glare behind him subsided so that he became more than the faceless silhouette he had been up to this time. He had Martha Holland's gun in his hand. Trumbull began to struggle instinctively against the ropes again.

"I brung his own gun, Pa," the son giggled.

"You done right, son. He would've used it on you if'n you'd've given him a chance."

"I didn't pull a gun on either of you," Trumbull protested.

"That's 'cause we didn't give you no chance to," the son said.

"C'mon, son. We's runnin' out of time with this Communist dope runner." The old man stuffed the gag into Trumbull's mouth and tied it behind his head. "Untie his feet, and let's walk him down through the mangrove. You know the place."

Trumbull was wild-eyed and shouting muffled and incoherent words against the gag as the crabman's son pushed him toward the door of the shed.

Chapter Fifteen

BRUCE LAFONTAINE SAT ALONE at the corner table in the bar area of the Spanish Park Restaurant. At lunchtime, prominent Tampa lawyers and businessmen were willing to spend half an hour in the bar waiting for a table in the dining room. The bar was similarly overrun around five P.M., when the lawyers, the contractors, and the owners of the Ruskin tomato farms called it a day and gathered for a drink. But in midafternoon, the place was deserted.

It was three P.M., and LaFontaine knew that he would be safe. He wasn't a regular there and Betsy, the bar manager, didn't feel obliged to entertain him with chitchat. It was obvious that he wanted to sit alone at the farthest table.

He sipped his old-fashioned, made correctly with blended bourbon, granular sugar muddled with bitters, no water or soda, and a balanced display of garbage. LaFontaine savored the aroma of bitters, the bourbon and the orange as he sipped. His eyes were glued to the door.

It was obvious to Betsy that he had not come in to get drunk. She had seen, but carefully not noticed, many afternoon rendezvous in the dark corner of the bar.

Dr. LaFontaine did not have long to wait. The door opened. A bright triangle of sunlight streamed across the floor and blinded him and Betsy until the door closed and the darkness peacefully returned. The intruder found the sudden light change equally disturbing. Agnes Trumbull stood there, alone near the door, waiting for someone to speak or for her eyes to adjust to the darkness.

LaFontaine got up quickly and crossed the room to touch her. Betsy was careful not to pay any attention to either of them.

"Agnes," he said softly as he approached.

"Oh, there you are, Bruce. I can't see a thing!"

"It certainly is bright out there, what? Here, give me your hand. I'll show you to our table." He led her to the corner table. By the time they were seated, her eyes had partially adjusted, and she was able to see that they were practically alone in the bar.

"Agnes. How are you coping?" His tone was serious and genuine.

"I'm not sure I'm over the shock, Bruce. Are you?"

He slid his hand across the table and touched hers again. "No, perhaps not. But, we will have to look for the best in it."

"Oh, Bruce, I—"

She was interrupted by Betsy's prompt attention and the clean ashtray that she had placed quietly on the table. "May I get you something?" Betsy asked Agnes.

"No, I don't think I—"

"Go on, Agnes," LaFontaine encouraged her. "It will do you good." He nodded encouragingly.

Agnes hesitated for a moment and then agreed. "Perhaps you're right, Bruce. Let me have a vodka martini on the rocks."

"And another for you, sir?" Betsy inquired, gently.

"I've got enough for now, thank you, miss," he said. He waited until she had returned to the bar before he took Agnes's hand again.

"Bruce," she said, biting her lip to keep from crying. "What am I going to do?"

"You are going to manage, Agnes, because you are who you are. Do you understand?" He spoke to her in firm, masculine tones that steadied her, even though his voice was hushed.

"I'm not that strong, Bruce. I've always had . . . Bill to lean on." She paused, swallowed, and tried to continue. "And now, I just—"

"Agnes. I know what you are going through. And you *are* that strong. But you need the encouragement that friends can offer. That's why I called you and asked you to meet me here today."

"I wouldn't have come except that you said that it was terribly important."

"I know. And I wouldn't have asked you to come if it weren't." He retracted his hand and sat stiffly upright in his chair as Betsy brought the martini. She placed it on the table on a fresh napkin and returned to the bar without speaking.

"Why, here, Bruce? Why the Spanish Park Restaurant bar, where everyone can see us?"

He glanced around the empty room to encourage her to do the same. "Do you see anyone?"

"No, but Bill used to come here, sometimes, and you never know who might show up." She glanced over her shoulder.

"That's just it, Agnes. That's why I asked you to come here. This way, if anyone is watching you, or me for that matter, there would be no suspicions generated by our meeting together this way."

She frowned slightly. "Suspicions about what, Bruce?"

"Oh, the usual thing," he said lightly. "You know the so-called police mentality."

"I'm beginning to. They have been haunting me ever since Bill's disappearance." She took a generous sip of her martini and closed her eyes as she swallowed it.

"You can be quite sure that they are not yet finished," he said. "You've met this Captain What's-his-name?"

"Rizzolo?"

"Yes, I believe it is. Italian, isn't it?"

"I think so," she nodded.

"What a bore! He came to my office and asked perfectly outlandish things." LaFontaine closed his eyes and shuddered slightly.

"About Bill?"

"Yes, yes. Of course. All about Bill, don't you see. That's why I suggest that they haven't finished asking their pesky questions. Not at all."

"I'm sure they have to do that as part of their investigation, Bruce." Agnes always seemed to understand everyone else's problems. Bill Trumbull used to complain about that, from time to time, but she had never understood what he meant.

"Oh, most assuredly. But I was concerned that their investigation and the dreadful newspaper publicity that has attended this incident might tend to discourage you when, really, you needn't feel depressed at all."

"What do you mean, Bruce?" She had been ready to sip her drink again, but she quickly put it down on the table.

"I mean . . ." He leaned close to her and dropped his voice to a coarse whisper. "I mean that I do not believe that Bill has been murdered at all."

She examined his face carefully for any crease or twitch that might indicate he was making some kind of morbid joke. There was nothing but calm sincerity in his expression. Her hopes and her heart leaped at this slight ray of encouragement. "Oh, Bruce. He's got to be alive. Somewhere."

"My sentiments exactly." Dr. LaFontaine took a smug and confident sip from his old-fashioned.

"Did Bill say anything to you or call you, or anything?" she asked hopefully.

"Oh, no, no, my dear. Nothing that blatant. Your

husband was a careful and clever man. I'm quite sure that *if* he were to deliver a message regarding his present welfare or whereabouts, he would do so in such a way that it would not constitute an embarrassment for anyone concerned."

"Well, how would I know about it, Bruce?"

"You would simply have to remain alert and attuned to any unusual message that might be brought to your attention by anyone. Besides, isn't that a far more wholesome attitude for you to assume than sitting around convincing yourself that Bill Trumbull is dead?"

"I do want to believe that he's all right. But . . . I'm so afraid."

"Drink your martini, Agnes. We really don't want to attract the attention of the barmaid. I'll order us another round." He raised his hand and gave a loud snap of his fingers that made Betsy repress the urge to tell him to kiss her ass. Instead, she quickly prepared two more drinks.

"But what about his car and all those things that the newspaper said? They think he's been murdered, don't they?" She didn't want to use the word. Saying it might make it so. She had known that since childhood.

"The *Tribune* is only interested in selling newspapers. You mustn't let them upset you. All they had was the terrible scene that was found by the phosphate pit. I'm sure that the homicide captain is no more convinced of Bill's death than we are." He smiled gently at the pathologist's wife as Betsy exchanged fresh drinks for the dregs of the old.

"Why would he do such a thing, Bruce?" Agnes searched his face for an answer.

"I'm afraid I don't have a reply for that one, Agnes. You'll have to come up with at least part of the answer yourself."

"What do you mean?"

"Agnes, we are both adults and sophisticated. We may as well accept certain realities in our lives. Ignoring them does not make them go away. In fact, I suspect that the inability to face certain of our personal difficulties may magnify them out of all proportion." He took a sip from his new drink and was surprised to find it as satisfying as the first. The second drink seldom was.

"What are you saying, Bruce?"

"You and Bill were having difficulties. Oh, I suppose I knew that for a long time, but you know how it is. People don't just barge in and start to talk about other people's personal difficulties with them. But, it was there. I could see it. I could see it in you and, of course, I could see it in Bill. I saw a lot more of Bill, of course, and perhaps that made it a bit more obvious to me."

Agnes lowered her eyes and lightly fingered the cold martini glass. "Did he . . . did he ever talk about it with you?" she asked.

"Not really. Bill wasn't much for talking out his personal problems. Oh, sometimes when we were having a quiet drink together in some pub, he might pass a remark or two that showed me that he wasn't all that happy at home, but then, as a physician, perhaps I was a bit more sensitive to some of his symptoms." It seemed to Bruce LaFontaine that Agnes was about to cry. He moved a little closer to her and took her hand in his own. The move fulfilled Betsy's expectations perfectly.

"I guess I wasn't very good at it, Bruce," she said sadly.

"You mustn't blame yourself. It was a lot of things, Agnes. His age, his job, the push of things around him . . . you know. I've seen a lot of cases like this one. Some of them turn out well enough in the end."

"*You* have?"

"Yes. Radiology is not my only interest, you know. I *am* a doctor, after all. And, I'm interested in the whole man, not just skiagrams of his bones. Radiology is simply a handy way to make a living, you see."

"You're sounding more like a psychiatrist."

"Well, we need all kinds of doctors, my dear." He

gave her a little laugh in an attempt to brighten her spirits. "Did I ever tell you my classification of doctors, by the way?"

"No."

"No? Well, listen to this. An internist is a doctor who knows everything and does nothing. A surgeon is a doctor who knows nothing and does everything. A psychiatrist is a doctor who knows nothing and does nothing. And, a pathologist is a doctor who knows everything and does everything, but one day too late."

Agnes laughed for the first time that week. "And a radiologist?"

"A doctor who sees right through everyone." He smiled broadly, happy that he had made her feel better, if only for a moment.

"Bruce," she said, suddenly serious again, "You didn't make me come all the way down here from Orange-burrow to tell me cute stories about doctors. There's something else." She sipped her martini to give him a chance to tell her exactly what.

"Yes, Agnes, you're right. I asked you to come here because I wanted to talk to you privately, before that awful Captain Rizzolo put two and two together, and began to embarrass you."

She nodded to encourage him. He was obviously reluctant to continue.

"Agnes, did Bill ever discuss another woman with you?"

"Another woman? Bill?"

"Oh, I don't think it was anything too serious, you understand. Just a diversion. The way men will, from time to time. But I thought—in view of the things that have happened lately, and the newspapers, and all . . ."

"Who, Bruce? Who's the other woman?"

"You've read the papers yesterday and today, I'm sure. While they haven't yet put the two stories together, I'm quite convinced that the death of Martha Holland is somehow connected to Bill's disappearance."

"Bruce!"

"I know it's hard to believe, but I think I know what I'm talking about. He'd been seeing her from time to time. I'm not sure that you ever knew."

"Martha Holland?"

"I'm afraid so. I knew it, so I'm sure that there are others who must have known. It's only a matter of time, you see, before the police get this kind of information and consider it as one, rather complicated case."

"But, Bruce, I don't believe it. The newspaper said that she was found on her sailboat. At first, *The Tribune* said she had been drowned when the boat sprung a leak, or something, and then, *The Times* changed it to a shooting." She gasped slightly, as if comprehending for the first time, the magnitude of the newspaper report. "Good God, Bruce! Do you think that Bill shot her?"

"Oh, heavens no, Agnes. Furthest from my thoughts," LaFontaine said lightly. "The worst I can imagine is that they were on the sailboat and got attacked or something."

"Attacked? Attacked by who?"

"Well, not Indians, certainly, but possibly someone interested in their money? Or perhaps, in Martha or hers—I'm just not sure."

"Interested in Martha? You mean, like a rapist?" Agnes put her hand to her mouth.

"Why not? There have been a lot of couples attacked in parked cars. Why not on a sailboat?"

"I still can't believe it, Bruce. I mean, I *want* to. God! Anything's better than thinking that he's been murdered and thrown into that phosphate pit."

"That's why I had to talk to you, Agnes."

"But, where is he now? How did he get off the sailboat, if she was raped when they were attacked?"

"Now, wait, Agnes. We don't really know what happened. I offered the rapist theory to give your mind something else to work on instead of Bill's apparent murder. I may have it all wrong. But I wanted you to be aware of this sort of theory before you were surprised by it when Captain Rizzolo jumped you with it. He hasn't, has he?"

"No. All their questions have been straightforward, so far. They haven't even mentioned Martha Holland's death. That's why I'm so surprised to hear you put the two of them together."

"I saw her, you know," LaFontaine said in a matter-of-fact way.

"Who?"

"Martha Holland. I bumped into her when she was evidently buying supplies for this trip in her boat. I didn't think anything of it at the time. She's always off on some sailing jaunt, or other. Not exactly my cup of tea."

"Was Bill with her?"

"Oh, my heavens no! She was quite alone. But she was in a strange part of town for the likes of her, if you know what I mean, and she acted a bit nervous."

"Did you tell that to the sheriff?"

"As a matter of fact, I did. At the time, you see, I had no reason to connect anything she was doing with the terrible reports we were getting about Bill. But now, as I think back over it all, I'm quite sure they must have been meeting somewhere to take a trip in that sailboat of hers. She seemed to have supplies enough in her little car to set sail around the world. Although I suspect that her planned itinerary was considerably shorter than that."

"So, Rizzolo knows too, then," she reasoned aloud.

"Possibly. But I'm not sure that he has managed to make the connection between Martha and Bill, as yet. I'm quite confident that he will, of course. There may still be time."

"Time? Time for what?" Agnes seemed puzzled.

"Time to help Bill, if he contacts you."

"Why would he contact me, Bruce? To hear you explain this whole mess, he left me to run off with Martha

Holland." She took a larger swallow of her martini and winced slightly as it went down. Drinking was not one of her larger talents.

"Because of his car, and all the trouble he must have gone to to make it look as if he were actually murdered."

"And you don't believe that he was murdered."

"Not for a moment," LaFontaine said, confidently. "Bill was too smart for all of that. If someone had abducted him from his office at the hospital, and forced him to withdraw his money from the bank, he would have devised a way to let someone know that it was happening. Bill was a difficult man to surprise or fool."

"I'll agree with that, at least," she conceded. "You think he will call me?"

"I rather doubt that. Too dangerous, you see. I rather suspect that whatever message he manages to get through to you will be a bit confusing, and anything but obvious. He couldn't afford discovery at this late juncture in the scheme."

"What scheme?"

"Bill carried insurance, didn't he?"

"You mean, for malpractice?"

"No, not malpractice. Insurance on his life."

"Oh, yes! Of course he did," Agnes admitted easily. "But I don't know much about all that. He took care of that sort of thing himself. I could call the insurance agent and check on it, I suppose." She sounded eager to help.

"No! That's the last thing you should do at this point. The sheriff is watching every move you make, I'm sure. He would love it if you suddenly ran off to contact the insurance agent."

'But it's my insurance, too," she said defensively.

"Sure it is, Agnes. But let it come to you. It will look so very much better for you that way." He signaled for another old-fashioned and gestured that a martini was not needed. Betsy had begun to make the drink before his hand was back on the table again.

"Why do you think the sheriff is watching me?" she asked.

"Wouldn't you, if you were assigned to the investigation of a local pathologist's murder?"

"That means they know I came here," she reasoned. "And it means they know that I'm meeting you here."

Betsy arrived with the old-fashioned and caught the last sentence. She was used to people who were concerned about being seen together in the bar.

"Of course, they do," LaFontaine said, softly. "That's why I chose such an obvious and public meeting place. They'll think nothing of it. Nothing at all."

Betsy shrugged and returned to the bar without comment.

"Bruce, you've made me feel a lot better," Agnes said.

"We all need something to hope for. But, you mustn't tell the children as yet."

"Oh? Oh, no of course," she agreed. It was clear that she had not considered that yet.

"They will be safer, if they think that Bill has been murdered. They are used to that story by now. That way, no matter what tricky questions the sheriff asks them, their answers will be consistent."

"It'll be harder on them, though," she said.

"That's why you'll have to be strong for them, too. Let them lean on you. You're all they have left."

"Am I really, Bruce?"

"None of us can be sure, Agnes. All we have at this point is our intuition and our hopes. At this very moment, however, my hopes are quite high."

"God. I hope you're right."

"So do I. Now—you've been here long enough for a woman who is grieving over the loss of her husband. The deputy outside will get suspicious if you stay much longer." LaFontaine stood up and took her hand tenderly.

"Where should I go?" she asked.

"Go downtown to Sacred Heart Church and light a candle at the altar to the Virgin Mary. If the deputy following you is a redneck, and sees you do it, he won't understand. And if he's an Italian deputy, he'll think it's quite normal." He gave a little shrug to explain his logic.

She smiled warmly and kissed him on the cheek. "You're a sweetheart, Bruce. Thanks for talking with me. Tell your Mary that I'll get over to see her soon."

"No, Agnes," he instructed once more. "Let Mary come to you. A visit *from* my wife is reasonable. She will come to help you with the children and the house."

"How come you think of everything, Bruce?"

"Obviously because I'm British," he said, smugly. He nodded his head toward the door and she quickly caught the hint. He watched her as she walked across the room with a lighter step than the one she had entered with. He took a deep breath and held it for a moment. "I hope I'm right," he said aloud to himself.

"Pardon me, sir?" Betsy said from the bar.

"Check, please."

Chapter Sixteen

DEPUTY SERGEANT ORVILLE GRUBBS had accepted some unusual assignments in his twenty-four years with the sheriff's department, but this one may have taken the cake, he thought. He was still grumbling about it to himself as he eased his shiny green-and-white cruiser along U.S. 41 toward the East Bay area.

"I guess, when a man gets into retirement years, they figger they can give him any damn fool assignment and get away with it," he said aloud to no one. "And, maybe they is right, 'cause here I am, chalkin' up overtime, burnin' the taxpayers' gasoline and tires, lookin' for some cracker that probably don't even live down this way." He shook his head sadly and threw half an ear to a radio transmission from the S.O. that didn't directly concern him. After that many years, his brain automatically paused for transmissions, regardless of what else he asked it to do.

Sergeant Grubbs kept his speed at a constant 55 miles per hour to conform with a recent directive from the sheriff himself. The sheriff didn't want the public to get upset about the green-and-whites whizzing around the county at speeds higher than those authorized by the governor. Conforming to the 55-mph limit had caused some incredible backups along the larger roads, since the citizens were afraid to pass the highway patrol and were, at the same time, generally hostile about the speed limit. There just didn't seem to be any way for the sheriff to win that one.

"That Captain Rizzolo must be plumb crazy," Grubbs continued to himself. "How's he 'spect me to hunt up one pertic'lar crabman down here without knowin' the one I'm s'posed to be lookin' for? Leastwise, he could have given me one of them floater things they pulled up. That way, maybe someone could have recognized the colors and tolt me whose it was."

Captain Rizzolo intended to beat the irate crab fisherman to the punch, explain the circumstances to him, apologize on behalf of the sheriff, and promise payment for all damages inflicted on the man's traps and floats. He had explained all that to Sergeant Grubbs and had acknowledged that one of the floats might have been a valuable lead in tracking down its rightful owner. However, the day was running out. The sun was threatening to disappear somewhere beyond St. Petersburg, and, with a little luck, the particular crabman might be identified by a routine survey of the area, even without one of his damned floats. It would have taken another hour to find the tugboat captain and ask him if he still had any of those floats that he cut off during the positioning of the barge. Rizzolo was confident that Capt. Coony Daggit would be at least half drunk by that time of day, and that, if asked, his sober half would spend at least two hours denying the whole incident anyway.

Rizzolo had picked Sergeant Grubbs because he knew that his down-home demeanor would be less offensive to a cracker crabman who would scream about police brutality the instant he was informed of the crab-trap accident. The captain was convinced that if he sent one of his New York transplants that the department seemed to be attracting regularly, the fisherman would carry his complaint all the way to the governor. Sergeant Grubbs was the best man for the job, even though the fact that he was scheduled to go off duty—a direct request from the captain himself—could not be ignored.

As he drove, Sergeant Grubbs noticed an open side window in a fruit stand that was closed for the day. He made a mental promise to check it out on the way back. Spotting that kind of small irregularity was what made Orville Grubbs a superior deputy, despite his unpolished, unschooled methods. It was that kind of simple alertness that had made him a good deputy originally and then, over the years, an outstanding patrol sergeant. He was not looking forward to retirement. He knew that when he had completed his twenty-fifth year, his name would come up for review again, just like it had when he had finished his twenty. He was hoping for thirty, but with the new federal standards, and the pressure on the sheriff to replace the older men with transfers from northern police departments, token blacks, and women, Grubbs was afraid that he would be put out to pasture. He blamed the whole thing on school busing, the news media, and the Northeastern Establishment. He was happy to tell anyone who cared to listen just why the whole country was going to hell.

As Grubbs saw it, forced school busing pushed the whites out of the cities up north, and the men who had been assigned to patrol the new, all-black downtown sections had rushed in to submit their resignations and moved to the quieter cities in the South. He thought it ironic that these younger cops were replacing the older men in the South who had been involved in the effort to force the blacks to move up north in the first place. Grubbs said that to complete the cycle, all the southern deputies should retire to Detroit.

Sergeant Grubbs was not sure where it was that he was supposed to go. Crab fishing was not one of his family's sources of income. He had been raised with cattle and strawberries near Plant City, and anticipated his return to a small farm when he finally got his pension. In fact, he already owned forty-seven acres of grazing land with fifteen Valencias in the eastern part of the county. Some years, he kept a few Black Angus on the land, but when the wholesale meat prices went down, he let it go to grass.

He turned the cruiser onto a narrow county road and headed for the bay. Even a farmboy like Orville Grubbs knew that you had to be near water to fish for crabs. But this part of the county was less familiar to him than the eastern parts, and he really didn't know the crab fishermen as well. Some of them came from old Cuban families that stuck together and didn't seek friends outside of their own Spanish-speaking groups. The others were old, sunbaked crackers who had fished the same mangroves for generations. Over the years, they had accounted for very few complaints to the sheriff and, consequently, their parts of the county were little known by members of the department. Newer trailer parks for retired mountain people from Tennessee and the Carolinas had invaded them in recent years, and increased the frequency of calls to the sheriff, with drunkenness, unsanitary conditions, and sexual assaults on minors leading the list of complaints. Actually, there were no real sexual "assaults" among these mountain people. It was simply that they introduced their children to sex earlier than others. None of the minor females had felt particularly assaulted, and none of the adult men had ever thought that their intimate gestures were offensive. It was more a misunderstanding between poor peoples with different life-styles who had now come to live close together in trailer homes near the bay.

Sergeant Grubbs had managed to ignore this type of offense when he was called to check out some other complaint at one of the trailer parks. As a result, he was now able to recognize responsible mothers, old before their time but not unloved for it, who would have been ruined early in their lives had they been branded as sexual-assault victims. Grubbs had kept dozens of these cases from his own juvenile bureau and had never regretted any of his judgments.

The county road was in need of repair, the edges crushed into turtle-sized pieces of tar by big produce trucks. On either side of the road, tomato and watermelon plants grew or died, depending on the rotation of the acreage and the market. After a mile or two, the road came to a "T". Grubbs stopped the cruiser and looked perplexedly in both directions. The sun was in his face and threatening to go down. The change in the trees and bushes told him that he was getting closer to the bay. He decided to turn south and to follow the road for a few more miles before quitting and turning back. A call into central communications would not have given him any information that he could use. No one in the radio room could tell him any more about where he was than the vista he saw through the lovebug smears on the windshield. He was in the lower bay area, off U.S. 41, and since his feet weren't wet, he must be east of the bay. That kind of dead reckoning was quite sufficient for Orville Grubbs.

Here and there, the backwash of the bay came up to the road and gave him a view of a dark, wet swamp that controlled its own overgrowth with brackish water and seasonal tide levels. Those were the areas that wiser men, like Sergeant Grubbs, preferred to leave to the raccoons, the snakes, and the gators.

The shadows were longer now, and the dark places beneath the trees were becoming black. Sergeant Grubbs was ready to turn his green-and-white around, and abandon his crazy search for this unknown, pissed-off crab fisherman, until the morning. But the swamp and the soft-looking sand on each side of the road kept him heading farther south while he searched for a place to turn around.

The turnaround came up after the next curve in the road. As did a small combination gas station and bait house. The sign over the entrance said, McCRAW's. Sergeant Grubbs swept his memory and found only a fragment of a recollection of McCraw's, attached to a low-key investigation of a child drowned on a Sunday school picnic, many years before. The child's body had been carried by the tide to the mangrove area off McCraw's landing, and Deputy Grubbs, then with only a year or two of service to his credit, had been assigned to a rowboat in the confusing backwater. There had, of course, been no prosecution, and Grubbs was unable to recall whether or not he had actually met any of the McCraws at that time.

There was no reason for Sergeant Grubbs to associate the younger McCraw, whom he had probably never met either, with the occasional drunk reports that had been filed on him with the city police department, and less frequently, with the county force. There were thousands of such reports every year, and for a teetotalling Baptist like Orville Grubbs, all these drunks looked alike.

Grubbs pulled the cruiser into the parking area beside the small gas station and waited for a break in the radio chatter to tell communications where he was. It was getting dark and there seemed to be endless bursts of words about a trailer truck that had turned over on route 574, causing a major traffic snarl and requiring an ambulance for the driver. The sergeant's professional courtesy and his appreciation of the seriousness of the truck accident kept him off the radio. After a few minutes of waiting for a break, he abandoned the attempt to report in, and got out of his car. He knew that it was a violation of departmental rules to be off his unit without calling in the location, but he was sure that he could get this routine check over with in a few minutes and be back in the car before he was called. Besides, the man on communications had known Grubbs for over fifteen years, and familiarity had a way of softening regulations.

The hot, still air of the mangrove area plastered Grubbs's damp shirt against his back as he stepped out of the patrol car and walked toward the gas station—bait house. There were no lights on, but it was a little early for them. The dark inside of the station contrasted sharply with the orange-red sunset that lit the cluttered yard. Grubbs squinted to sharpen his vision and walked noisily into the single room of the store. He hoped that someone would throw him a greeting from a darkened corner, but none came. He glanced around the room and saw the usual stock of a small store. It carried standard items that a storekeeper hopes to sell to a forgetful or poorly prepared fisherman when he finally gets near the water.

The stale air in the room reminded Sergeant Grubbs of the odor of cats, although the McCraws had not had one for years.

"Hellooo?" Grubbs called loudly. The ancient dog, still lying malnourished and motionless near the gas pump, emitted a noise that was somewhere between a bark and an anemic growl. It was impossible to tell whether it was a greeting or a warning, but Grubbs did not consider the animal to be the slightest threat, even though his leg still bore the irregular scars from a neurotic poodle that had leaped out at him from a house trailer in Sun City when he had responded to a woman's call for help. She had been unable to light the pilot in her oven.

Grubbs noticed the door in the rear of the store and assumed that the proprietor had temporarily left by it. The front door was still wide open and the cash register drawer was ajar. It was obvious to Grubbs that the place was not closed for the night. Above the rear door, there was a faded metal sign that advertised Garcia y Vega Cigars at a price that hadn't been in effect for two decades. Even Garcia couldn't buy them that cheap anymore, but since McCraw hadn't stocked cigars in years, it didn't matter what the sign said.

Grubbs expected to find a dark and musty storage room when he opened the rear door of the store. He was pleasantly surprised to find himself outside again, bathed in the warm light of the sunset, and partially surrounded by empty oil cans and greasy automobile parts that, evidently, had been thrown out the door when they were no longer of use. He stepped out carefully to avoid getting grease on his shoes. At one corner of the building, flies buzzed around an area that Grubbs correctly assumed had been a handy place to piss.

The only other building in sight was the small storage shed near the canal, some forty feet behind the gas station. If there were anyone around at all, Grubbs reasoned, he would either have to be in that little shed, or off in the swamp somewhere. Grubbs was willing to abandon the whole search if there were no one inside it; twilight swamp-walking was definitely not one of his favorite outdoor sports, crab traps or no crab traps. He took off his cowboy hat to run his hand through his sweaty hair, then replaced it at an angle that violated another departmental regulation. He preferred not wearing it at all, but he was willing to comply with the hat-on-out-of-the-car rule, provided that he did not have to wear it like Smokey Bear or some jaunty Marine drill sergeant.

About halfway across the junk-filled yard, Grubbs took an irregular step to avoid a front bumper from a forgotten wreck, and kicked an oil can. The oil can was not one of the newer cardboard replacements, but was metal, and rang in an E-flat as it bounced. The noise disturbed more than the blue jay that leaped from a limb in a nearby pine and flapped his way along the canal. It also disturbed the McCraw boy. He suddenly appeared in the doorway of the shed, let out a rebel yell, and shot Sergeant Grubbs in the stomach with Martha Holland's gun.

"Jesus," Grubbs sighed softly as he spun around, grabbed his belly, and stumbled through the trash toward the rear door of the gas station. The bullet burned in his stomach and his white shirt began to turn bright red along the belt line. During years of boring patrols, Grubbs had mentally rehearsed what his reaction would be if he were ever shot. He had seen himself quickly taking cover, whipping out his revolver, aiming carefully, and returning fire with deadly accuracy. Instead, he now found himself stumbling and falling across the main room of the store, spilling canned goods and fishing supplies from the display stacks, and finally lurching out the front door toward his car. His head was already feeling light, and he knew that he was bleeding internally.

He fumbled at the car door and threw it open clumsily. He was happy that he hadn't locked it, although that violated another departmental rule. His radio was still on, and there were more words being exchanged about the trailer truck accident. This time, he did not wait for clearance. He took the transmitter in his hand and pushed the button with his bloody thumb.

"Signal thirty-three, for Christ's sake. Signal thirty-three," he shouted. "This is car nine. This is Orville Grubbs and I've been hit." He was transmitting the signal for an officer in trouble and requesting assistance. This signal would take precedence over other radio traffic, if it was understood at headquarters, and Grubbs knew that the communications officer would send help as soon as he could. He knew that it would be picked up by any car in the area. The thought was comforting. What wasn't comforting was the fact that there probably weren't any other cars in that area.

"Car nine," headquarters responded. "What is your ten-twenty?" Communications was worried. They didn't know where the sergeant was.

"Jesus. I'm shot," Grubbs moaned into his transmitter. His ears were beginning to buzz. Grubbs wondered if that meant he was bleeding to death inside.

"Orville!" the communications officer shouted. "This

is Maxwell Appleyard. Where the hell are you, man?"

"McCraw's," Grubbs responded. He was feeling weaker and scared. "East Bay. Crabman's shack. Bait store. Get Rizzolo. He knows."

"Roger. Stay in the car, Orville. Repeat, stay in your car. I'm sending help."

"Yeah. OK, Max. Thanks. I'll hold on from here."

"Are you now under fire? Over."

"No. Hell, Max, I only saw the guy once."

"Hang on, Orville. I'll send everybody I've got." Corporal Appleyard adjusted his transmitter and started his emergency A.P.B. to all units. Simultaneously, he flipped on the intercom so that every deputy in the building could hear his voice transmission. He spun his chair around to face his transmitting computer and typed the same message into the machine. It instantly appeared on the display boxes of all the patrol cars equipped with the new visual communications setups. As soon as he had a free hand, he picked up the phone and dialed his counterpart in the Florida Highway Patrol. He explained the situation to the F.H.P. and asked for help. The highway patrol did not monitor the radio transmissions of the sheriff's office and vice versa. There was no formal agreement between them to supply assistance in emergency situations such as signal 33, but the report of an officer shot and under fire was one that no policeman could ignore. Corporal Appleyard hoped that a highway patrolman was cruising somewhere in the east bay area. As far as Appleyard could figure it, Sergeant Grubbs was the only sheriff's unit anywhere near McCraw's, and even that estimate depended on Appleyard's dim recollection of that part of the county. He had pulled routine patrol in that area, but it had been years before. Still, some things stick in your memory if they are not crowded out by other masses of trivia, and Corporal Appleyard hadn't entertained very many new thoughts in a long while.

Captain Rizzolo was halfway to Fatman's Barbecue for his supper when he heard the emergency transmissions. The transmissions from Sergeant Grubbs had been faint and erratic due to the distance, but the messages from headquarters had come in loud and clear. Rizzolo had repressed the urge to call back immediately. He knew that additional radio traffic would only clutter the airways and possibly obscure an essential part of Grubbs's call.

He knew the general area where he had sent Sergeant Grubbs. He turned his unmarked unit around to head south along U.S. 41. He brought his blue flasher up onto the dashboard in front of him, turned it on, and pushed his car up to eighty.

He found a space in the radio chatter. "Seven-fifty," he said tersely.

"Seven-fifty. Go," Appleyard responded.

"I caught your signal thirty-three, and am responding. I'm on 41 south, just clearing the city limits. I'll be ten-fifty-six with Grubbs in ten minutes."

"Roger, seven-fifty. Are you assuming command of the signal thirty-three?" Appleyard was searching for a ranking officer to take over this operation. The most he had expected for the moment was a circulating patrol sergeant or maybe a lieutenant on his way home. A homicide captain was more than he had hoped for.

"This is seven-fifty, that's ten-four with me. I'll take it over from here. And, Max . . ." Rizzolo became almost human for a moment.

"Yes, Captain?"

"Get an ambulance down there, will you?"

"Yes, sir. Ten-four."

Rizzolo got off the air and concentrated on driving his unmarked unit through the early-evening traffic. He used his flashing blue light and siren whenever it looked like either of them would help. The road was four-lane, but without a separating median, and the drivers weren't in any particular hurry. Only a few of them spotted his blue light and moved over; the stereos and tape decks didn't give his anemic siren a chance. To persuade some of the more reluctant idiots to move over, he pushed his front bumper almost onto the rear of the car in the lane in front of him, flashed his headlights, and leaned on his horn and siren, all at the same time. One by one, they leaped out of the way when they finally got the message. A couple of the civilian drivers muttered something like "Goddamned cowboys," as he roared by.

He picked up his transmitter and called in again.

"Yes sir, Captain," Appleyard responded.

"Max, I want the chopper in the air over that place as soon as you can get him up. He can monitor the location for me."

"Ten-four, Captain."

"We may need his lights in a little while," Rizzolo added.

"Roger, seven-fifty."

"Max, can you raise anybody from the F.H.P.?" The captain didn't know that Corporal Appleyard had already called the highway patrol.

"That's affirmative, seven-fifty. But the F.H.P. hasn't got anyone ten-eight in that sector. Sorry."

"OK, thanks," Rizzolo said. He swerved around a slow MG midget. The couple inside the little car were more interested in making love than in driving. Rizzolo took them on the right and flipped back into the left lane in front of them before his blue light and siren had registered on the young man's distracted brain. "Move over, asshole," Rizzolo muttered through his teeth. "You can play those kind of games at the Holiday Inn."

The radio traffic told him that other units had picked up the signal 33, and were responding to the scene. He remembered the city motorcycle cop who was responding to a plane crash at the airport and had hit a fire truck at an intersection. The motorcycle cop was a vegetable now, and was farmed out, at full-duty pay, to a state institution. It was hard for an officer, responding to a scene with a red light and siren, to hear the sirens of other emergency units on the road. Rizzolo hoped that the other deputies rushing to help Grubbs remembered the story about the motorcycle cop. Rizzolo threw it into all of his training lectures for just that purpose.

During a stretch of straight road Rizzolo reached over and flipped open his glove compartment. He was glad to see a box of Winchester .357 magnums. He hadn't been sure that the box was still in there, and without them, he would have only the bullets in his gun and the six in his belt pouch. He hated to wear the little belt pouch, with its awkward, upside-down snap flap, but it was a good regulation and he insisted that all the men obey it.

"Seven-fifty," the radio said, suddenly.

"Seven-fifty," Rizzolo responded.

"Captain, the chopper's down with a broken something-or-other in the engine," Appleyard said. There was obvious frustration in his voice.

"Goddamn tinker toy," Rizzolo said aloud before he depressed his transmission button. "Ah, ten-four. What about the city's?"

"The location is outside the city limits, Captain."

"I know that, Corporal. Christ! Call 'em up and ask for Major Kleinfelter in homicide. Tell him what's comin' down. Tell him I told you to call and tell him that I need his help. See if he can swing it, Max."

"Ten-four, Captain. Sorry."

"And, Max . . ."

"Yes sir?"

"Did you raise the ambulance?"

"That's affirmative, Captain. I've got two units en route. They'll probably need help finding the place when they get to the area. They're coming from all the way downtown."

"Keep 'em coming, Max. By the time they get there, it'll look like a parade. They'll find the place."

"Roger, seven-fifty."

"Have you heard anything more from Orville, Max?" Rizzolo was worried. It was easier to be busy and worried than just worried.

"Let me try, Captain. Car nine. Car nine." He paused to give time for an answer, but none came. "Car nine, please acknowledge. Car nine."

There was silence as every unit en route shot a glance at the radio and waited for Sergeant Grubbs to respond. Each of the deputies had mentally traded places with Orville Grubbs, and each of them could feel the burning of the bullet, although they had not all imagined the wound in the same location. The silence from Orville Grubbs was ominous and even more nerve-racking than the combat-ready chatter that had preceded it.

"Come on, Orville, you big, stupid, red-necked son of a bitch," Rizzolo said to himself with surprising tenderness and concern. "Answer the goddamned phone."

"Car nine. Calling car nine," Appleyard continued. "Do you read?"

Ears strained and lumps appeared in throats simultaneously all over the county. A weak voice broke through the silence to say, "I'm sure thirsty, Max." It was unmistakably Orville Grubbs.

"Tell him I'm almost there, Max," Rizzolo said. He wiped his eyes with the back of his hand to clear the blur that suddenly appeared during Grubbs's response, and bit the inside of his cheek to keep it from returning.

Chapter Seventeen

THE YOUNGER McCRAW did not know why his father was angry over the shooting of Sergeant Grubbs. The old man had hit him with his fist, making the area around the boy's eye a puffy, blue mass. He took the gun out of his son's hand as if it were a forbidden toy.

"You idiot! You ain't got brains enough to . . ." the old man shouted at him, angry and frustrated. Bill Trumbull had crouched in his corner, his hands still tied and his mouth tightly gagged, when the boy had fired the shot. Trumbull had anticipated a hail of bullets in return and didn't want to be caught in the crossfire. He hugged the floor, making as small a target of himself as he could, and watched the old man beat and disarm his son. The boy cowered in front of his father like a small child.

"He was comin' after us, Pa," the son squealed between blows. Most of the father's punches fell harmlessly on the boy's strong arms and shoulders.

"That was a sheriff!" the old man shouted. "Don't you know what you done?"

Bill Trumbull felt his heart leap for joy at the announcement. Even discovery and arrest by a deputy would be better than further imprisonment at the hands

241

of this unpredictable crab fisherman and his demented son.

"They ain't no good, Pa. They is just like them fish and game wardens. They is always nosin' around, causin' trouble."

"They'll cause trouble, all right, now that you done shot one of 'em," the old man snarled.

"We can hide him, Pa," the boy pleaded. "Just like the others."

"They wasn't sheriffs, boy. When you shoots a sheriff, they send out a whole swarm of 'em to see what happened. He's probably out there, gettin' on his radio right this minute." The old man went to the open door of the shed and looked out without exposing himself. "Leastwise, he ain't layin' out there in the yard."

The son joined his father in the doorway. "But I winged him, Pa. I knowed I winged him."

"Yep. I 'spect you did. But now, we got to worry 'bout whether he is dead or whether he is only winged, 'cause if he is only winged, he is goin' to call for more deputies, and that's for sure."

"You think I should go see, Pa?"

"Sneak out there around the lee-side of the store and get us a look." The old man thrust his head toward the main building. The boy made a move toward Martha Holland's gun, but the old man pulled it back abruptly. "I'll keep a holt to this here gun, boy. You done 'bout enough shootin' for one day." He gave a quick glance at Bill Trumbull and satisfied himself that the pathologist was behaving himself in the corner.

The son gave the yard the once-over from the doorway, and started out for the other side of the store. He picked his way noiselessly through the trash in the yard, and cautiously rounded the corner of the building. The old man squatted in the doorway as he watched his progress. He held Martha's gun in an awkward way that told Bill Trumbull that he was not used to handguns.

The green-and-white stood silently in the parking area. The younger McCraw peeked around the corner of the main building, and looked for signs of life. There were none visible. The doors of the cruiser were closed and the car appeared empty.

"He's still in the store," the boy whispered softly to himself. He crouched low enough to half-crawl across the front of the store without being seen through the windows. He made it to the open front door without any noise to signal his approach. There, on his hands and knees, he slowly peeked inside around the corner made by the doorway. He had carelessly turned his back toward the patrol car, but Sergeant Grubbs did not see it. At that moment, Grubbs lay on his back, across the front seat of the car. His shirt had become wet and sticky with his own blood, and the chatter on the radio had become a confused blur. He felt cold and thirsty and his mind was strangely distant, like in those last moments of consciousness before falling asleep. As if by reflex, he had taken his revolver out of its holster. He could feel the butt of the gun in his right hand, but it seemed as if the hand itself had fallen asleep. He wanted to use the radio to call headquarters. He knew he had to report more of the details of the incident, but he felt confused and totally lacking in initiative.

The McCraw boy looked around the darkened interior of the store and listened for noises that did not come. The spilled canned goods and fishing supplies convinced him that he had really shot the deputy and that his body was somewhere inside. He wished his father had let him bring the gun so that he could shoot the deputy again, just in case. But he was used to his father spoiling his fun. The silence inside the store made him excited and strangely brave. He wanted to see the deputy's body and to look at the place where he had shot him. When he had been younger, he used to have fun by shooting stray dogs and cats with an old .22 single-shot rifle. The gun had since been broken and discarded somewhere in the debris of the bait house. He remembered how he used to poke sticks into the round, bloody holes that his .22 had made in the fur of his animal victims. The thought of the bullet hole in the deputy's body made his penis quiver and he suddenly wanted to masturbate, but he put it off until later.

Half bent over, he cautiously entered the store; yet he was convinced that there was nothing to fear. He knew then that he had killed the man in the uniform, and now he wanted to touch the body. He wondered if his father would let him keep the deputy's badge. He decided to take it anyway, and to put it in the little wooden cigar box that he kept hidden in a hollow place in the old pine tree that lightning had struck. He had other things in the cigar box—a .22 bullet, a credit card that he had failed to return to a customer, a used condom that he had found floating in the mangrove, and most of a pack of cards. Sometimes, he would hide from his father and his chores, and take these things out of the box and play with them. His father had forbidden him to ever touch cards because he said that they were sinful. He knew that the rubber would make his father mad too—especially when he put it on and masturbated while fantasizing about the salesman he had killed one day when his father had gone to Tampa in the pickup. They had buried him when his father got back. His father had hit him that day too.

He began to creep around the store, fully expecting the dead body to turn up behind one of the piles of fishing supplies or in one of the dark corners where he had crawled before dying. He saw the sergeant's blood on the floor. The boy did not know that the fact that blood drops were star-shaped and symmetrical indicated that they had fallen vertically. Had he been brighter and more alert, he would have also seen the blood spots on the front steps, and known that Sergeant Grubbs was not in the store.

His search for the body became frantic and then

angry, when he realized that the deputy had escaped. He picked up a can of Campbell's pork and beans and threw it against the wall.

"You son of a bitch," he shouted at the deputy's memory. "Where did you get to?" He turned and walked boldly out of the store, pausing for a moment in the front door, half expecting to see the deputy lying face down in the gravel. He looked across the road and wondered if the deputy had escaped into the deepening shadows of the swamp. He knew that if night came, he would have a hard time tracking the deputy through the mud and soft sand that filled the spaces between the cedars and cypress trees in the swamp. For a moment, he considered returning to the shed and asking his father for the gun, telling him that he was going to look for the deputy in the mangrove, but he could see his father refusing to let him track the deputy in there at night. His father would spoil everything, if he let him. He squinted for a moment and stumbled down the front steps, heavily clumping his way toward the edge of the swamp.

As he neared the road in front of the station, the radio in the car blurted a message to one of the units en route to the scene. The boy did not hear the message distinctly and would not have comprehended the meaning of it if he had. However, the metallic sound of the transmission and the splatter of the static at the end of it attracted his childlike attention. He had never seen a police radio before and he was suddenly consumed by a desire to look this one over. He grinned spontaneously and turned toward the patrol car, suddenly abandoning the idea of searching for the deputy in the swamp.

The radio emitted another burst of coded words and all thoughts of caution suddenly left the boy's mind. He eagerly reached for the handle on the driver's side door.

"Ten-four," he giggled childishly. Images from television programs flashed in his head. He opened the door without hesitation. For an instant, he saw the sergeant's black shoe and the green of his trousers. He may have also seen the bloodied shirtfront, but he probably did not see the badge that he wanted to add to his collection of favorite things, because Sergeant Grubbs raised his revolver from the floor and blew a massive hole through the young man's right shoulder. The .38 caliber bullet had been hollow pointed and half-jacketed. It mushroomed, but did not fragment as it struck the boy's humeral head, shattered the shoulder socket, and severed the right subclavian artery.

Sergeant Grubbs's shot had been an unaimed reflex and had not been completely comprehended by his blood-starved brain. The crabman's son was blown back some fifteen feet from the open car door, and his shoulder registered incredible pain. Bony splinters had been blasted into the wound from the inside. He scrambled for the store, holding his wounded arm with his left hand, and not looking back. He did not see Grubbs drop the revolver on the floor of the cruiser, surrendering to the weakness of an impending state of shock.

The old dog stood up, walked a half a dozen lazy steps to his right, sniffled the ground, and flopped down again, oblivious to the boy's wound or the excitement in the yard.

The son staggered through the debris inside the store, screaming for his father, and pausing only long enough to fumble open the back door. He crashed through the junk in the backyard and burst into the shed, spurting blood, and yelling frantically that he had been shot.

Incongruously, the old man began to beat him again, this time for being stupid enough to get shot. Punching had been his parental response to every problem that his son presented. But when he saw the blood spurting from his son's shoulder, he stopped hitting him and began to panic.

Trumbull was still lying on the floor. He had begun

shouting through his gag the instant he saw the bleeding boy.

"Sit down here, son," the old man shouted at the struggling boy. "Here, hold your hand tight up here to where the blood's comin' out." He took a jackknife out of his pocket and extended the blade with his stubby fingernail. He moved quickly to Bill Trumbull and rolled him over, face down.

"You said you was a doctor," he shouted at the pathologist. "Get over there and do somethin' for that boy."

Dr. Trumbull pulled the gag out of his mouth as soon as his hands were free, and scrambled toward the boy. "It looks like he's been shot through the artery," the pathologist said hoarsely.

"Don't give us no fancy doctorin' words," the crabman said. "Jest stop that bleedin'." He closed the jackknife, slipped it into his pants pocket, and picked up Martha Holland's gun again. He pointed the gun at Bill Trumbull, not realizing that it was powerful enough to send a bullet all the way through the pathologist and into his son.

"I'm shot, Pa," the son screamed hysterically. "I'm shot, I'm shot." He struggled against the arterial pressure that the pathologist was applying above his entrance wound.

"Hold still," Trumbull said, finding the pressure point again. "Otherwise, you'll bleed to death!" He felt weak and somewhat dizzy himself, and blinked his eyes forcefully to clear his vision.

"Set still, boy," the crabman said. He cuffed the young man on the ear, which did nothing to restore his calm. "This fella here said he was a doctor. Now, you let him tend to ya." He took a few steps toward the open door of the shed and looked out cautiously, keeping the gun pointed in Trumbull's general direction. The yard was still empty. There were no deputies in sight.

"That deputy shot me from inside his car, Pa," the boy whined indignantly. "He didn't give me no chance at all. All I done was to open the door of his car. He was in there, Pa. Waitin' for me. He didn't give me no chance."

"Them bastards," the old man said, condemning everyone.

"He's going to need some medical attention in an emergency room," Dr. Trumbull announced. The boy's blood had already turned the doctor's hands red. "We're going to have to get a surgeon to go in there and tie off that artery. This pressure treatment won't be enough."

"I don't want no operation, Pa," the boy screamed.

"Shut up, boy," the crabman said. "We'll get him to the hospital just as soon as it looks safe."

"And if that deputy's still alive," Trumbull added, "he'll need some medical attention, too. Why don't you go in and call an ambulance for the both of them?"

"An ambulance for that goddamned deputy?" the old man shouted. "After he's gone and done that to my boy, here? Huh! Let the bastard die, that's what I'll do for him."

In the distance, Trumbull thought that he heard a siren but he dismissed the idea after he concentrated on the sound and found that it had disappeared. He didn't know that Captain Rizzolo had just switched off his siren and ordered a silent approach by all the units converging on the area.

A combination of luck and intuition helped Rizzolo avoid wrong turns and brought him within sight of Grubbs's green-and-white in the least time possible. The captain piloted his car to a noiseless halt a few hundred feet down the road from the cruiser, and got out. He knew that the other units would arrive in a few minutes, and when they did and saw his car they would not proceed beyond it until they had grouped, looked over the situation, and received some orders.

Rizzolo decided not to sign off the air. He was afraid that his signal would be picked up by Grubbs's unit and be broadcast, much too loudly, all over the front yard.

He took the box of .357's out of the glove compartment and dumped them loose into his left-hand jacket pocket. He knew that his snub-nosed revolver was loaded. He slipped it out of his belt holster and snapped the hammer back quietly.

If he played the situation by the book, Rizzolo knew that he should wait for help to arrive, set up a command post, and direct the approach to the scene from some protected vantage point. But, he also knew Orville Smithfield Grubbs. They had served together with the sheriff's department for many years, and while the differences in their personalities had never attracted them to each other as friends, they shared a mutual respect for one another. It was because of his respect for Grubbs and the gravity of his present situation that Rizzolo suddenly decided that he would move in on Grubbs's car without waiting for the others to arrive. It was a choice that he would have never allowed another officer to make without severe criticism.

Rizzolo assumed a hunter's crouch and crept quietly toward the green-and-white. He carried his gun at a ready angle in front of him. His eyes swept the yard constantly, straining to detect the slightest motion that might give away the gunman who had shot Sergeant Grubbs. The silence in the yard was almost palpable, and the sounds of his own breathing and the pounding of his heart seemed to the captain to be loud enough to be heard across the bay. His mouth was dry and his sweat had taken on a disagreeable odor. He could almost taste adrenaline.

He made it to the back of the cruiser and hunched down behind it, pausing to listen. Not even a bird challenged the silence of the evening.

Rizzolo was not sure that he wasn't being watched

from some hidden place—a target on the end of an unseen gun somewhere out in the yard or from within the darkness of the store. He rolled across the trunk to the passenger side of the car. He had always taught his men to do the unexpected and thereby reduce the ability of the other guy to anticipate movements. At that moment he hoped he had been right.

From the right side of the car, he could see the other side of the empty yard—still all his. He eased himself along the passenger-side door and stole a glance into the patrol car. Sergeant Grubbs was sprawled across the front seat. His shirt was bloody. His eyes were closed and Rizzolo waited anxiously for him to prove he was alive by taking a breath. It came after a long, painful delay in which Rizzolo himself did not breathe. They exhaled together, but the sergeant's breath was shallower than the captain's.

Rizzolo raised his snub-nosed revolver to the window and gave two quick taps on the glass. Grubbs opened his eyes and looked back over his forehead at the upper half of the captain's face. He smiled painfully. Rizzolo winked at the deputy and crossed his lips with his gun barrel, a sign to keep quiet.

Rizzolo lowered himself beside the passenger door again, and depressed the door latch silently. It was unlocked. The captain thanked God and Grubbs for being careless enough to drive around in a cruiser with an unlocked door. He eased the door open and stuck his face into the crack.

"Orville," he whispered. "It's me, Rizzolo. Are you all right?"

"Yeah, Captain." His hoarse voice made it clear that he was hurt. "I think I stopped one."

"You're going to be all right, Orville. There's a lot more help comin' down the road behind me." He smiled at the sergeant, not realizing that his upside-down face made his mouth appear grotesque.

"Cover your ass, Captain."

"Where is he, Orville?"

The sergeant shook his head helplessly. "Out back, somewheres. He got the drop on me. But I think I winged him." He raised his .38 a few inches off the floor next to him as if to prove his shot to Rizzolo.

"You got off a shot at him?" Rizzolo asked.

The sergeant nodded. "Yeah, Captain. Right here from the car. He came out after me."

"Out here? Where'd he go then? Back to the store?" Rizzolo raised up slightly and got an abbreviated look at the front of the store. There was still no movement anywhere.

"I dunno, Captain. Maybe. Maybe he went back in the store. I didn't see where he went." The sergeant seemed to have trouble breathing, and spoke in short grunts. "Go around . . . to the side. . . . There's a . . . shed."

"Is he alone?"

"I only saw the one. . . . I think he's alone. . . . I didn't hear nobody else." Grubbs winced again. He was obviously in pain. Rizzolo began to worry about making him talk so much. In the detective movies, the intern in the hospital scene would always come in and tell the cop not to make the wounded suspect talk too much. Rizzolo didn't understand why the talking made the wound so much worse, but it seemed to be a hallowed medical tradition.

"You hang on, Orville. I've got an ambulance showing up in a couple of minutes. I'll get back to you." He quietly eased the car door closed, and crept to the right front fender. The empty yard stretched out in front of him. Rizzolo could easily identify the corner that Grubbs had indicated when he told him to go around to the side. The front door to the store was open and it was dark inside. Rizzolo wondered if there was a gun pointing at him from that darkness.

He looked back toward the road and saw that it would be the same exposed shot if he tried to return to his car. There did not seem to be any greater danger going forward, across the open yard, than back to his own unit. Rizzolo was not known for going backward in anything that he attempted. The sight of Sergeant Grubbs lying wounded on the car seat was enough to push him on, regardless of the risks.

He resumed his crouch and went into a half-run that took him across the front yard like a fullback. He kept his gun pointed at the open front doorway as he ran, holding his fire. He wasn't sure who, or just where his target was, and he needed the element of surprise, if he could preserve it.

Somewhere, deep inside himself, Rizzolo hoped that he would be challenged by the gunman, and that he could get a clean shot at him to vindicate Grubbs's suffering. Rizzolo knew that if he killed the gunman, he would have to justify the death to the state attorney's office. To get by that kind of an inquisition, he would need a clean challenge that could not later be construed as an opportunity for capture. Rizzolo would rather dodge a dozen bullets than explain the death of an unarmed criminal to the liberal element of the S.A.O., the mental health board, and the local newspaper. Of those, the only one he was sure of was the newspaper, because he was confident that they didn't give a damn whether he shot a man or not, as long as it sold copies in the morning.

The captain put his back against the side wall of the store and made his way toward the rear corner. When he got there, he crouched low again and carefully looked around the corner. The theory was that no one would expect a knee-high face to appear around a corner, and if anyone was waiting, Rizzolo might get a split-second advantage.

There was no one waiting. There was no one in sight. There was only the shed that Grubbs had prepared him for. He was reasonably sure that the gunman, if he was anywhere at all, was inside the shed. Grubbs had thought that the gunman was alone, and so far, Rizzolo had not discovered any reason to doubt it.

Inside his regulation-filled heart, he knew somehow that he should go back to one of the cars, wait for his reinforcements, locate a bullhorn, and order the man in the shed to surrender. He would want every one of his men to do it that way. He knew that there was no hurry, and he knew that a mistake at this point would only produce a second wounded officer. At the same time, he could not get the picture of Sergeant Grubbs out of his mind.

Up to that point, Captain Rizzolo had not considered that he just might be killed.

After he recognized that possibility, Rizzolo paused to think of others. If Grubbs had shot the man out front, by the car, Rizzolo had to assume that the gunman knew that the deputy was still alive, and that he had probably radioed for help. If his reasoning was correct, then Rizzolo had to assume further that the gunman was either waiting for the reinforcements to arrive, or that he had headed out through the swamp in an effort to escape before they got there. Rizzolo was willing to bet on the escape option. A wounded man might reconsider a nighttime run through a mosquito- and snake-infested swamp. Under the circumstances, the shed was becoming less threatening and more inviting to the captain.

Rizzolo squinted at the horizon. The light was getting worse. The sun would be totally gone in a little while, and that would complicate the whole scene. He strained his ears for the sounds of any of his patrol cars but heard nothing. Rizzolo looked into the sky and wondered if the T.P.D. was going to lend their chopper and if it would get there before dark. His mind was filling with if's.

Then, with a suddenness that characterized his approach to many problems, he stepped out from his protected position and began to pick his way across the yard. He held his gun just above eye level, its muzzle pointed slightly upward, the hammer cocked.

Inside the shed, the bleeding had been temporarily brought under control, and with it the panic and the noise. Bill Trumbull had begun to develop cramps in the small muscles of his hands and forearms from the effort of exerting a steady pressure grip on the boy's wound. The young man's complaints had been reduced to whimpers that could not be heard beyond the four walls of the hot, humid shed. The old man stood with his back to the door and watched the doctor at work. He kept Martha Holland's gun pointed in the general direction of the pathologist.

Rizzolo's approach to the shed was noiseless. He did not stumble over any of the junk in the yard, as Sergeant Grubbs had done. The crabman's discovery of the homicide captain had to be attributed solely to plain, bad luck. The old man had turned casually to look across the yard from the doorway just as Rizzolo reached the halfway point. For an instant, the captain's plain blue suit fooled the old man. He did not recognize him as a cop.

"Here comes one of them damned gas-company agents, son," McCraw announced. He squinted to bring Rizzolo into sharper focus. "And, he's got a gun!" The old man brought Martha Holland's .38 into firing position and began to tremble as he aimed at the homicide captain.

Rizzolo had not yet seen the old man, who was hidden by the deepening shadows of the oncoming evening.

Trumbull looked up from his patient and saw the old man aiming the gun. He could not see Captain Rizzolo, but he knew instantly what was about to happen. He knew that the old man's shaking hand and poor eyesight would not prevent another person from being shot. The doctor's action was sudden and instinctive. There was no time to plan heroics. He released his pressure grip on the boy's shoulder and leaped at the aged crabman, taking him through the open doorway like a linebacker stopping a halfback. There was a tangle of bodies as the two men burst out of the shed and onto the ground in front of the door. The old man pulled the trigger of the .38 and the explosion of the gun produced a massive ringing in Trumbull's ears. Simultaneously, Trumbull felt sudden burning in his left thigh as the leg gave way beneath him. His hands grabbed for the gun, as they rolled into the junk in the yard.

Rizzolo had been more than surprised by the sudden appearance of the two men in front of him. He had been startled and had almost fired a shot into them as they flew out of the doorway and onto the ground. His professionalism had overcome his basic human reaction to shoot, and he had dived to his right, rolling quickly away to regain a firing position on the ground.

The boy began to scream that he was bleeding to death. He came running out of the shed, ignoring the fight between his father and the doctor, and started begging Rizzolo for medical assistance. There was blood spurting from his shoulder and Rizzolo knew that this was Grubbs's man.

"Get the gun," Trumbull shouted as he wrestled with the old man. Blood poured from the pathologist's thigh wound and quickly soaked his pants. "The boy hasn't got a gun!" Trumbull struggled to maintain his grip on the .38, but the old man twisted and fought like a squealing frightened animal.

Rizzolo assessed the scene quickly. He ran to the two grappling men and stepped heavily on the gun. The crabman screamed in pain as the captain's big foot crushed his hand into the hard ground and instantly fractured two fingers. At the same time, Rizzolo pointed his own gun at the boy's head.

"Hold it right there," Rizzolo said loudly.

"I'm bleedin' to death!" the boy screamed.

"Put your goddamned hand on the bleedin'," Rizzolo ordered. "And stay where you are or I swear to Christ I'll blow your head right off."

"My hand!" the old man screamed. "You're breakin' my hand!" He was lying on his back now, and Trumbull had begun to untangle from him.

"You move very slowly too, mister," Rizzolo said to the pathologist. "And stay right there on the ground where I can see you."

"Are you from the sheriff?" Trumbull asked. He spreadeagled himself on the ground in front of the captain.

"I am Captain Rizzolo."

"I'm Bill Trumbull," the pathologist said.

"I'm bleedin'," the boy put in frantically.

"Trumbull?" the captain asked, astonished. "We thought you were dead, in a phosphate pit."

"I'm not dead yet," Trumbull groaned. He grabbed for his bleeding thigh with both hands and squeezed the femoral artery. He was not able to feel any broken bones.

Rizzolo took his foot off the crabman's hand and kicked the .38 away. "You hit bad?" he asked the doctor.

"I think it's all in the soft tissue," Trumbull said. He grunted from the pain and the effort of controlling the bleeding.

"What about me?" the boy screamed. "I'm bleedin' to death!" His hand pressure was poorly applied, and the blood gushed between his fingers and ran down his arm and onto his shirt.

"Bleed to death, you maniac!" Trumbull shouted. "He's the one that shot the deputy."

Rizzolo felt a reflexive half-squeeze in his trigger finger, but he stopped it before he had blown a hole in the boy's face. "You son of a bitch," he said through his teeth. "If I only had you out here alone."

"That one's his father," Trumbull said. "Crazy. Absolutely out of his mind. And dangerous."

"He would have got me surer than hell, if you hadn't jumped him, Doctor," the captain said. "What the hell have we got goin' on here, anyway. Who the hell are these assholes?"

"You busted my fingers," the crabman whined.

"They run this place," Trumbull explained. "They had me tied up in the shed."

"Tied up?" Rizzolo asked. "What the—?" He was interrupted by the sudden appearance of four uniformed deputies who came around both sides of the store simultaneously. They were armed with pump-action, 12-gauge shotguns.

"Are you all right, Captain?" the first deputy asked. The four of them pointed their shotguns at the three men on the ground.

"Yeah, I'm OK," Rizzolo said. "Grubbs is shot. He's out front in his car. Front seat."

"We found him. The ambulance crew is taking a look at him right now," a deputy said. "He'll be OK."

"Check out the doctor, here," Rizzolo said. "He's caught one in the thigh."

"The doctor?" the nearest deputy asked. He seemed surprised. He had set his police mind on three criminals.

"Yeah. This here is Dr. Trumbull," Rizzolo explained. "The pathologist that we thought was dumped in the phosphate pit?"

"What's he doin' down here, Captain?" a deputy asked. He put his shotgun on safety and bent down to look at the pathologist's thigh wound.

"Saving my life, for one thing," Rizzolo said.

"Excuse me, Captain?" the deputy asked.

"Nothin'," Rizzolo said, looking beyond the deputy into Bill Trumbull's eyes. "There's got to be a lot more to all this than I see from right here, but let's get some medical help in here for these wounded men, and we'll sort it all out later." He turned and pointed at the two McCraws. "Book these two for assault with intent to commit murder, for openers. And get one of the ambulance guys to look at this bastard's shoulder. I don't want him to bleed to death before he tells me why he shot Sergeant Grubbs or, for that matter, why he abducted the doctor from his office at the hospital."

"Captain, I—" Trumbull began.

"Doctor—" Rizzolo interrupted, "I think you'd be better off just shuttin' up and waitin' till you've had a chance to think everything over carefully. You'll probably want to talk to your lawyer. About a lot of things, maybe."

Bill Trumbull looked at Captain Rizzolo and nodded in agreement. He was sure that the captain was offering him some kind of a deal, but he wasn't sure what it was.

Chapter Eighteen

THE NEXT DAY, Rizzolo used his influence to get an appointment with the state attorney himself. John Nolan preferred to see police personnel only after one of his assistants had thoroughly worked up a case, pigeon-holed each of the witnesses, prepared an in-house brief on all the legal issues involved, and told him what his official stand should be. Nolan had been a good lawyer in his younger days, but now, insulated by a battery of forty-five junior attorneys, most of whom wanted only a year or two of experience in the S.A.O., he had become an executive and politician. Mostly a politician. He did, after all, run for office every four years.

John Nolan was approaching fifty, and still maintained the slim body that helped him capture the overall track medal at Hillsborough High School, in Tampa, and go on to run varsity at Florida State. He had a preference for the three-piece, Wolf Brothers suits that made him look older and more professional than he really was. He had joined the state attorney's office after law school at Stetson, as a post-graduate opportunity for practical experience, and had stayed five years, rising to the position of second assistant before leaving to try his luck with a large, downtown corporate firm. In that firm, he had been assigned to the anonymous slot of sixty-fifth attorney, and been given several of their not-too-important cases to work on. John Nolan quickly missed the excitement of criminal law. He tolerated the gentlemanly hypocrisies, the better pay, and the rigid organizational structure for eighteen months before he reapplied to the S.A.O. He was eagerly re-accepted, of course, and had stayed on ever since.

Some years after his return and the retirement of his boss, he ran, unopposed, for the office of state attorney itself, and now he could not imagine himself doing anything else with his life. Neither could anyone else.

Rizzolo parked his car in one of the slots reserved for bailiffs, and entered the Courthouse Annex Building. Criminal trials were held on the ground floor, and offices associated with the criminal justice system took up the five floors above. The state attorney's office was on the fifth floor, either to show its importance, or to keep the assistants as far away from the courtrooms as possible. John Nolan might give one interpretation, but Chief Judge Walker would offer another entirely.

There were hellos and familiar nods from all corners as the homicide chief walked the full length of the courthouse and punched the elevator button. He was almost lost in the small crowd of secretaries and clerks that suddenly gathered to fill the elevator the moment the door opened, and he suffered in silence as it stopped at every floor from the ground to the top, discharging middle-aged ladies with paper cups of coffee, until, alone, he was delivered to the S.A.O.

Ordinarily, the receptionist would have asked him to wait in the anteroom until she could check with Nolan's private secretary, or buzz the assistant state attorney that Rizzolo had business with. But this day, Nolan had recognized the urgency in Rizzolo's call, and had cleared the way for him out front. "Good morning, Captain. You may go right in," the receptionist said, cupping her hand over the phone.

"Thanks," Rizzolo grunted. He pushed the swinging doors open athletically, and walked into the state attorney's office complex with an air of disdain, bordering on contempt. His attitude had been honed by many disappointments after his men had delivered a homicide case, closed tighter than a drum, wrapped like a gift, and packaged neater than eggs in a crate, only to watch a junior assistant state attorney plea bargain it away or lose it outright in one of the downstairs courtrooms. With that kind of a track record, Rizzolo could no longer allow himself any chances. He worked his cases to a state of perfection that would allow only an idiot to lose them. Unfortunately, with the turnover at the S.A.O. every year, idiots had to be given their postgraduate chances too, and the results were never perfect. Surgical residents at the hospital put their first stitches in the wrong places, interns at the E.R. injected the wrong drugs, and assistant state attorneys filed the wrong motions. In both professions, the system left a great deal to be desired, but so far no one had been able to think of a better way to change university graduates with M.D.'s and J.D.'s into real doctors and lawyers.

Rizzolo made his way through the labyrinth of inner corridors that separated the assistants' cubicles and gave the office a superficial resemblance to a monastery with each monk in his cell, pouring over thick, dusty books. At the end of the hallway was a closed door. Behind it, in an office three times larger than those of any of his assistants, except the number-two man, sat John Nolan, smoking one of Tampa's best hand-rolled cigars and reading one of the five newspapers he received every morning.

The walls were covered by framed photos of John Nolan with just about everybody, always shaking hands, invariably facing the flag, and never smiling. There was John Nolan with J. Edgar Hoover; John Nolan with the chief of the narcotics bureau; John Nolan and a governor, and the next governor, and the next governor; John Nolan and the chief of police; John Nolan and the sheriff; John Nolan and the previous senator, in front of the Washington monument; John Nolan and Bobby Kennedy. The photographs were frequently signed, and everyone seemed proud and happy to know John Nolan.

Rizzolo stopped at Nolan's secretary's desk. She had obviously been alerted by the receptionist.

"Oh, hello, Captain Rizzolo. Mr. Nolan is expecting you." She waved her hand toward the state attorney's private office and announced the arrival of the sheriff's captain in one, smooth, professional motion. There was no doubt in anyone's mind that Nolan needed her at that desk to contrast with his own, often abrupt ways.

By the time Rizzolo had opened the big door and stepped in John Nolan had folded his newspaper, picked up his cigar, and taken two steps into the center of the room.

"Captain, how are you?" Nolan asked, extending his hand. He was always running for office.

"Fine, sir, fine," Rizzolo said. "Thank you for seeing me this way. So quick, and all."

"Not at all, Captain. I'm always pleased to see you. Anytime. Anytime at all." The state attorney motioned toward one of the two comfortable leather chairs in front of his oversized and very cluttered desk. Rizzolo sat down in it without hesitation.

"As you know, Mr. Nolan," he began, without further preamble, "I've been working with one of your assistants, Elton Majors, on the Trumbull case."

"Oh, it's the 'Trumbull Case,' now?" Nolan asked sharply.

"Well, *we* call it the Trumbull case. Over at the sheriff's office, I mean. Just a way of classifying it for our own reference, Mr. Nolan."

"Certainly, Captain. But, for an official file, we might try to be a little more circumspect with our terminology, you see." John Nolan was already being defensive, and

Rizzolo knew that he might have wasted his time in coming to see the state attorney.

"Yeah, well, anyway, Mr. Nolan, I've tried to explain this case to Mr. Majors, and—well, quite frankly, sir, I haven't had too much luck." Rizzolo leaned forward in his leather chair, causing it to squeak.

John Nolan had retreated to his chair behind the big desk, and loosened his tie. The tie was not particularly tight, but he wanted to give Rizzolo the impression that he was being informal and confidential. Rizzolo assumed that the tie was too tight. His own was.

"According to Mr. Majors, sir," Rizzolo continued, "your office does not seem to think that there is sufficient evidence against Dr. Trumbull to make a charge."

"Something like that, yes."

"Well sir, that's why I came over here this morning to see you," Rizzolo explained. "I thought I owed it to you to lay out everything we had on this here . . . er, Trumbull case, and let you make up your own mind about it."

"Elton Majors and I spoke about it late last night, Captain," Nolan warned.

"Yes sir. I know."

"You know?"

"Well, not really 'know.' What I meant was, I assumed that you had talked about it with Mr. Majors."

"He said so?"

"Not exactly, but I got the message," Rizzolo explained. "I mean, I figured that he was speaking for you when he told me how he intended to handle the case."

"And how was that, Captain?" Nolan reached for his cigar and took a rolling puff.

"Mr. Majors said that there wasn't enough to tie the doctor into the case, and that there was plenty to use against the McCraws, if we wanted to file."

"And you disagree?"

"Well, yes and no, Mr. Nolan. Yes and no."

"What have *you* got for a theory, Captain?" Nolan sounded superior. He was convinced that he was.

Rizzolo sat back in his leather chair and glanced at the ceiling. He wanted to select his facts carefully, knowing that he would probably get only one shot at John Nolan. "We've got a bunch of loose ends, if you know what I mean, and some of 'em just don't add up to the McCraws. Not in my mind, at least."

"Like . . . ?"

"Like, for one thing, the known association between Dr. Trumbull and Martha Holland."

"Martha Holland was a highly respected female lawyer," Nolan observed somberly.

"Yes, sir," Rizzolo agreed. "But, she wasn't the kind of lady—lawyer or not—who would have known the McCraws. Y'know what I mean? I mean, the boy got into a few scrapes with my office and with the P.D., from time to time. Nothing much, of course. Some fights, some drunk charges. Things like that. But, she— Martha Holland—never defended him, or anything like that. Even her secretary couldn't identify a picture of the McCraws, father or son. So, I don't think they'd ever been to see Miss Holland at all. Least, not in her office."

"You checked it out?" Noland asked.

"Yes, *sir*," Rizzolo said triumphantly. "I sent a couple of detectives over to interview just about everybody in her office. And they came up with zilch."

"You apparently didn't like the idea that she could have annoyed these crab fishermen with her weekend sailing, and that they came to complain about damage to their traps?" Nolan asked.

"The old man's too crazy to follow through with something like that. Even if you assume that he was smart enough to pick up her registration number off the boat, look it up in the tax records at the courthouse, and then pay her a visit to complain."

"But what if he just rows out there in that little boat of his with his son, boards Martha Holland's sailboat, and starts an argument with her? Couldn't that erupt into a fight with her winding up shot? And then them sinking her boat to hide the evidence?"

"The McCraws knew every inch of that part of Tampa Bay, Mr. Nolan."

"So?"

"So, they knew how deep it was where the sailboat was sunk. They would know that the stick on the top—"

"Mast," Nolan corrected.

"—mast on the top would stick up out of the water and be seen."

"But, *you* said the old man was a psycho, and that the boy is a defective," Nolan offered. "Would a psycho and a defective necessarily be expected to calculate the depth before they sank a sailboat to hide a woman they had just murdered?" The state attorney spread his hands out to encourage agreement.

"Well, maybe not," Rizzolo conceded reluctantly. "But that doesn't explain the wood alcohol."

"Wood alcohol, Captain? I'm afraid I don't—"

"The autopsy. Doc Flood, over at the M.E. office says that the stuff he found in her stomach was wood alcohol. He had a chemical name for it. Methyl, or something like that."

"And where would Miss Holland get wood alcohol on a sailboat?" Nolan teased.

"They burn it in those little stoves that they have on sailboats. Elton Majors told me that," Rizzolo explained.

"Oh, yes. Majors sails in the Southern Ocean Racing Conference. He'd know about that kind of thing," Nolan agreed. "But, why would she drink wood alcohol? Didn't you find other things to drink on board? Where's that list that your crime lab prepared for me?" He rummaged through the papers on his desk without success.

"There were several canned cocktails, Mr. Nolan, but they were all opened."

"So why would she drink the alcohol for the stove, Captain?"

"Well, sir, I don't believe she really did. I think it was planted on her to throw us off."

"Planted? By whom?" Nolan asked, squinting.

"Who knows?" Rizzolo asked with him. "That's why I'm interested in the fact that there is wood alcohol in her stomach. Now, to me, that don't sound like no psychotic crab fisherman or his screwball son to me." He shook his head to agree with his own denial.

"Who then? Trumbull?"

"Uh-huh. That's who I think," Rizzolo said. He began to count on his fingers. "The doctor knows the lady lawyer. We made that connection with no trouble at all. The radiologist, LaFontaine, gave us that early in the case. He could have been out there with Miss Holland for perfectly normal reasons—like, y'know . . ." The captain shrugged to express his idea that there may have been a sexual motive for the cruise.

The state attorney nodded knowingly.

"She had a carful of groceries and tackle, like she was expecting to go on a long cruise," Rizzolo added, using up another explanatory finger.

"But that was in her car, wasn't it?"

"Yeah. That's a problem," Rizzolo agreed. "Well, my theory is that for some reason, she didn't get time to put none of this stuff on her boat."

"She was shanghaied?"

"Sort of," Rizzolo agreed. "But it was *after* she showed up at her yacht club with all the stuff."

"Why after?"

"Because, there wasn't no room for all that food and booze and stuff to fit in her little car, and still leave room for someone to be in there with her."

The state attorney nodded comfortably.

"So maybe," Rizzolo continued, "she showed up at

the boat and got jumped before she had a chance to transfer the stuff. And that's when she was forced to sail across the bay."

"But why do you think she was forced to sail the boat?" Nolan asked.

"Because, if you follow me with my theory that Dr. Trumbull was involved, he didn't know enough about sailing to navigate the boat from the yacht club to the McCraw part of the bay at night."

"You insist that it was all done at night?"

"Oh, yeah. We're sure about that. We found them two kids that the dockmaster remembered seeing run into Miss Holland's boat with their pram. It left at night, all right."

"You were explaining about the wood alcohol?" Nolan asked, glancing at the clock.

"OK. The way I see it, that alcohol was put into her stomach after she was dead."

"After she was dead? Why?" Nolan asked.

"To throw us off the track. We're sure it was put down there after she was dead."

"How can you be sure, Captain?"

"Because we had Dr. Flood run a wood alcohol level on her blood, and it was negative."

"So?"

"So, if she had drank that wood alcohol before she died, some of it would have been absorbed into her bloodstream. But if she had it put into her stomach *after* she was dead, it would all stay in her stomach. Like it all was."

"Doc Flood says all that about the blood alcohol?" Nolan asked. "I mean, about it not being absorbed into the bloodstream if she were dead?"

"Yes sir, he does." Rizzolo assured him. "And that's not all. We found a short length of plastic hose beneath the stove cabinet. And it could fit into her nose and down into her stomach, if you knew how to do it."

"Trumbull?"

"Why not? He'd be a lot better at it than the Mc-Craw boys." The captain allowed himself a large shrug that announced that not every loose end was tied up.

The state attorney made a face and turned to face the window. He didn't need to be persuaded that Rizzolo's idea was easier to buy than the McCraw theory. This Trumbull business was disconcerting at best. "But, Captain Rizzolo, didn't you find the doctor's car at the phosphate pit, with blood and hair on the tire iron?"

"Yes, sir, we did. But—"

"But what? Doesn't that sound to you like an assault?" Nolan swiveled his chair around to face Rizzolo again.

"Sure. It has some of the earmarks of an assault, but the doctor's a pathologist."

"What's that got to do with it?"

"As a pathologist, Mr. Nolan, he would be trained in what a murder weapon looks like."

"Trumbull is a hospital pathologist, not a medical examiner," Nolan argued.

"That's just it," Rizzolo agreed. "He could put his own blood on the tire iron and stick some of his own hairs in it to make it look like he had been hit over the head with it, but not being a forensic pathologist, like Dr. Flood, he might not have known how to do it right."

"And do you think it was done right, Captain?"

"Well, almost," Rizzolo said. "You see, sir, the hairs on the tire iron were pulled out of the head. The crime lab came up with that. The ends were still intact and the hair shafts didn't look cracked or crushed."

"So?"

"So, the crime lab boys think that if someone was hit on the head hard enough to stick hairs to a blood splatter on the weapon, the hairs ought to be a little more battered than the ones we found on Trumbull's tire iron."

"Will that stand up, or is that just crime-lab bullshit?" Nolan asked.

"Well, it's not incontestable, if that's what you mean."

John Nolan stood up, exasperated. "You mean, Captain, that the hairs and the blood on the tire iron *could* have gotten there when Dr. Trumbull was struck on the head with it. Isn't that right?"

"Yes, sir," Rizzolo conceded. "But that's only one of the points I want to make."

"Captain, I'm frankly a little tired' of this whole theory that the sheriff's office has developed. We find a local doctor, alive and reasonably well, in the shed of a couple of crazy crab fishermen, and you yourself admit that their whole bait house area is filled with skeletons of various people they have done away with over the years, and now you want me to abandon these two psychos and go after their own victim." He threw his hands toward the ceiling and let them fall against his thighs with a loud slapping noise.

"We've never seen the wound on Dr. Trumbull's head," Rizzolo offered.

"His lawyer happens to be a damned good criminal defense lawyer, Captain. He won't let us even talk to his client unless the conditions are favorable. And, by the way, he would like us to come over to the hospital and do just that. He wants to talk to me about the whole case. I think that if I am willing to show him what I plan to do with the McCraws, he's willing to let Dr. Trumbull clear a few things up for us."

"When?" Rizzolo asked.

"I told him tomorrow was OK with me, and that I would check with you."

"Whatever you say, Nolan," Rizzolo said, wearily. "I'll go along with whatever you set up with them."

"Well, look at it this way, Rizzolo. We haven't got anything that will really stick against Dr. Trumbull. I mean, you've got your theories, and believe me, I really appreciate all the time you and your men have put into this case—and you've got a bunch of inconsistencies that you would like cleared up for you. Who wouldn't? But hell's bells, man, you haven't got to go into that courtroom and present the evidence. And in this case, you'd like to have the evidence presented against a local doctor. A pathologist, for Christ's sake! How will that look?"

"We got other things, too, Mr. Nolan," Rizzolo argued, gently. "All I need is a little more time."

"You can take all the time you want, Captain. All the time you please. But in the meantime, I'm going to file murder-one charges against the old man and his son. And if you come up with some ironclad evidence against Dr. Trumbull at some later date, you come back and lay it on me. There's no statute of limitations for murder, you know." John Nolan paced the room, telegraphing his impatience.

"But the old man, McCraw, is crazier'n a loon," Rizzolo said.

"And I'll accept his plea of insanity. That'll put him in Chattahoochee for the rest of his life," Nolan promised.

"Or until some homosexual psychiatrist lets him out in six months," Rizzolo said bitterly.

"If he does, we'll try the old bastard on one of those skeletons you dug up down there behind his bait house." He winked at the homicide captain to reassure him.

"What about the boy?" Rizzolo asked. "Is he too crazy to try too?"

"You ever heard of the M'Naghten Rule, Captain?" Nolan asked smugly.

"McNaghten?"

"Not, *Mc*-Naghten. It's M-apostrophe-Naghten. Some Scottish name, I guess," Nolan explained. "Anyway, in this state, that's the basis for our insanity excuse. The M'Naghten Rule says that a defendant is sane enough to try if he knew right from wrong."

"Even if he's nuts?" Rizzolo asked.

"If he knew right from wrong, he's not nuts," Nolan explained, resuming his seat, "at least, not according to M'Naghten."

"But that boy's pretty sick, Mr. Nolan," Rizzolo said. "He's not all there."

"He's enough there to stand trial for Martha Holland's death, Captain."

Rizzolo cupped his brow in his hand and became silent.

"You don't like that idea, Captain?" the state attorney asked.

"No, sir, I don't," Rizzolo said. "That McCraw boy's been a problem to us for a long time, and there's no doubt in my mind that he's involved up to his ears in some of them dead bodies we dug up out back of the bait house, but I can't put him into the Holland case." He shook his head sadly.

"Captain, that won't be necessary," Nolan said. "All you've got to do is deliver me the evidence that you already have, and I'll decide who we charge, and who gets tried." His tone made it clear that he wasn't inviting a debate on the subject.

"I'll give you everything I've got, Mr. Nolan," Rizzolo promised. "Only . . ."

"Only what?"

"Only, it seems to me like we're going after the wrong guys. I mean, that crazy old coot and his kid."

"You go after anybody you want, Captain," Nolan said. "All I'm talking about is the trial that I've got to put on to clear this mess up. If I do it your way, and charge Dr. Trumbull with the murder of Martha Holland, I'll have to go in with a damned weak case, and Barry Ackerman will beat the pants off of me."

"Ackerman's tough, all right," Rizzolo agreed.

"You bet your ass, he is," Nolan said. "And if I go against the McCraws, I'll get somebody from the public defender's office." He allowed himself a wry grin.

"Sounds like you're stacking the deck," Rizzolo said.

"This job demands convictions, Captain. The public doesn't really care how I get 'em, as long as the results are there." Nolan nursed his cigar, and wiped the ashes into the center of the tray.

"That's not the way it is on television," Rizzolo said.

"They don't have to run for office, Captain." Nolan stood up and paced back and forth in front of the window. He watched the people on the street below. "Oh, come on, Captain. You know that the McCraws deserve to be sent up for what they did to those other bodies you dug up."

Rizzolo nodded slowly. "I'll go along with that. But I promise you something. I'm going to stay on this Trumbull angle and make something out of it someday. I *know* it's there."

"Stay right with it, Rizzolo," Nolan said. "When you get all the pieces put together, you bring it back to me and we'll take a long look at it together. Just don't push it too hard right now. Let me run with the McCraws. Let's clean the case up with those two psychos, pack 'em off to a mental hospital, or send the young one to prison for a while, if the judge agrees that he's sane enough to stand trial, and avoid tangling with Barry Ackerman. OK?" He turned away from the window and faced the homicide captain.

"Then you won't object if I continue to watch the good doctor even after you put the McCraws on trial?" Rizzolo asked. He stood up because Nolan seemed to demand it.

"You have my permission to follow him every day for the rest of his life," Nolan said. "Providing—"

"Providing what?" Rizzolo asked, cautiously.

"Providing that you don't harass him. I don't want to get one single phone call from Dr. Trumbull, or his wife, or Dr. LaFontaine, or anyone else you see as a possible suspect, complaining that your men are watching them. Understand? I mean that to be particularly true after the trial. It won't do for me to convict the McCraws and then have you running around hounding other people about the same damned case. Get it?" There was no apology in the state attorney's voice. He was in charge, and Rizzolo was given no alternative but to honor his wishes.

"What if the good doctor spots one of my men and puts two and two together?" Rizzolo asked.

"It's your ass. That's what," Nolan said. "By then, I will have done whatever I can do with the McCraws, and you can't really expect me to step up and admit that I let you continue an investigation of Dr. Trumbull after we've convicted somebody else for the same crime, can you?"

"I get it," Rizzolo said, adjusting his coat. "If I come up with something, you'll back me if we can put it on without embarrassing your office. And if we don't come up with anything, you've already gotten your pound of flesh to satisfy the public."

"Very astute of you, Captain," Nolan said, offering his hand.

"And, 'Don't get caught'—is that your last words of advice?" Rizzolo asked. He shook the state attorney's hand limply and looked directly into his eyes.

"I couldn't have said it better myself," Nolan said, looking away from the captain's hard gaze. He put his arm around the homicide captain's shoulder and led him to the door.

As Nolan led Rizzolo into the anteroom, the state attorney's secretary broke into a practiced smile. "Did Barry Ackerman say when he wanted to meet with me and Captain Rizzolo, Peggy?" Nolan asked the young woman.

"He said he'd call back when he had set it up with Dr. Trumbull, Mr. Nolan," Peggy said.

"Are they coming here?" Rizzolo asked.

"Oh, no," Peggy said, somewhat surprised at the captain's question. "Mr. Ackerman said that his client was in no condition to come here, and that you two gentlemen were to meet him at the hospital." She was obviously impressed by Barry Ackerman's reputation.

"Well, whatever's convenient for Barry Ackerman and his client," Rizzolo said, almost unpleasantly. "I'm sure Mr. Nolan will accommodate him."

John Nolan ignored the remark and slapped the captain on the back. "Come back again, Captain Rizzolo," he said loudly, playing to the other people waiting in the anteroom. "It's always a pleasure to have the chief of the homicide section as a visitor and as an advisor. I'll tell the sheriff that you came by. I'm sure he's proud to have you on his staff."

"Yeah, well, OK, Mr. Nolan," Rizzolo said simply. "I'll wait for you to call with the details about our meeting with Ackerman and his client." He turned to leave.

"That's fine, Captain," Nolan said. "I'll have Mr. Majors get together with you to coordinate the details for this case. I'm sure he'll enjoy working with you."

The secretary began to wave her hand at the captain when the phone rang. After a short pause, she said, "It's for you, Captain Rizzolo. It's Lieutenant Turner."

Rizzolo walked back to the desk and took the phone. John Nolan, obviously curious about Rizzolo's call, busied himself reading a stack of telephone messages his secretary handed him.

"Rizzolo," he said gruffly.

"Captain? This is Turner. I got the lab report back on that gas stain. The one in the trunk of Trumbull's T-bird?"

"Yeah, Lieutenant. What did you find?" Rizzolo asked. He held the phone tight to his ear. No one else in the room could hear what his caller told him.

"The lab says that the gas chromatograph pattern shows gasoline and motor oil," Turner said excitedly.

"So?"

"The gasoline contained lead, Captain, and the oil was mixed in with it."

"Meaning?"

"Meaning it's probably not from a lawn mower at all. A lawn mower would have spilled the gas and oil in different places, like two separate spots. I think it was something else entirely."

"Like what?" Rizzolo asked, frowning.

"Who knows, Captain. Maybe it was a motorcycle or

a scooter. That's what the chemist says the lab pattern looks like," Turner said.

"OK," Rizzolo said. "Tell you what, Lieutenant. For now, let's just sit on it. I'm coming back to the office and I'll go over all the evidence in the case with you again. Maybe something will fall out, this time around."

"OK, Captain," Turner said. "I just thought you'd like to know about that report while you were talking to the state attorney. I thought it might be something important."

"It is, Lieutenant," Rizzolo said. "It is. But I'm not sure that Mr. Nolan would like to be bothered with any more facts this morning. I'll see you soon." He handed the phone to the secretary, and threw one more look at the state attorney. John Nolan did not look up as the homicide captain turned and left the room.

Chapter Nineteen

IN THE HILLSBOROUGH RIVER, outside Tampa General Hospital, two tugs struggled with the massive bulk phosphate carrier, *Torm Gerd,* out of Oslo. Bill Trumbull could see the entire maritime operation from his room. Across the river, the docks of the Luckenback Shipping Company faced Seddon Island, now abandoned. The harbor in Tampa was totally devoted to commercial shipping because it was one of the best deep-water ports on the Gulf of Mexico. As a harbor, it had nothing at all to offer the hometown pleasure boater. The million-dollar yacht basin in St. Petersburg captured all of that business.

"It would scare the hell out of me to have to bring one of those big ones into this harbor," Trumbull said to his wife Agnes. She fluffed up his pillow and joined him in looking out of the hospital window.

"They have harbor pilots, or something like that, don't they?" she asked without really caring.

"Even so. That's a lot of boat."

"More than a single sailboat, huh?" She smiled at him to lessen the embarrassment of her remark.

"Oh, come on, Agnes. We've been all over that. You've got to let it drop."

"*I* can let it drop, but what about the state attorney's office?"

"Well, you know what Barry Ackerman told us to do about that." The starboard tug had reversed its engines and the water in the harbor churned like transient soapsuds.

"Barry Ackerman is a good criminal lawyer," she said simply.

"But I'm not a criminal," he replied. He took her hand and brought it close to his bandaged thigh.

"I know that." She patted him tenderly. "I'm glad you're safe."

"I wish I could tell you the whole story," he sighed. "But you know what Barry Ackerman said about that."

"I don't know why you called Barry Ackerman, anyway. Everyone will think you're automatically guilty of something, if he's representing you."

"Because he's one smart lawyer, that's why. But I know what you mean," he said. "Criminal lawyers scare the shit out of me, too. They're always showing up on the evening news with some gangster, coming out of the courthouse. Y'know, with the guys in the foreground covering their faces with their hands?" He mimicked the gesture.

"How about if they decide to charge you with something, like Barry talked about?" she asked.

"Now you're sounding like Ackerman. Only, he made it seem like a real possibility. And remember, he said he's not at all sure how the state attorney will see it."

"How much did you tell Barry Ackerman, anyway?"

"I told him everything. Having a lawyer is like having a priest. If you're not going to tell him the whole story, why bother wasting his time?"

"You thought that up?" she asked.

"No, Ackerman did. But it makes sense. Look, I wanted him to go to the state attorney and straighten out this whole mess, and he told me that I didn't have to tell Captain Rizzolo anything, and I didn't."

"You can thank Captain Rizzolo for that as much as anybody," Agnes said.

"He's not a bad guy, y'know?"

"He's also aware that that crazy crabman would have killed him if you hadn't jumped him just in time."

"You think that's why Rizzolo gave me a chance to see Barry Ackerman before he called the state attorney?"

"Wouldn't you?" she asked. "Wouldn't you give a chance to a guy who had just saved your life?"

"I guess it might influence me a little."

"You're such a sentimentalist."

"Thanks," he said, sharing a smile with her. He knew that he had put Agnes and the children through a lot of suffering, and he felt guilty about it. He wouldn't have blamed her if she had told him to keep on going, as she probably would have, had she known about his insane plan to escape the life they shared. He knew that he needed Agnes and the children, and he welcomed a chance to patch things up between them. So far, Agnes was giving him that chance.

"Are you sure that you're ready to talk to all these lawyers today?" she asked.

"Why put it off?"

"It's just that you've been through so much over the past few days. Maybe you could get Barry Ackerman to stall them for the rest of the week."

"Barry says that I should get it cleared up, the sooner the better. He says it looks better that way."

Agnes busied herself with straightening up the newspapers and the magazines that had accumulated on the bedside chair and on the floor. Even in Tampa General, she was the tidy housewife. "I guess that's right. Even the children have had a tough time answering the questions from the other kids at school, and not really knowing what to say."

"What did you tell them?"

"They think the crabman and his son made you take

the money out of the bank and that they kidnapped you to their shack to hold you for ransom. It's just about the same thing that the newspapers and the TV are saying." She offered a small but helpless shrug.

"But, I never told the news media that story," he protested.

"You didn't have to. All they need is one loose fact. They are perfectly capable of inventing their own 'news.'"

An overweight nurse opened the door and stuck her head into the room. She was in her mid-thirties, but her weight made her look older. She spent just a moment inspecting Agnes Trumbull's trim figure and then turned toward Bill Trumbull. "Excuse me, Doctor," she said formally. She had never felt comfortable with a doctor for a patient. "There are some men here to see you."

"Thank you, nurse," Bill Trumbull said. "I think the doctor has made special arrangements for this meeting?"

"Yes sir. There's a note on your chart allowing it." The nurse was being quite correct and fussy in the face of unusual instructions. She did not personally approve of business meetings in patients' rooms, but this one had been authorized by the chief of surgery himself. The nurse had not been told that the "business" involved the state attorney, the sheriff's homicide captain, and one of the city's sharpest criminal defense lawyers. On the other hand, there was nothing in her attitude that said she would have given a damn, had she known who these men were.

"We'll need a few more chairs, nurse," Trumbull called after her as she left the room.

"They'll each carry their own," she shot back. She was not a maid, she quickly assured herself.

Agnes Trumbull exchanged a knowing glance with her husband, but did not speak. She was secretly happy that there were still nurses like that in hospitals where her husband might have to work. It was the cute and friendly nurses who made medical wives worry.

There was a sudden commotion at the door as Ackerman, Nolan and Rizzolo bumped their way into the hospital room. Each of them carried a straight-backed wooden chair, and the lawyers also struggled with attaché cases. There was a mumbling of incomplete greetings and renewed introductions between the men and the Trumbulls. Everyone acknowledged that they more or less knew everyone else, and was glad to see all the others. Under the circumstances, the amenities were more than hard to believe.

The sight of the two lawyers immediately reminded Bill Trumbull of Martha Holland. He was filled with the hollow feeling of loss. He knew, within himself, that if a full confession would bring her back to life, he would not hesitate. He could still see her smile, hear her laugh, smell her hair. It was clear that her memory was not going to fade away quickly. With her death, he had fashioned for himself a kind of earthly purgatory in which he heard her voice in every lawyer's logic, and turned to look for her whenever he heard the click of a feminine heel behind him. In life, he could have told her "Enough," and put a halt to her erosion of his peace of mind. But in death, she would always be with him.

Barry Ackerman brought his chair close to Bill Trumbull's bedside. Agnes stood near the window at the head of the bed, while Nolan and Rizzolo sat at the foot, facing the pathologist. The opposing teams were clearly squared off. Ackerman did not wait for a polite lull in the small talk to get the meeting off the ground. He walked all over Agnes Trumbull's attempted commentary on the weather.

"On behalf of Dr. Trumbull," Ackerman said, louder than necessary, "I want to thank you, Mr. Nolan, and you, Captain Rizzolo, for agreeing to meet with me and my client under these unusual circumstances." Everyone acknowledged his opening remarks with little nods and smiles in the appropriate directions. "There's no one taking down any testimony here, today, Dr. Trumbull, but these gentlemen and I have agreed that we would conduct ourselves in a reasonable manner that would afford an opportunity for an adequate exchange of information, without compromising anyone's position in any subsequent legal proceedings. Am I correct, gentlemen?"

"Absolutely," John Nolan said, smiling at Bill Trumbull and his wife.

"Whatever Mr. Nolan says is OK with me," Rizzolo added, stretching his neck uncomfortably in his tight collar.

"And of course, I'll reserve my right to object, and will instruct my client not to answer, whenever it becomes necessary," Ackerman added casually.

"No problem," Nolan agreed.

Agnes Trumbull wondered why these lawyers had to say all those things in what seemed to her to be the most complicated way they could find, but she knew better than to ask.

"Does Mrs. Trumbull intend to stay?" Captain Rizzolo asked pleasantly.

"Why not?" Bill Trumbull wanted to know. He felt Barry Ackerman's hand move across the sheet that covered his wounded thigh. There was a slight squeeze and a sharp pain.

"Do you object to Mrs. Trumbull's presence, Captain?" Ackerman asked.

"Oh, no," Rizzolo said quickly. "It's just that there may be some things brought up that—well, y'know, might be a little embarrassing for the doctor." Rizzolo wished he had kept his mouth shut.

"My wife can hear anything you have to say, Captain," Trumbull said heroically. He reached up to pat her hand. He knew that everyone in the room could see Martha Holland standing there beside his bed, as well.

He wondered if she would always intrude herself so obviously.

"Perhaps, Captain, you can let me know when you get to a sensitive area," Ackerman suggested, "and I will confer with Dr. Trumbull and Mrs. Trumbull at that time." He gave a plastic smile that told the homicide captain that he thought he was an idiot for raising the subject. The captain silently agreed.

Barry Ackerman preferred loud plaid jackets and solid trousers of alarming but perfectly matching colors. Several judges had felt that he was more appropriately dressed for the country club than the courtroom, but his comportment was always so correct, that they came to overlook his taste in clothes. He was similarly theatrical in his style of defense. He was a master of the unexpected; a genius at demonstrative evidence; incredible in his cross-examination of scientific experts—and terribly expensive. Trumbull didn't doubt that the price of his shoes alone would have bought Rizzolo's entire outfit. That acknowledgment did not make anyone unhappy or uncomfortable. Not even Captain Rizzolo, although the comparison never entered his mind.

"Dr. Trumbull," John Nolan began, "it is our hope that you can be of assistance to us in clearing up several confusing events that have occurred over the past several days. Your attorney, Mr. Ackerman, has indicated that he does not prefer the simpler method of having you provide us with a narrative statement, covering your experiences during this time period." He paused to nod gently to Barry Ackerman. The defense lawyer rummaged through his attaché case in mute response.

"We are therefore faced with this alternative method of arriving at this information," Nolan continued. "Namely, questions and answers."

"I understand," Trumbull said. He felt that a more intelligent-sounding response was required at that point, and hoped that none of his answers would make Barry Ackerman wince. Trumbull knew that he would

be too self-conscious to hold each of his answers until
he had conferred, behind his hand, with his attorney,
the way that the big witnesses did at televised Con-
gressional hearings.

"It may save us all considerable time if we provide
you with a general narration of our understanding of
some of those events, and then indicate those areas in
which we feel that your cooperation and information
could be of value," the state attorney explained, flatly.
John Nolan had a style that could make the invasion
of the east coast of the United States sound dull and
uninteresting. What was worse, he knew this, and tried
desperately to overcome it.

"That's certainly agreeable with me," Ackerman offered quickly. "Please do that. It may save time for us
all." The pathologist was pleased to see that the suggested method had been acceptable to his attorney. He
was emotionally ready to get it over with. His wife remained inflexibly skeptical. She did not like questions
or answers from lawyers, regardless of which side of
the case they seemed to be on.

"According to our information, Dr. Trumbull, "Nolan
intoned nasally, "you left the hospital at which you are
employed, under abrupt and somewhat unusual circumstances. Incidentally, we have not, as yet, been
able to come up with anyone who actually saw you
leave the hospital, or who has direct knowledge of the
circumstances under which you left. We would appreciate your help in *that* area." He paused to glance at
Captain Rizzolo for confirmation and received an appropriate nod of the head. "Shortly thereafter, you arrived at the bank where you have maintained your personal account for some—"

"Six years," Rizzolo said. He looked at Agnes Trumbull with automatic police curiosity. She was unmoved.

"—some six years," Nolan continued, "and withdrew
the balance of your account, some seventeen thousand
dollars."

Rizzolo nodded silently. He had the exact amount withdrawn written on an index card in his pocket, but he was smart enough not to jump in on his state attorney at every opportunity.

"You were then apparently taken, or forced to drive your car, a Thunderbird, to a rather remote area near Seffner, where the car was later found by the sheriff's department, noted to be abandoned, along with one shoe, later identified by Mrs. Trumbull as your own." Agnes received another nod at the mention of the shoe. John Nolan then looked at Dr. Trumbull over his half-glasses. There was no response from either the doctor or his wife. Ackerman had done his coaching well.

"There was a tire tool found at the scene that showed some evidence of a physical struggle," Nolan droned. "Right, Captain Rizzolo?" The state attorney was obviously handing over the floor to the captain.

"The tire tool," Rizzolo said, "showed blood and hair that we have determined to be compatible with your blood type and hair structure, Dr. Trumbull. We obtained your blood from your own hospital blood bank, and samples of your hair from the hairbrush in your office." He was careful not to smile smugly, but he felt like it.

"And then," Nolan took over, "you were apparently taken to a fishing shack—"

"Bait house," Rizzolo corrected.

"Yes. Bait house," Nolan said. "In a remote section of the eastern part of Tampa Bay, and held prisoner by a one Liam McCraw and his son, Quentin. Is that not correct?"

"Excuse me," Barry Ackerman said, holding his hand in the air in front of Bill Trumbull, like a traffic cop. "We agreed to listen to your narration, John. We did *not* agree to confirm it as you go along."

"Oh, yes! Excuse *me*," Nolan said rapidly. "That was more of a mode of speech than a request for confirmation. But, let me go on with this. Sometime during your captivity, these same men, Liam and Quentin McCraw, left the bait house with you in it, apparently, and went to the nearby beach, located some distance from said bait house, proceeded through a mangrove area, and discovered a sailboat, anchored offshore."

"We have never confirmed the actual anchoring," Rizzolo said testily.

"The McCraws went out to this sailboat, using their own smaller boat," Nolan went on, glancing at Rizzolo and showing signs of being slightly annoyed, "found its owner, Martha Holland, a local lawyer and sometime acquaintance of yours, I believe, and killed her with a single shot from a revolver."

"Hers," Rizzolo suggested.

"Yes," Nolan agreed. "The revolver belonged to Ms. Holland, and the bullet recovered from her body by Dr. Flood matched the ballistics from the same gun. It was this same gun that we later found in the possession of Liam McCraw at the bait house. But, I'm quite sure that you're well aware of that part of the story." Nolan allowed an awkward smile.

Trumbull mentally inspected the wound in his thigh, and nodded quickly. Once more he saw Martha Holland's last, astonished look at him. He saw her fall to the floor of the sailboat again and saw her dead body lying on the starboard bunk. He saw the water rising to her outstretched fingers.

"The motive for your abduction, Dr. Trumbull," Nolan continued, "was apparently robbery, although we have not yet ruled out an unborn extortion plot. Apparently, no calls or demands were made by the McCraws to Mrs. Trumbull during this time."

Agnes was careful not to nod or shake her head, even though every eye in the room had automatically turned toward her at the end of the state attorney's statement. John Nolan recognized that there would be no response from Mrs. Trumbull, and went on. "The motive in the killing of Martha Holland seems to be a mixture of anger from her trespass into the crab nets—"

"Crab *traps*," Rizzolo said, exasperated.

"—crab traps, and robbery," Nolan said. "We have been unable to establish any proof of sexual attack on the body of Ms. Holland. Too decomposed, you see."

Trumbull and Ackerman nodded in unison. Both of them maintained placid faces that neither confirmed nor denied anything. Both of them knew that there had been no real motive for the killing of Martha Holland. Trumbull had explained every detail to Barry Ackerman, and the lawyer had gone over the incident with the pathologist several times. At first, the grief that Bill Trumbull had experienced during the retelling of Martha Holland's death had made him refuse to accept it as an accident. Barry Ackerman had seen it as an accident from the first time he had heard the pathologist explain it. After that, it had taken the criminal lawyer many hours of patient conversation with the pathologist to make him see that he had not intended Martha's death in any way. Ackerman had eventually convinced the pathologist that a reasonable jury would have seen it that way, and had finally gotten the doctor to agree. The lawyer's persuasive reasoning had overcome the pathologist's emotional blockade, and Bill Trumbull had agreed to remain silent while Ackerman represented him.

"The McCraws then sank the sailboat, in an effort to conceal the murder, leaving the body of Martha Holland on board. Unfortunately for them, the water proved to be too shallow to totally conceal the boat, and it was seen by a passing fisherman, sometime later."

"The mast was sticking up out of the water," Rizzolo added.

"There was a sizable sum of money recovered in the back of the bait house, Dr. Trumbull," Nolan said. "Your bank had no record of the serial numbers of the money which you withdrew, but we have no reason to doubt that it represents the same currency. The McCraws' business records, such as they are, did not reflect that their business generated that kind of income."

"And, there is no evidence of any losses in Ms. Holland's accounts," Rizzolo added. "But *we* have a slightly different theory on one point, Mr. Nolan. Do you want me to tell them about that now?"

Barry Ackerman's eyebrows raised slightly. He knew that it had been, so far, so good. He wondered if the captain was about to pitch the curve.

"Yes, please, Captain," Nolan said. "We want to clear up as much of this as we can. Don't we, Barry?"

Ackerman nodded ever so slightly.

"Yes sir," Rizzolo said. "We recovered Ms. Holland's car at the yacht club and found that it was still loaded with the kind of stuff that you would take on a cruise. Now, I'm not a sailor myself, you understand, but there was groceries, liquor, and some of them little doodads that you have to use to make a sailboat run. Y'know, like little pulleys and clamps, and ropes. Stuff like that. So, we figure that somebody might have jumped her before she shoved off, and forced her to steer the boat over by the McCraws' place. The rope suggests that, too."

"What rope?" Ackerman asked, cautiously.

"The rope that she used to tie the sailboat up with at the yacht club. Seems like the rope was left in a sloppy mess at the dock," Rizzolo said, twisting his hands to show the sloppy mess. "Miss Holland was known as a bug on doing that kind of thing right. The dockmaster is convinced that someone else must have taken the boat out that night."

"Night? Why night?" Ackerman asked.

"Oh, yes sir. It was at night," Rizzolo said. "We definitely established that the boat left the yacht club during the night. Two kids, fooling around in a little boat, remember seeing it there during the day. They bumped into it with their boat and were scared that my deputy was going to bring 'em in for causing some damage to Miss Holland's sailboat when we went out to talk to them."

John Nolan felt compelled to make a point. It was, after all, his case. "The presumption is that one or both of the McCraws forced Ms. Holland to make that voyage to their area of the bay, if the captain's theory is correct, and if she did not, in fact, sail out of the yacht club by herself." It was obvious that the state attorney had heard much of the sheriff's theory before and had not bought it.

"Did, er—" Ackerman hesitated. "Did either of the McCraws know Martha Holland?"

"That's a good question," Rizzolo said. "We have not been able to establish any link between Miss Holland and the McCraws prior to the incident. However, we know that Miss Holland did a lot of sailing in the bay, and that she probably had sailed into their area on several previous occasions."

"And damaged their crab nets?" Ackerman suggested.

"Crab traps," Rizzolo corrected. "Yes, sir, we think that she might have sailed in there before, caused some damage to their crab traps, and then made them mad when they complained to her about it."

"Why made them mad?" Ackerman asked.

Captain Rizzolo hesitated and looked at Barry Ackerman for a moment and then at the state attorney. "Well, if you will excuse me, it was because she was a lady lawyer. We figure that if she sailed in there and busted some of the McCraws' crab traps or their ropes and floats, that she would have given them a lot of smart lawyer talk when they come to complain. And, we figure that those McCraws didn't appreciate being talked to that way by a female, even if she was a lawyer. And they probably didn't know she was a lawyer."

Bill Trumbull could imagine the scolding that Martha Holland would have handed out to those two demented crab fishermen after they had rejected her apology for running over their crab lines, and after they had attempted to abuse her verbally. He knew that

Rizzolo's narrative, while dead wrong, presented an incredibly accurate portrait of Martha Holland under attack.

"The McCraws said that?" Ackerman asked.

"Barry," John Nolan offered, gently, "the McCraws are one step away from an institution. The old man is as crazy as a loon, and the son is a known mental defective. We are not relying on any of their statements."

"And what's worse," Rizzolo said, "is that after we got pokin' around down there in the mangrove behind the McCraws' bait house, we come across a whole mess of old bones and buried skeletons."

"Human skeletons?" Agnes asked.

"Hell, yeah, human skeletons. Excuse me, ma'am," Rizzolo said, all at once. "We found enough bones down there to keep Doc Flood, the medical examiner, busy for a couple of months. Leastwise, enough to close out a bunch of old homicides and missing-persons records."

"The McCraws killed them?" Trumbull asked. Some of the things that the younger McCraw had said in the shack began to make sense to him.

"Killed 'em and buried 'em," Rizzolo said. "Them McCraws were bad people. Real bad. I only wish they was sane, so's we could send 'em up for a long, long time."

"They'll be sent away, all right," Nolan said. "It may be the mental hospital instead of prison, but I can promise you that they'll be locked up."

"You are apparently considering accepting a plea of insanity for the McCraws?" Ackerman inquired.

"Don't you agree?" the state attorney asked. "I mean, do you see any profit in our cranking up a long, expensive trial over any of this, and then having one of your colleagues from the defense bar blow us out of court with a plea of insanity that any junior law student could think up? I mean, after all, Barry, I've got what I need out of this case. I've got two mental cases that are clearly guilty but can't stand trial. What else do I need?" He held his hands wide to assist the defense attorney in his search for something else.

Barry Ackerman looked into John Nolan's eyes. It was lawyer to lawyer and there was no hint of insincerity. Ackerman had to agree with Nolan's theory. What else *did* he need? He certainly did not have to look in the direction of a respected pathologist to initiate a case that would be almost impossible to prove and, at best, would generate adverse publicity for everyone involved. Barry Ackerman could sympathize with the state attorney's position without hesitation. It was Rizzolo who worried him. Captain Rizzolo was a tough cop who had dedicated himself to law enforcement. He lacked the subtle discretion that guided the state attorney in the performance of his job. Rizzolo painted his own pictures in bold, primary colors and left the pastels and shadows for the lawyers and judges. Ackerman knew that the homicide captain could be a problem.

"And you, Captain Rizzolo?" Ackerman asked. "How do you feel about the case?"

"Me?" Rizzolo asked. "I'm more or less satisfied. I went over the whole case with Mr. Nolan, here, and I told him we ain't got much on Dr. Trumbull." He turned to the state attorney for clearance. "Is it OK, Mr. Nolan? Can I tell 'em?"

"You may express your own theories, if you wish, Captain. I'm sure that Mr. Ackerman realizes that your statements do not necessarily reflect the opinions or positions of the state attorney's office at this time." Nolan looked quickly at Barry Ackerman and gave a slight shrug.

"Yeah, well, OK," Rizzolo said. He was not sure whether the state attorney's disclaimer was intended as an aid or a hindrance to his proposed explanation. "There's a lot of loose ends, y'know what I mean? Take, for instance, the fact that the doctor, here, and Miss

Holland was good friends. Excuse me, Mrs. Trumbull, but I got to say it the way I see it. OK?"

Agnes Trumbull nodded, and gave her husband's shoulder a squeeze. It told the pathologist that, somehow, it would be all right.

"This is too much of a coincidence, for me," Rizzolo said. "Y'know what I mean? I mean, here's a sailboat from clear over on the other side of the bay, and it ends up off the mangrove backwash near the place where the McCraws have the doc stashed away. But, we checked out the sailboat and we find nothing to put the doc on board. Nothing at all. Of course, the sinking and the lapsed time helped to cover any fingerprints that might have been left on the boat, but that's the way it is."

"Captain, I hope you're not accusing—" Ackerman interrupted.

"No, no," Rizzolo said, quickly. "I'm not accusing the doc, here, of anything. I told all of this to Mr. Nolan and he wants to go his way with the case, and that's OK with me. I just want to give you my theory, that's all."

"I'm sorry, Captain," Ackerman said. "Please continue."

"We got nobody that sees the doctor leave the hospital with anybody else. Now, it doesn't seem right to me that two guys as unclever and crazy as the McCraws would be able to get the doc out to the bank without somebody seeing them. Get it? OK, so maybe they did it by phone. Y'know, with a threat? But what's the difference? I can live with that part of it too, if that's the way Mr. Nolan wants it."

"And the car, Captain?" John Nolan prodded, slightly annoyed. "I believe you were dissatisfied with that, too?" He raised his eyebrows to show Barry Ackerman that he was getting a little exasperated with the homicide chief and his doubts.

"Yes, sir, I'm a little bit concerned about the car," Rizzolo said, defensively.

"In what way?" Ackerman asked.

"Well, sir, the doctor's car was only driven to Seffner before it was ditched at the phosphate pit. Now, that's not very far from the hospital. I mean, why wouldn't the McCraws drive the car all the way down into the East Bay area before they got rid of it?"

"Maybe they didn't want to attract attention to their part of the county, Captain," Ackerman offered. "After all, it would be a stolen car at that point, wouldn't it? And they would not be sure that they hadn't been seen somewhere along the way. Right?" Ackerman began to wonder if he weren't offering too much. He did not want to get sucked into the theorizing or offer false explanations that would cause him ethical problems later, if the truth came out. Yet, he couldn't let the captain air all of his suspicions without at least offering a small disclaimer on behalf of his client.

"Yeah, we thought of that, and it kinda makes sense," Rizzolo agreed. "But, it makes the McCraws too smart, if you ask me. And the tire iron. Now, that's a setup by a real pro, *if* it wasn't used to hit the doc over the head with."

"And you think they may not have struck Dr. Trumbull with the tire tool?" Ackerman asked.

"I kinda hoped that the doc would fill us in on that, Mr. Ackerman, but I guess he's not goin' to do much talking," Rizzolo said. "At least, the radio was on the right station."

The son of a bitch doesn't miss a thing, Trumbull thought to himself.

"What radio station are you talking about?" Nolan asked.

"Well, the doctor here, he likes that long-hair stuff. The kind the University of South Florida puts out? But, the car radio was on a country-and-western slot," Rizzolo said. "Sounds more like the McCraws, don't you think?" He winked at the pathologist, but no one else saw him.

"Sounds good to me," Nolan said.

"So, what are your plans, John?" Ackerman asked. It was time to get the captain back into his corner. He had run with the ball long enough.

"Well, Barry, I've given the whole case a considerable amount of thought," the state attorney said. "The captain and I have been over the facts several times, and I'm convinced that justice will be served by prosecuting the McCraws. As much as I can, of course."

Bill Trumbull felt a weight leave his chest. He tried desperately to avoid heaving a sigh of relief.

"We have two defendants that are involved in several previous homicides and now, in the abduction of Dr. Trumbull," Nolan continued. "And, one of these defendants is obviously too demented to stand trial. As far as I am concerned, the doctor is nothing more than an unwitting victim."

Bill Trumbull bit the inside of his lower lip to keep himself from smiling. He wondered if the state attorney was often as wrong as he was at that moment. The prospect gave the pathologist a sudden chill.

"Your conclusions are certainly acceptable to me," Ackerman said, leaning forward to shake hands with the state attorney. "Under the circumstances, I think your attitude is more than reasonable." He avoided looking at his client.

"If we agree then," John Nolan said, "I don't see why we should disturb the doctor's rest any longer. We want him to heal that leg as soon as possible, don't we?" He gave a patronizing nod in Agnes Trumbull's direction. Nolan stood up and touched Captain Rizzolo on the shoulder to encourage him to do the same. "It's clear to me that you are not going to allow Dr. Trumbull to make a voluntary statement at this time, Barry."

"I'm sure you understand, John," Ackerman said. "You and Captain Rizzolo have developed what appears to be an adequate explanation for this unusual case, and I don't think it would be appropriate for the doctor to add any statements of his own, right now."

Captain Rizzolo began to struggle with the chairs. Ackerman moved to the foot of the bed, as if to offer general assistance. He was happy to see Nolan and Rizzolo preparing to leave, and he didn't want to do anything that would prolong their visit. He moved toward the door with John Nolan and expressed encouraging best wishes for the state attorney's success in the next election. Their conversation continued into the hospital corridor as the homicide captain fussed with the chairs.

"Captain Rizzolo," Bill Trumbull said softly. He threw his head to one side.

The captain put down the chair he was carrying, and came to the doctor's bedside. It was obvious that the pathologist did not want to speak loudly.

"Yes, Dr. Trumbull?" Rizzolo asked.

"How's Sergeant Grubbs?"

Rizzolo's eyes met Trumbull's and found no insincerity. The doctor was genuinely concerned. "He'll be fine, Doctor. The bullet made a hole in a piece of his gut and then through the vein that comes up from someplace inside, but they fixed both of them."

"I'm glad, Captain," Trumbull said.

"I know you are, Doc. I'll tell Sergeant Grubbs that you was asking for him. He'll want to know that."

"And I'm glad you made it through all right, too, Captain."

"Thanks to you, Doc. That crazy old fool could have dropped me like a ground squirrel, if you hadn't jumped him."

"He probably wasn't too sure of what he was doing," Trumbull added. There was sympathy for the old man in his voice.

"I probably shouldn't have been out there alone, but I guess the sight of Orville Grubbs layin' there in that patrol car pushed me to where I didn't belong." He shook his head regretfully.

"We all make mistakes, Captain," Trumbull said, offering him a smile.

Captain Rizzolo looked at Agnes and then at the pathologist. He nodded his head in agreement. His gaze burned deeply into the pathologist's eyes. "You're right enough, there, Doc." He continued to look at the doctor and then turned away. He gathered the chairs together and bumped them out of the room without speaking again.

Bill Trumbull and his wife watched the homicide captain leave the room with the chairs. The pathologist swept his eyes past his wife's face and looked out of the hospital window again. The tugboat had managed to push the big phosphate carrier into the appropriate dock area, and the harbor looked inactive once more. Seagulls dove for tiny fish that had been stunned to the surface by the churning of the massive engines.

He looked at his thigh and ran his hand over the bandages. He felt Agnes's hand cover his own, and he knew that in time his leg would heal, and that when it did, there might still be time for Chichicastenango, and Brother Timothy, S.J.

A CAPITOL CRIME

LAWRENCE MEYER

 AVON/37150/$1.95   CC 5–78